REMNANT AWAKENS

A FRACTAL FORSAKEN BOOK

J. LLOREN QUILL

Follow me @ www.facebook.com/jllorenquill

Published by Jason Quill
www.facebook.com/jllorenquill

Publisher's Note: This is a work of fiction. Names, characters, places, and incidents are a product of the author's imagination. Locales and public names are sometimes used for atmospheric purposes. Any resemblance to actual people, living or dead, or to businesses, companies, events, institutions, or locales is completely coincidental.

Cover design and map by Abby Haddican
Book Layout © 2015 BookDesignTemplates.com

Remnant Awakens / J. Lloren Quill – 1st ed. Published 2021.
ISBN 978-0-9979887-9-6

For those that continue to find opportunity when doors are shut to them. For those that open doors.

THE KINGDOM OF
MALETHYA

PILLAR

MINOT

THE NOMADIC TRIBES

Ispirtu

Rue St.

Regallo Estate

Darik's Palace

Bellator

RAVINAI

Arena

Slate's Apartment

Infirmary

Catalpa Grove

PORTSWAIN

THE DISENITES

CONTENTS

REFLECTIONS

Duty. Loyalty. Honor.

Rainier laughed as he walked from Minot to the tiny hunter's cottage on the edge of Minot, drawing looks from everyone around him. He gave his best Remnant smile and laughed even louder. Why would he care if they looked at him? These soldiers and wizards took everything too seriously anyway. This was all just a game. That they never realized the lies hidden within those words made the whole thing even more funny.

Take duty, for example. Growing up in the nomadic Tallow clan, Rainier was taught all about duty. He lived it. Every member of the Remnant lived it.

After Malethya defeated the Disenite army in the Twice-Broken Wars, someone needed to stay behind. Someone needed to watch Malethya for signs of blood magic, so a solitary squadron of paladins shed their armor and slipped into the countryside. They moved from town to town, never staying anywhere long enough to create suspicion, but their differences still attracted attention. The soldiers chose to accentuate those differences, traveling in caravans with pillows for chairs and silks for every occasion. Malethya called them nomadic tribesmen, but this remnant of Disenite soldiers never forgot their duty. The Remnant stayed hidden in enemy lands and vowed only to return home if the threat of blood magic

2 J. Lloren Quill

returned.

Rainier never questioned the teachings of the Remnant. He was Remnant, and this was his duty. When Lattimer revealed himself as a blood mage, Rainier did what he was trained to do. He returned home to Disentia. He warned his people that blood magic had returned to Malethya, and everything he thought he knew about duty, loyalty, and honor came unraveled.

Now he walked to the hunter's cottage, the home of the biggest secret in the history of Malethya, and he found it funny. The most important task in Malethya's history fell to Rainier Tallow, born in Malethya, descended from Disentia, and duty-bound to no one.

CHAPTER ONE

HANG THE MESSENGER

"Rainier Tallow, you are charged with high treason." The pronouncement came from the high priest of the Disenite court. He stood as he spoke, which gave the priest an air of even greater authority within the courtroom. In case someone misconstrued the obvious, Rainier had no power here, and neither did the rest of his tribe that waited behind him, knowing that their fate was tied to his. "You have only been kept alive this long because you spoke the sacred words of the oracles. Explain how you came to our shores and explain where you heard the sacred words. You will be killed if your answers do not satisfy my curiosity."

Apparently the Disentia Court had never heard the phrase burden of proof. "We set sail..."

A sharp, discreet elbow cracked him in the ribs, courtesy of his court-appointed priest. Rainier bit his tongue and then recalled the titles these fractal-forsaken bastards demanded to be called. *Did I just refer to a high priest as a fractal-forsaken bastard? Ah well, the man obviously had an affinity for titles, so what was one more? Besides, the title fits a man that seizes my ship, jails me, and puts me to trial. I expected a parade in my honor when I came home, or at least a hot meal. Instead, I get Mr. Robes of Righteousness before me.* "Your excellency," Rainier began again, "we set sail from Malethya two months ago to fulfill our duty to Disentia."

The high priest interrupted him. "What was your duty? The court is unaware of anyone left behind in Malethya." The biting tone made it clear that the court was never left unaware of Disentia's plans.

This is starting poorly. What did I do to deserve such anger? Rainier looked up at the priests in their elevated seats and tried to understand their perspective. Each priest on the court represented one of Disentia's tribes. The priests representing the Scorched, Frozen, and Charged factions looked upon him with skepticism that bordered on disdain. None of them approached the open hostility of the high priest, however. The heavily tattooed priest bore the sacred ink of the Marked faction, from which Rainier had descended. Rainier didn't find a friendly face in the Marked priest despite their supposed brotherhood.

Rainier decided to keep his explanation simple and to the facts while he tried to understand where the anger originated. "We are the Remnant. When Disentia's forces attacked Malethya, they attacked a people with a pagan's understanding of magic – they used the spark to cast spells and the pattern served only as a link in the process. The oracle that led the Disenite forces predicted that since the pagan wizards of Malethya didn't hold the pattern while using the least amount of spark necessary to cast a spell, they were destined to fall from fractal's grace completely. It would only be a matter of time before they forgot their own history and fell back into blood magic, the casting of spells using only the spark. This prophecy demanded that our priests and paladins cleanse the land of Malethya.

As the war continued, the oracle's prophecy increased in strength as the pagan wizards used magic in battle against our holy forces and relied upon increasing levels of spark with every battle. Before the final battle of the war, the oracle made another prophecy – the war must end to save the land of Malethya from its own people. The pagans' use of magic would scar the land so greatly, that it could never be cleansed, recovered, or converted. The oracle commanded the Disenite forces to sail home and chose to stay behind with a group of brave paladins to cover the retreat of their friends, knowing their demise was already foreseen.

It was only after the Disenite ships sailed and the final battle began, that the oracle saw another vision – a vision of blood magic in Malethya's future. The prophecy would not be realized soon, he knew that war with the Disenites would leave the land of Malethya in great upheaval, so he ordered a small group of the remaining paladins to leave the final battle. They disappeared into the countryside, charged with the duty of watching Malethya for the return of blood magic to the land. I was born to their number, and I now lead them. I am Rainier Tallow, leader of the Remnant."

"The tale you tell is quite astounding, Rainier. I question the validity of the tale, but it is interesting enough that I'll allow you to continue. But first, who was the oracle you speak of?"

"Trabon Tallow, my father." Muffled laughter filled the courtroom, but the serious priests managed to maintain their stoicism.

"So, you claim to be the descendant of Disentia's most

famous oracle and former leader of Julian the Immortal's troops." Mention of Julian the Immortal caused all the priests to bow their head in reverence towards the man seated above the high priest. Julian had not spoken as Rainier's court-appointed priest had told him to expect. In Disentia, the pattern was power, and words were a powerful pattern. Julian appointed the high priest to be the Immortal's Voice and to speak for him in public. The priest said the arrangement was intended to keep anyone from learning the pattern of Julian's speech and use it to control him. It was good to see paranoia wasn't limited to the leaders of Malethya. "That is quite the claim, but we'll get to that in a minute. You have yet to tell me how you reached Disentia's shores."

Rainier spoke clearly and assuredly to push past the skepticism of the court, "The Remnant hid under the guise of a clan of nomadic tribesmen and watched Malethya for signs of blood magic. After waiting patiently, my father's prophesy became realized. At first, small towns were wiped out without any evidence, but as the blood mage grew in power, he grew more brazen. An army of Furies was observed during an attack on a small town, confirming the presence of the blood mage in Malethya."

"Excuse me, but I thought you said the Remnant was watching Malethya dutifully. Are you telling me that it took the presence of an army before you took notice?"

Rainier countered tactfully, given that the man held his fate in his hands, "With all due respect, your excellency, I ask you to consider the welcome I have received since my arrival." *Who steals a man's ship? Bastard!* "I thought it was important to gather more evidence before returning."

"Then please present the evidence you gathered while this threat to Disentia grew in power."

Rainier had to bite his tongue to keep a biting remark down. *What was I supposed to do - carve out the eye of a Fury and pocket it during my journey across the sea?* "I'm afraid I don't have any physical evidence, but I stayed in Malethya long enough to identify the blood mage. Lattimer Regallo has taken control of Malethya and is ruling the country from the shadows. He controls the mind of King Darik, he has an army of trained Furies at his disposal, and the people of Malethya don't even know he has taken power. You may judge that I stayed too long in Malethya, but I left as soon as I could direct the Disenite forces to their target and not a moment longer."

"You stayed until you knew where to direct the Disenite forces? Do you presume to lead the Immortal's troops? I believe I am the Immortal's Voice and only I can appoint someone to that position." Laughter filled the courtroom and Rainier received another elbow from his court-appointed priest. "Now, how did you get to our shores?"

"The Remnant was known as a nomadic tribe within Malethya, but we were prosperous in our businesses, and we secured a ship at Portswain under the name of a holding company. It was kept in dry dock until I needed it. After identifying Lattimer Regallo as the blood mage, I returned to the Remnant and told them to prepare for our journey home. The ship was in harbor by the time we reached Portswain, and we sailed straight here, at least until our ship was identified in Disentia's waters." Then his ship was stolen, he was imprisoned and half-starved before standing trial for treason, but he left out those details.

The high priest then said, "You were fortunate to be found by the captain you did. When you spoke the sacred words of the oracles, he did not recognize them, but he found an old flag from the Immortal's army and an oracle's ring while appropriating rations from your seized ship." *Appropriating rations? How about pillaging?* Rainier kept his mouth shut and the high priest continued. "He brought the items to his superior's attention, and they are one of the few reasons you have been granted this trial. I would now have you speak the sacred words again, in front of the court's well-trained ears."

Rainier took a deep breath and recalled the words he had repeated back to his father every night before bed, "The world is a pattern of ever-changing life. The pattern cannot be seen. The pattern cannot be described. It is only through familiarity with the world that a sense of the pattern can be understood. It is only through familiarity with life that the pattern can be predicted." Rainier stopped himself before saying aloud the words that his father always said back to him, but that didn't stop the words from floating through his head. *You are a part of the pattern, young son. Everything you need in this life has already been given to you.* Those words didn't seem any more applicable to his current situation than the sacred words, even if he felt a deep truth buried amongst the confusing riddles.

How can something be true and confusing?   As contradictory as it seemed, Rainier didn't have to look too far into his past for an example. Rainier's friend was his Teacher of the pattern and a walking testimony to the power of blood magic. Slate had an innate power to sense the pattern around him, but his lack of training made him completely ignorant of it. His soul was true, and he fought blood magic with the dedication of the Remnant, but he fought with power bestowed by Lattimer. He fought with the tools of the enemy. *What are Slate and his friends doing now? Has Sana healed Slate completely or is he still only partially saved from the grip Lattimer holds on his mind? I wish I could see my friends again, but the best way to help them fight Lattimer is to return with an army at my back. That sounded a lot easier to do before I got held for treason...best to get out of the noose before making too many future plans.*

The high priest called upon the priest representing each faction of Julian's domain. They all wore expensive robes styled in the manner of their own faction. The stylistic differences contrasted sharply with the expressions on the faces of the priests. They all wore the same look of bemusement intermingled with condescension and indifference. *These are the people that hold my life in their hands. How can they care so little about the proceedings? How can they care so little about me?* The high priest asked formally, "Scorched faction, how do you judge the testimony?"

The Scorched priest, dressed in an elaborate mix of yellows, oranges, and reds, stated loudly, "The words spoken burn with the heat of wizard's fire and smolder with the truth of an oracle. He speaks true."

Next to Rainier, his court-appointed priest exhaled slightly in relief and the high priest moved onto the next priest. "Frozen faction, do you agree with that assessment?"

The Frozen priest stood, and Rainier failed to appreciate the translucent robes that shimmered in all the wrong places. "The words spoken sting like a foot stepping on the morning frost and bite with the truth of an oracle. He speaks true."

The high priest must have agreed with Rainier's aversion to the sight before him. "Thank you. Please take a seat." He then moved onto the next priest. "Charged faction, what did you hear?"

The priest stood in his robes that darted out in seemingly random directions like a lightning bolt. It reminded Rainier of the Sicarius Headmaster when erupted in spark that knocked back Lattimer and allowed her to escape the clutches of the blood mage. The priest said, "The words spoken arc from one truth to another. He has the capacitance of knowledge reserved for an oracle."

"That only leaves one faction. As the head priest of the Marked faction, I too, shall pass judgment of the sacred words." the high priest announced.

The Marked priest's plain robe emphasized the ink covering his skin. Rainier knew the meaning of the tattoos instantly since the Tallow tribe descended from the Marked faction. The Marked cover the portions of the body that describe their mission in life. The priest's inked skin declared his devotion to the pattern itself, the highest declaration a member of the Marked could make. The priest looked down upon Rainier and said, "The words spoken sting like the needle and hold with the permanence of ink."

The court-appointed priest next to Rainier almost

choked at the proclamation and an audible sigh of relief could be heard from his tribe standing behind him. All four factions had validated the truth of Rainier's words. *Now they have to believe my story. When is the parade? Break out the confetti and pour the drinks.*

The Marked priest continued before any celebrations began. "However, the man speaking does not bear the ink of the Marked. He does not know the pattern and therefore cannot speak as an oracle."

Curses. His father had always pushed him to name a Teacher, complete his training, and declare his devotion to the pattern. Rainier had named Slate Severance to be his Teacher, but he had severed that relationship before completing the devotion ceremony. Even though Slate's abilities as a Perceptor made him more than qualified for the role, Slate hadn't known his responsibilities as a Teacher, and Rainier wasn't anxious to fill him in on the process. The guy was already a tournament champion and all-around badass – he couldn't give Slate any more titles to fuel his ego. Besides, it hadn't seemed that important when they had been chasing down a blood mage; now it did.

"I have named a Teacher, but your statement is true. I have not completed my training."

Silence hung in the courtroom as Rainier tallied the implications. *Will the sacred words carry enough weight with the high priest to overlook my lack of formal training?*

Finally, the high priest stood up. "Rainier Tallow – The court has reached its verdict." He looked around the courtroom at his fellow priests and then raised his voice, no longer speaking as the high priest of the Marked faction but as the Voice of Julian the Immortal. "You speak the undeniable truth of the sacred words and warn of a grave threat to Disentia. The sacrifices you and the rest of the Remnant have made in the service of Disentia are commendable, but I fear your lack of training and the time you spent away from Disentia has led you astray. There is no threat to Disentia. Before this trial, I spoke with the oracles. They do not foresee a rise in blood magic on our shores or any of our neighbors. You have invoked the sacred words and soiled the pattern with lies. You are sentenced to death by hanging."

What? They are going to kill me because I don't have ink on my skin, and my warning caught them off-guard? Pattern-soiling or not, I don't plan to go down that way. Rainier relied on his Sicarius training to play the part of the confused and condemned prisoner contemplating the end of his life. He hung his head in his hands and shook it from side-to-side, which gave him a chance to formulate a plan. A paladin approached him from his right, probably tasked with leading him back to his cell. He would see a dejected, unarmed man too shook up to mount an attack. When he got close, Rainier could incapacitate the man and steal the short swords from his back before the paladin realized he intended to fight back. After that, things would get ugly. The priests would surely cut him down since he was used to facing the fireballs of Ispirtu wizards and didn't know what spells to anticipate from the priests, but if he were lucky, he could bury his sword into Mr. Robes of Righteousness before he fell. The paladin neared and Rainier readied himself to spring into action and strike a blow into the soft spot of the paladin's neck when a raspy, age-ravaged voice stopped the paladin in his tracks.

Julian the Immortal spoke from on high, "As my Voice has said, the boy will be sentenced to death...unless he completes the Oracle Trials." *Boy? I've put my pubescent years behind me, but I won't argue with the old man while he is saving my life. Besides, everyone probably seems like a boy to someone older than dust.* Regardless, the simple act of speaking seemed to stir a spark of life within Julian, and he continued. "He will be fed, prepped for the trials, and given comfortable rest while under guard. The Oracle Trials are scheduled for tomorrow. Let them determine his fate. If he passes the trials, he will obtain the title of oracle, his warning will be believed, and we will act."

The courtroom was stunned, but not by the words spoken by Julian but rather the fact that he spoke at all. The high priest recovered first. "While I speak for the Immortal, I cannot always interpret his wisdom correctly. I hang my head in shame and will receive any punishment for my failure you see fit." The high priest did indeed hang his head, but Rainier failed to see any shame on his face. It looked more like annoyance at the interruption and a healthy dose of fear – Julian was old but apparently still immensely powerful.

Julian spoke, "Learn from your shame and continue as my Voice. Redeem yourself by carrying out my orders and ensuring the boy is properly trained. Then, meet me in my chambers and we will prepare for war."

CHAPTER TWO

OUT OF THE NOOSE AND INTO THE ORACLE FIRE

Rainier waited impatiently in his new, opulent prison cell. The room in Julian's palace was decorated without concern for coin, but the Disenite tastes in décor had diverged from the more practical considerations of his nomadic tribe. "I'll take some comfortable lounging pillows any day," Rainier said to himself. A paladin stood watch within the room, but the woman refused to engage in conversation. Naturally, Rainier took that as a challenge and tried to get a response, so he kicked a gilded loveseat and said, "I could trade this monstrosity to a Ravinai businessman for half a year's rent." The paladin didn't respond to vandalism, but she did set her jaw – that was progress. Rainier tried a different tactic by boasting about the tribe's reputation for making a deal. The reputation was well-earned, so why not spread it overseas. He revised his asking price for the chair. "Make that half a year's rent and a date with the businessman's daughter." At that comment, the paladin's eyes nearly bulged out of her head, but she kept her silence. Rainier only laughed and said, "Besides being tried for treason and this whole oracle debacle, getting you to talk to me is a close third on my list of challenges for the day. Once I pass this testing tomorrow..."

The door opened and the high priest, the leader of the Marked faction, interrupted him as he came into the room, "That is quite a presumption, Rainier Tallow."

"If you had your way, my tribesman and I would be dead already." The high priest's eyes went wide, and he nodded to the paladin in the corner. She stepped forward and struck him in the jaw. *What is that all about? I just tried making friends with the woman.* After his head stopped ringing, Rainier realized the paladin's hit was less about his overtures of friendship and more about Mr. Righteousness' affinity for titles. "Your Excellency," Rainier stated with grandiosity, "if I can survive a rigged trial with you as the judge, then I can surely survive whatever further tests are in store for me."

The paladin waited for her orders to strike Rainier again, but the high priest kept his composure. "Let me speak plainly so that you understand. We receive dozens of sailors, thieves, and general miscreants every year that invoke the sacred words of the oracle to avoid capture or to stay their sentences. It is a waste of my time and that of the other priests. For whatever reason, your story struck a chord with Julian the Immortal, and he has offered you the slimmest of chances to prove yourself. The Oracle Trials have been unchanged for hundreds of years, and while the trials have not changed, the number of people that pass has dropped considerably. In fact, no one has passed the trials in over a decade. You think Julian saved you, but he did not. You are a dead man." The high priest paused to let the words sink in.

"Despite the fate that awaits you, Julian's intervention, and your claim that you are Trabon Tallow's son requires even more of my attention than your trial did. I promised to ensure that you received the best training possible between now and tomorrow morning. To fulfill my end of the bargain, you will have the honor of being taught by myself, the head of the Marked faction. I will not have anyone accuse me of providing inadequate schooling after you fail and are hanged."

Whatever happened to visualizing success? Rainier didn't expect much of a pep talk from his teachers after a preamble like that. "What do I need to know? Let's start with your name. If you'll be teaching me, I need to know what to call you." Rainier asked.

"You need to know more than I have time to teach you." the high priest said. "Your first question is a waste of your own precious time, but since you asked and you'll be dead tomorrow anyway, my name is Jamison. Now, let's start with the basics."

Jamison stepped forward and dove straight into a lecture. It was going to be a long night. "The Oracle Trials were developed to test an exceedingly rare talent – the ability to predict future events. Anyone that passes the trials is held with the highest regard within Disentia. Past oracles have been responsible for the greatest achievements in our kingdom's history, whether it be through advancements in technology or any other areas that the oracle specializes in. Your...father, Trabon Tallow, applied his talents on the battlefield to predict troop movements and always placed his troops in the optimal positions for success."

"History is great, but what do I need to know for tomorrow?" Rainier asked, before remembering to add,

"...your excellency."

"There are three stages to the Oracle Trials. The first stage is a simple test of the spark. Magic comes from recognition of the pattern, but we are imperfect in our casting and every individual needs some spark to make up for our imperfections. The second stage of the trials tests the ability to sense your surroundings with the pattern. If you pass the second stage, then you will enter the third trial – where magic defines everything around you. If you use logic or deductive reasoning in the third stage, it will inevitably lead to failure. The only way to pass is if you know what will happen next. The only way to pass is to be an oracle."

"So, the only way to become an oracle is to pass the Oracle Trials and the only way to pass the Oracle Trials is to be an oracle. Why are you here again, your excellency?" Rainier's frustration with the paradox spilled over in the form of a rhetorical question, but then a sense of peace calmed him. He knew he had the spark because his father had Lucus test him for it at an early age. That only left two trials, and from the sounds of it, he would be tested on his decisions and reactions in certain situations. That was the type of test that didn't require book knowledge or an evening full of lectures. He would either pass or he wouldn't, and his experience with Sicarius techniques and adventures with Slate Severance would help his chances considerably.

"I said you must be an oracle to pass the Oracle Trials, but that doesn't preclude a brash individual from failing spectacularly through complete ignorance." The high priest scolded Rainier, and Rainier responded with a lopsided grin that hid his building frustration. Years of hiding who he truly was from the Malethyans gave him lots of practice at hiding his emotions when needed. Besides, the man had made his point. If this jerk had information that could improve his chances of survival even a small amount, Rainier would bite his tongue and use the information.

"Can you tell me about stage 2? You said I would need to use the pattern to sense my surroundings. What does that mean?" Rainier asked.

"We can't tell you what the trial will be because Julian directs the trial himself. However, all initiates are instructed to learn a Sensing spell. It's a way to monitor the patterns around you without affecting them or changing them. Have you not had this training?" Jamison asked questioningly. *Was that a hint of concern creeping into Mr. Righteousness' questions? Certainly not.*

Rainier didn't trust these men enough to share too much of his family history, so he simply said, "I have received training, but we called the spell by a different name." That was more or less true. The spell sounded a lot like the probing spells used for healing, which he had studied the pattern for even though he had never actually cast a spell. His father had told him the Remnant's job was to stay vigilant and report back when trouble arose – he worried that casting spells would tempt Rainier to act instead of returning home. *Maybe father hadn't looked far enough into the future to determine my need for the spell at this moment? Or maybe he had and considered my imminent death the best possible outcome given the alternatives?* His father was funny that way, and it made arguments around the campfire rather one-sided when you knew he could predict the future. *Maybe that's why I rebelled and chose Slate as my Teacher? Was I really rebelling if father knew I was going to do it beforehand? Maybe the choosing of a Teacher was exactly what Trabon wanted since control of the Remnant passed to Rainier upon Slate's choosing.* Rainier stopped himself — trying to sort through what his father did and did not know always threw him for a loop. He refocused his thoughts and asked a question about the Sensing spell. "In most spells you need to hold the pattern in your mind, but with this one, it is more ephemeral, right? You want to read the differences in the pattern around you, so if you hold it too tightly, you can't discern it correctly." *After that, you just throw a little spark at it to cast the spell. How hard could it be?*

"That is a valid description," the high priest said, "but a better analogy comes from mathematics. If you define the pattern and hold it too closely, you have over constrained the spell and there is no longer a unique solution. Conversely, if you hold the pattern too loosely, the spell is under constrained and there are infinite solutions."

Rainier was sure the analogy was a good one for someone who cared about math. He had pushed that garbage out of his head as soon as the lessons progressed past advanced sums — they always helped with negotiations when making a deal. He just nodded towards the high priest and tried to keep an interested look on his face while remembering his lessons from Lucus. Lucus had always said a spell could reach similar outcomes with different combinations of spark and pattern, which was basically what the high priest was saying.

Jamison turned towards the paladin, "Please have someone fetch a bowl of wanderleaf from stores. This is a lesson Rainier needs to have before the trials." The paladin left momentarily to relay the message.

While waiting for the wanderleaf to arrive, Rainier soaked up as much information as he could manage about the upcoming trials. From what he could gather, Julian had established the trials early in his reign, although the exact date of that was difficult to tell since Julian had the title of Immortal after his name. And even though the trials had remained unchanged, little was known about them and not everyone that entered the trials was heard from again. *Maybe I'm not the only one they are trying to kill off.* Most Disenites that passed stage one of the trials entered service for Julian in some capacity and those that passed stage two were short tracked for promising careers within the priesthood. The high priest had even taken a spare moment to point out the features of the city from the window in his room. The highlight of the tourism speech was when Jamison kindly pointed out the gallows near the dock where he would be hanged when he failed his test. Rainier thought that summed up the night's activities acutely – highly informative with a heavy dose of pending doom.

The conversation regained some pragmatism when the wanderleaf arrived. *Where did they need to get the stuff from that it had taken hours to obtain? It had been hours!*

"Ah, here we go," the high priest acknowledged receipt of the wanderleaf from the Paladin. Without prompting, the paladin lit the wanderleaf into a slow, smoldering fire and smoke curled upwards towards the ceiling. The high priest instructed Rainier, "Inhale a small amount and hold your breath for a few seconds. The effects will only last a minute or two."

Rainier leaned over the small plate of smoldering wanderleaf and took a deep breath. He closed his eyes and held his breath. When he opened his eyes, the room streaked with golden opulence and swirled with condescending power.

"Do not try to focus on individual objects. Let your eyes relax and wander where they please."

Rainier tried to relax his eyes, but the swirling of the room was unnerving. The unease worked its way to his stomach and Rainier began fighting a battle on two fronts – the swirling images assaulted his eyes and queasiness threatened his insides.

"You are fighting against the wanderleaf. Wanderleaf can be disorienting, but the disorientation is the point of the exercise. Do not let your mind force what you see to be something you already know. Open your mind to a new possibility. Maybe the walls you once knew are not really walls. Maybe the chair is not for sitting. Maybe it has a different purpose."

What is this crackpot smoking? Oh yeah...wanderleaf. Stupid question. It's hard to be witty when you need a convenient place to empty your stomach. *Would the paladin at the door lend me her helmet?* Rainier imagined the look on the all-too-serious woman's face when he handed the helmet filled with the contents of his stomach back to her. His internal joke had an unintended benefit – it diverted his attention from the swirling images in front of him. His distracted brain took in the movement around him instead of trying to find the objects through the swirls. The second he did that the nauseating feeling began to temper.

"You are learning. Release your mind from what it thinks it knows and focus on what could be."

Rainier heard the high priest's words, but the swirls never reached a level of prophecy that was demanded of an oracle. They were simply beautiful swirls that he enjoyed watching. As the wanderleaf's temporary effects faded and the walls became solid once again, fear of the following day's trial and some anger at his father for failing to prepare him for this critical moment intermingled.

"Can you teach me anything other than getting high? That didn't seem to work." Rainier said with a healthy dose of sarcasm that hid his worry.

"You saw the pattern. That is a good first step and one that should not be taken lightly."

"I lost my senses for two minutes and will probably feel terrible in the morning, right when the trial begins. Do you have anything to teach me that may actually help me?" Rainier asked.

The high priest evidently felt that his teachings were at an end for the evening, as he said, "It is apparent that your ways are not our ways. Maybe this will serve you well in the trials. Good evening, Rainier Tallow, and I hope our next meeting is not at the gallows."

Jamison turned to leave, and he wasn't convinced to stay by Rainier's ineloquent and half-buzzed arguments to the contrary. "I didn't mean to..." His argument was drowned out by the shutting of the door, leaving Rainier alone with the mute Paladin. "Well, isn't that a fractal-forsaken…"

The paladin smacked him across the face before he could get out another word. Rainier looked at the condemnation in her face and realized just how seriously the Disenites took the pattern. If mentioning a fractal in the same sentence as forsaken deserved a slap, he'd have to be more careful with his words, but he didn't feel like being cautious when this might be his last night with the privilege of breathing.

"Do you have anything to say to help me, paladin, or just more righteous condemnation? I'm about to go to the gallows for no real reason, so I just want to know what to expect from you."

The paladin's face flashed with emotion and her armor lit up in unison with the glow of some magical enchantment. Rainier, the experienced negotiator, knew when to push his luck. He took his opportunity with her display of raw emotion and pushed it further, hoping to break her bond of silence. "Do you think that some fancy armor is going to scare me paladin? I'm about to die tomorrow. I'm going to go to some fractal-forsaken…" This time Rainier blocked her blow and stepped inside her guard, leaving his face inches from hers as he said, "I'm going to go to some fractal-forsaken Oracle Trial, breathe in some wanderleaf, and hope they put me out of my misery."

The paladin shoved Rainier away from her, but not before Rainier grasped the leather straps for her armor. He landed on the bed, pulling the paladin on top of him. Rainier couldn't help the comment that came out next,

"You'll have to talk me up more than that if you hope to get me in bed, paladin."

Rainier's words drove the paladin's emotions past the point of temperance and her vow of silence, "I would not bed a blasphemous foreigner like you if you passed the Oracle Trials and became the Immortal's Voice."

Her words were meant as an insult, but Rainier only laughed, and then said, "Good. Then we're on the same page. I have devoted my life to serving Disentia without ever stepping foot on its lands. Now that I have returned and warned all of you, I have been greeted with the noose. If the Immortal offered to make me his Voice, I would accept, only to use the position to dethrone the bastard."

The shock on the paladin's face carried into her words as she said, "I have never heard such blasphemous words spoken."

Rainier knew from previous negotiations that shock was the perfect state of mind for planting an idea. He said to the paladin, "I have devoted my life to Disentia. I have disowned my own ambitions, my own wants, my own desires, to serve the Remnant. You, the mute paladin that would probably be killed if I told a priest of our conversation, should know of this sacrifice better than anyone. Imagine how you would feel if your devotion to the Immortal was rewarded with a noose simply because you spoke to me tonight..."

Shock turned to anger which turned into a helmet to the forehead. Rainier's eyes rolled backward.

"Rainier Tallow, the Oracle Trials begin now!" The high priest's voice disrupted Rainier's dreamless slumber. He awoke to a throbbing headache and confusion about how he ended up tucked under the covers of a wonderfully comfortable bed. After months on a ship, followed by several evenings in a jail cell, Rainier would have enjoyed the extravagance of a comfortable bed. Annoyed at the missed opportunity, he threw back the covers and stood up, only to find he had been stripped to his undergarments.

Fractal's curses. He always wanted to maintain the upper hand in a conversation, and it was difficult to do that when you were nearly naked. If you commented on it and made a joke, you lost authority. If you dressed too quickly, you appeared embarrassed or shy. His best course of action was to casually dress himself in the fresh set of clothes laid before him, ignoring the presence of the high priest and the paladin, and treating them as if they were serving maids. Rainier's casualness probably angered the high priest, but it was the only way to display self-confidence while standing in his trousers.

He looked over to the paladin and saw that she was stoic as usual, not even bothering to divert her eyes in his direction. He said to her, "I can forgive the headbutt, but you cost me a night of sleep in that bed. You owe me one." Her eyes darted in his direction, but a set jaw and years of training held back any comments from the paladin.

"If you don't hurry up, you'll miss the Trials, and the debt you owe will be paid in the gallows," the high priest warned Rainier needlessly. When someone threatened to put a noose around your neck, it was a threat that didn't need repeating.

"The Immortal wants me to be tested. The Trials won't begin without me." Rainier knew less about his homeland than he cared to admit, but one thing he knew to be true – the Immortal's words ruled. He finished getting dressed under the watchful scowl of the high priest, who turned to leave the room without asking Rainier to follow.

Rainier followed anyway but took a moment to tease the paladin as he passed, "The next time you want to see me naked, don't knock me out. I'm a lot more fun when I'm conscious." The paladin didn't say a word, but she didn't need to. Her enchanted armor flashed a bright blue as her emotions got the better of her. Rainier laughed. He didn't know if the flash of color was anger or a different emotion, but the unexpected reaction was better than anything he had hoped to get.

In the hallway, the high priest said, "If you are through degrading the honor of the Immortal's holy troops with your shameless advances, I would suggest you focus your attention on the task at hand."

Rainier kept his mouth shut while silently wondering who had sucked the fun out of this guy's life. As he followed the high priest through the palace, he reflected again on the differences in Disentia from the way he was raised within the Remnant. *My father taught me the beliefs of Disentia, but now they seem foreign. I grew up in Malethya but always considered myself a Disenite. Why then, do I find so much pleasure in tormenting this paladin and aggravating the high priest?* Rainier shrugged off the thoughts as a consequence of his current predicament. In different circumstances, the high priest might share a drink with his tribesmen around a campfire and the paladin might take her helmet off to feel the wind through her hair as she rode through the Malethyan plains. *Right — and maybe I really can predict the future and just decided not to do it until this very moment. Why am I being so random? Is this what people do right before they die?*

Jamison exited the palace and headed directly across a manicured mall. In front of them, a domed building blocked out the morning sun, leaving two sets of wet footprints amid the dew-covered grass. *I feel as alone on my home soil as those footprints look in that sea of grass.*

"The building before us is the home of the oracles. Since we haven't had a true oracle in some time, it has been repurposed for training. Candidates live here from an early age until they are ready to undergo the Trials," the high priest said.

"Thanks for the reminder that I am woefully unprepared. Would you like to strangle me before we go in as a reminder of what happens if I fail?" Rainier asked with all the petulance he felt the high priest deserved to hear.

The double doors carved from large catalpa trees swung open to reveal the Immortal standing at the center of the domed room. The high priest ran up to join Julian and resumed his role as the Immortal's Voice. He said, "You are late."

"Jamison overslept and failed to wake me." Rainier grinned at the mortification that spread across the face of the high priest. Rainier strode into the chamber like he owned the place, saw a crowd of serious looking teenagers in robes, and said, "It looks like I have a cheering section.

Let's start this thing. Test me for the spark."

Julian held his gaze, and Rainier felt the weight of years and years of judgment bearing down on him. Jamison, the Immortal's Voice said, "These are the other candidates, Rainier Tallow of Malethya. Join their ranks and do not speak unless asked a question. The Trials will determine if you are worthy of sharing your voice more liberally."

Fractal's curses. Another miscalculation. Rainier assumed the Immortal believed his story and was an ally. At the very least, he had hoped to use his famed powers of persuasion to invoke some leniency. Without being able to speak, the high priest had used his role as Julian's voice to remove Rainier's best weapon and chance of escaping his situation.

Julian said, "The Oracle Trials are a sacred ritual. They were devised to evaluate the potential of the most devout within my kingdom."

Devotion? Rainier had been thinking of this as a test of magic. *If the Oracle Trials are truly a test of devotion, I will pass. No one else has sacrificed their entire life to Disentia like I have.* The trickle of hope he had been clinging to grew into a small stream.

"The first trial will test your abilities with the pattern. The pattern is sacred and can never be fully understood by those that tread the soils of this kingdom. The most devout of you will hold the pattern and only require a small amount of spark to summon a spell. Hold the pattern, step before me, and be tested." *This Voice thing is confusing. Am I supposed to stand before the high priest or Julian?*

Thankfully, he didn't have to go first. One by one, the

robed candidates stood before Julian, who laid his ancient hands upon them. After a second or two he would nod his head and the robed figure would step aside. Since all the students were chosen based on their ability to become oracles, they all passed without surprise. When it was Rainier's turn, he stepped up and held the pattern of a probing spell that Lucus had taught him and stepped forward. Julian smelled of mothballs and power. He laid his wrinkled hands on his head, and... nothing. Rainier didn't feel a thing. He was just standing there with a creepy old guy grabbing his head. A few seconds later, Julian nodded, and Rainier stepped aside.

That was anticlimactic.

Even though Rainier knew that magic couldn't be felt when it was being used on you, it was different when you knew someone was casting a spell on you. Rainier wanted to feel *something*. He had known Slate Severance and heard his tales of Brannon's spells ripping through his body and Ibson's calculating powers of healing. Slate was a Perceptor, a rare gift that allowed him to feel magic and manipulate its use on him, even though he didn't have the spark or the ability to cast a spell. After hearing Slate talk, he wanted to feel Julian's magic, if only to know the silent man better so that he could manipulate him enough to save his own neck.

Oh well, at least he had passed the first test.

Julian said, "Congratulations, you have all passed a test that I screened you for as babies. Now, let's see if the years of training have borne any fruit." He nodded towards his Voice, signaling for the wanderleaf to be offered. The Voice walked around and held the smoking weed in front of the first robed oracle-to-be. Rainier saw the student inhale deeper than a drowning man gasping for air. The next student did the same. Meanwhile, Julian explained the second trial. "Around this room are thirty-two doors. They are spaced evenly apart and are identical in every way. To choose the correct door, you will need to see the pattern around you. Pick the correct door and walk through. For those of you lucky enough or talented enough to pass this test, the final stage of the Oracle Trial awaits you on the other side. It will require you to not only see the pattern but also see possible permutations of the future pattern and to act accordingly. The path to becoming an oracle will be clear to only the truly enlightened. If you fail to choose the correct door, your Trial will be at an end. Whatever fate awaits you outside of these Trials will meet you once you pass through the door."

Rainier looked around the circular room in incredulity. *My life hangs in the balance of some game that belongs in a travelling carnival.* The only thing that ruined the image was that he could not picture the powerful and crusty Julian handing him a prize if he won. At the carnival, if he lost, he may have opened a door to find the bearded lady waiting to kiss him. Now if he failed, he had the noose waiting for him.

The wanderleaf slowly made its way towards him. After Julian's speech finished, Rainier saw the same look of despondency in the students' eyes that he tried to hide in his own as they looked around the room. Rainier didn't think it was possible, but the students started inhaling the wanderleaf even more deeply. Rainier had barely sniffed the stuff the previous night and the whole room swirled. He still had a headache from the experience. Nothing about the sight of these students inhaling smoke to the point of delirium inspired the words "sacred" or "devout." Rainier questioned the high priest's description of the Oracle Trials and the small stream of hope that his years of devotion would help him in these trials ran dry.

The high priest finished delivering the drug to the student in line next to him and then turned expectantly to Rainier. His father's words, spoken to him as a child, echoed in his head, *"You are a part of the pattern, young son. Everything you need in this life has already been given to you."* Rainier didn't have anyone to trust in the Disentia, but his father had never led him astray. He looked to Jamison and refused the wanderleaf with a shake of his head.

"The wanderleaf will help you to see the pattern. Take it." The high priest demanded.

Rainier shook his head again as reverently as someone could shake their head. In this decision, he wasn't trying to ruffle the high priest's feathers. The high priest obviously had no idea what to do with him, so he looked to Julian. Julian simply raised an eyebrow towards Rainier and nodded. The high priest said, "The choice has been made."

Julian snapped the would-be oracles out of their drug-induced stupor by casting a spell and saying, "I have blinded your movements and muted your footsteps from the other contestants, so that you will not be swayed by the decisions of others. You have five minutes to complete this stage of the trial. Any delay will forfeit your Trial. Choose your door."

Rainier looked down the line of contestants and saw nothing, proving the effectiveness of Julian's spell. Alone, Rainier fought down the panic of having to come to a solution within minutes. He imagined the other students either rushing to a decision or waiting in paralysis until the time was about to expire. Rainier promised himself he would do neither. *I am part of the pattern. I have everything I need.*

Rainier held the pattern of the probing spell and applied a small amount of spark. Although he was practiced at the pattern of the probing spell, the only time he had applied it had been under the influence of wanderleaf. Rainier expected the walls to swirl around him, but that wasn't the case. His vision didn't change at all, except everything seemed more vibrant. Colors became sharper and architectural features became more pronounced.

"Four minutes remain. Choose your door," the Immortal's Voice resonated through the room.

Rainier scanned the doors of the room, looking for any markings that weren't visible without the aid of the spell —— no luck. The doors were identical, just as Julian had promised. Rainier looked to the walls and tapestries adorning them. The colors of the tapestries jumped from the fabric, making every one of them look like a masterpiece. Every masterpiece was maddeningly identical.

"Three minutes remain. Choose your door."

I am part of the pattern. I have everything I need. Rainier begged to differ, but he trusted the words, nonetheless. *What do I know about these Trials?* Rainier thought back to Julian's words. He had said the doors and the walls were identical, which Rainier had just verified. *The information I need has already been given.*

"Two minutes remain. Choose your door."

Time! Jamison's words hit Rainier like a blow to the head from Magnus. *Why is time so important?* Julian had been extremely strict about the five-minute deadline. Rainier looked around the room quickly for anything moving or changing with time. After already looking at the doors, he used the probe to look higher and higher up the walls until his eyes rested on the oculus of the domed ceiling. *Why does the Trial hall have an oculus?* It was early morning with the sun's rays barely peaking over the horizon, so the powerful rays of the sun barely contributed to the lighting of the Oracle Trials.

"One minute remains. Choose your door or forfeit the Trial."

Rainier looked closely at the occulus, thinking there may be a hidden compass or indication on the rim of the opening but found no clues. *Why are the Trials held at sunrise?* The high priest couldn't usher him into the circular room fast enough when he was worried about Rainier being late, so the timing had to be important. The only explanation was that the timing had to do with the sun. Rainier changed the focus of his probing spell from probing the walls to probing the light around him – the early rays of the morning light came through the occulus and bent towards a door like a shimmering arrow, pointing him towards survival. He sprinted for the door before time ran out, opened the door, and leapt through the threshold before he had time to process what was on the other side.

Rainier landed awkwardly onto a wooden platform. A raucous crowd gathered before the stage and cheered at the sight of him. *I've done it! I made it through stage two of the trials! It's no parade and it's a little later than I would have preferred, but it's nice to finally be recognized for my efforts.* Rainier threw an arm in the air and the crowd went wild.

"Rainier Tallow has been charged with high treason and sentenced to death, pending the outcome of his Oracle Trials." Rainier looked to find the speaker.

He was wearing a black hood and carrying an axe. "He has failed."

Fractal's curses.

Rainier looked behind him, but the threshold of the doorway he had just crossed had disappeared. In its place hung a noose. Rainier stared at it for a moment, and then his focus shifted to the men and women standing behind the noose – his friends. The Remnant, for all their sacrifice and loyalty, would be strung up like common thieves.

How did this happen? The light pointed to the doorway. I passed the second trial! His mind screamed despite the noose hanging before him.

"As penalty for high treason, Rainier Tallow is sentenced to death." The nooseman slid the rope around Rainier's neck and continued to address the crowd, "The accomplices that helped to perpetrate this crime will share his fate. Joining him will be Hanna Rodica, Jarma Nurwu, Luca Graxis, ..."

Rainier stopped listening to the names of the Remnant. As their leader and the only member of the Remnant not currently shackled, he had to keep his wits. *How can I save them? How can I save myself?* He scanned the crowd. The crowd was too tightly packed to escape into, and a ring of archers stood upon the walls surrounding the gallows. He'd be shot dead before he made it halfway through the crowd, and that was even if he ignored his friends.

You are a part of the pattern. Everything you need has already been given to you. The words of his father sounded hollow after failing him in the Oracle Trials. *I had to have been right. The light bent and showed me the path.*

"Lara Bodier, Vera Grundlow, Kalen Hadlow..."

He considered going for the nooseman's axe, but it would do little good against arrows loosed from all directions around him. *Think Rainier!* He was running out of time and options, but he couldn't let it out of his head...he had solved the riddle of the second Oracle Trial...

Rainier stopped. *What if I DID pass the second trial?* If he did pass it, then this hanging was the third Oracle Trial. Julian had said that if he failed the trial his fate would await him. He couldn't have been more honest, in his own twisted way, then setting the third trial at the gallows. *What else did Julian say? Something about not only seeing the pattern around him but also future permutations of the pattern.* Rainier cast the probing spell on the light shining in the gallows. The colors brightened but nothing like the path he had seen from the oculus.

"...Kalus Straker..." The name of Rainier's childhood friend made him look up. He met Rainier with an expectant gaze, waiting for his friend and leader to solve the riddle of the pending deaths. Rainier smirked to let him know everything was under control. A leader had to inspire confidence in every situation, even if he knew it to be a lie...another great lesson from his father. "This concludes the list of traitors to Disentia. Let us now remove them from our sacred soil." The nooseman played to the crowd by sharpening his axe on a grindstone in an entertaining display of sparks.

Rainier modified his spell to look at his surroundings, using the nooseman's grandstanding for a little extra time. Frantically searching his surroundings yielded nothing of interest. He closed his eyes in frustration. The light showed the way in the second trial when he cast the probing spell upon it because he already knew the sun's rays and the timing of the sun's angle was important. *What's important to me now? I don't give two coppers about my surroundings, and all I really want is to keep the noose from squeezing around my neck when that platform drops away. All I really care about is myself.* Rainier cast the spell on himself while focusing on the pattern of the bent light he had seen in the previous trial and coupled it with his very urgent sense of survival. *What spell am I casting?* Rainier felt like a child playing too close to a raging fire. Without experience and training in magic, one false move could kill him as surely as the noose.

Given the circumstances, he didn't have too many options. Rainier poured spark into the spell and opened his eyes.

Soft light streamed out from his body in every direction. It didn't inhibit his vision, but the new experience was disorienting. *Could everyone see the light? What do the streams of light tell me?* While all the streams of light originated from him, they didn't branch out evenly away from him.

A thick stream of light headed towards the axe held by the nooseman and then the streams of light dispersed within feet of the axe. *Am I supposed to run and capture the axe?* Rainier almost removed the noose hanging loosely around his neck and darted for the nooseman, but his Sicarius training stopped him. *Trying to retrieve the axe is certain death.*

Rainier looked across the mass of spectators and saw that the streams of light heading in that direction all terminated about halfway through the crowd. *Death by arrows.* Checking his theory, Rainier looked down at his feet. A bright spot surrounded where he stood. *Death by noose.* Suddenly, Julian's words came back to him, "The path to becoming an oracle will be clear to only the truly enlightened." *Enlightened paths...paths of light.* That bastard Julian had been giving a hint all along. *Which one of these paths leads away from death?*

Rainier turned his head, looking for any path of light that led to safety. Focusing on the end goal, Rainier looked for a stream of light that went the furthest. Beyond the crowd, no light reached past the archers. He looked to his side – no doors or exits that way. Finally, he looked behind him, above the rest of the Remnant. A small stream of light cleared the wall. *One chance in a million. I don't suppose I could have asked for better odds from an Immortal.* Rainier tried to trace the light backwards, but the trouble was that there were so many paths crossing over each other. *What would Sana do? She'd change the pattern.* Rainier stared at the path of light going over the wall and shifted his focus to be entirely on that pathway. As he did so, the other paths dropped away, leaving a clear, if impossible, course of action. The light traversed the entire platform, zigzagging chaotically, leaping high and diving low. *It may not be the easiest path to survival, but I'll take it.*

"Rainier Tallow, your failure to live within the pattern is now forgiven. Return to the pattern in peace." He swung his axe and cut the rope that held the platform beneath his feet.

Rainier dropped.

Before the rope tightened and snapped his neck, Rainier reached out to grab the edge of the platform, stopping his descent, just as the enlightened path predicted. The path went upwards next, so Rainier heaved his legs up onto the platform. As he did so, a volley of arrows embedded in the wooden structure supporting the platform of the gallows beneath. He looked up just in time to see the nooseman, who realized he had forgotten to tie Rainier's arms, rushing towards him with his axe raised overhead. Rainier fought every urge and ounce of training that told him to sweep his opponent's leg and kill the nooseman before the next volley of arrows came towards him because the enlightened path before him didn't stay on the platform. It moved slightly towards the nooseman and then launched towards the crowd. *What good is an enlightened path if I don't know how to read it?* Despite his training, he trusted the lighted path that had so far let him escape certain death on two occasions and waited until the axe descended towards him. At the last possible instant, he rolled towards the light.

The axe cut into the wooden platform in the location his neck had previously occupied. Instead of cutting flesh, it snapped the rope around his neck. If he had rolled in any other direction, the rope wouldn't have been in the blade's path. *Enlightened path is right.* Rainier kicked the backside of the nooseman's knee to drop him to the ground and then jumped to his feet. The path before him curved out and around the crowd, which didn't make sense unless...

Rainier sprinted towards the crowd, grabbed the dangling rope that had previously been attached to his neck and leapt as far as he could leap. His momentum took him out over the crowd, whose lust for a good old-fashioned hanging had turned into loud cheers for the unanticipated entertainment his harrowing escape provided. As he flew over the heads of the cheering Disenite citizens, the second volley of arrows flew by him. The skilled archers aimed true, but Rainier was no longer where they had aimed when they released their arrows from distant walls. The arrows rained onto the platform, embedding in the wood everywhere they didn't meet the flesh of the nooseman.

Rainier's feet touched the wooden platform and he cut in sharp angles across the gallows wherever the enlightened path took him, which appeared to be a very circuitous route towards the dead jailer. As he darted around, arrows landed by his feet or whistled by his ear, but he never got hit. When he got closer to the jailer, two things caught his eye: the axe the jailer had pulled free from the platform and a ring of keys sparkled in the sunlight. *The enlightened path goes straight through them as well, so I guess that's as good of a sign as I'm going to get.* Rainier slid across the wooden planks as he approached the jailer, following a dip in the enlightened path. His hand reached the jailer's keys and tightened around them as an arrow flew within a hair's width of his face. *That was too close. The next time the path tells me to slide, I'm going to slide a little lower.*

Rainier then grabbed the axe and slung the dead jailer on his back as he stood, using his body as a flesh shield while he made his way towards Kalus and the Remnant. Rainier could see more guards fighting through the crowd to get to the platform. He was running out of time, but he knew he had enough to survive, so long as he kept following the enlightened path ahead of him.

Rainier tossed Kalus the keys to his manacles and Kalus said, "It took you long enough." Kalus bent down to remove the shackles from his ankles first.

Rainier dropped the dead jailer near Kalus to provide some cover and then took advantage of Kalus' hunched over position by jumping off his back onto the shoulders of the Remnant standing next to him. Without breaking stride, Rainier yelled back to Kalus, "I was fast enough to save you. Now try being more useful than a stepstool and free everyone else before those guards make it through the crowd. Then meet me up on the wall." Rainier raced along the shoulders of the Remnant and leapt over the parapeted wall into relative safety from the archers surrounding the platform. The parapet didn't provide him with cover from the archers atop this wall, though, so Rainier charged at the nearest one, chopping with the bulky axe before the archer could drop his bow and unsheathe his sword. Rainier grabbed the sword as he ran past. *I'll take that. I'd prefer two short swords, but even one is better than wielding a timber slicer like Magnus.*

Kalus and the first few members of the Remnant had begun clearing the parapeted wall while the Remnant below freed themselves under a barrage of arrows. *They better not suffer any casualties. Even a single death is an insult to the devotion we have shown and the lives we have surrendered in the name of the Remnant.* Up on the parapet wall, Rainier tossed Kalus the axe. "Do your worst. Hold that side of the wall."

Kalus laughed and said, "I'm always at my best when I'm doing my worst." He thrust the axe in the air and yelled, "We are the Remnant! We will survive as we always have – on our own!" Then he launched himself at a guard with savage intent.

Rainier ran in the opposite direction, slicing through archers as he followed the enlightened path. The archers were trained soldiers, but an archer was no match for a master swordsman at close range. They barely slowed him down. Near the end of the parapeted wall, Rainier crouched in an alcove because the light on the path before him pulsed in this location. A half second later, two guards rushed around the corner. Rainier sliced through their hamstrings as they ran by. A few of the Remnant came up behind him and took their weapons. "Hold this position," he commanded of them.

He turned back towards the direction Kalus had ran and took a deep breath. The Remnant had taken the wall, but the soldiers below had worked their way through the crowd and even more joined the fight atop the wall. The Remnant wouldn't hold for long once all those soldiers joined the fight. *At least the light is still shining in front of me and the noose is no longer around my neck...well, that's not quite true.* The loop still dangled around his neck, but the danger was gone. *Follow the enlightened path.* That sounded simple, and the path was clear, but the choice was not. He looked out over the wall and saw the ships lining the bay some fifty feet below him. *Ah well, it's worked up until now. I might as well follow the path again.* "Remnant – Take a swim!"

Rainier ran down the wall, jumped onto a merlon atop the parapet and leapt as far as he could leap. He pointed his toes and held the sword above his head so that contact with the water wouldn't impale the blade into him, and then held his breath, hoping a rock didn't greet him at the bottom.

Whoosh! The cold water rushed by him as he plunged into the depths of the bay. He tumbled in circles and started to swim to the surface when he realized the enlightened path didn't lead him upwards. Rainier immediately changed course to follow it, holding the blade between his teeth so that he could swim faster. His lungs began to burn when the path turned skyward, and Rainier broke through the surface of the water to gasp in the sweet air.

Rainier found himself beneath the docks, out of view from everyone. From his vantage point, his saw his friends fly en masse through the air and he cringed at the number of broken bones they would suffer as they collided with each other under water. He heard footsteps on the dock above and he peeked around the corner to find that one of the soldiers guarding the dock was running down the dock with a bow in his hands. *My friends will be completely defenseless.* Rainier grabbed the edge of the dock and reached up high enough to grab the soldier by the leg as he ran by, pulling him into the water. From there, it was the simple matter of sword versus bow and the water turned red.

Next, Rainier followed the enlightened path beneath the docks to where a ship was tied. He chuckled when he saw the name on the stern – *Remnant Awakens.* His escape had led him right back to his commandeered ship. At least it wouldn't be heavily defended if it hadn't been put into active duty yet. Rainier climbed the rope holding the stern of the ship to the dock without anyone noticing and landed on the ship's deck. Only two guards were stationed on the ship, and they were occupied watching the commotion his crew caused by suddenly jumping into the bay. He dispatched them before they could even turn around to notice his presence. Then he followed the enlightened path to the armory and obtained an exploding orb. Rainier triggered the timer on the orb and threw it towards shore. It demolished the pier as it connected to the rest of the docks, cutting off any soldiers from blocking their escape.

Rainier climbed upwards and clung to the mast so that the Remnant that were swimming towards the end of the pier that remained intact could see him and yelled, "I hope you've enjoyed your dip in the waters of Disentia, but I've had enough of this place. Let's go back to Malethya."

A cheer went up from the Remnant when they saw Rainier alive and standing on the Remnant Awakens. A long journey can make even the hardiest seamen feel the confines of their ship, but at that moment, the Remnant

Awakens looked more like home than anything they had experienced since reaching the Disenite shores.

"Toss the lines and set sail. We need some distance between us and this shore if Julian decides to give chase." Rainier's men eagerly obliged and they cleared the bay at full sail. Rainier commanded his troops, "Tend to the wounded and chart a course to somewhere remote that we can stock up on supplies. I'm going to the captain's quarters."

Rainier shut the door to the captain's quarters and before he could process what had just happened, a doorway appeared within the room and Julian stepped through. Rainier grabbed his sword instinctively, but he didn't have a chance to use it, and even if had the opportunity to try, he was sure that Julian was wrapped in a lot of wards and defensive magic.

The Immortal said, "You have passed the third Oracle Trial. Drop the sword and come with me. We have much to discuss."

CHAPTER THREE

ORACLE OF THE UNNAMED

Rainier followed Julian through the doorway into an immaculate office with décor that hadn't changed in several decades. The doorway disappeared behind him.

Julian addressed him formally, "Rainier Tallow, for completion of the Oracle Trials, I congratulate you. It is a rare gift to see the pattern in the world around you and rarer still to walk the enlightened path."

"Was that real or part of some magical test? If I failed the test, would I have met the noose?" Rainier had to ask. He knew he was still being tested, but everything seemed too real to be contrived by magic, even from someone as powerful as Julian.

Julian thought for a moment before answering. "For what I need you to do, for the role I wish you to have, a magical trial would not suffice. I need the leader of my army to use his powers in the real world. I need you to act decisively when your life is on the line."

"...and the arrows that pierced the flesh of my friends and family as they stood manacled and awaiting death?" Rainier could not let their loss be wiped away as part of some test. "As part of the Remnant, they devoted their lives to Disentia. They deserved better."

Julian frowned, and the creases of his paper-thin skin doubled upon themselves in folds that had been formed over hundreds of years. He said, "I will heal those that have injuries and I regret that any member of the Remnant needed to die, but I needed to be sure of who you are. There is much you don't understand. As for the Remnant, your father created your group, and I trusted your father's judgment. He asked a lot of the Remnant, and you have fulfilled the purpose he intended, but I'm afraid I will ask more."

"My father sent us to warn you of a blood mage in Malethya. He sent us to warn you about Lattimer Regallo. We are the messengers. Our task is complete." The words sounded hollow even as Rainier said them. The task wouldn't be complete until Lattimer was removed from power.

"You are much more than a messenger, and don't pretend otherwise. The task initially set before you may be complete, but the need remains. And if there is one thing I know about Trabon Tallow, it is that he probably anticipated the need when he formed the Remnant. I will assume he sent you here, at this time, to serve me once again." Julian looked to Rainier and waited for him to refuse the stated assumption.

As much as Rainier wanted to deny the Immortal, he could not. His father was maddeningly correct and impossible to argue with even beyond the grave. For something as important to him as forming the Remnant, he would have thought through all the future possibilities of its formation. Trabon had a reason. He just didn't share it with anyone else. Rainier nodded his head in concession of the point and waited for Julian to go on.

Julian sat upon the top of his ornate desk, apparently

needing to rest his ancient muscles. In explanation, he said, "I can use magic to hide the aches in my bones or to give my muscle the strength it once had, but I tire of it. Sometimes I want to feel the pain in my joints and the weakness in my legs. It helps me to remember that things have changed since I first came to these shores. What do you know of the blood mages and the Twice-Broken Wars?"

Rainier thought back to his lessons from Lucus and his heart ached at the memory of his dead teacher. He gathered his thoughts and restated the history lesson succinctly. "Candor researched the relationship between the pattern and the spark, founding a form of study called spark-based magic that did not rely upon the pattern. Without being limited by the pattern, the students that studied spark-based magic under Candor were capable of great deeds and powerful spells. They were only limited by their imagination. These times were called the Golden Ages of Candor. After some time passed, the students of Candor grew greedy and used their powers against each other in a quest for ultimate power. They used spark-based magic in wars against each other, turning people into armies of mindless Furies whose sole purpose was to attack, reeking such devastation upon Malethya that the people began calling them blood mages. Candor saw the evil his research had created and called his former students together. At the dinner, he used blood magic for the first time, turning their wine to arsenic after they swallowed it and killing the last of the blood mages.

All was peaceful in Malethya, at least as peaceful as Malethya ever is, until my father and his Disenite army appeared on its shores. The Disenites traded peacefully with the Malethyans until they discovered the matter in which they taught magic. They allowed their wizards to cast spells without a strong affiliation with the pattern. Our priests would not tolerate such a blasphemy and we invaded. The Malethyans turned back my father's army by using magic in battle, and the devastation set off a second civil war within Malethya. Malethyans refer to that period of their history as the Twice-Broken Wars."

Julian sat as still as a stone gargoyle atop a castle, but Rainier didn't dare assume the man wasn't listening. When he finished, Julian said, "Good. You know all the common histories. Let me fill you in on the relevant parts they left out of the story."

Rainier sensed Julian was settling in for a story. Rainier hoped his ship didn't reach Malethya before the old man finished his hundred-year oration. *Old man stories are the worst.*

Julian opened his mouth, stopped, and then closed it again. Then he reached to place his hands upon Rainier's head. Rainier recoiled at the thought of Julian touching him with his leathery skin. The Immortal said, "Sit still. I don't have time to share all my wisdom with you and only have you retain a tenth of it." When Julian's hand touched him a moment later, Rainier would have recoiled again, but the Immortal had an iron grip.

Images and words flooded into Rainier's brain, overflowing his capacity to understand or process any of the information. He squirmed and fought against the Immortal, but it did no good. The memories kept coming. As they did, the sights and sounds of Julian's memories overstimulated his senses, causing excruciating pain. Somewhere in the part of his brain that was still processing his own thoughts, he laughed perversely – he'd have to tell the Sicarius Headmaster about the pain that sensory overload could cause so that she could add it to her arsenal of torturous techniques. The small joke distracted him for a moment, and in that moment the stream of memories came to a blissful end.

"What did you do to me?" a dazed Rainier asked the obvious.

"I've just given you a century's worth of knowledge. No amount of education could prepare you more adequately for the tasks that await you." Julian spoke to Rainier who was trying to listen even though his mind felt ready to explode. "The only problem is that you will fight against my memories and will try to exclude them from your mind. You won't be able to recall all the details of my life as you would recall your own. However, when you find yourself in a situation where you are looking for answers, you may access a memory of mine that aids you. For now, I will help you access the most important ones."

Flash. *"Raise your glasses." Around the table, my former friends sit in adulation of Candor. I can't help but be disturbed to see these practitioners of spark-based magic in their overly elaborate robes and golden rings. They had all once been pious students with nothing to their names, wearing the simple robes that Candor and I still wore. Now that they were all powerful wizards, greed and power had changed them, but not enough to refuse an invitation and to celebrate the life's work of the man responsible for the power they now wielded. I smile at Candor and raise my* glass, "To Candor, the greatest wizard who ever lived." I toast Candor and then clink my glass with the wizards beside me. "To Candor!!!" a chorus echoed around the table as I raise my glass to my lips. I closed my eyes to savor the taste and then opened them upon hearing the gurgling fits of dying men.

Candor said, "The poison will kill you within minutes. If you feel its effects, I offer you a simple choice – repent and live your lives in service to me or die." The gurgling didn't stop even as spastic hands reached overhead for salvation.

"What have you done?" I didn't feel the effects of the poison. Was I safe? I asked my mentor, "What becomes of me?"

"They went too far. I could not allow them to spill the blood of Malethya for one more day. These wars will not be the legacy I leave." Candor then said the haunting words, "As for you, you shall have a different fate...I'm sorry Julian. There is no one else I can trust with this burden."

Rainier was pulled from the memory back into Julian's office. The abrupt change disoriented him, so the questions in his mind never reached his lips. *Julian the Immortal was one of Candor's original students? Candor didn't kill him like all the stories said. Instead, Candor did...what, exactly? What burden did Julian bear? And Candor...Julian's memory showed him the face of Candor. It was a face he knew well...*

Before the questions could make their way from his mind to his lips, Julian started answering them, and he did so with a release of years upon years of anger. "I was Candor's best student. He taught me everything he knew, and I stuck to the rules he required. When the other students were seduced by power and greed, I stayed the course. I watched helplessly as my former friends and colleagues turned into blood mages, a blight upon humanity. When their treachery reached unspeakable heights, Candor finally acted. He imprisoned the blood mages, and only he holds the key to their cell." Julian's anger subsided slightly, but Rainier got the sense that Julian had merely succumbed to his new reality, rather than actually letting go of his anger. "As for me, Candor made me immortal and banished me from Malethya. I am only able to set foot upon Malethya's shores if the threat of blood magic returns." He paused, and then smiled knowingly at Rainier. "You speak of the sacrifices of the Remnant — I understand them well. The Remnant has spent their lives away from the only home they knew — I have spent lifetimes away from my home. You thought you protected Disentia from a blood mage — you were protecting Malethya from itself. Your warning did not fall on deaf ears. It was a call to me. It was a call to return to Malethya and to act upon the burden Candor placed upon me. I will cleanse the land of blood magic and be banished from its shores once again."

Before Rainier could empathize with the plight of Julian, he touched his forehead and pushed another memory upon him.

I stepped foot on the shores of a distant land, a land that would be my new home. The natives saw the arrival of my ship and greeted me with the threat of spears and arrows. They didn't realize how inconsequential their weapons were. I amplified my voice so that it would carry for miles past the seashore and said, "I am Julian the Immortal, and I claim this land. It shall be called Disentia, because if I could dissent from the vows I have taken, I would, and I would leave these shores immediately. You will follow me."

Someone who considered himself a hero let loose an arrow. It curved around me and struck the sand, guided to safety by the defensive magic I held in place. I looked up to the man and fulfilled his death wish by casting a spell that lifted the arrow, turned it around, and sent it through his heart. I said, "I do not wish to harm any of you, but this is the fate of all that would seek to kill me. I bring you knowledge of magic and the pattern. You will learn to respect the pattern above all things."

Rainier was again ripped from the memory, and the sudden changes still disoriented him when Julian began chuckling in a nostalgic way. "When I came to these shores, I was still young and naïve. I was so determined to prevent spark-based magic in any form within Disentia that my first order upon arriving was to respect the pattern above all things." The nostalgia turned to melancholy as he explained the consequences of his actions. "The people here were so shaken by my arrival that they took the words I spoke literally. Their innocent praise of the pattern, for which they knew nothing about, turned into some form of religion...and religion is a funny thing. If you tried to start a religious movement, it would be difficult to do. I would argue that the challenge of starting a religion pales in comparison to the challenge of ending one. My first words here have manifested and shaped the culture of Disentia in ways I never could have predicted."

Your first declaration was that you are immortal, you demonstrate arcane powers beyond the knowledge of anyone around you, and then declare the pattern to be held above all else...and you wonder why the people started to treat you like a god? Thankfully, Rainier had collected enough of his wits to keep his thoughts to himself. Instead, he said, "My people are on a ship leaving these shores. What is it you ask of us to do? You are considered an all-powerful, living representation of what Disenites worship. What do you need from me that you can't ask of your priests?"

Julian sighed, contemplating how to answer the question. "I need someone to wield the power of the empire I have created without the...pretenses that are too deeply ingrained in my priests." Before Julian could continue, an explosion rocked the walls of the office. Julian said, "Ah. That would be the demonstration I ordered when it became clear that you held the gifts of an oracle. I want you to understand the power of the Unnamed Army. They are the sword and the spear of Disentia. They have given up their names and devoted their lives to protect the pattern." He then stood up and walked onto his balcony, beckoning Rainier to join him.

In a field below him, the shining metal armor of Julian's holy army reflected the morning sun so brightly he had to squint to see the details. When he did, he realized the paladin's armor was so bright because it created its own light. Rainier thought back to the paladin in his room, whose armor changed color when he embarrassed her. Seeing the demonstration below him gave Rainier a new appreciation for her abilities. Two groups of paladins engaged in battle, but it was unlike any battle Rainier had ever seen. The paladins jumped abnormally high in the air and landed with such force that it shook the ground. Their swords were bathed in light, and when they parried a blow from another paladin, it created a blinding flash of light. Rainier finally spoke, "I see an army that the greatest fighters of Bellator could not meet in battle..." Boom! Beyond the sparring paladins, a glowing orb launched into the air from some contraption. It flew further than any catapult could reach and when it landed in the distance, it exploded with the force of a hundred exploding orbs, throwing the earth into the air. "Only the strongest wizards could cast a spell of significant power to that distance. The Ispirtu wizards would be wiped out if they joined the battle." Rainier paused, and said with a heavy heart as reality set in, "All of Malethya will be destroyed. No one will survive this war. You can't send the Unnamed Army to Malethya."

Julian nodded slowly and said, "Now you are beginning to realize the predicament I face. I performed my duties too well. I created a culture whose primary purpose was to oppose blood magic. Duty turned to religion and religion turned to fanaticism. The soldiers are obedient to the orders of the priests in all ways and the priests are unreasonable zealots."

"Why don't you put an end to it?" Rainier couldn't help but blurt out. "Speak and tell them they've gone too far."

"Think on it, Rainier. You don't need to be an oracle to see what their course of action would be. They have been told the dangers of blood magic their entire lives. It is so engrained in them that they would be more likely to believe the sky was green and the grass was blue than to believe that practitioners of spark-based magic didn't deserve to die a terrible death. And the priests...they have become too powerful to let any alternate truths enter their ears. They control the people and the armies...at least they did until you became an oracle and the duty of leading the Unnamed Army became yours..."

Rainier's head was spinning, and he wasn't entirely sure if it was from Julian's memories being jammed into his brain or from trying to process all the complications of his new reality. With a million questions tumbling about in his brain, only a simple comment came out. "My men are on a ship sailing away from here..."

"Yes, and you will join them soon. I will send you back to the ship before it is too far away for me to create a portal." Julian said. "It was necessary..."

Rainier's head started to clear enough to finish the thought, "It was necessary to have the third Oracle Trial in a public setting. There needed to be enough witnesses that the priests could not deny me. The people needed to see me live. They needed to see me live when everyone expected me to die. They needed to see proof that I am an oracle."

"Yes. The priests do not take kindly to threats to their power. You would have suffered an 'accident' and life would resume as usual in Disentia." Julian smiled at Rainier for the first time, and Rainier struggled to stop from gagging at the sight of Julian's decayed and rotten teeth. "Now that the people have witnessed your gifts in action, your position is safe. Your life is not."

"That's why my men are on a boat right now? To preserve their safety?" Rainier asked.

Julian nodded. "Did you really think it was a coincidence that the Remnant Awakens was moored next to the gallows with only a handful of guards on hand? I helped you where I could, but I could only arrange for so much aid. Regardless, you do speak some truth. I believe I have grown complacent in my position...it may be time to reassert my authority." Julian clapped his hands, producing the sound of a hand bell. Instantly his door opened, and a paladin entered. "Summon the high priest," Julian commanded.

The paladin left and Julian turned back to Rainier. "Say nothing. I will do the talking."

Rainier thought back to the words he had already spoken to the high priest and the tone in which he had spoken them. Having already ruined any chance of diplomacy with the man, he was perfectly happy to sit back and let Julian the Immortal carry the conversation. Moments later, Jamison entered the room with robes flowing. He gave a perfunctory bow towards Julian and said, "Your Voice comes with open ears to hear your words and spread your message to the land." It had the sound of a phrase repeated so often that it lost its meaning.

"Rainier Tallow will be named the Oracle of the Unnamed Army."

The high priest's eyes settled on Rainier with disgust, a feeling he didn't try to hide from Julian when he replied. "This simpleton will never be named Oracle of the Unnamed Army. I tolerated your games during his trial, and I allowed him to be tested in the Trials, but I will not abide..."

Julian raised his hand, and Jamison's voice cut off. He gasped for breath and reached for his neck to remove the constriction blocking his airway, but there was nothing to grasp. Julian squeezed his hand tighter and said, "You *tolerated*...you *allowed*...you will not *abide*..." His voice grew louder with each of the words. "These are not the words of a humble servant. These are the words of someone who has forgotten their master." At his last word, Julian extended his arm outwards and released his grip. The high priest flew backwards and hit the wall of Julian's office, sending age old artifacts to the ground in the process.

Anger flashed in the high priest's eyes as he stood, trying to hide his obvious pain. He said between gasps of air, "I have ruled your kingdom for years while you sat in silence. Now you dare to tell me that I don't know my place. Perhaps you are the one who has lost touch with his proper place." Jamison weaved his arms in an intricate pattern and prepared a complex spell. Julian looked unperturbed, and his only action was to stand between the high priest and Rainier. The high priest said some words of power and pushed his arms outwards, unleashing a torrent of ice, fire, and lightning towards Julian the Immortal. When it neared him, the flames dispersed, the electricity arced to nearby metal objects, and the ice vaporized into a harmless cloud of fog.

Julian said, "I have lived too long for you to kill me with that elementary spell, you pathetic excuse for a wizard. I *tolerated* your political games because they are of no consequence to me. I *allowed* you to rule my kingdom, and I will not *abide* your disobedience. Now, show me that you are still a useful tool despite your ineptitude. Join me on the balcony."

The anger in Jamison's eyes never left, but he did as commanded. When he reached the balcony, Julian told him, "Amplify your voice and proclaim Rainier Tallow to the be the Oracle of the Unnamed Army. Do it with the joy of someone who has waited for this day for years and the gravitas of someone accustomed to speaking with authority. Finally, speak of Rainier in the riddles that you have made popular in my silence."

The high priest tried to rationalize with Julian by saying, "The army will not respond to him. He cannot speak with the pattern, and he does not know our ways. He will…"

"Say the words, Voice. Now." Julian cut him off and the conversation reached its end.

A pained look came over Julian's face as he weighed his options, but the previous encounter discouraged him from any further brave acts against Julian. Julian leaned towards Rainier and whispered, "Listen carefully to the manner in which he speaks. The alternating speech is called speaking with the pattern. The more conversations weaved within each other demonstrate a greater proficiency in the so-called art. It is another example of contrived power created by people who lack true ability." The high priest turned towards the army below and spoke in a voice that carried far beyond the fields of the demonstration.

"I am the Voice of Julian the Immortal, and I have a proclamation." The commanding voice silenced the demonstration below, and everyone turned towards the balcony to hear the pronouncement. The high priest then switched his tone to that of an excited commoner, "We have awaited someone capable of passing the Oracle Trials for far too long." Finally, he switched tones again to give voice to the silent armies below, "We have awaited a commander worthy of our might." As the commoner, he said, "Today in the gallows, we witnessed someone escape certain death by slipping the noose, running through a storm of arrows without being hit, freeing his friends, and escaping to the sea." As the army, the high priest said, "Such a man is capable of guiding the swords and spears of the Unnamed Army." The high priest then ushered Rainier in front of the balcony and said as the Voice, "The man that accomplished these feats stands before you. Rainier Tallow, leader of the Remnant, survivor of the gallows, and walker of the enlightened path, in the name of Julian the Immortal, I proclaim you to be the Oracle of the Unnamed Army."

The army below banged sword to shield in approval and a cheer rose from the city beyond. The high priest, turned to him and said, "They await your orders."

Rainier looked to the army below him. When he spoke, his voice carried as the high priest had done. He kept his message short and to the point. "Prepare for war. A blood mage lives in Malethya." Now the shields and swords banged in random appreciation from the silent Unnamed Army below, who had just been given the opportunity to utilize the skills they had devoted their lives to honing. Rainier turned away and walked back into Julian's office.

The high priest followed, and Julian shut the door. He said to the high priest, "Summon the chief of my Guards like the obedient priest you claim to be. Then come back in. I'll have use of you." It had obviously been a long time since the high priest had taken orders, but he begrudgingly followed suit.

When he left, Julian said, "Despite his arrogance, the high priest spoke some truth. The Unnamed Army takes orders using patterned speech, and it will take time for you to learn this art. I will send Jamison with you. As head priest of the Marked faction, he will command the respect of the troops and keep things orderly."

"I thought the priests would try to prevent me from commanding the troops." Rainier couldn't help but ask the question, "Will he obey me and accept my position?"

"Do not be so ignorant!" Julian scoffed at the absurdity of the question. "I thought I had made myself clear. His power is threatened by the presence of an oracle. However, while he plots to kill you, he will keep the troops in order so that he can safely assume command when you die."

"Then why are you sending him with me?" The stupid questions kept pouring out of Rainier. His father had always said he needed a better filter.

"When you proclaimed the Remnant to have ties to the Marked faction, you made Jamison a direct enemy. I'm sending him with you because his intentions are clear. He wants you out of the way. Sometimes knowing you have an enemy is preferable to wondering if you have an enemy, and the politics of Disentia and the Priests are foreign to you. I am protecting you."

"But if I kill him, I lose control of the army?"

"You are a fractal-forsaken oracle. Use it. Walk the enlightened path. Avoid his knives in the night until you have control over the army, and then dispose of him."

The door opened again, and the high priest returned. Jamison bowed deeply to Julian and spoke with too much sincerity when he said, "How may I serve?"

"The Oracle of the Unnamed Army will set sail for Malethya. I ask that you serve as his Voice and accompany him."

The statement was the last thing anyone in the room expected, least of all Rainier. *I don't want some priest acting like a parrot on my shoulder...especially one that wants me dead.* Jamison looked like he was about to give a rebuttal but thought better of it. After a moment of reflection, Jamison said, "I humbly accept the position as the Oracle's Voice and pledge the armies of the Marked faction to his cause." Nothing in the way he looked at Rainier suggested the humble intentions he proclaimed.

Julian finalized the process by saying, "Rainier Tallow, do you accept Jamison of the Marked faction as your Voice, with all the duties and responsibilities of the position passed to him?"

Julian who nodded slightly towards Rainier in encouragement. Without too many other options, Rainier said, "I accept Jamison as my Voice." *Even though it is the last thing in Malethya I'd wish for.* "I pass duties and responsibilities associated with the position to him." *What duties and responsibilities? With some fractal's luck, Jamison will lose his voice or his life before I ever have to find out.*

The high priest placed a hand on Rainier's mouth and a second hand on Jamison's mouth and muttered some words that could only be a spell. Rainier stood in awkward silence until the man finished. His cold, clammy, and possibly decaying hand dropped, and Rainier wiped his sleeve across his mouth in a not-so-subtle way of removing the man's sweat from his face.

Julian spoke to the high priest, "I will be sending Rainier back to the ship via a portal. You will go to the barracks and make sure my wishes are carried out. I expect the ships of the Marked faction to be loaded with troops and sails to be set by the time the sun rises tomorrow. The Marked faction's ships can easily catch the Remnant Awakens in open water. When they do, the Oracle of the Unnamed Army will have devised a plan of attack for the coming battle with Malethya."

"As you command..." The high priest bowed and backed towards the door. *He is probably plotting my death with each step.*

After they exited, Julian turned to Rainier. "That should buy you a few weeks on the ship to learn our customs and prepare to lead the Unnamed Army." The Immortal searched quickly through a bookshelf before deciding upon an unfairly thick text. "Ah, here we go. *A Life in the Pattern* was written by a pious priest, a long dead friend whose life's work has been taken completely out of context. It is complete rubbish, but it does a fair job of explaining the mindset of the priests and the paladin army that serves them. More importantly, a lot of the narrative in this book has been interpreted literally by the priesthood and used more as doctrine or laws than it was ever intended. And once you know the rules of the game..."

"...I can use them to my advantage," Rainier said.

Julian's thin lips nearly cracked as they stretched across his ancient teeth into a smile.

Rainier thought back to his tribe's reputation in Malethya. They were considered fierce negotiators from their frequent transactions as they moved from town to town, and Rainier was no exception. The thought of relying upon his finely-honed skills of persuasion brought some comfort to Rainier's current predicament. If persuasion was the skill he needed to survive the next part of this journey, at least he was prepared for once. That was one step in the right direction from the Oracle Trials.

"When you aren't reading this book or devising a plan of attack for when you reach Malethya..." Julian started. *Like that leaves any time for another life-threatening task.* Julian continued, "...I expect you to hold onto the enlightened path at all times. It will fatigue you at first, but as you learn from your experiences..." *Experiences like surviving Jamison's attempts to take me life?* "...you become accustomed to the pattern and your strength will not wane." *Maybe I'll be able to fight for my life when people are trying to kill me then.* "Eventually, you have the potential to expand the power past yourself. It is this potential that makes you the right person to lead my armies. You will see the enlightened path for not just yourself, but the entire army, and you will direct them accordingly. Do you understand me?"

Don't get killed. "I understand. I will train with diligence." *After that, well...we'll see.* Rainier grew tired of people directing his life like he was a tool at their disposal. His father always knew best, which was a common curse among rebellious boys as they grew into men, but it took on an entirely new meaning when your father could predict the future. He'd be a fractal-forsaken fool if he escaped the strings of his father just to hand the strings to another. *If I am going to escape Julian's reach, I'll need allies.* "Is there anyone that I can trust to protect me as I learn to walk the enlightened path? If I am in a weakened state, Jamison has a better chance of burying a knife in my back. Having some muscle at my side would at least force him to be creative."

Julian scratched the grey stubble on his face that somehow managed to avoid tearing his parchment thin skin as it pushed through the surface and said, "Your point is well-taken. I do not want to underestimate the effort it will take for you to hone your abilities." He stopped scratching his chin as a thought came to mind. "The Disenite religion allows for priests to name fighters as their Hand. I think the practice was put in place for silver-tongued priests to maintain their power, but it may be useful in this situation."

"I choose Kalus Straker, a member of the Remnant. He has fought with me in skirmishes since our youth."

Julian shook his head slowly. "Do not be hasty." The condemnation softened as Julian expanded upon his thoughts by saying, "You will need someone familiar with the Disenite ways since you will likely be attacked in the manner of a Disenite, not a Malethyan. A member of my personal guard would fit that need." *It would also tighten the strings that hold me to you.* Then Julian reconsidered his stance and said, "However, Jamison will have tricks of his own, and having this Kalus as your hand will ensure your communication back to the Remnant and those faithful to you." Reaching a conclusion without consulting Rainier, he smiled and said, "You should name both. You have two hands, so you should be able to name two people as your Hands. Any rules forbidding it would go against the pattern, and not even Jamison will risk that."

Rainier thought frantically for a way to influence the decision of who was named his Hand from the personal guard. *I can't let Julian name one of his most loyal paladins to be at my side night and day. The last thing I want is someone I'm not able to influence.* The problem was that he didn't know any of the paladins...or did he? The girl that stood guard in his room had Julian's infinity insignia on her armor. *She seemed to have a large distaste for my sense of humor, but she did have a strong right hook, and I know my words penetrated her armor. She might do the job of protecting me well if she doesn't kill me first.* "What is the name of the paladin who protected me in my room before the Oracle Trials? Could she be named my Hand?"

"She is a paladin in the Unnamed Army – she sacrificed her name a long time ago. When the members of the Unnamed Army have a need to talk to each other, they address each other by their rank within their unit. However, I have no idea who guarded your door last night. I haven't spoken in years, and I stopped memorizing guard schedules years before that." Julian clapped his hands again to the sound of a bell and a paladin appeared.

"How may I serve?" he asked. The man looked like he could punch through a wall without overly exerting himself. He also gazed upon Julian like a deity and looked like he would drown a puppy without a second thought, if ordered to do so.

"One, who was assigned to Rainier's room last night?" Julian demanded.

"Six."

"What is your assessment of her?"

"She possesses impressive skills in battle, but she has been held back from advancing further within the ranks of the Unnamed Army."

"Why is that?"

"Her temperament, your grace. She lacks the ability to lead without emotion." *Perfect, that is what I need.* "Despite this limitation, she is loyal to the pattern and to you." *Maybe not quite perfect then. That whole loyalty part could be a problem.*

Julian said, "Send for her. And tell her to pack her belongings. She has a long trip ahead of her."

One nodded and left the room to fetch her.

Julian then turned towards Rainier and said, "This may be the last chance we have to speak privately until I arrive in Malethya. There is one part of your mission that I wanted to remain unknown. I did not wish to speak of it in front of the priests or the paladins. Do you remember the faces of the men in my memory?"

"Yes." The vision from Julian's past was burned into his memory as if it were his own. Men of power. Women of entitled grace. One face stood out amongst all of them – Ibson.

"After Candor forced his former students to obey him, he locked them away and told them they needed to earn their release. They were tasked with researching magic, and specifically the pattern. The cell that held them would not open until the occupants found a magic powerful enough to make up for the devastation they caused with their wars and greed or until someone personally attuned to the pattern released them."

"You want me to find Candor and release them?"

"No." Julian shook his head emphatically. "Candor is known for being the founder of spark-based magic, but later in his career he changed the direction of his studies to pattern-based magic, as he forced the blood mages to study. Candor didn't share the results of his research with anyone, not even me, but I know enough to realize he was successful in some areas. Candor became a master of different dimensions, including time. He would come and go as he pleased, without ever aging. I do not know where he is, but he is not worth chasing." *Ibson could travel through time? I thought he was just a wizened old wizard that ended up in the Infirmary with a head injury.* The two descriptions didn't quite add up to Rainier. Julian moved on before Rainier could sort through his thoughts and Rainier had learned enough from his Sicarius training to know that information was powerful and not to be given freely. "I do not want you to find Candor. I want you to gain a foothold in Malethya with the Marked faction's forces so that the rest of my invading army has a friendly beachhead. Then I want you to penetrate into Malethya with a small group of soldiers and find the cell Candor locked the blood mages in and destroy it, with the people inside, before Lattimer discovers a way to release them. The blood mages, if they are released, are the only people capable of standing in the way of the Unnamed Army. If they are released, the world will not recover from the powerful forces that will oppose each other. It is better that the armies of Malethya be crushed beneath the Unnamed Army than the kingdom of Malethya be destroyed by a battle between blood mages and my paladins. If you can find and destroy this cell, then I will arrive with the remaining factions of the Unnamed army – the Scorched, Frozen, and Charged soldiers – and put an end to the blood mages in Malethya once and for all."

The door opened, ending their private conversation, and One came in with the paladin known as Six. She wore full armor and carried a small travel sack that looked like it contained enough supplies to last for all of a single day.

"I told One that you should pack for a long trip, Six." Julian stated.

"As did I," One added.

"I am told that my duty will be to serve as *his* Hand," Six tried to keep the sneer from her face at the sight of him, but she couldn't hide it completely. "All I need for that duty is my armor."

Julian raised an eyebrow but didn't openly question Rainier's choice in protection. Rainier said, "I see you are speaking to me now. That's a start. Just keep the pointy end of your sword aimed at the people trying to kill me and away from my neck..."

Julian explained, "The hand is not effective unless it communicates and acts with the rest of the body. As your Hand, Six can converse with you, just as One may converse with me."

"If you can converse with me, then I'd like to know your real name. You may be used to being nameless, but I'll need something to call you, and the number Six just won't do." Rainier put on his winningest smile.

Six was unmoved, and she looked questioningly to Julian.

He said, "You are no longer in the ranks of the Nameless Army. You are the Hand of the Oracle. You can use your name if you wish." He waved his hand dismissively, trying to speed things up.

Six formed her name as if it were foreign, but she said, "Lira. My name is Lira."

Julian wasted no more time. He waved his hands and expanded them outwards. As they expanded, a portal ripped through the air in his office and Rainier could see the inside of his cabin on the *Remnant Awakens.* "As the ship leaves these shores, it will be impossible for me to create a portal. Once you walk through this portal, you are on your own until I come with the rest of my army."

Lira drew her sword and jumped through the portal without hesitation, searching for enemies in the empty cabin. Rainier walked through slowly, letting his natural confidence be displayed as he assumed his role as leader of the Remnant.

After passing through the portal, he looked back. Julian said, "You know your mission, Rainier. Go now. Succeed. Ensure the success of the Unnamed Army." The portal snapped shut.

I know my mission. I will stay alive and keep the members of the Remnant from dying at the hands of Jamison or anger Lira enough that she does the job for him. Once I assume command of the Marked faction's troops who currently won't take orders from me, I will storm the beaches of Malethya, but that will only be to disguise my real mission of locating the thought-to-be-

long-dead blood mages of yore and to kill them while they are protected in an impenetrable cell. No problem. Oh, and that doesn't even consider that Ibson, a friendly wizard that was currently speaking in simple rhymes in the Infirmary, was likely the founder of spark-based magic with the capability of performing magic in higher dimensions and traveling through time or the fact that Slate and Sana had probably gotten into all sorts of trouble while I was away. This will be easy.

INTERLUDE

REFLECTIONS

It took Rainier a moment to find the hunter's cottage in the clearing. The amount of security around its small structure made it comically hard to find, but Rainier was with people that knew the cottage well. He walked past Guards, and he could almost see the conflict in their dutiful hearts. He didn't belong here, but they had been told what he came to do, and they let him pass. Was it dishonorable for them to let him pass? Rainier smiled, thinking that he didn't have to worry about that one. His duty was to himself, but who was he loyal to? What ideals did he honor?

Rainier passed through the threshold of the cottage and his world transformed into a beautiful library extending upwards and outwards, exquisite in all forms. Dutiful wizards sat at tables cataloging the contents and trying to regain some of the lost spark-based knowledge. They were all loyal to Lattimer, but in the worst kind of way. They were compelled to do his bidding, trading their own minds for power.

Rainier had been loyal to Slate once, but he saw the price of loyalty. Slate trusted Lattimer, and Lattimer used Slate's loyalty against him. Without Slate fighting in Ispirtu, Lattimer never could have defeated Brannon. Where did Slate's loyalty get him? Slate was a split second and one lucky spell from Lucus away from turning into another one of Lattimer's vegetable brains.

Rainier kept smiling as he walked past the scribes, ignorant people who gave away their loyalty for something as fleeting as power, writing in their notebooks. Up ahead, he saw a doorway leading to a vast desert. It could only be the infamous storage room that Sana had escaped.

Escape was a word that entered my mind quite frequently aboard the ships of the Marked faction, but why did I need to escape? Instead of trying to kill me, they should have thrown me a fractal-forsaken parade for the loyalty I showed to Julian and Disentia.

Who wants loyalty? I don't want anything to do with it.

CHAPTER FOUR

AFLOAT BUT NOT ADRIFT

"Lira!" Rainier bellowed across the deck of the Remnant Awakens. "Kalus claims he can beat you in battle. Care to prove him wrong with some friendly sparring?" It had been several weeks alone on the sea and the crew needed some entertainment. More importantly, Rainier needed a break from reading *A Life in the Pattern*. It should have been named *A Life Without Fun* – don't cheat, don't swindle, repetition breeds excellence, devotion leads to everlasting life. Blah.

Lira, who so far had led a perfectly boring life in the pattern, at least by Rainier's assessment, took a break from silently glowering at Rainier to look towards Kalus. Rainier's childhood friend had grown into a formidable fighter, but he lacked the expertise and Bellator training of Slate or a member of the Crimson Guard back in Malethya.

"You may have shiny armor, but we aren't strangers to a good fight in the Remnant." Kalus warmed up by stretching and going through his daily forms with his axe, foregoing the preferred short swords of many fighters in the Remnant.

She shrugged, apparently deciding that some sport was preferable to another lonely day on the ship. She stood, with the light glistening off her shining armor, and promptly began taking it off.

Rainier laughed and said, "She not only accepts your

challenge, but she also wants to shut you up for good. She's going to fight you without armor!"

"Maybe she doesn't want to fight. Maybe she has a different activity in mind." Kalus smirked at the innuendo, and Rainier smirked back for an entirely different reason. Kalus was his friend, but when it came to fighting, he wasn't on Lira's level, or anywhere close to it. He was going to get a beatdown worth remembering.

"You better not be getting any other activities on your mind, Kalus Straker!" Hanna Lodicum pushed her way through a crowd and yelled at her man. How any woman could stand to be with Kalus was beyond Rainier, but Hanna wasn't just any woman. She could hold her own in a fight and could more than hold her own around Kalus. "And you better not sully my name by losing your fight either. Don't make me have to step in and save you like I did at that tavern in Portswain before we set sail!"

Kalus cringed at the memory, which drew bouts of laughter from the Remnant. It didn't draw so much as a chuckle from Lira. She was all business, and once she was free of her armor, Lira picked up a practice sword and shield, banged them together, and lowered herself into a defensive stance.

Kalus charged forward with a smirk, rushing towards defeat with the unknowing happiness of a lemming approaching a cliff. He feinted to his right and then darted left while delivering a sweeping blow from his axe. Lira dropped low, swinging her shield into his knee to knock him off balance. As his axe flew overhead, she reached up and grabbed his arm, twisting him towards her. She elevated quickly from her crouched position, connecting a knee with the delicate region between his legs. He toppled to the deck of the *Remnant Awakens*. Innuendo answered.

The men of the Remnant that gathered to watch the sparring session laughed at Kalus' expense. The women laughed harder.

Hanna yelled to Kalus, "That was a sorry display of manhood. You lasted about as long as you did last night when we were rolling around on the deck in your miserable attempts to pleasure me."

The laughter rolled in again and drowned out Kalus' moans of misery as he lay in the fetal position on the deck.

Lira banged her shield and pointed her sword at Rainier in challenge. *It was bad enough when I had to worry about an errant stonehand cracking a rib while sparring with Slate. Now I have to worry about a low blow from Lira cracking something much more precious. No thanks.* "I'd like to keep that part of my anatomy intact, Lira. I'll sit this one out."

"Oracle, show honor." Lira banged her shield again and Rainier groaned. As his Hand, Lira was free to speak to him, but that didn't mean she took the opportunity very often. If she was resorting to speech in a public setting, then she was serious about this. Rainier stood up and began to stretch. It also gave him a moment to try holding the pattern again — maybe that shiny yellow enlightened path would keep his manhood intact.

Rainier held the pattern of the probing spell, centered it on him, invoked some spark and...nothing.

No shiny light, no enlightened path, no help whatsoever. The colors around him became more enhanced, and he knew the probing spell was working, but that fractal forsaken light refused to enlighten him.

It had been the same ever since he got on this ship. Whatever magic he had invoked at the Oracle Trials under the threat of his pending death was more luck than skill, and Rainier had been unable to repeat it, despite going through the same steps. Of course, he didn't plan on telling that bit of news to Lira or anyone else, considering the title of oracle was the only reason she tolerated him.

Kalus tossed him two short swords after picking himself up from the ground and said, "You sure know how to pick 'em. Your lady is calling."

"Thanks for the swords. I'd trade you for some ice, but ice is tough to find out here. I guess you'll have to grit your teeth in pain and shut your mouth instead." Rainier heard Kalus laugh at the comment as he caught the swords and moved swiftly into an attack, shifting forms as he did so. The Remnant cheered in appreciation of the skilled and fluid movements of their leader. Despite the encouragement, Rainier didn't expect Lira to be awed.

Lira matched his movements and the two danced around the deck, fighting each other in an intricate display of balance. Each small shift in balance needed to counteract the movements of the other, all while combatting the shifts of the deck as it floated upon the sea. It became apparent with each blocked strike that the two's skills were nearly matched. Rainier's strength in battle had always been his speed and unpredictability, but Lira matched his aggressive style to a stalemate. The problem was that Rainier began to tire, while the conditioning of Nameless Army kept Lira fresh...he was fighting a losing battle.

Rainier poured his remaining energy into a final flurry of short swords that nearly broke the guard of Lira, but nearly breaking someone's guard is as useful as nearly escaping the noose. She knocked his sword away and took the advantage, pressing him towards the edge of the deck. She bashed her shield into his arm, forcing him to drop his sword.

Lira leaned against her shield, pinning him against the rail and said, "You are a skilled fighter, but you are not fighting as an oracle. It is said that an oracle will know the movements of an opponent in battle before their opponents lift a sword to strike." It was the longest statement Lira had ever made. Then she asked the question that Rainier hoped to avoid. "Are you truly an oracle?" *I'm a nomad. I swindle, persuade, or talk my way out of trouble when I can and fight my way out of trouble when I can't. I'm a man that escaped the noose and doesn't know how he did it or if he could do it again.* None of those answers seemed like they would end with Lira being satisfied. He looked at her and the earnest expression on Lira's face made Rainier want to do something totally out of character – tell the uninhibited truth. He opened his mouth to explain that he couldn't hold the enlightened path as Julian described, "I …"

"Ships! Ships approach from the stern!" A call came from the crow's nest of the ship, drawing Lira's attention. Rainer took the opportunity to escape her iron grip and the even stronger stare she held. *That was close…I would've rather taken a shot like Kalus than admit weakness to Lira.* He moved away and started barking orders to the crew so that Lira wouldn't ask any other serious questions.

"Swab the deck! Tighten those lines!" Rainier yelled to the crew something that sounded captain-ey, but they all knew he was completely useless on a ship. He held the title because he was their leader, but the men manning the sails had become tone deaf to his nonsensical commands, which was fine. He simply used the tactic to avoid Lira for a moment. *I think I liked her better before she started speaking. I can go for some friendly banter or slightly veiled advances, but her straightforward questions are too much.*

Before the ships arrived, Rainier tracked down Kalus. "Remember you are my Hand. Don't say anything in front of the Nameless Army. That isn't your role."

Kalus said, "I didn't ask for that role, and I'm not good at holding my tongue."

Rainier looked at his childhood friend and said, "I need someone I can trust. The second Jamison shows up, my life is in danger. And my trust in Lira is...tenuous at best." *If she decides I'm a fraud, she'll gut me like a fish.*

"I have your back, mate." The bond between childhood friends prevailed the travails of the immediate situation.

"So, you'll come with me if we need to board one of those ships?"

Kalus laughed. "Are you kidding me? Hanna won't give me the night off tonight if I begged. After that blow from Lira, you'll be doing me a favor."

Rainier laughed and clasped him on the back as he watched the approaching ships. *Loyalty is earned over time, and once earned, it is a difficult bond to break.* The words of Trabon Tallow echoed in Rainier's head. Times hadn't been great between Rainier and Kalus since Rainier left for the tournament and then joined Slate's adventures, but some bonds stood the test of time. He trusted Kalus. He trusted Kalus with his life.

The ship bearing the flag of the Marked drew closer with unnatural speed, propelled by majestic sails that lit with the same glow of Lira's armor during battle. Whatever magic gave the paladins their armor also powered the sails of their fleet. Jamison hailed them from the deck of the *Inked Tides*, the Marked faction's flagship.

"Let the Marked faction witness the Oracle of the Unnamed Army, the Slipper of the Noose, Rainier Tallow!"

A cheer rose from the depths of the *Inked Tides* and in the ships beyond, articulated in the form of metal against armor. Rainier welcomed Jamison and his ships, despite the immediate threat to his ability to breathe. "Hail the Marked faction, the paladins of the Unnamed Army, and the conquerors of Malethya!"

An even louder banging of metal arose from the depths of Jamison's ship in approval. During the pounding of weapons against shields, Lira arrived at his side, warning Rainier that the bravado of his hailing wasn't taken as acceptance of his lack of response to her previous question. *I'll deal with her later...after I figure out how to keep Jamison from killing me, and how I can summon the enlightened path at will. After that, I can answer her questions.*

A boarding party consisting of Jamison and a glut of paladins in full armor crossed the water between ships. Rainier tried in vain to hold the enlightened path, but the best he was able to manage was short bursts of yellow light that disappeared before he could interpret their meaning. *Frackin' magic*. The boarding party stepped onto the deck of the *Remnant Awakens*, and thankfully no one tried to kill him on the spot.

Jamison pronounced in an amplified voice for the benefit of all ships to hear, "The Oracle of the Unnamed wishes to board the Inked Tides so that he may direct the Unnamed Armies as Julian prescribed!" Another cheer rose from the depths of the fleet's ships. Rainier didn't join them. By using his position as Rainier's voice to speak on his behalf, Jamison had managed to isolate him from those most loyal to him, the Remnant. He would have little choice but to board the *Inked Tides* to demonstrate his position of leadership within the Unnamed Army. By doing so, Rainier would open himself to innumerable opportunities for Jamison to plot against him. Slate had always told him to try to control the location of the battlefield, but he didn't have much choice in this instance.

Rainier responded, "My place is aboard the *Inked Tides* where I can be with the Nameless Army. With Jamison as my Voice, and Lira and Kalus as my Hands, I can serve as your oracle and lead you to victory against the Defiler of the Pattern, Lattimer Regallo." *At least, I would serve as your oracle if I can get the fractal-forsaken enlightened path to show up occasionally.*

Rainier patted Jamison for theatrical effect and the leader of the Marked faction returned the hug for longer than social norms intended. While in the not-so-warm embrace of his intended killer, Jamison said, "Well played, Rainier Tallow." *I disagreed. Bringing Kalus and Lira with me to the Inked Tides is better than going alone, but I'm still facing a stacked deck. My situation is dire at best.*

Jamison released Rainier from his tattooed clutches – *awkward bastard* – and pronounced to everyone as Rainier's Voice, using the regimented cadence of speech the priests developed to speak to the army, "Our leader will join his troops. Captains are to provide daily updates to the oracle aboard the *Inked Tides*." *How does stating two completely independent statements bring someone closer to the pattern?* Rainier hated the sound of patterned speech, but he knew enough of it now to listen for those two subjects to be continued in the proclamation. "Our leader is a true Oracle to the Unnamed Army and his arrival will be celebrated with a feast tonight. Captains are to air grievances during their daily updates and the grievances will be judged by myself, the Marked priest, with consultation of the oracle." Jamison halted the spell that amplified his voice and said to the paladins of the boarding party, "Four will row me back to the *Inked Tides* to prepare for the oracle's arrival. Three will protect the oracle. Two will stow the last boarding vessel until needed. One will signal the *Inked Tides* when the oracle has gathered his belongings." *Another nuance of patterned speech. By counting down, Jamison issued commands without jumping between subjects.* That seemed more reasonable to Rainier, and he stowed it away as a means of communication with his future troops, if he lived long enough to use it.

Rainier watched a few seconds as the paladins rowed Jamison back to his ship, where he could put into motion the murderous plans he had imagined over the last few weeks. *Let the games begin. I have a few tricks of my own.*

"I need to pack my things. Lira and Kalus, come with me." Rainier turned towards his cabin and walked swiftly there. "Close the door." Rainier ordered before the armored footsteps of the three unwanted paladins could enter the room. Kalus quickly complied, shutting the door in the face of a particularly serious looking paladin.

A knock at the door was followed by a patterned banging of shield against sword. Rainier looked to Lira for an interpretation. "The paladins are here under orders from your Voice. They wish to protect you."

Rainier had no desire for the protection of Jamison's hand-picked paladins. "I have my Hands to protect me while inside my cabin. They may watch the door for any potential trouble from my friends and family." Rainier couldn't keep the heavy sarcasm from lacing his words, but Lira simply pounded out the response. Confirmation came from the other side of the door.

Rainier started grabbing his supplies immediately, meager though they were. He had some clothes, the book *A Life in the Pattern* from Julian's office, and his short swords in addition to the trunk of his own belongings Julian had stored aboard the ship prior to the Oracle Trials. In it were the keys to his plans. The trunk contained disguises of limited use, since he would be aboard a very confined space and he didn't own any paladin armor, his lockpick kit, a Stratego medallion to contact Slate when he reached Malethya, various mirrors for covertly navigating around corners without notice, and...most importantly...his Sicarius mask. The enchanted mask made the wearer immemorable. Anyone who saw him wearing the Sicarius artifact diverted their eyes from the mask. The end effect was that if Rainier dressed as a peasant, people would remember a peasant passed by, but they wouldn't care to look more closely unless there was a reason for a peasant to be out of place in the situation. In that case, even the Sicarius mask couldn't stop someone from noticing something was amiss and raising an alarm. He patted the trunk containing the black mask affectionately. *If I can't get this sparkly enlightened path to make an appearance, at least I can still place my trust in the darkness of the night.*

Rainier brought his thoughts back to the immediate tasks at hand. He said, "The moment I step aboard the *Inked Tides,* I will be in danger. Jamison will attempt to end my life so that he can retain control of the Marked faction."

Lira's cheeks turned red in anger and her armor lit up right before she erupted with an emotional outburst. "A priest of the pattern would never commit such a sin! What you say is blasphemy of the highest order!" *There's that temperament One had mentioned. It's good to know I can still rile her up occasionally even if she got the better of me while sparring. And two sentences! That's progress.*

Before she drew a blue sword on him, Rainier held his hands out in what was hopefully an appeasing manner and said, "I don't expect you to believe me. All I ask is that you protect me so that I can survive long enough for you to reconsider. Can you do that?"

Neither the red nor the blue colors faded, but Lira said through gritted teeth, "I am your hand. I will do my duty and serve the pattern." *Fractal's blessings for blind faith in an ideal. That's something I'll never have.*

Rainier looked over to Kalus and found him lounging with remarkable ease, especially considering the knee to the groin he suffered not too long ago. "You don't seem too worried, Kalus."

"I didn't sign up to be your Hand. You volunteered me for the job." He smiled and said with a laugh, "If I'm not any good at the job and you die, I guess I get to go back to being a philandering nomad in Malethya."

"Hanna might have something to say about those plans. Besides, I saw how your forward advances towards Lira ended up. I think you are using the word philandering rather optimistically, my old friend." Rainier shared a laugh and then continued on by saying, "I chose you to be my Hand because I needed someone I could trust. You probably noticed on the deck, but the first thing Jamison will do is isolate me from the Remnant. By naming you my Hand, I've guaranteed that I can at least maintain communication with you. Hopefully, I'll be able to maintain communication with the Remnant through you as well."

"Ha! I knew you didn't want me to be silent! Can you imagine one of us banging on a shield? What a way to waste your life!" Kalus laughed again before Lira turned her red face towards him. "You are the obvious exception, my elusive rabbit. I will chase you through any forest until you are mine." She kicked at him, but Kalus was expecting it and managed to move before he spoke in a higher octave again.

"Enough of that. We don't have much time before those guards get anxious." He grabbed his things and turned to Kalus. "Protect me. The Remnant is family. Family first." Kalus nodded with a degree of seriousness that rarely showed upon his face. Rainier turned to Lira. "Protect me. Do it for the honor of the pattern." *That sounds like the gibberish I read in A Life in the Pattern.* The nonsense worked as the colors faded from Lira's armor and she set her jaw in determined resolution. "Good. Now let's go win control of an army."

He pounded on the door and did his best to mimic the patterned speech he heard from Jamison when ordering troops. "Two paladins will carry my things to the ship and if you drop it in the water, you better hope you can swim with armor on because you'll be diving in after it. One paladin will sit atop the trunk while it is carried." *If I need to issue commands using a stupid pattern, then I'm going to issue stupid commands with the pattern. Maybe they'll realize the foolishness of their ways.*

Rainier walked past the confused paladins without bothering to explain himself and climbed aboard the small boarding ship, setting his front foot on the prow like a conquering hero from the legends. He wanted anyone on the *Inked Tides* that was watching, and he was sure they would be, to see a figure worth remembering.

Lira and Kalus joined him momentarily, with Hanna yelling from the deck, "Don't die over there, Kalus, or I'll have to find someone else to roll around with!"

Kalus yelled back, "You'd never find a man like me!"

Hanna waved him off replying, "Aye, but I bet I could find someone who's twice the man you are. It's hard work to find someone as inadequate as you!"

The biting humor at Kalus' expense was followed up by

the comical sight of two warriors straining to carry a trunk with a fully-armored paladin atop it. Rainier managed to maintain his heroic pose without buckling over in laughter during the loading process and for the ride across the calm sea to the Inked Tides, where Jamison was waiting.

"Welcome to the *Inked Tides*, the commanding vessel of your Marked fleet." Rainier stepped onto the deck of the ship. The first thing Rainier noticed was the size, which was impossible to ignore. On the deck, three full-size fighting rings had been set up for the training of the Unnamed Army. The second thing Rainier noticed was the number of soldiers, whom Jamison had brought aboard from multiple ships and lined up in rank and file for an impressive display of might. *I will win control of this army before we reach Malethya.* Jamison marched him to the front of the troops and amplified his voice with patterned speech, first speaking as a priest and then as a commoner. He said, "The pattern is all around us, and we devote our lives to understanding it through dutifully playing our role, whether it be as a priest, a paladin, or a commoner. We are blessed today to be in the presence of Rainier Tallow, a true oracle. No one has had the chance to hear the words of someone so close to the pattern that he can predict where the pattern will take us. Listen to our wise leader as he proclaims the brilliant plan that will lead the Unnamed Army to victory." *That bastard set me up! My plan? I don't have a plan, and he is supposed to be my Voice until I can learn patterned speech!* Jamison switched his tone to that of a commoner, and he said with eager anticipation, "I am excited to hear what plans he has for this great army! Rainier Tallow, please tell us how you will use our power and might to erase the blood mage from Malethya and bring honor to us all!" Jamison stepped aside with exaggerated pomp and circumstance to make room for Rainier's address to the troops.

Rainier stepped forward and did what anyone in the Tallow faction would do...stall and lie wherever necessary. Thankfully, he had plenty of practice at both of those tactics from his youth. He hadn't prepared a speech, and he didn't know the proper way to address the troops, so he copied Jamison's tone by first speaking as an oracle and then as a commoner. The best he was hoping for was to speak enough to appease the troops without actually saying anything. He said, "The pattern holds endless possibilities for all of us, and the time has not yet arrived to decide our actions. The pattern must unfold and unveil its mysteries to me, and when it does, we will act decisively." A stomp of feet showed agreement from the soldiers. "We will act within the pattern." A second stomp, louder this time, emboldening Rainier to raise his voice like a preacher in a pulpit. "We will honor the pattern with our actions!" A third stomp, followed by the banging of shield against swords. *There. Vague. Non-committal. Appropriately motivating and mysteriously oracle-like. Now move on before you mess it up.* As a commoner, he spoke to the troops, "I will stow my gear and look forward to dining with you all this evening. I hear that you have prepared a feast. Let us fill our stomachs, drink, and be merry. Enjoy this evening before the battles begin!" Stomping demonstrated the troops approval, and Rainier turned to Jamison, signaling he was done speaking.

Jamison led the way towards Rainier's room with a

small contingent of Marked priests and paladins in tow. Like Jamison, the priests had covered their skin with tattoos to signify their devotion to the pattern. They wore robes that cut off at the shoulders to display their inked arms and the plainness of the robes contrasted with the tattoos in a way that highlighted their intricacies. Jamison stopped in front of a luxurious cabin and said, "We have prepared the finest room aboard the *Inked Tide* for your use. Your two hands have been given adjacent rooms."

The word prepared hung in Rainier's mind. He didn't want part of any preparations Jamison had concocted, but *A Life in the Pattern* had taught him the importance of such trivialities to the Disenite priests. It would be against the pattern of things to stay in a room below his station. "The hospitality of the Marked faction is appreciated, but I would prefer if my hands stayed in the same room as me. I find the bond between us strengthens the more time we spend together." By claiming the bond would bring them closer together, Rainier made it impossible to contradict the request because the action was linked to the pattern. Lira kept her face neutral, but her eyes failed to hide her displeasure at the pronouncement and the realization she'd be sharing quarters with Rainier and Kalus. *I'd rather have her mad at me and by my side to protect me than happily sleeping in the room next to me while an assassin slits my throat.* "I would also extend an invitation to you, Jamison, to share our quarters. As my Voice, the proximity may strengthen our bond as well, although I have predicted that your duties as a priest will prevent it."

Here was the first trap Rainier had prepared, and the words of his father echoed in his head from the first time he was sent into town to negotiate on behalf of the Remnant. *Do not start off by making demands. Start by strengthening your position.* He had forced Jamison into a simple decision, and Rainier would benefit regardless of the response. *If he contradicts me, I'll limit Jamison's ability to scheme against me and force him into a setting in which I hold the upper hand. If he agrees with me, he'll be acknowledging my wisdom as an oracle.* Rainier would be happy with either response.

With his priests surrounding him, Jamison spoke carefully to sidestep the proposal. He wouldn't want to refuse an offer that could help him to better serve an oracle. "You honor me with your offer, but I'm afraid my role as high priest of the Marked faction requires time away from my duties as your Voice so that I may meditate and reflect on the pattern around me. It is the best way for me to lead my flock." He expanded his arms to the priests surrounding him.

"It is as I have foreseen then," Rainier said in his most wise and fatherly tone. He grabbed his trunk from the paladin carrying it and stepped through the circle of priests into his cabin, splitting the group in two. Kalus and Lira joined him without prompting. He said with much more command than he had previously used, "Leave the adjacent rooms empty and place a guard at my door. Do not disturb me until the feast." He swung the cabin door closed and turned his back on Jamison before it slammed shut.

Inside the cabin, Lira challenged him. "Why would you speak in such a way to a high priest?"

"Because that high priest wants me dead, and I need to

gain control of the army before he gets what he wants." Rainier could hear the group disbanding outside his door with the exception of two armored feet that stationed themselves to guard his door. Rainier smiled at the sound.

"A high priest would not commit murder. And why would you order a guard to be stationed at your door if you thought Jamison would do such a thing? One of us would make more sense."

Kalus laughed and answered on behalf of Rainier. "Rainier ordered the guard to be stationed outside our door before Jamison gave the order. It was an order Jamison was going to give anyway, but this way the soldiers are obeying Rainier. He lost nothing and gained a measure of authority...it's simple negotiation." Kalus clasped his friend on the shoulder. "Anyone in the Remnant worth his salt could have done that, but that bit where you tricked Jamison into confirming your claim as an oracle in front of his most trusted priests and paladins, now that was just beautiful."

Lira gave a discerning look before acknowledging, "I have a lot to learn about your ways. You fight with more than just swords." Then she looked to Kalus. "This is a good thing, because you do not fight well with swords."

"Lira, I think you and Hanna would get along swimmingly." Rainier laughed at Kalus' expense and said, "Jamison will fight with weapons other than swords as well. That begins with this room. If he *prepared* it for my arrival, there may be a surprise waiting for us." He looked to Kalus, who was familiar with the intricate details of ransacking a room. "Tear this place apart. I want to know what's under every loose floorboard or sewn into every piece of fabric."

Kalus set to work with the efficiency and thoroughness of a professional coupled with the care and delicacy of a tornado. Rainier turned away from him, confident that nothing unusual would be overlooked.

Lira said in her clipped manner of speaking, "I do not believe the high priest would end the pattern of your life."

Rainier responded, "That sounds like a fancy way of saying murder. And yes, he would murder me. People do surprising things with the proper motivation. Jamison is definitely motivated, and he has the authority and power to carry out his will. That is a dangerous combination."

"What is his motivation?" Lira asked.

Rainier smiled. "He has the strongest motivation of all. I have threatened his position of power. He would do anything to keep it, and quietly eliminating me is the best option." Rainier read skepticism on Lira's face, but her ears were open. That was a beginning. He said, "I don't expect to convince you right away. All I ask is that you keep your eyes open for trouble and your mind open to the possibility." Sometimes the best strategy for persuading someone was to stop talking. *I hate that part of negotiations, but if it's the best way of gaining Lira as an ally instead of an unwilling bodyguard, it's worth it.*

Rainier's restraint was rewarded with a nod from Lira after several excruciating seconds of silence. Of course, that was a relative silence because Kalus-the-tornado created enough noise to wake the dead as he dug through drawers and tossed out their contents. Rainier switched topics to keep Lira engaged in conversation. She rarely talked this much, and he wanted to take advantage of the opportunity. He asked, "What methods would someone use to quietly 'end someone's pattern' in Disentia? Poison? Knives in the night?"

Lira spat on the floor in disgust and said, "These things go against the pattern. They would not be done."

"Then what else..."

Lira cut him off with a shove to the shoulder. "No more. I will not answer these questions when you have not answered my own." Lira fixed him with a stare that pierced deep within his soul into places Rainier didn't even like to visit. Dark things happened down there, and they were best buried from sight. Rainier preferred people to stay focused on his shiny exterior. "Are you an oracle? You do not fight as one, and you scheme like someone that belongs in the stockade. If you hadn't escaped from the noose, I would not even ask the question. Because of that deed, I will ask again. Can you see the pattern? Can you lead the Nameless Army?"

Once again, Rainier found himself wanting to tell her the truth. Then his better judgment and a lifetime of negotiations kicked in, and he held his tongue.

"Look at this!" Kalus saved Rainier from a response. In his hands, he held a small sphere with the insignia of the Marked faction on it. Within it, an inky substance swirled in an ever-changing pattern. "Any idea what it is?"

"That is a holy artifact that priests have filled with the pattern. It..."

Lira kept talking but Rainier had heard enough. He opened the window in his cabin and threw it into the sea.

Kalus stuck his head out the window and said, "It looks like the holy pattern doesn't float."

Rainier laughed at his friend's joke. Lira didn't. She turned red and stewed in the corner. *Oh well, at least I won't need to explain my intermittent abilities as an oracle yet. She's too angry to keep talking. Maybe if I explain why I pitched a holy artifact into the sea she'll come back around.* "That sphere looks like the exploding orbs we have in Malethya. I can't have a magical artifact in my room when I don't know who put it there, what it does, how to activate it, or what it might do to me." Silence from Lira.

Rainier gave up on his conversation with Lira and helped Kalus finish tossing the room. Their efforts didn't produce any more exploding orbs of the holy variety, but their efforts weren't in vain. You can't put a price on piece of mind.

After several awkward minutes of silence courtesy of the angry paladin in the corner, a rap on the door was followed by a priest's voice announcing, "The feast will now commence."

Rainier opened the door and managed to keep a straight face as the priest and the paladin looked in to see the room completely destroyed. Clothes and furniture lay strewn across the floor. In his most authoritative voice, Rainier said, "Leave everything as it is. I worked hard to decorate it to my exact tastes, and I know where everything is." He walked out of the room like a king, dutifully joined by his two hands, one on either side, and left the young priest to scramble to keep up. *I'd love to know what that priest is thinking right now and what he plans to report back to Jamison. He must think I'm insane.*

In the short time they had been locked in their cabin,

the Marked faction's soldiers had transformed the main deck. Jamison had packed the troops so tightly for his display of military might that there wasn't room for anything but soldiers on the deck. Now, barrels had been brought from the storage holds and wooden planks were laid across them, forming massive tables that spanned the length of the deck. Normally the tables would have looked plain, but it served the same purpose as the robes of the priests. The simple nature contrasted with the elaborate patterns etched in the paladin armor and the inked arms of the priests. The simple metal mugs and plates were similarly etched in patterns that alit and swirled as they watched. "Remind me that the cups really are swirling after I have a few drinks of wine tonight," Kalus said.

"I don't think that's a sight I'll forget, even after a few drinks," Rainier responded. The magical display also reminded Rainier to try holding the enlightened path. He started with the probing spell and concentrated on himself, as he had done in the gallows. He applied some spark, and a yellow light momentarily streamed in front of him. It flickered before Rainier could comprehend any of it, and then faded away. *Great. One more bout with magical impotence.*

Without any enlightened guidance, Rainier followed the young priest to their seats of honor. Rainier was directed towards a seat at the right hand of the center table. Jamison held court at the head of the table, and he explained the seating situation as soon as Rainier arrived. He rose from his seat and said to the crowd, "I am honored to have Rainier Tallow join this gathering of the Marked faction as our special guest." *He also wants his troops to see me as being subservient to him. By setting this feast up as a gathering of the Marked faction, he is justified in sitting at the head of the table. Every member of the Nameless Army will see me being subservient to him. I can't let that happen.*

Rainier followed up Jamison's announcement with one of his own, hoping that his imitation of Jamison's sentence structure and cadence of speech would qualify as patterned speech. He said, "I am honored to be a special guest at this gathering of the Marked faction. To further acquaint myself to the soldiers under my command, I will be joining various tables throughout the course of the evening."

Jamison retook control by raising his glass of wine. Rainier saw a cup had already been poured for him, so he reached for it, tapping the table with his left middle finger while doing so. Kalus picked up on the hand signal and whispered in Lira's ear Rainier's unspoken command. Jamison said, "In two days, we will reach Malethya's shores. We have one night to prepare for our arrival. Tonight, we celebrate the opportunity to serve the pattern." *Two days? That guy must have gotten into the wanderleaf before the feast. It will take weeks to reach Malethya.* Metal cups swirled as they were raised in unison, the lighted patterns sparking in a beautiful display as the cups clinked together. "Enjoy yourselves while the food is served." Rainier toasted Jamison and matched his smug smile. A clink and a spark later, Rainier raised the cup to his lips, tilting it back as far as he could without allowing the wine to touch his lips. *Never drink a pre-poured cup.* Thankfully, Kalus and Lira had followed his instructions, and their cups also remained full, but he needed to fix that before it was noticed.

"I think this is the perfect time to meet the troops. As my Voice, please accompany me and speak on my behalf," Rainier requested of Jamison.

"Of course, I will lead you to a table of paladins for introductions." Jamison smiled in an all-knowing sort of way, and then left the table without waiting to see if Rainier would follow. The abrupt dismissal by Jamison gave Rainier a moment to clasp Kalus on his shoulder and whisper his next instructions without raising Jamison's suspicions.

Jamison led them to a table of paladins who were talking quietly among themselves and sharing a quiet laugh, but when they saw Rainier approaching, all talking stopped and backs went rigid. Jamison said, "The Oracle of the Unnamed Army would like to make your acquaintances."

He stepped to the side and the reason for the smug smile became clear. These soldiers would not speak to him and a look from Lira warned against pushing the issue. He had already made the situation uncomfortable for the soldiers who were torn between wanting to impress him and holding to their codes. *It would be so much easier to win these soldiers over if I could just get them drunk and play a few rounds of cards. I can make any man trust my sense of strategy after a night of emptying his pockets.* Instead, Rainier clasped the shoulder of the soldier in front of him and set his cup of wine down on the table next to his as he said, "You honor your oaths with your silence. You honor your oaths with your training, and you will soon honor your oaths with the blood of our enemies in battle." *This patterned speech stuff was growing tiresome. The paladins stomped their feet against the floorboards and remained at attention.*

Kalus and Lira stood at the far end of the table, indicating to Rainier which way he should divert the soldiers' attention. Rainier said, "The power of the pattern is great. It is reflected in might on the Nameless Army. It is reflected in your devotion, and it dwarves the miniscule armies of Malethya." Rainier gestured to the back of the deck, away from Kalus, where the mast of the *Remnant Awakens* could be seen peeking above the deck of the massive *Inked Tides*. The tiny Malethyan ship served as the perfect example of Disenite power. All the soldiers' eyes looked towards the mast of the *Remnant Awakens*. As they did, Rainier reached down and grabbed the soldier's cup next to his. He didn't need to look towards Kalus to know that he had switched his own cup and Lira's cup for the cups of the soldiers at the end of the table. "Despite our advantages, it is only through the pattern that we will be victorious. Despite your skill, the enemy will use blasphemous means to level the playing field. Tomorrow, you must remain diligent in your training and diligent in your devotion to the pattern. Tonight, you must enjoy the company of your friends." Lira gave him the slightest of nods, indicating he hadn't butchered patterned speech too terribly. Rainier knew to stop while he was ahead. He raised his cup and created a shower of magical patterns as he toasted the soldiers at the table. Then he took a deep drink of wine. *I deserve that drink.*

Jamison led them back to the head table and said as he

walked, "You've been practicing your patterned speech. Just so you know, it won't matter. You will never have control of this army. Julian named me your Voice, and with that title, I speak on your behalf. Anything you say that contradicts me will be ignored as a private discussion between the two of us, and my orders will be carried out." Then Jamison gave another smile and said, "Besides, I think your time as an oracle will be short-lived."

Jamison stopped to greet a table of priests, and the openly hostile looks in his direction left little doubt about whether he should join Jamison or continue to the head table. Rainier took the unexpected opportunity to walk without an escort to sneak in conversation with Kalus and Lira. "Did you switch your cups?"

"It was too easy. If the soldier would have stared at the *Remnant Awakens* any longer, I could have taken his armor and had my own shiny breastplate to go with my glowing personality."

"Yes, the light of your ego precedes your every word Kalus."

"Hmph." Lira stifled a giggle. *A giggle! Who knew the woman giggled? I thought she spent her days glowering and playing with sharp objects.*

Kalus said, "It won't be so funny when those soldiers are doubling over sick later."

Lira was appalled, which means she held the same blank stare on her face that she usually maintained. "Your efforts were wasted. A Marked priest would not resort to poison. I have told you this already."

Rainier stopped the argument. "Keep your eye on that table, and we'll get our answer soon enough."

They reached the head table as their food was being plated. They cut the meat from the same roast that they served everyone else at the head table, so unless Jamison was willing to kill all his closest advisors just to get to Rainier, it was safe to eat. He bit into a mouth-watering cut of meat and the simple pleasure was only slightly spoiled as Jamison rejoined the group.

Jamison ate a few bites and then stood to address the group one more time. *What's the next surprise he has in store for me?* Rainier tried to find the enlightened path again as protection. The probing spell didn't fail him, but when he tried to focus on himself, the light shot out at random directions and couldn't focus. It flickered out before he could determine its meaning. Jamison proclaimed, "The time has come to meet your responsibility. The time has come to meet your destiny."

Several tables of priests stood and spread out around the deck. They stretched their arms and gesticulated in some wizardly patterns that made their tattoos shine in divine light. As the light grew too bright to see, their arms shot upwards and blue light passed through the air to the sails of the ship, lighting them up in swirling patterns like the cups on the dinner tables. *That is an incredibly large amount of magic.* The ship launched forward so smoothly that the sudden acceleration was only noticeable by the feeling in Rainier's stomach and the shifting of his wine in his cup. A second later, the sails of the other ships in the Marked fleet alit and pushed forward, striving to keep pace with the *Inked Tides*.

Jamison sat back down to the stomping of approvals from the Nameless Army. Rainier said, "This is quite the display – more impressive even than the glowing armor. I haven't seen that type of power from too many wizards." *It's a short list - Ibson, Lucus, Lattimer, Brannon, and Sana.* "What is the source of your power?"

Jamison raised an eyebrow in surprise but only said, "The pattern is the source of all power." *Priests are terrible liars.*

The sight of a soldier with a ghostly pallor leaving a table to rush below deck interrupted the conversation. It happened to be the soldier who was the original owner of the cup from which Rainier now drank. A feeling of dread came over him as he realized he had just survived his first attempt on his life. *That bastard tried to poison me. A part of me didn't think he had it in him. I can't underestimate him again.* Rainier elbowed Lira at his side to make sure she noticed the soldier disappearing below deck.

With a renewed sense of urgency, Rainier tried to find the enlightened path again. He held the probing spell, concentrated on his own pattern, and applied some spark. It flickered a bit and then grew steady. The little light eventually streamed in front of him! *It's about fracken' time!* The light glowed in every direction. He could only ascertain that his life wasn't in immediate danger because he had so many paths in front of him. While the initial thought comforted him, he didn't want to waste the enlightened path while he held it. A thought struck him. *I can look for the shortest path of light. I can put myself in just enough danger to trigger Jamison's next trap. I can force Jamison's hand while I have the power to avoid it.*

Rainier probed outwards and when he found the string of light that ended first, he held and focused on it. The other enlightened paths fell away. The shortest path that remained led towards the priests Jamison had just been talking to. Rainier said to Jamison, "I'd like to meet the priests of the Marked faction responsible for such a display of power. Will you introduce me?"

Jamison seemed genuinely surprised, but he could hardly say no. "They would all wish to know you, oracle." *Of course, they would - know thy enemy.* Rainier chastised his line of thinking. While several of the priests were undoubtedly loyal to Jamison, that didn't mean that all the priests were under his influence. He may be able to win a few over with the right words.

Jamison set down his dinnerware with the precision of a Malethyan noble and led their small group towards the table of priests as the very picture of grace. *I don't know if he's going to introduce me or start a sermon.* Jamison said, "The oracle wishes to meet the Marked priests. Please take advantage of this blessing by asking any questions you may have from the one who sees the pattern." Jamison bowed his head in reverence. Rainier wanted to punch him. He may have surprised Jamison with his request, but this was obviously a trap he had in waiting. *That's why I'm doing this now. The enlightened path stretches beyond this table, so I am not in immediate harm. This will be a war of words, but at least I can fight it with my own tongue. These aren't soldiers of the Nameless Army forcing me to use patterned speech.*

Rainier looked beneath the tattooed faces of the priests and found general skepticism upon most of the faces and open hostility in a few of the robed men and women. Rainier expected some skepticism to his presence, but even taking that into consideration, there was something odd about the group.

A priest across the table broke the silence and asked, "As an oracle, do you place yourself above the priests of the Marked faction?"

The first of many loaded questions. Thankfully, Rainier could tap dance with the best of them. "I have not placed myself in any position. Julian has named me an oracle and bestowed the title upon me."

A second priest took up the line of questioning. He asked, "And why is it that the Immortal sent you away so quickly after finding the first true oracle in years?"

"The reason for my departure should be clear. It has been proclaimed by Julian's Voice, your own high priest, for all of Disentia to hear. I am to lead the Nameless Army against the army of Lattimer Regallo." The enlightened path he was following started to fade. *What am I doing wrong?*

"So, you do consider yourself the leader of this voyage? As such, you must consider yourself the leader of us." A smug look accompanied the finality of the statement.

Rainier was about to respond when a young priestess next to him twitched slightly, and then broke from the line of questioning. She sounded earnest, bordering on desperate as she said, "I heard you attained the enlightened path without the aid of wanderleaf. How did you do that?"

Rainier looked the priestess in the eye and realized what the twitch was. The woman was going through withdrawal. He looked around the table and saw stained fingers from years of crushing the leaf to inhale it. These priests and priestesses were all addicts. "What's your name, priestess?"

"I am Kalana," she replied.

"Have you ever attained the enlightened path?" Rainier questioned her as the enlightened path faded even more from his own view. He focused harder on it, but it kept slipping slowly away.

"I glimpsed it once. I'll never forget the light streaming away from me." Kalana said wistfully. "I'd do anything to see it again." *The poor thing tried so hard to grab it that she snuffed out any chance of seeing it again in a cloud of wanderleaf smoke.* Her plight made him realize that he was doing the same thing, but without the smoke. Rainier quit trying to hold a single path and follow it. The path grew brighter, and other paths broke away from it, but he still wasn't doing something right.

The smug priest brought the conversation back to the main topic at hand – trying to trap Rainier in a web of words. "Do you admit that you consider yourself our leader? What visions do you have to guide us?"

Rainier was tired of watching his words and the fractal-forsaken path wasn't helping him anyway, so he quit holding his tongue. "I am not your leader. If I were your leader, I would not allow you or anyone else in the Marked faction to ever touch wanderleaf again. Whatever benefit you gain from it has been negated by years of abuse." Most of the priests and priestesses around the table stared at him behind practiced masks of blank expression, and as they did, a strange thing happened. The enlightened path grew brighter and several of the branching paths terminated a short distance from the table. *Success is a funny thing. I never thought I'd measure my own success by the number of people that want to kill me within fifty feet of where I stand.*

Rainier identified one of the paths that brought him towards the stern of the ship, where he could get a closer look at the *Remnant Awakens*. He focused on the path, dropping the other paths away, but he didn't try to hold it tight and smother it this time. He then concentrated on meeting the gaze of the few priests and priestesses that didn't appear intent on murdering him. He said, "When you choose to follow me, you will choose me despite my ignorance of your ways. Because even though I am an outsider, I have grown up as a member of the Marked faction. I share your ideals, if not your practices, and it is plain to see that wanderleaf smoke has clouded your sense of the pattern around you. It's time for you to clear your vision and answer your true callings."

Some of the priests and priestesses around the table regarded him behind blank faces, but Rainier felt his words had reached their ears. He doubted he had any allies from his speech, but some priests were willing to listen. Others were not.

"You know nothing of what we have been called to do." The priest with the disconcerting series of tattooed spikes radiating from his eyes said as he pounded the table in anger. "You know nothing of us!"

Rainier met the intensity of the man's stare and said, "I know that you have been teaching people to pass the Oracle Trials with the aid of wanderleaf, and you have all failed. Now I am here. I passed the Oracle Trials. I passed them without wanderleaf or your ways. Consider the possibility that my perspective could help you on your own journey to enlightenment."

Rainier turned his back to the group and started walking away, showing immense disrespect to the priests directing their objections towards him. Along with the flurry of objections, a string of light paths shortened in front of him, many of them ending all too soon. *Did I overdo it by turning my back on them?* With so many possibilities of dying within a hundred feet of where he stood, Rainier shifted his focus away from the short pathways of light. *How about I focus on a nice long pathway that makes sure I make it through the evening?*

That done, now he just needed to give people the opportunity to act. He said to Lira, Kalus and Jamison, "I'll be taking a walk to reflect. Alone."

Jamison said with a smile, "As you wish." Kalus and Lira hesitated but then carried out his order, leaving Rainier alone.

Rainier followed the enlightened path towards the stern of the ship, noticing that the evening's spirits lightened the soldiers' mood considerably, in their own silent way. Many of them rolled dice and gave grunts of approval or stomps of anger at the outcome of the rolls. *Compared to their previously stiff behavior, these soldiers are downright raucous.* The enlightened path led him towards the table, and as he approached, they halted the game and waited for him to pass by with silent stares.

The same silence met him at each table he passed, making the relatively short walk feel uncomfortable. *It's like this is a funeral procession, and I'm the casket.* Rainier stopped himself from following that analogy too much further and instead focused on following the enlightened path.

The last set of tables held soldiers that took their drinking seriously, and the grunts almost bordered on intelligible syllables. Their games, like their drinking, were more serious than the soldiers near the head table as well. This last table had a set of daggers out along with their dice. Rainier couldn't make out the dice game they played, but the loser of each round had to lay his hand on the table. Then the winner of the round would grab a set of daggers and plunge the tip into the table, with grunts of approval rising from the crowd whenever the dagger was placed particularly close to the webbing between the loser's fingers.

Rainier gave a wide berth to the drunk soldiers as he rounded the table towards a location against the railing of the ship indicated by the enlightened path. The view at the railing gave him a healthy appreciation for the might of the Disenite fleet as the number of glowing sails following the *Inked Tides* stretched towards the horizon, but Rainier's attention was drawn towards the tiny *Remnant Awakens* in tow behind the Inked Tides.

Though the sun had set, and the decking was only illuminated by lantern light, the lack of activity concerned Rainier. It wasn't just the dark sail that bothered Rainier. *Whatever magic is propelling these ships forward doesn't work on my ship.* On a normal evening, the members of the Remnant would be telling tales and enjoying themselves. On this evening, the lantern lights predominantly emitted from the cabins. Even more concerning, the light reflected off the armor of soldiers standing guard on the deck. *My friends are as much a prisoner as I am.*

The enlightened path shifted suddenly and broke Rainier from his reverie. The light pulsed and shot downwards to his right. Rainier followed without thinking, diving for the floorboards, and grabbing the rail. As he did so, a huge swell hit the side of the *Inked Tides*, causing the ship to sway towards Rainier. The drunken soldiers at the table next to him were thrown off balance from the deluge of water, but it was the winner of the last round of dice that became the ultimate loser. He was standing and holding a dagger, ready to plunge it into the table as close to the loser's hand as he could without hitting it, when the wave hit. He flew overboard, arms outstretched, and dagger extended right over the rail at the stern of the ship. *Right where I was standing.* Then a series of tabletops, barrels, and soldiers came sliding towards his side of the ship, crashing into the railing, which thankfully was built from fine construction that could withstand the weight. Even more importantly, Rainier wasn't crushed in the malaise. *Bless this oracle thing.*

Rainier was still counting his blessings as he tried to shield his face from the water pelting his skin. Before he could wipe it away, the ship started to roll back in the opposite direction, and he felt himself being lifted into the air. The ship continued to roll, and he hooked a foot on the railing and clung tightly as objects slid away from him, rushing into the scattered troops and towards the opposite railing. Many objects and soldiers weren't lucky enough to grab hold of anything on the deck, and they fell into the dark sea. *It could swallow this entire ship. I am going to die.* Just when Rainier thought the mighty ship would capsize, it began to roll back again. With each roll, the bottom of the ship aligned a bit more with gravity, and the pure terror in Rainier subsided.

Rainier used the railing to steady himself on the swaying ship as the soldiers picked themselves up from the deck. The frantic dive had made him lose his concentration, and the probing spell failed. He could no longer hold the enlightened path, so he settled on the shortest possible route to Lira and Kalus, taking a split second to look at the *Remnant Awakens* to ensure it was still in one piece. His ship was and, miraculously, so was he. *I've tempted fate enough for one night.* Enlightened path or no, the combination of the dagger piercing the air where his heart once beat, and the sea swallowing soldiers and priests indiscriminately left his sense for adventure waning.

Kalus and Lira rushed towards him, with a robed Jamison lagging behind the sprinting warriors. Despite arriving last, he spoke first, saying loudly for the soldiers to hear, "Fractal's blessings that our oracle is safe. I saw you by the railing when the wave hit, and I feared the worst." *Feared the worst or hoped for the best? It can be a fine line.*

Before responding, Rainier took a moment to quietly greet Lira and Kalus. "I'm glad you are well."

Lira responded quietly, "Jamison cast a spell that held our table and chairs against the decking when the wave hit. He saved us." Lira's kind words contrasted with her readied stance. She could draw her blade in a heartbeat. *Tonight's events may have convinced Lira of the truth.*

Rainier looked past Lira and Kalus to see the head table in perfect order. Even the plates and food remained in place. *That's a quick piece of spellcasting if you aren't prepared for it in advance.*

Jamison smiled in gracious appreciation for Lira's acknowledgment of his work and said, "My only regret is that I wasn't quick enough to save everyone."

First, he tries to kill me, and then he sets himself up to be a hero in the process. It was a good plan, and one that would have worked even better if I hadn't been holding the enlightened path. Rainier stowed his thoughts until later.

Rainier finally addressed Jamison's initial proclamation. With a loud voice, he said, "My undoing will not come from a stray wave. My abilities as an oracle protected me, but I was unable to protect you. I will get better." *What was that saying about making promises you couldn't keep?* Rainier continued solemnly, "Take tonight to mourn the dead. Pick up the broken pieces and mend what can be fixed. Our path still points forwards, where more sinister enemies await us in Malethya, enemies with blood magic. Be ready." A few soggy boots stomped on the wet deck in approval, even though he spoke without patterned speech. He didn't care, as long as his point got across.

Rainier then turned back to Jamison and said in a conversational volume, "I will retire for the evening and my Hands will join me. As my Voice, I'd like for you to arrange for the leaders of the Nameless Army to give a demonstration of the capabilities of these ships. With these sails powering us towards Malethya, I need to know our options upon arrival."

"That is most wise, Oracle of the Unnamed Army, for

we shall arrive in Malethyan port in two night's time, and we have yet to hear your enlightened plan." Jamison bowed his head in mock reverence to Rainier. *Two days. It took me weeks to reach Disentia aboard the Remnant Awakens.* The thought of crossing the sea in two days astounded Rainier, even when he was staring at the blue sails propelling them forward at impossible speeds.

Instead of responding, Rainier gave a nod of acknowledgment and walked back to the safety and quiet of his cabin. Once inside, he turned to Kalus and simply said, "Report. What did you take out of tonight's activities?"

"I thought the exploding orb in the bedroom was a friendly welcome. The poisoned wine was a rookie move, but that wave...that wave wasn't your garden variety type of murder. That was art." Kalus gave a devil-may-care smile and lounged in a chair. "That man really wants you dead." *Leave it to Kalus to take a grave situation and turn it into a joke.* From anyone else, the comment would have been offensive, but Rainier had spent too many evenings around a campfire with Kalus to be offended. His friend was just trying to keep him loose.

"Really? I hardly even noticed..." Rainier slipped into his childhood habit of matching Kalus' laid-back demeanor and the stress of the situation became more manageable. He looked to Lira and said, "You looked like you were a second away from drawing iron against your faction's high priest only a moment ago."

"I am your Hand. It is my duty to protect you."

"This morning you wouldn't have considered the possibility that I needed protection from Jamison." Rainier pushed her for further explanation.

"I saw the soldier drink the wine intended for us and get sick. The wave hit. I am not a sailor, but it didn't seem ...natural... for that large of a wave to strike in a calm sea."

"I don't consider myself a sailor either, but I can tell you that on the way from Malethya to Disentia, we didn't encounter any swells that size. We certainly didn't encounter any waves close to that size on a clear, starry night without a cloud in the sky." Rainier let the words linger as his mind sifted through the day's activities, since Lira was accustomed to long silences.

I am imprisoned on a ship by a group of wanderleaf-crazed priests and priestesses hell-bent on killing me before I have a chance to upend their way of life and assume control of the Unnamed Army. If I manage to get control of the army, Lattimer and his army of Furies await on the shores of Malethya, and my only allies are Slate and a group of friends that have already been defeated by the blood mage once.

"I believe you are telling the truth. If others are to believe you, we will need proof against the priests. How will we obtain it?" Lira asked Rainier and Kalus.

Rainier's worries were temporarily eased by Lira's words – he had one more ally on this ship. He smiled at her and said, "That is a problem for tomorrow." He had already started formulating a plan, using Jamison's attempted poisoning as a basis for his scheme. "I just hope you are able to fake an illness and wear a mask. Everything else should fall within the duties of a soldier. I am too exhausted to explain more tonight." Rainier found the cabin's bed and collapsed face-first into it.

Before succumbing to his weariness, he heard Kalus say, "I guess that only leaves the question of where you and I are going to sleep, my silent sweetheart. May I suggest we stay close for warmth since there are no extra blankets?"

"I would rather freeze." Lira answered. Rainier heard Kalus grunt, which he assumed was the results of a blow to a tender area. Rainier closed his eyes.

Rainier's worried thoughts led to troubled dreams.

Rainier was back in the gallows, awaiting execution in front of a crowd of cheering people. A noose was slipped around his neck, and it tightened as he fell. The rope failed to snap his neck on the initial drop, but the pressure made his eyes bulge, and his tongue rolled out of his mouth in an unflattering and totally uncontrolled fashion. While gasping for breath that would not come, he looked up at the beam supporting his noose. It transformed into the mast of the *Inked Tides*, and his body started swinging in a slow circle. He looked back down from the mast to see that the cheering crowd was replaced by the immensity of the ocean, and a whirlpool had ensnared the *Inked Tides* within its currents. Cargo and soldiers flew from its deck, inspired by the horrors of dinnertime. As the ship spiraled inwards, Rainier swung in faster circles and the eye of the whirlpool became visible. The depths of the ocean took the form of Julian the Immortal's face – as old as time and as uncompromising as death. The ocean's mouth opened into complete darkness and uttered words that shook his entire being. "Your journey hangs by a thread. Win the Nameless Army. Secure a port. Find and destroy the hidden blood mages." The Inked Tides spiraled faster and faster towards the source of the voice. "Do. Not. Fail. Me." The ship entered Julian's mouth, and Rainier felt the pressure of the ocean's depths close around him.

CHAPTER FIVE

SHOOTING CANNONS, STANDING STONES

Rainier awoke drenched in sweat.

He was simply happy to have awakened.

He pushed himself up from his drenched sheets and savored a deep breath that filled his lungs. He groaned when he realized his tongue was in its normal place within his mouth, and then he said, "If I never see a rope or go swimming again, it will be too soon."

Kalus sat up in the far corner of the room, where he had been exiled by Lira. He looked at the soaked sheets and asked, "What happened to you? Is that all sweat?"

Lira had rested between the bed and the cabin door in case any visitors came in the middle of the night. She looked quizzically in Rainier's direction but chose not to speak. She was always quieter in the morning.

"Julian the Immortal visited my dreams last night," Rainier said.

At this news, Lira's jaw dropped in awe. "What an honor the Immortal has bestowed upon you. What was his message?"

The fate I escaped in the gallows is nothing compared to what awaits me if I fail this mission? When you are older than dirt, you start eating ships just to experiment with new foods? Regardless of Julian's intent, Rainier intended to capitalize on his ability to communicate with Julian based on the look of wonder on Lira's face. There was no need to tell her that Julian threatened his life. "He stressed the importance of our mission and blessed the three of us in our efforts."

Lira touched her fingertips to her heart, spread them out, and then twisted them back upon themselves into a fist, the Disenites' formal sign of a fractal's blessing. It symbolized that the pattern was both infinitely expanding and infinitely complex at even its smallest level. By encircling the heart, the blessing protected you from both large events outside your control and complex events in which you don't fully understand, at least according to *A Life in the Pattern*.

Kalus ignored the blessing and said, "So tell us your plan. How are we going to pay back these priests for last nights' efforts?"

"Jamison played his high cards too early." Rainier smirked at Kalus, who had partnered with him to fleece many traveling merchants of their coin and wares during their time as nomads. "He put on a grand magical display of awesome power, but he overdid it. He showed his hand. Not even Lucus could have powered an entire fleet across the sea with a single spell, and he knew the pattern better than any wizard I've met, with Ibson being the exception, of course. Which means..."

"...they had some help." Kalus finished for him. "But who? Or what? Some ancient artifact or enchanted button? Maybe he has a magical wand shoved us his ass so far we didn't notice it?"

Rainier chuckled as he dug through his trunk of

belongings. His hands grasped what he was looking for and he pulled out the Sicarius mask. "That is what Lira is going to find out for us."

"What is that?" Lira asked.

"This mask has the power to make you unnoticeable. Dressed as a soldier, you could blend into the rank and file of the Unnamed Army without anyone noticing."

"I am already a soldier. I do not need to blend in."

"You will need to blend in to sneak aboard the captains' ships and discover what powers the Unnamed Army." Rainier smirked. "Last night I requested a display of the Army's capabilities. I want you on one of those ships when the demonstration takes place."

"How do I get onto one of the ships when I am locked in here with a guard outside the door?" Lira asked.

"I feel like this is the part where you show us how clever you are..." Kalus added in.

"Jamison was kind enough to arrange transport. By requiring the captains to air their grievances aboard the Inked Tides, he has given us access to the entire Marked fleet."

Kalus laughed and shouted, "Don't mess with the Remnant!" It was loud enough to be heard from two decks below their cabin, but Rainier didn't mind. People were already trying to kill him. Would it really matter if Kalus got reprimanded for yelling aboard the ship?

Rainier clarified his plan to Lira. "You will appear to be sick this morning when Jamison arrives to bring us to the meeting with the captains. When we leave, wear the mask with your armor and walk out the door. Tell the guard something generic, like 'all clear' and keep walking. He won't think anything of it. Then head straight for the transport boats that bring the captains to the *Inked Tides*. Return with the crew of one of the transport boats. When the demonstration of the Marked fleet takes place, look for signs of magic and investigate their source. Come back to the *Inked Tides* with the transport ships following the demonstration and report to me. Is that clear?"

Lira saluted and confirmed, "Your commands are clear. I shall not fail." She proceeded to lie on the floor and curl up in her armor. It wasn't convincing enough.

Rainier said to Kalus, "Help her appear appropriately wretched. I've heard you have a talent for wretchedness." Kalus grunted as he crossed the room to help Lira with her acting. By the time Rainier looked back, she had been stripped of her armor and wrapped in his sweaty, dream-soaked sheets. Her hair was matted in an undesirable fashion, and he had found a bucket to place next to her. Rainier had to hand it to Kalus – those sweat soaked sheets were a convincing touch.

Rainier was dressing when a knock preceded the opening of the door. Jamison walked in with several escorts and ordered one of the priests at his side, "Open that window. This place smells like death." He looked down at the pitiful heap of sweat-stained sheets and asked with a knowing smile, "Did you eat or drink something that didn't agree with you?"

Kalus answered for her by responding, "She must be seasick."

"Ah. Well, that's a shame." Jamison managed to say without a trace of sarcasm. "It would appear that our oracle must attend the meeting of the captains without one of his Hands then." Jamison nodded to another priest, who handed Rainier some folded garments. He said to Rainier, "You'll need to appear in clothes more befitting an oracle."

Rainier took the stack of white linens and tossed them on the bed. "I won't placate someone's perception of my appearance by dressing the part. I'll wear my leathers." *And I'll bring my short swords.*

The priests beside Jamison looked deeply offended, but Jamison bowed his head and said, "As you wish, my oracle."

Rainier gave one last command to Kalus before he exited, "Stay here and tend to Lira." Before Kalus could object, Rainier added, "That's an order." Kalus let his displeasure show upon his face, but he stayed behind. As much as Rainier wished to have Kalus by his side, he was short on time and was hoping Kalus could find a way to gather some information today.

Jamison led Rainier onto the brightly lit deck. Its ordered cleanliness contrasted from the chaos of last night's near capsizing. The crew must have gotten up incredibly early, or not gone to bed at all, to clean up the destruction. All that remained was scrubbed floors and soldiers training in the three fighting rings. Past the controlled chaos of clashing swords, several captains in shining armor waited for Jamison to approach.

The first was a short man with piercing eyes that took in everything around him. The second captain was a statuesque woman that looked down upon Rainier with critical evaluation. The final captain was a non-descript woman who held her evaluations behind a mask of stoicism. Jamison managed the greetings using patterned speech, tying together the end of one sentence with the beginning of the next. "The captains of the Marked fleet are to be presented. I present to you Captain Filios, Captain Tera, and Captain Sharan."

"I am pleased to finally meet you," Captain Filios offered with a slight bow of his head and a look that was far more calculated than pleased.

"Things have been quite…eventful…since you came aboard," Captain Tera offered with a frown. *Translation – I lost a lot of troops at dinner last night, and I blame you. Great.*

"We hope your guidance proves enlightening," Captain Sharan stated diplomatically. *At least she is giving me a chance.*

Rainier listened attentively to the captains while stealing the occasional glance towards his cabin. During the introductions, the door opened, and a non-descript soldier exited with a quick comment to the guard at the door. Rainier watched Lira in the Sicarius mask pass undetected and join the captains' guardsmen as they loaded the smallboats to return to their ships.

With that part of his plan in place, he tried to assert some control over his situation. "My father always told me that guidance is only useful when it is coupled with wisdom." Rainier said, despite his father never having said such a thing. It sounded wise though, and he got a small nod of appreciation from Captain Sharan. "Last night, I requested a demonstration of the fleet's abilities. Is it prepared?"

"A smallboat was sent adrift early this morning,"

Captain Filios said as he pointed into the distance. Rainier could make out a speck in the sea when he stared into the morning light. *It can shoot that far?!?* "My ship is prepared to fire on my command."

Rainier looked over and saw that Filios' ship positioned its cannons to face the distant smallboat. *That's a problem for Lira.* If Lira didn't choose the smallboat returning to Filios' ship, she wouldn't be in position to see the Nameless Army in action.

"That's not good enough. I want each of the ships you captain to fire upon the target."

Tera's and Sharan's eyebrows lifted towards the crow's nest. Filios' pride got the better of him, and he blurted out, "Oracle, I assure you that my crew is perfectly capable of hitting the target."

Jamison saw the opportunity to play the pacifier and said calmly, "I am sure our young oracle did not mean to offend you, Captain Filios. He is still learning our ways." *Ease the tension and strike a blow against my credibility, huh? I can't have that now.*

"Jamison is correct. I did not mean to offend you, but I did mean what I said." Rainier jumped into the conversation before Jamison could continue. "Captain Filios, I assume you assigned your best men and women to this demonstration?"

"Of course..." Filios' curiosity demanded that he hear Rainier's explanation.

"Then I will pose you a question. What good does it do me to know that the best unit in our fleet can hit a difficult shot? If we engage in battle, am I to assume that all the ships in the fleet are equally talented? Or will all the others miss the mark?"

Tera answered for Filios by saying, "All of our troops train with diligence and pride in serving the pattern."

Rainier smiled and said, "Show me."

Sharan nodded and turned towards the guardsmen boarding the smallboats. "When you reach our ships, order them to prepare the cannons while positioning the ships. When we signal, fire upon the smallboat." *A small victory. The captains obeyed their first order from me and now Lira is guaranteed to be on a ship that is firing its cannons. If she makes the most of the opportunity and comes back with some solid information, my small victory may not be that small.*

The party of five waited in awkward silence for the smallboat to return to the ship. Jamison couldn't take the silence any longer and started droning on mindlessly about the infinite wisdom of the Immortal. *What drivel. That man thinks every situation calls for more talking.* Rainier recalled Julian's words to him – Disentia has forgotten how to do what needs to be done.

After several minutes of priestly propaganda, the ships in the fleet turned to aim their cannons at the distant target, which was barely visible against the horizon. *There's no way they can hit a smallboat at that distance.* "Are we ready to give the signal to fire?" Rainier asked.

"The ships have aligned, but the cannons are not prepared," Captain Tera said.

How long does it take to prepare a cannon? Then Rainier understood. The cannons took on a dim blue hue. It grew steadily brighter until they luminesced like Lira's armor during battle. "What is that?" Rainier asked with incredulity.

"That is the full might of the Marked fleet," Sharan responded with obvious pride. She then yelled an order to the crow's nest. "Raise the flag!"

High above them, a soldier held aloft a red flag that would be visible to every other ship in the fleet. "Fire!" she yelled. The flag dropped.

The blue cannons thundered and recoiled, their momentum carrying them backwards as a chorus of blue cannonballs shot forwards with blinding speed. A moment later, a concussive wave rolled over the group, deafening Rainier, but he kept his eyes on the smallboat as a sky of cannonballs arced towards it. They converged as they fell through the sky in a blue arrowhead of destruction. The tip of the arrowhead touched the horizon and the smallboat turned into flotsam and shrapnel. Before the other cannonballs even touched the water, their target was gone, and instead they were met with an eruption of water shooting skyward. By the time the cannonballs had finished exploding, the only thing left was a steam cloud of vaporized water marking the event.

Rainier instinctively reached for the enlightened path, only to find it sputter out. Rainier was surprised that his first reaction was to reach for the path when only a few days ago his hand would have reached for his sword hilt. *When did I get so dependent on the enlightened path?*

Rainier managed to keep his mouth from gaping open at the destruction, and he appreciated the ringing in his ears that prevented conversation. It gave him a moment to collect his thoughts.

The ringing subsided and Filios asked Rainier, "Are you

satisfied with the demonstration?"

Are you kidding me? Who wouldn't be impressed with that display? How many fish did they just boil in the ocean with exploding cannonballs? Rainier responded to Filios, "The training and diligence you described is apparent. The army's capabilities are impressive."

Sharan then said, "Good. Then let us meet and describe strategy."

Jamison concurred and led the group up to the captain's quarters. He said, "Follow me and we shall settle all grievances while preparing for our upcoming invasion of Malethya."

Rainier made sure to walk at Jamison's side, so that the captains would not view him as Jamison's inferior. Jamison led the group to an elaborate room with a raised chair and a heavy wooden table in the room's center. The raised chair emanated power. Jamison gestured for Rainier to sit upon it.

Rainier sat in the fancy chair. It was carved with elaborate swirls and patterns that clearly identified it as a seat of prominence within the Marked faction. *It's a seat for a figurehead – all show and no real power. I can see why they wanted me to wear the robes. I'd be an impressive figurehead sitting in this chair in flowing robes.* Rainier looked down to where the captains positioned themselves around the table in the center of the room. The table contained intricate maps, papers, and other materials necessary for planning a war. *That's where I need to be. I'm no figurehead, and I don't need robes to be impressive.*

Rainier said in a voice filled with command, "I will be

joining you at your table. Is there another chair available for me to sit in?"

Jamison was aghast as he said, "The chair you sit in is reserved for the most revered guests of the Marked faction. It is centuries old, and you show disrespect to everyone here..."

Rainier cut him off and said, "It's a beautiful chair, and I'm happy to sit in it. But I will be joining you at your table." He stood up and tried to lift the chair off the raised platform only to find it was every bit as heavy as it was ornate. After struggling for a moment, Rainier gave up every attempt at manners and gave the chair a good push. It inched across the raised platform and produced a cringeworthy screech.

Rainier was about to give it another push when Captain Sharan stood up and said, "Let me help you with that." She looked over to Jamison and explained, "I'd hate to see such an important chair damaged." She had to pass by Rainier to get to the other side of the chair and she whispered as she walked by, "It was also the right thing to do." Sharan grabbed the other side of the chair and, together, they lifted the chair off the raised platform and placed it at the head of the table, forcing Jamison to move his chair in the process.

They settled into their chairs under the annoyed stare of the Marked faction's high priest. Jamison reasserted control by kicking off the meeting. "This is the first of our daily meetings in which our esteemed oracle will participate and we will use his unique abilities to guide our war strategy. As such, I have asked Captain Tera to lead a detailed summary of the state of our entire army. Captain

Tera, will you run through the list of items to be discussed."

"Of course, my priest. Today we will discuss food and water rations, inventory lists for supplies, weapons, and armor, and the list of the infirmed." *How long will that take? There must be thousands of soldiers on these ships?* "After that, we must discuss training formations for the coming week, battle readiness, and areas of deficiency noted within the development of our army." She paused to look at Rainier and then said, "It goes without saying that our training would be much more efficient if we had an overall plan of attack." She then turned back to Jamison to finish, "Finally, we will decide upon any proposed rank changes for the officers and finish with an airing of grievances." *All day...this will take the entire day.* "Captain Filios, I believe you have prepared the inventory lists?"

Captain Filios motioned towards an attendant who marched over with a thick stack of papers and set them before Filios. Filios straightened in his chair, tugged on his pristine uniform as if it were wrinkled, and launched into tireless recitation.

"341 cook sets, consisting of 2 pots, cutlery and stirring spoons – 129 cook sets lost in last night's storm. 3,747 cups – 2,358 cups lost to the sea. 2,844 plates – 1,190 plates broken last night. 2,260 place settings..." Rainier's attention was lost. *If Filios wants to discuss place settings, that's fine with me, but I'm not going to waste my energy on that.*

Instead, Rainier practiced holding the enlightened path. If he was expected to deliver oracle-worthy foresight to the captains and Jamison after the litany of common household items ended, it might be beneficial to actually be holding the enlightened path before he opened his mouth. Rainier cast the now-familiar probing spell and focused on himself. For the first time today, prophetic light shot away from him. He tried not to focus on any one path too strongly, hoping that he wouldn't strangle his opportunity as he had done last night. Diffuse light streamed in every direction, with a soft glow emanating from his current seat. *Is this what the enlightened path looks like when no one is actively trying to kill you? I could get used to this, but I bet these moments will be rare in the coming days.*

"Our water supply is sufficient, although fifty barrels of fresh water were lost. I have ordered the soldiers to prepare rain catchers to fill more barrels if the weather chooses to cooperate," Filios continued. Rainier went back to his thoughts.

How do I use the enlightened path to do anything useful for the army? Julian wants me to command his forces, but so far all I've managed to do is keep my head attached to my neck. As important of a skill as that is, it doesn't really help me to lead an army. The large map at the center of the table caught Rainier's attention. It showed the Marked faction ships sailing towards Malethya. Two things caught his attention — the first was that the map's borders stretched well beyond any map Rainier had studied in Malethya. *The Disenites sure have expanded their reach since the Twice-Broken Wars.* The second point on the map to grab his attention were the tiny ships. *Could I focus on them while using the enlightened path?* Rainier tried to transfer his probing spell towards the ships, and it immediately snuffed out. *I guess there isn't room on the enlightened path for inanimate objects. It was worth a try, though.*

"This concludes our list of supplies. In summary, the near capsizing of the *Inked Tides* damaged our stores, but with the speed we are currently traveling, it will not be an issue before we reach the shores of Malethya," Captain Filios finished. The report had taken so long that the shadows in the room had shortened as the sun rose higher in the sky.

"Thank you for that detailed report. You are as diligent as ever, Captain Filios," Jamison nodded towards Filios, who tried to hide his pride in the priest's praise. Jamison said, "Captain Tera, please begin your report of our armaments."

Captain Tera received a second stack of papers from the assistant and began her report. She said, "The Marked faction's fleet contains 12 ships, including 7 fighting vessels and 5 support ships. The seven fighting vessels include the *Inked Tides* under the command of Jamison as well as two ships under the command of each captain. No vessels were lost in last night's unexpected storm, although minor repairs were required to the hull of the *Inked Tides.*" *Someone had to stay awake all night to fix the hull. I wouldn't want that job.* "The cannons for each fighting vessel are fully working, although a significant loss of munitions occurred this morning during the demonstration requested by our oracle."

Captain Tera droned on with occasional undertones that indicated her displeasure with the waste of supplies that the demonstration cost the Marked fleet. Rainier ignored it and continued experimenting with ways to use the enlightened path in some prophetic way that would actually help the army. Everything he tried failed quite spectacularly. *I can't wait to be done with these meetings. This is such a waste of time!*

"1500 bucklers, 4,178 short swords, 2,100 long swords, 654 great swords, …" Captain Tera continued listing out the armaments of the Marked fleet.

This is a bit more interesting than spoons and water barrels but sitting through this is like a death by a thousand paper cuts. Rainier tried to hide the boredom and despair from his face as he made eye contact with each of the captains. He stopped when he got to Jamison. *Is he enjoying this?* The beginning of a smirk danced at the corner of his mouth. *What is he getting out of this? We are all trapped here in this room.* Suddenly, Rainier realized why Jamison was smiling. He didn't enjoy being in here anymore than Rainier, but the slow march of time was exactly what he needed. *Every minute that passes, I am closer to Malethya, and he is still in command of the army. I need to end this!*

"…4,238 studded bracers. That concludes our list of armaments," Captain Tera finished.

"Thank you for providing that exhaustive report to our oracle, who I am sure finds the information regarding our army invaluable," Jamison said. "We will continue these updates daily so that our oracle can stay well informed." He then turned to Captain Sharan and asked, "Captain Sharan, have you prepared a list of the infirmed?"

"I have prepared the list, as you requested, my priest," Sharan acknowledged. "As you may imagine, the near-capsizing of the *Inked Tides* left quite a few soldiers with serious injuries that required healing from the priests and an even larger number of soldiers requiring dressings. Of course, neither of these lists is as important as the soldiers that fell overboard and were lost to the sea. I will begin with them, to honor their memory..."

Rainier saw his opportunity to jump into the conversation and said, "I believe the best way to honor the fallen soldiers is to prepare for our future battles and to limit future losses. Let's discuss battle strategy for when we reach Malethya."

Jamison stammered in disbelief as he said, "This is highly unusual. The pattern's agenda for the day is rarely altered, and it would require a seconded motion to be implemented."

"What have I done so far that can be considered usual?" Rainier asked. "I motion to talk about battle strategy."

"I second the oracle's motion to bypass the list of the infirmed and proceed to battle strategy." Sharan stated before Jamison could issue any cautionary looks. *I could give that tough, calculating woman a hug right now, even if she stood there like a statue while I did it.*

Attendants cleared the table of the lists and clutter that had served as Rainier's prison for the better part of a day. Left behind was the map with the Marked fleet vessels upon it. The second map, with a dated but detailed depiction of Malethya, was also placed upon the table.

Filios started the conversation by saying, "The Marked fleet is less than a day away from Malethya, but as you can see, we do not know where we are attacking when we get there. Does our oracle have any insight in the matter?"

There it is — an open challenge right out of the gate. "What are the tactical assessments of my esteemed captains?" Rainier had been leading the Remnant for too long to fall into that trap so easily. *Deflect and gather more information.*

Captain Tera said, "I suggest we approach the southern shores of Malethya where the country is less populated. That way we can preserve our numbers and fortify our beachhead without much resistance."

Captain Filios objected by saying, "That ignores the might of our fleet." *It takes little intelligence to object to someone else's' ideas without proposing one of your own.* Rainier's negative initial impression of Filios intensified from the man's comment.

Rainier saw Sharan looking thoughtfully at the map. "What do you suggest, Captain Sharan?"

Captain Sharan looked up and said, "I have been studying these maps since we left Disentia. I believe Portswain would be the most strategic city to capture. It is closer to Ravinai than the southern shores, and if we can control the city, we will also have access to the river, giving us a direct route to Ravinai." She then shook her head and said, "But of course, I have no knowledge of their defenses, and I doubt the river will be deep enough for our fighting vessels."

Jamison took advantage of her indecision by saying, "The risk is too great. Captain Tera's plan is the safest."

Rainier saw an opportunity to undercut Jamison and maybe gain an ally. He closed his eyes and held up his hands in mock meditation. The room quieted, and after a period of silence that felt appropriately prophetic, Rainier opened his eyes and said, "Captain Sharan has chosen wisely. The enlightened path points us towards Portswain."

"But we are unsure of their defenses..." Filios objected.

"YOU are unsure of their defenses. I have spent my entire life in Malethya. We will sail to Portswain and come no closer to their shores than the smallboat was from our fleet at today's demonstration. Portswain has many cannons defending her walls, but none have the range of your fleet." *I've never seen ANY cannons with the range I saw this morning.*

Jamison asked acidly, "And what does the enlightened path tell us to do when we get to Portswain, my oracle?"

Buy time. "The enlightened path only stretches to Portswain and there are too many options for me to decipher from this distance. Maybe when we get closer, the path will become clearer."

"Our path is set," Sharan concluded, dropping a marker upon Portswain's location on the map.

Jamison maintained his composure, but he needed to fight to do it. Obviously, he had hoped for a bigger blow against Rainier during this portion of the meeting. *A small win. Keep getting the small ones until larger opportunities present themselves.* Jamison said, "Let us move on to the listing of grievances. This is an historical practice that provides commoners a chance to petition the oracle over any grievances they've suffered. If you decide that the grievance caused the petitioner to stray from the enlightened path, you can provide recompense in any form you feel fit to restore the petitioner's path to the light."

They want me to be a judge?

An attendant opened the doors of the cabin, making the long line of petitioner's visible. *How long will this take?* The captains gathered themselves and began to rise from the table. *I will be stuck here all-night listening to stories of petty theft or star-crossed lovers! I need to do something to get out of here.* Rainier, who was always quick on his feet said, "Jamison, as my Voice, I delegate you to this task."

Rainier stood up and started walking away from the table. At his announcement, Sharan paused ever so slightly, which concerned Rainier a great deal. *Did I just say something foolish?* Rainier looked back over his shoulder as he exited the room.

Jamison was smiling from ear to ear.

I have done something wrong. After surviving most of the day and even getting some minor wins in his battle with Jamison, Rainier got the feeling he had lost badly.

Guards welcomed him at the door and escorted him to his own cabin, where he found Kalus waiting with a set of standing stones, a childhood game from his days with the Remnant.

Rainier couldn't help but laugh, despite his slip up with Jamison. "You have a single travel sack to your name, and you brought with a game of standing stones?"

"Come sit down and play a game with me. Lira isn't back yet, so I don't think we have anything better to do. You can fill me in on your day, and I have something I'd like to talk with you about as well," Kalus said.

Kalus has something serious to talk with me about? I

don't know if he's ever said a serious word in all the years that I've known him...a manipulative word or an outright lie sure, but never a serious word. Rainier sat down as Kalus started passing him half of the stones. The purpose of the game was simple. Three red stones were placed on the board as targets and each player had a starting point. They alternated turns placing pieces on the floor in any configuration they chose. At the start of a player's turn, they could choose to attack, which meant they toppled the standing stone at the start location. If done correctly, the stones would topple in sequential order until finishing by knocking over an opponent's stone or a red target stone. If an opponent's stone was knocked over, it was replaced with one of your own. The first person to knock down two red stones was the winner.

Rainier remembered spending countless hours playing the game in the back of a caravan as the tribesmen moved across the plains. It usually ended with one of the children throwing the stones at his opponent after realizing he couldn't win. It was the only time in his life Rainier could remember a stone being thrown at him with nostalgia.

"What happened with our marked-up priest and his entourage of captains? Did Jamison convince you of his righteousness and bend you to his will?" Kalus asked. He laid down his first stone near one of the red markers. It was a common move to start the game.

Rainier matched his move by placing a stone next to another red marker. "I think I can turn Captain Sharan into an ally. All it takes is a little Remnant charm."

Kalus chuckled and said, "I hope your charm is more effective than mine has been with Lira. So far, all I've received for my efforts is swelling in a sensitive spot." More pieces fell on the board and a general pattern started to form, hinting at Kalus' strategy.

"I think Lira is doing you a favor by spurning your advances. A kick to the groin now is much better than whatever Hanna would do to you when she found out." Rainier devised a counter strategy that played along with Kalus' placement of stones and didn't let him on to his plan. He continued his description of the meeting by saying, "I also broke tradition by moving a fractal-forsaken chair, and then I pretended to draw upon my powers of mysticism while declaring that Portswain will be our point of attack."

"You never were one for tradition. Why else would you have left your family and named Slate Severance as your Teacher? He knew nothing of the Remnant." *How long has Kalus been holding this in? He's never said a word about me leaving before this.* Kalus slammed a standing stone onto the floor, aimed straight at a red marker. It was a move that dropped any subterfuge and turned it into a race to the marker.

"I saw something when I fought him in the tournament. He moved...like one of us. He moved with the pattern." Rainier started laying stones from his starting location, acting as if he were joining Kalus' race.

"You had him beat. He landed a lucky blow. There was nothing more to it than that." Kalus started playing his stones faster now that he had made his intention clear. Festering anger may have played a role as well.

"It was more than that. Although in all the time I spent with Slate, I don't think he ever realized his talent. His heart was always in the right place, but he made a mistake. Blood magic was used on Slate, and his abilities as a Perceptor made him think he could control it. In the end, he got deceived and used by Lattimer, someone he mistook for a friend. Slate's biggest weakness is his loyalty and trust in his friends. Lattimer used his loyalty against him, and now he's in power." Rainier placed his standing stone at a slight angle, veering away from the first red stone towards the second.

"You're conceding the first red mark? Don't make this too easy for me." Kalus laughed, but there was no joy in it. The emotions he had held within him were finally being released, and there wasn't room for joy. He placed another stone and said, "What about you? Do you trust Slate and his friends?"

Rainier said, "I trust Slate to always do the right thing. If he needed to get into a locked room, he would run through a brick wall to get there with the power of his good intentions. Sana would take the time to assassinate the guard and steal his key. Neither of them would consider the possibility that they could bribe the poor guardsmen with enough money to buy a necklace in the market that might win him the affections of the girl he's been pining after, and that he'd open the door for you after a five-minute conversation. Slate hasn't learned that sometimes the world needs someone to do the wrong thing. Sometimes the world needs someone who can look you in the eye, shake hands to finalize a deal, and leave you walking away with a smile on your face, only to find yourself wondering how'd you been fleeced three days later. Lattimer is too smart to be fooled by Slate and his trustworthy heart. He won't find me as easy to predict." His stones now split between the two remaining markers, not targeting either of them.

"You always were difficult to predict. I for one did not think you would abandon all of us and become a city boy. But I wonder, have you gotten too unpredictable for your own good?" Kalus said. Then he attacked, knocking down his first standing stone, which created a chain reaction ending with the fall of a red mark. "1-0," Kalus stated and then said, "Tomorrow we arrive in Malethya. Where will your loyalties lie when we get there? Will it be to Slate, to Sana, to the cause you abandoned us for? Will you stay loyal to that bag-of-dust Julian that left us to rot in Malethya, only to imprison us when we fulfilled our duty? Or will you place your trust in the Remnant, the people that have placed their trust in you?" Kalus challenged Rainier with a stare that was sharper than the point of any sword.

Rainier played his stones, choosing not to respond while he gathered his thoughts. *Where was this coming from? More importantly, how do I respond? Am I loyal to all of them? Or does that make me loyal to no one.*

In the meantime, Kalus pounded down stones without breaking his death stare. After a few minutes of back-and-forth plays, Kalus had positioned his stones near a second target. "I will have you beat in two moves," he claimed.

"If you are questioning my loyalty, then why do you still follow me?" Rainier placed a single stone on the outskirts of the board that connected a line of his white stones to Kalus' grey stones.

"My opinions don't change in the timespan of a single

fight. I have known you my whole life, but maybe I don't know you as well as I think I do?" Kalus didn't respond directly to Rainier's question, which Rainier fully expected. *Why would you give away information in a negotiation?* Instead, Kalus placed one more grey stone next to a red mark, completing a path back to his starting point. On his next play, he would attack, capture the red mark, and win the game.

In response, Rainier toppled over his first standing stone, but instead of directing it towards the red markers, he attacked towards the outside of the board. His standing stones toppled one by one in a complex and circuitous pattern until they reached the last standing stone he had played. That stone knocked down one of Kalus' grey stones on a pathway he had considered blocked. The blocked path did go all the way back to his starting point though and as his stones started falling in that direction, Kalus' eyes got wide in recognition of what was happening. His stones fell one after the other until it reached his starting point, and that triggered the fall of all his other standing stones he had aimed at the red marks. The grey stones on the board toppled one after the other until his own grey stone toppled the red mark that would have won him the game. Rainier simply said, "1-1."

Kalus looked across the board as the full realization hit him. The score may have been tied, but all his stones were knocked down and now belonged to Rainier. He had no way of attacking to reach the final red mark. He was beat. He reached down and threw some stones at Rainier, before breaking into a laugh, and this laugh was from the bottom of his soul, shaking him from head to toe. He said excitedly, "I had you beat! And that, Rainier Tallow, is why we follow you!" Between laughter he said, "You've done this since we were kids. No one else could have done that."

Rainier allowed himself a genuine smile that seemed to occur too rarely these days. When Kalus started to calm down, he said in a more serious tone, "You see things differently than those around you. Anyone else would have been fixated on the red marks, but you saw the whole board and won the match by using my own stones against me." He paused for a minute, but Rainier didn't interrupt him. He had known Kalus long enough to recognize that he had more to say. Finally, he looked Rainier in the eye and said, "I know we're in a tough situation. We should be living a life of ease after fulfilling our duty, and instead Julian threw us back into a deadly game where we don't understand the rules or the pieces. You will see us through, Rainier. Right now, you might still be understanding the lay of the board, but you will see the pieces soon enough. When you do, I know you'll tip things in our favor. You are the leader of the Remnant, and we are all behind you. We are family." He clasped hands with Rainier and pulled him in for an embrace.

Right in the middle of that display of manly emotions, the door opened, and a guard walked in. She closed the door and said rather rigidly, "I did not expect to enter and find this. I can come back later..." The guard took a mask off to reveal a rather bewildered Lira.

Rainier laughed and said, "Welcome back, Lira. You aren't interrupting anything but a moment between friends. I'm so glad you made it back from the captain's ship, and I'm looking forward to hear what you discovered."

Kalus pulled back from the hug and said jokingly, "Dearest Lira, I am deeply offended that you haven't taken my advances seriously. If a simple embrace with a friend has made you question me, then I need to be more direct in my advances in the future. I would be happy to do so, so that my intentions are clear."

"No! That won't be necessary!" Lira said way too quickly for Kalus' liking. She turned to Rainier and said, "I would be happy to give my report."

"Any insight you can provide would be most appreciated. But first, come sit down. I'm sure your day has been tiring since you aren't used to clandestine work." Rainier gestured to the desk chair, which was the only proper place to sit in the cabin. "I would also like to ask your opinion on something. I fear I made a mistake in my meetings with Jamison today. It may be too late to correct my mistake, but maybe you will have some information that can help me deal with the damage I've unknowingly done."

"I will try to help." Lira said while removing her heavy armor and sitting in the chair. She had too much honor and grace to fall into the chair as Rainier would have done, but she exhaled deeply as she sat, releasing the pressure of a long day. Rainier knew the feeling well. His early training with Slate in the game of Stratego, with their daily battles of subterfuge in the heart of Ravinai, were some of the most mentally taxing days of his life. Even with the aid of the Sicarius mask, Lira had no formal training and must be exhausted. Like the professional soldier she was though, she pushed ahead with her report. She said, "I joined the guards on the smallboats used to transfer the ship captains to the *Inked Tides* this morning without consequence, although I was unsure of which ship the smallboat would take me to. It arrived at one of Captain Tera's ships, and I boarded, trying to stick to places where groups of guards had gathered." Rainier had instructed her that the mask would be most effective this way. *The soldier can follow instructions. That isn't a ringing endorsement of her potential for future Sicarius work, but it's a start.* She continued, "Shortly after I arrived, there was a signal from the *Inked Tides* that caused quite the commotion, and everyone began to hurriedly prepare to fire upon a smallboat in the distance. I took the opportunity to go below deck by the cannons. I saw soldiers open the portholes, advance the cannons through them, and set blocking behind the wheels to keep them in place. Crates of cannonballs were opened. The cannons were loaded with a swirling blue ignition orb, and the bombardiers took aim at the target. When they were ready, a group of Marked priests entered. They each carried a few small, ornate boxes. The priests set one box upon each cannon in rigging that looked specifically designed for the purpose. Then they spread amongst the bombardiers and said a prayer. The cannons lit up." The word prayer bothered Rainier. *I know a spell when I see one. Also, that ignition orb sounds a lot like an exploding orb, and what's up with the boxes?* "When the order came to fire, the bombardiers pulled a rope, which drove a pin into the ignition orb and the cannonballs hurled through the air. The recoil drove the cannons backwards and they skidded across the floor, despite their blocking. The bombardiers were well trained and ran to push the cannon back to its firing location even while our ears were still deafened."

"You said the priests said a prayer. Were they holding scepters or wearing amulets or anything?" *Did they have any enchanted artifacts at their disposal?*

"They were dressed in their typical robes and did not carry any items in their hands," Lira confirmed. *That just leaves the boxes. Too bad Lira didn't see where they came from.* She then said, "I thought the boxes were important, so after the demonstration I waited and tried to see where the priests took them."

"Nicely done, Lira," Rainier said with genuine compliment. *Maybe I should consider that ringing endorsement to Sicarius when I see Sana next.* "What did you find?"

"I could not follow closely, because no soldiers followed the priests deeper below deck, and I feared I would be discovered. By the time I reached the bottom of the steps, the priests were no longer in sight, and I found myself in a small cargo hold. The room had only one door at the far end. I tried to open it, but it was locked. Being unable to go further without kicking down the door, I looked through the cargo quickly and headed back up to the deck, where I awaited the transport ship's return to the *Inked Tides*."

"You did the right thing by following slowly. I can't risk you being caught." Rainier confirmed. He then asked, "Did you see anything interesting in the cargo hold?"

Lira shrugged and said, "Nothing useful to me. The priests brought with a lot of wanderleaf. I wouldn't have recognized it by sight, but the smell of wanderleaf smoke came from behind the locked door. There was little doubt after that."

Kalus laughed and said, "Those priests had a very taxing day apparently. They could hardly make it back to their smoking lounge before lighting up."

Rainier wanted to know one more detail and asked, "What about the boxes? Were they located in the cargo hold or did the priests keep them with them?"

"I did not see the boxes in the cargo hold," Lira said and then signaled the conclusion of her report by saying, "You mentioned that you needed my advice."

Rainier summarized his day for Lira's benefit. She nodded in understanding, but rarely interrupted him, not even touching the food that was brought to them for dinner. Her stoicism didn't stop Kalus from making a comment, however.

"Thanks for the daily rations!" Kalus yelled to the Guard who opened the door. "It feels just like my time behind bars in Disentia." The door shut hard without a rebuke. Kalus sneered at the guard's lack of wit.

Rainier got to the point in his story when he made a misstep. "I delegated responsibility to judge the petitions of the people to Jamison as my Voice." Lira's eyebrows raised to the ceiling. Coming from Lira, who was trained to show emotional restraint, Rainier could tell she was aghast. He hurriedly explained himself by saying, "I knew Jamison was using the listing of grievances to waste time and keep me locked away, where I couldn't assume control or win anyone to my side. I had to get out of there."

The explanation didn't assuage Lira's initial reaction as she said, "Do you know what you've done?"

Rainier didn't. *Sometimes the best course of action is to admit defeat and ask for help.* The words of Rainier's dad floated into his head, although he had rarely ever seen his dad admit failure or ask for help in anything. He knew he needed help though, so the words rung true. *If I don't want to ask for help again, I guess I shouldn't make a practice of losing.* Rainier let the pain of failure show on his face and said, "I do not know what I've done. Will you tell me, and help me fix it?"

Lira said, "The oracle's word during the listing of grievances is considered final. Since an oracle can see the enlightened path, his word is considered the ultimate truth when deciding between disputes. When people agree to go to the oracle, they are agreeing to settle their dispute based on the overall good of the community. They waive their right to justice and accept the outcome that is best for all. The oracle decides the outcome that will lead all of us closer to the enlightened path."

Kalus interrupted Lira, which left her visibly annoyed, but Kalus couldn't stop from interrupting people any more than the sun could stop from rising in the morning. He said, "Wait a minute. Are you telling me that someone could commit murder, be sentenced by the priests, wait in line outside of Rainier's door, and if Rainier decided that the murder was justified, the man wouldn't be punished?"

Lira frowned. She said, "The situation you describe is highly unlikely, but the answer to your question is yes. If the oracle decided that the murder and the murderer's continued existence brought Disentia closer to the enlightened path, then he could prevent the punishment ordered by the priests." She looked thoughtful and said, "Your implausible story does illustrate the problem at hand though. By delegating your responsibilities to Jamison, you have given him extraordinary power."

"Then I'll speak up tomorrow and take back my role." Rainier said, almost hopefully.

"Your proclamation was heard by all three captains. It is done." She then said, "A normal person would attempt to right this wrong by attending the list of grievances, but even then, your case would be heard by Jamison."

The enormity of his mistake began to sink in. He had thought of the listing of grievances as a stall tactic by Jamison. He was stalling all right, but he was stalling to delay the list of grievances, the one place where Rainier would have power over him. *And I gave it away.*

"How could this happen? Did the enlightened path really lead you in this direction?" Lira asked incredulously. "Are you truly an oracle?"

There's that question again. *When all else fails, try the truth.* Those weren't the words of Rainier's father. That was all Rainier, and the outcome was the same. He had failed and had to fess up and hope for her help. *I have to stop making this a habit.* He looked Lira in the eyes and said, "I'm still learning how to use the path. Sometimes I hold it and can see it clearly. I held the enlightened path during the Oracle Trials. I held it last night during dinner and decided to force Jamison's hand while I was able to hold it. Even today, I held the path during the listing of inventory by the captains. Other times I reach for it, and it feels like it's just beyond my reach."

"You're an impotent oracle!?!" Kalus blurted out with a laugh that lasted way too long. *I've used that same word to describe me, but what gives him the right to call me impotent?*

The frustration Rainier had been hiding finally broke through. He continued, "When I can't hold the path, my only defenses are my sword and my wit. I wasn't holding the enlightened path when I delegated my power to Jamison. My sword and my wit failed to protect me today."

Lira's silence lingered in stark contrast to Kalus' background of laughter following Rainier's admission. He was left trying to read the expression behind Lira's stony face. *What have I done? Who ever said that telling the truth was a good idea? She's probably a split second away from drawing her sword and cutting me down as a blaspheming infidel.* Rainier took a half-step back and dropped his hands to his sides, trying to stay non-confrontational while still gaining reaction time to draw his own blade if it came to that. Kalus was too busy laughing to be of any help if it came to blows.

After several agonizing seconds, Lira said, "I do not know the troubles of an oracle, but I have heard tales of priests that claim to have held the path once and could never find it again. Usually, they go mad. Others look for help from things such as wanderleaf – I believe you met one such priest by the name of Kalana." She nodded towards Rainier, and he didn't want to admit the huge relief he felt at her slight affirmation of loyalty. "What I do know is that you've held the path three times in two days, which is more than any priest I have ever met, and you have passed the Oracle Trials. You are a true oracle, Rainier, even if you need some practice." She turned thoughtful and then said, "Someday you will see all the possibilities upon the battlefield and maneuver our troops to victory even when facing incredible odds. When you learn to use your power fully, you will be the greatest general to ever command an army."

Rainier blurted out, "But to do that, I'd need to be able to see the enlightened path for an entire army. So far, all I've been able to do is to save my own skin." *More confessions? What am I doing?*

"You haven't been too great at that either. You've been cutting it way too close for comfort these past few days." Kalus chimed in with one of his ever-helpful comments.

"And we arrive in Portswain tomorrow morning. We are out of time for you to practice your skills as an oracle. What shall we do?" Lira asked.

"We stall." Rainier said, starting his plan with the most basic need. "Jamison set up these daily meetings to keep me tucked away doing useless inventory. I'll use the mandatory meetings against him. I'll ask details about the condition of every pot and pan in the fleet. I will inquire about the grade of steel used to produce our shields and the quality of the ore from which they came. I'll be such a pain in the ass..."

"You'll be good at that," Kalus said with a smile.

"...that we won't ever get to battle strategy and the deployment of troops before the listing of grievances, which is too important of a ritual for Jamison to ignore." *That should bring the contest to a stalemate, but that isn't good enough. I need to win.* "That brings me to your roles in this plan. Kalus, I want you to borrow the Sicarius mask and use your innate ability for mischief to wreak havoc upon the fleet. I want the line of soldiers with grievances to be so long that Jamison needs to stay up all night to hear the disputes."

Kalus smiled and said, "I can manage that."

Rainier then turned to Lira and said, "I need you to find any archaic ritual, process, loophole, or trickery within the pages of A Life in the Pattern that will allow me to disavow..."

Lira stopped him. "I am no scholar and I do not resort to trickery. It is against the pattern."

"You're right. Leave that to me. I can read it during my days sequestered with Jamison and the captains." Rainier reconsidered his position and said, "Would you be willing to continue your work with the Sicarius mask? You and Kalus would have to coordinate who would use it, but you could investigate the priests and try to find out more information on how they power this army."

"This is important, and if they are breaking the pattern, they must be stopped. This is an honorable mission, but where do I start?" Lira asked.

"You start where the trail ended. Follow the wanderleaf."

CHAPTER SIX

PORTSWAIN

The cityscape of Portswain rose above the docks, just asking to be invaded. Rainier sat in the captains' meeting and could feel the frustration of everyone in the room. They had been sitting outside the range of Portswain's coastal defenses, doing nothing more than float and flap their flags for days now. With each flap of the breeze, the tension in the air grew.

"We are running low on fresh water. We brought with enough barrels to make the journey, but we did not plan to sit in harbor for weeks on end. We need to attack..." Captain Tera made her case before Rainier jumped in.

"This is not the portion of the meeting in which we discuss battle strategy. Please continue with the list of supplies and do not disrupt the daily pattern again." Referencing the pattern was the only way to keep things in order, and even that argument was wearing thin.

"We have 50 barrels of water left. That is enough for two days at reduced rations." Captain Tera stated more formally but without bothering to hide the underlying anger. Festering hostility had replaced the niceties of diplomatic tension days ago. The hostility grew with each rising tide that the fleet sat bobbing in the harbor of Portswain.

Captain Tera continued her inventory list while Rainier took stock of his situation. Over the last few weeks, Kalus had proven his worth. The line of soldiers that Jamison was forced to deal with now wrapped around the corner and got longer every night.

Rainier looked down at the book in his lap. He had read *A Life in the Pattern* several times from cover to cover, sometimes even stopping the captains' meeting to read aloud from the book if the day's meeting happened to be going a little too fast for comfort. So far, all he had been able to do was confirm that the listing of grievances was a near-sacred event to Disenites, and that it could be used to resolve any situation, regardless of circumstances. *I doubt they considered the need for the oracle to use the listing of grievances when they wrote that rule.* As for his abilities as an oracle, he was able to hold the enlightened path more consistently, but he had no luck in applying the path to anyone besides himself. Most days the path diffused around him, comforting him that the tension in the room, although thick, was not life-threatening.

"Captain Filios, please begin your report, and try to be brief." Jamison implored as Tera concluded her list.

Rainier went back to his thoughts, occasionally asking a random question without relevance that required a lengthy or detailed response. Lira had taken to her mission with fervor and had located all the wanderleaf stores on each ship. In each instance, the priests resided behind locked doors, and entire sections of the ships were off limits. Rainier had encouraged Kalus to obtain some priestly robes during his days of mischief, and the stolen robes in combination with the Sicarius mask had allowed Lira to gain access to one of the rooms. Inside, she found the priest's quarters, but the boxes that powered the cannons went deeper into the bowels of the ship, and she couldn't gain access even with the mask. Only one priest ever entered at a time, which made it impossible to blend in with a group. *Maybe the Sicarius Headmaster could find a way, but Lira doesn't have any training.*

"How are your stores of wanderleaf?" Rainier asked Jamison when Filios had finished. "I did not hear them listed in Filios' report."

"The priests have sufficient wanderleaf." Jamison stated curtly, but thanks to Lira, Rainier knew better. She had seen the supplies of wanderleaf dwindle and several priests and priestesses began shaking and becoming physically ill while going through withdrawal in the confines of their quarters. Lira had reported that priests were stealing each other's rations, and in some instances, even resorting to violence to obtain more of the drug.

"That concludes my report. Let us next talk of battle strategy," Filios said. *How did that go by so fast? I got lost in my thoughts and failed to string out his report.* Rainier looked at the sun in the window. It was still too high in the sky for the listing of grievances to begin.

"Motion seconded." Captain Sharan said before Rainier could think of a way to divert the conversation. "What plan has our oracle devised?"

All eyes turned to Rainier. In truth, he had been devising plans – plans for Kalus to create mischief, plans for Lira to infiltrate the tight-knit group of the priests, and, most importantly, plans to escape this boat with his life. Of course, those plans didn't prepare Rainier to face Lattimer the blood mage and to fulfill Julian the Immortal's demand to destroy the hidden blood mages that Ibson had locked away years ago. Sounds simple. No problem. Rainier lied to himself and tried to focus on the task in front of him — Portswain.

"Your cannons are beyond the range of any of their defenses. Take out these locations," Rainier said, as he pointed to the various Malethyan defensive posts. *I have to give them something, but I don't have to attack yet. I can hold them off a few more days.* "After that, you can take the port. I would expect much heavier resistance on land. Malethyans are not known for their naval prowess."

Captain Tera said, "Then we should support our troops with continuous fire beyond the docks to prevent a coordinated counterattack as the army gains a foothold in the city." It will also kill many Malethyans. Rainier could hardly imagine the damage those cannons would cause if they fired freely into the city of Portswain. *Why am I concerning myself with the lives of Malethyans? I'm the leader of the fractal-forsaken army invading them.*

"That is sound strategy, but we should localize our fire to strategically cut off the docks from any additional support. Otherwise, there will not be much city left to take, and we need the supplies to replenish our troops." Captain Sharan amended.

"Our troops are eagerly awaiting the order to attack," Captain Filios said.

"Then it is agreed," said Jamison. "Tomorrow will be a day of preparation. The attack will commence the morning after next, with the sun against our backs."

Rainier used his most prophetic voice to say, "The strategy is clear, but the timing deviates from the pattern. We will wait." Rainier assumed a chorus of protests would follow, but Jamison held up his hands and said, "Our oracle has spoken. This concludes our discussion on battle strategy. Shall we close the meetings for today and begin the list of grievances early?"

"Motion seconded," Captain Filios said. Rainier started to stand up, thankful for an easy finish to his day, when Filios said, "and I have a grievance to be heard by the oracle."

Rainier sat back down, on high alert. *What is Filios planning?* Jamison said, "As the appointed delegate of the oracle, I will hear your grievance."

Filios said, "I have a grievance with the oracle, who is defying all logic by delaying an attack on Malethya. I believe his previous affiliations, namely his childhood spent in the country, are affecting his ability to carry out our mission and that he should be removed from power." *Fractal's curses. Jamison finally found a way around my stalemate.*

Jamison turned to Rainier and said, "Oracle, this grievance is most disturbing. Do you have anything to say for yourself?"

"I am appointed by Julian the Immortal. If you defy me, you are defying the Immortal one." *Perhaps by evoking the name of Julian, I can inspire some fear in them. With any luck, they've awoken in pools of sweat from dreams of the old bastard, too.*

Jamison nodded solemnly and said, "And this is why it is so disturbing to see you turn from the path. As the delegate of the oracle, I order Rainier Tallow to be detained indefinitely, until Julian can hear this accusation himself. This grievance is sided with Captain Filios. The fleet shall prepare for the invasion and will attack the morning after tomorrow. The troops under the oracle's command shall pass to the next leader in line, the high priest of the Marked faction, Jamison." *If the fractal-forsaken fool had a crown handy, he no doubt would have placed it upon his own head.* Jamison rose to his feet under the power of his legs, or maybe it was the power of his own self-righteousness. It was difficult to tell in that moment. "Guards, take Rainier Tallow and lock him in his room."

Guards came and escorted him away. Jamison and Filios immediately began congratulating each other on their successful coup, while Tera stared at the map. Only Sharan looked in Rainier's direction as he was dragged away.

Rainier entered his cabin with all the grace he could muster after the soldier's foot kicked him in the back and sent him sprawling across the wooden floor. Lira popped up and drew her sword, but the soldier slammed the door shut before any further confrontation could take place.

"Are you hurt? What has happened?" Lira asked.

"I'm fine. The corner of the table broke my fall when my face hit it." Rainier said as he gingerly touched his cheek. "Jamison had Filios list a grievance against me. Jamison used his authority as my delegate during the listing of grievances to take over the army and lock me away. Oh...and Malethya is about to be invaded." Rainier looked around the room and asked, "Where's Kalus?"

"He took the Sicarius mask today and hasn't returned," Lira said with a hint of concern.

"Do you know what he was planning to do?" Rainier asked.

"No, but the priest robes are gone," Lira said.

Rainier didn't know what to make of that, but he had known Kalus for a long time. He always managed to get himself out of tough spots. "He'll be ok. Kalus knows how to take care of himself."

Lira nodded but the concern didn't leave her face. "What will you do now?" she asked.

"I didn't come all the way across the sea just to show up without an army at my back. You said I will be the greatest general this world has ever seen. I can't do that without an army."

Rainier started talking through different scenarios and their current options, as limited as they were. They could throw open the window and swim for shore, hoping they survived the swim and the imminent attack, but that wouldn't help them win over the army. The more they discussed, Rainier could see only one option, the listing of grievances. For it to work though, he needed the listing of grievances to be in a public setting, where he could convince the masses to turn against Jamison. Rainier and Lira stayed up all night plotting new ways to make the argument against Jamison, but they could never get past the fact that Jamison was Rainier's Voice, and they had no means to discredit him while he maintained that role. Anything he said would be taken as if Rainier himself were speaking. The plan became bleaker as the night got darker, and not just because Rainier couldn't formulate a strategy for the next day. The door never opened. No footsteps entered the cabin. Kalus was gone.

Rainier awoke in a stress-fueled state and reached for the enlightened path out of reflex. Thankfully, it held, and he expertly scanned the streams of light emanating from him. There were a lot fewer paths than normal, and it wasn't until he looked down that he realized why. His Stratego medallion that he wore on a necklace around his neck shone with enlightened light.

Rainier immediately ripped it off his neck, threw it to the ground and smashed it with the pommel of his short sword. Sana had given him that medallion when he left Malethya and had said it was one half of a pair. She called them entangled particles or some such nonsense, but however it worked, she had promised that she would know when he broke it and that he needed help.

"Open the cabin window," Rainier commanded.

"I thought you decided against swimming to shore last night. You plan to make an exit now?" Lira asked with disdain. She would view the strategy as dishonorable. Rainier had no such qualms with the move, but that wasn't why he needed the window open.

"The window isn't an exit. It's an entrance. I have some friends that will be visiting." Rainier then added, "Try not to be surprised when they come in, or you might not live long enough for introductions."

Sana would be coming, and if Sana came, she'd be coming as the Sicarius Headmaster, the world's greatest assassin and the Shadow of the Night. With her, she'd be bringing Slate Severance, the ghostly demi-god with blood-stained eyes who didn't bleed when he was cut and moved with inhuman speed. May the pattern help any fractal-forsaken fools who stood in their way.

Gasp! Lira startled in the most uncharacteristic way. Rainier turned around and saw Slate Severance with a knife against her throat and the Sicarius Headmaster poised with a throwing knife in case things got out of hand.

Rainier smiled and said, "You can let her go. This is Lira. She's on our side."

Slate dropped the knife and rushed over to envelope Rainier in a manly embrace. *I hate when you hug me like this! I'm smaller than you, I get it.* Rainier recoiled slightly and then let go of his initial height-restricted reaction. *...Forget it, you fractal fool. You know you miss this devil like no other.* Rainier embraced Slate and patted him on the back. "Do you know how many campfire stories I've told of you to Disenite children?" Rainier joked.

"I hope you scared them with stories...stories that are true." Slate said in his most ominous voice, before laughing.

"It wouldn't be fair to keep the legend of Slate 'Stonehands' Severance constrained to Malethya. I couldn't help but spread word of your wrongdoings. You are the most nefarious criminal in all the land, after all. I'm scared just being in your presence."

Slate laughed but then said, "You may need to retell your stories from Sana's perspective. She's done some stuff that put my stories to shame. Just ask her about Phoenix."

"Phoenix?" Rainier asked and turned his attention to Sana. He gave her a hug and said, "I thought you were going to keep Slate out of trouble. What's this story about?"

The Sicarius Headmaster said, "I had to tie him to a tree to keep him out of trouble, but I did it." Rosana continued, "It didn't sit well with him when he missed out on all the fun, but I made up for it later." Rose blushed. Sana responded logically, "And it was the solution that gave us the best chance of beating Lattimer. He's the only one that has shown the ability to resist Lattimer's blood magic. I couldn't risk it."

"It sounds like we have a lot to catch up on," Rainier said.

"I'd say," Slate said. "For instance, how does a tribesman from Malethya show up with a fleet of Disenite ships in the harbor of Portswain?"

"You'd have to be an imprisoned but legendary general with the gift of foresight to truly understand," Rainier joked. He then spent the remainder of the morning filling in Slate and Sana on his exploits, starting with the details of the Remnant.

"So, you are the leader of the last standing battalion of the army my father fought to eradicate?" Slate asked.

"Life's funny," Rainier said with a shrug.

"Maybe we can get it right this time around. We have an entire war to figure things out." Slate offered with a smile. Rainier then described his time on the shores of Disentia and the lack of parades in his name, omitting any disparaging remarks for the sake of Lira, who was listening intently.

"It sounds like you were able to get the Marked faction here and pointed towards Lattimer, but you broke your medallion. What do you need?" Sana asked. "And it better be important!" Rosana added, "You interrupted a very pleasant breakfast at a fancy inn where Slate was in the process of showering me with gifts."

"Well, for starters, I'm locked in my cabin. The imposed privacy has given us the opportunity to catch up, but I don't want to stay locked away while Portswain gets destroyed." Rainier admitted. "After that, I'm not entirely sure. I looked along the enlightened path, and it pointed me to the Stratego medallion. I've learned to trust my abilities when they appear, so I broke the medallion." He then described all the events of the last few days to Slate and Sana in exacting detail, hoping they could see a way out of the situation. They soaked up the knowledge as only members trained in Sicarius could.

Slate nodded thoughtfully after processing all the information, shrugged, and said, "Well, I can help you break out of this cabin if you'd like. Just don't make me swim again."

The Sicarius Headmaster scolded him by saying, "It wasn't that far. And if we need to swim again, we will."

Slate responded by saying, "Easy for you to say. You don't have to swim with a hand made of stone. I'd rather break through this door and take over the ship...but that's just me."

Rainier sought the enlightened path, and it blissfully held. *Am I getting better at this?* The light went towards the window and towards the door, either path was an option for survival, but he knew only one path gave him a chance to leave the ship with an army. He said, "All right, if you prefer the door, then let's break out of here."

"Do you know what awaits us on the other side?"

"Yes." Rainier said. "An army with enchanted armor that enhances their movements, a whole bunch of fractal-forsaken political intrigue with the captains, and a group of magic wielding priests that want me dead. Oh, and my friend Kalus is missing."

"Next time just say you have no idea," Rosana said. She turned to Slate, "Should we stir things up a bit?"

"Do it, and we'll look for Kalus in the meantime. He'll be the only one that doesn't try to put a sword in you." Rainier smirked and then said, "And try to keep everyone breathing. Remember, I'm supposed to lead this army. It wouldn't do to kill them all before they get off the ship."

The Sicarius Headmaster twirled a knife and placed it back in the folds of her outfit. "Fine by me. Darts it is."

"As for Jamison and the captains, a little violence has a way of sorting out petty drama." Slate said with a smile before kicking down the door. Splintered fragments shot forward, and Slate followed right behind them, locating the guard, and chopping down at the base of her neck. She crumpled to the ground and Slate said, "Don't worry, I used my left hand!"

Rainier didn't have time to ponder how the scene would have looked different had Slate used his Stonehand, because he was rushing out the door. Lira, his Hand, was at his side drawing her sword, but they were two steps behind the Sicarius Headmaster, and everyone trailed the blur of motion known as Slate Severance.

By the time Rainier burst into the sunlight and let his

eyes adjust, Slate and the Headmaster had cleared half the deck. Darts flew into flesh with magical precision, and Slate flashed from soldier to soldier, incapacitating them before they even had time to react.

Rainier held the enlightened path, which led him towards a stack of barrels. Beyond the barrels was a staircase that held a warm yellow light. *That seems straightforward enough.* Rainier pushed the stack of barrels unceremoniously towards the top step. Lira followed his lead, and the bouncing of barrels was soon met with the thud of barrels against armor. They continued tossing the barrels down the stairwell until it was completely blocked. No one would be helping from below deck until they could clear all of that out, and, judging by the speed Slate and the Headmaster moved, it would be far too late.

"Attack!" A cry arose from the crow's nest from a soldier with a bird's eye view of the action. She had just enough time to raise the alarm before a dart hit her, and she fell into the netting below. The alarm alerted the rest of the soldiers, though, and they drew steel. A second later, everyone's armor and weaponry glowed bright blue, undoubtedly from some "prayer" cast by a priest below deck.

The paladins moved much quicker with their enchanted armor, and they put up a stout defense against Malethya's finest. As they adjusted to Slate's speed though, Slate and Sana adjusted their strategy as well. He fell back towards the Sicarius Headmaster, keeping the area clear of soldiers around her. That gave her room to throw her darts, and as fast as the soldiers were, they couldn't outrun a dart imbued with the pattern of an attacking falcon. Soldiers continued to fall.

Rainier dove to the side, following the sudden shift in the enlightened path, just as a soldier jumped from the quarter deck with ill intentions and a pointy sword. Lira put an armored foot into the man's face, and he crumpled to the ground. Rainier nodded his appreciation and made his way up the steps of the quarterdeck to where the captains' meeting was being held, just as they burst out the doors, drawn by the sounds of battle.

Jamison saw him and yelled, "Kill him!" without hesitation. The captains drew their swords and advanced while Jamison prepared a spell.

Lira stepped in front of him, but Rainier knew the captains were too skilled and would overpower his Hand. They spread out and advanced with the clear advantage. Captain Tera engaged Lira in a loud crossing of blue swords, while Filios and Sharan swept around to reach Rainier, the traitorous oracle. Rainier held his short swords at the ready, but his focus was on the enlightened path. Aided by its comforting light, he feinted forward as if he were trying to fight back-to-back with Lira and instead leaned backwards, just as two blades sliced the air where he would have been. He rolled to his right, avoiding an armored kick from Sharan, and as he stood up to face the duo again, Slate Severance vaulted over the railing of the quarterdeck and punched Filios' shield with his Stonehand so that it crumpled. The force of the blow knocked Filios over, and before he could get up, Slate had launched himself into Jamison and interrupted his spell.

The Headmaster appeared at the top of the steps with a

knife in hand and said to Tera and Sharan, "Take one more step and it'll be your last, ladies." They wisely stepped away from Lira and Rainier while holding their shields high. The Headmaster lithely climbed the mizenmast, giving her the upper ground and a clear kill shot on anyone below her.

Slate stood Jamison up and asked Rainier, "Are these the people causing you so much trouble?"

Rainier smiled and said, "These would be them." He then turned to Jamison and said, "We have control of your ship. Step down and acknowledge my right to lead this army."

Jamison frantically looked around to assess his situation, and to Rainier's dismay, the smug confidence the priest always displayed returned quickly. He said, "You have overestimated the situation. You may have taken the ship, but you can't hold it with your numbers, and you forgot about the fleet." Rainier followed his gaze and saw blue cannons encircling the ship. "If I don't give the signal to call off the attack, they will level this ship faster than you or your pet demon can jump off it."

Below them, soldiers began to stream onto the main deck, as they had finally cleared or carved through the pile of barrels in the stairwell. Jamison said, "Besides, the pattern is being restored as we speak." He gave a sinister smile and said, "And I have a little surprise for you as well. Tell my priests to bring the prisoner to me."

More soldiers streamed out of the stairwell and filled the deck below, pointing swords threateningly. Their numbers grew even more rapidly as the incapacitated soldiers awakened. *These are impossible odds, but this is all I wanted – a chance to make my case to the army.* A few seconds later, a large group of priests came up the stairs, pushing a tied-up Kalus ahead of them. The man holding Kalus was the spiky haired priest that wanted to kill Rainier at the welcome dinner. Rainier also recognized Kalana in the group, the priestess who had once held the enlightened path and would do anything to find it again. They moved as one towards Jamison, who tried to look confident even though he was within striking distance of Slate Severance and a wrist flick away from one of the Headmaster's darts.

He addressed the crowd with an amplified voice and a form of patterned speech, "Today is a day of truths. We will bring the truth of the pattern to the people of Malethya." He gestured to the city walls of Portswain and boots stomped in appreciation. "Tomorrow, we will tear the city down and rebuild it as the pattern intended." Giving speeches was Jamison's strength, and he gained confidence as he spoke, ignoring the immediate threats to his life. *The man is a professional blowhard. I'll give him that much.* Jamison turned somber and said, "Unfortunately, this day has brought another truth to light – Rainier Tallow is a traitor." Silence followed.

Is that shock I'm seeing in the soldiers? Disbelief? I'm getting really tired of people calling me a traitor.

The spiky-haired priest shoved Kalus forward so that he was visible to the troops on the deck below. "This truth became apparent when this man, one of the so-called Remnant that appeared with Rainier Tallow, was apprehended in the priest quarters yesterday. I do not know what he was doing, or why he was dressed in the robes of a priest, but I do know he wore an enchanted mask." The spiky-haired priest held Rainier's Sicarius mask in the air for all to see. "The truth is that this mask is not of the pattern!" Jamison increased the volume of his voice to new heights and all the drawn swords suddenly looked a little pointier.

This is getting bad. Even I might not be able to talk my way out of this one.

Jamison continued with impassioned anger, "And now the ultimate truth about Rainier Tallow is revealed. He not only spies upon his own priests, but he also attacks his own people!" Swords crossed down below. Rainier didn't know what it meant, but it couldn't be good. "Look at who he consorts with..." Jamison gestured to Sana and Slate, "...one wears a mask created with blood magic and the other looks to be more demon than man." The tension in the air had risen with the volume of Jamison's voice and now he lowered it dramatically, knowing everyone hung on his words. "It is with sadness that I bring you these truths, and, as the high priest of the Marked faction, I motion for Rainier Tallow and everyone associated with him, to be executed for his crimes."

Rainier looked out on the Nameless Army, the men and women he was supposed to lead. They held swords against their own necks, a clear and silent death sentence. Rainier held the enlightened path, but there was no yellow light. There was no path forward.

A sword unsheathed behind him, and Rainier had no doubt it would be aimed straight at his neck.

"I wish to join the Listing of Grievances!" Rainier the tribesman shouted. This wasn't Rainier Tallow, the leader of the Remnant, or Rainier the Oracle. All those titles and their presumed authority had failed him. This was the shout of a practiced swindler who had been caught making an unfair deal. This was pure desperation.

Jamison raised his hand. Rainier assumed the sword behind him stopped its motion as well because his head was still attached to his neck.

"It is the right of every person to be heard at the Listing of Grievances. As I am the appointed delegate in this matter, we can hold the trial right now and be done with this charade. What is your grievance?"

People keep trying to kill me. Rainier pushed aside his actual thoughts and frantically thought through the text of *A Life in the Pattern* for something more useful. "I claim to have been misrepresented by my Voice, the high priest Jamison. This man promised to serve me and instead he attempted to kill me, used his position to keep me from performing my abilities as oracle, and has deviated the entire army away from the enlightened path."

Jamison gave a low whistle and a shake of the head. Then he said, "These are serious claims. Before they can be made in a public setting though, they will need to be given by your Voice, and since your initial grievance was being misrepresented by your Voice, we will settle that one first. You have become a fan of *A Life in the Pattern* recently, have you not? We will borrow a section from that book and settle this dispute by arguing within the pattern."

Rainier cringed. The premise was that a moderator would choose a topic that both parties would debate. Since Rainier never got the knack for patterned speech, it would be a quick debate.

"Captain Sharan will moderate and choose the topic."

Captain Sharan stepped forward and looked Rainier in the eyes. She studied him for a moment and said, "The topic is the morality of war, and Jamison shall go first."

Jamison straightened his back, inflated his chest, and exhaled an oration fit for a pulpit. "The way of the pattern is the way of morality. When the pattern calls for war, the question of morality may not be questioned..." He continued with eloquent alliteration, changing his cadence, and easily switching from one style of patterned speech to another, all within the same testimonial.

I'm a dead man.

Rainier stopped listening and concentrated on escape. He held the enlightened pattern, but he was surrounded by an army of soldiers with enhanced weaponry that had already decided his fate. There would be no escape from the gallows this time.

Jamison finished his speech to the sound of rabid stomping from the soldiers below. Captain Sharan turned to Rainier and said, "Rainier Tallow will now speak regarding the morality of war."

Rainier stepped forward and tried to collect his thoughts. *Save yourself first. Escape is a great option – use it whenever possible. A knife in the back is a good option if you are a poor swordsman.* Nothing from his father's teachings or his Sicarius training seemed to help him. He looked up to the sky in frustration.

His frustration melted away in the form of the Sicarius Headmaster perched upon the mizenmast. She radiated the yellow light of foresight as brightly as a sun.

"I name Rosana Regallo as my true Voice. She will represent me in this debate." Rainier announced and pointed towards the robed and masked figure above them.

"That is absurd!" Jamison interjected. "The debate is between Rainier and me. Make the man speak so we can finish this."

Sharan thought long and hard before saying, "The oracle has the right to name his own Voice. Since the matter at hand is the misrepresentation of the oracle by his assigned Voice, I will hear the argument from Rosana Regallo."

Jamison shook his head in disgust, but all eyes were on the Headmaster as she flipped off the mast and landed on one knee of the quarterdeck. *If she were holding a staff, she could have passed for Slate entering the arena during my tournament bout all that time ago.* She stood and walked up to Rainier, asking, "What do you want from me?"

Rainier answered honestly, "I don't know. I only know that you will win the crowd, and you can beat Jamison." He gave his best Remnant grin to the shadowy Sicarius mask hiding Sana's face and said, "Just be you." She turned her head quizzically at the words, and they obviously carried more meaning than he had intended. *What does 'Just be you' mean to Rosana? She is easily the most complicated woman I have ever met, but that look had meaning. I guess I'm about to find out.*

The Sicarius Headmaster stepped forward, looked across the crowd, and stated with resolute certainty, "There is no morality in war." Shocked silence followed the blasphemous statement. "Morality is spoken of by those who seek reason for the acts of war they have committed or have ordered others to do on their behalf. I seek no such false promises. I am the shadow in the night, the Sicarius Headmaster, the most feared assassin in Malethya, and I know of the atrocities of war. An act of war is no different than the work of an assassin carried out on a larger scale. I know death. I know killing, and to me, morality is best seen in my enemies' eyes when they see me enter the room. It drives their fear and makes them search for reasons at a time they should be acting. It causes them to hesitate just long enough for one of my daggers to open their throats. Morality is death."

The Sicarius Headmaster removed her mask, looked out on the silent crowd, and spoke again. "Morality clouds the minds of everyone at war. It prevents them from being strategic and forces them into irrational decisions." Her voice changed as she spoke, almost imperceptibly, but it lost its previous edge. Now is sounded scholarly, if not academic. She said, "I am Sana, a wizard. My master Lucus taught me morality and taught me to use the pattern. I call upon the pattern to cast spells…" Sana turned her palm upwards and electricity jumped from one hand to the other, almost as if juggling. She continued her lecture on magic and the pattern as she tossed the electricity back and forth in demonstration. "…and I assure you that knowledge of the pattern has nothing to do with morality. I can call upon the pattern to produce spells as easily as your priests, and I know of wizards with the same abilities as me that have highly questionable morals. The two issues are distinct and independent. To address them together is to cloud your mind with frivolity."

"Blasphemer!" Jamison cried and the crowd pounded the deck in unison. It took the raised hands of Sharan to bring order to the masses.

While they settled down, Sana removed the pins from her hair and let it hang down to her shoulders. Once she could be heard, she said above the murmur of the crowd, "Morality is often the cause of war, if anyone was observant enough to see." Her voice changed again. Now, it inspired trust but was simultaneously immemorable. It sounded as if she could scan the crowd and see everyone's thoughts. "I am Rosana Regallo, and I have been called a master of my environment. I see what is in front of everyone but goes unnoticed. I see things from angles and perspectives that others miss. I have learned that morality is often as simple as a matter of perspective. A fruit merchant will condemn the actions of a child who steals fruit from his cart as immoral, but the morality of taking a single apple from a man who has so many is lost on a child with an empty belly. War is no different, it just plays out on a larger scale. Powerful leaders take offense at the actions of another group, often calling them immoral, and seek 'justice' using the tools at their disposal. The tools at their disposal are usually the lives of their soldiers." Rosana paused for a second, giving the crowd time to think. She finally said, "I do not know you or your beliefs, but I ask you to consider whether you truly understand the actions of your leaders. Do you know why you are being asked to endanger your lives? Is it for some theoretical argument regarding the pattern or because you genuinely want to stop a blood mage? Do you want to stop him from burning out the minds of more soldiers and adding numbers to his army of Furies? Do you really want to stop my brother?"

"She admits to being the sister of the man we are sent to stop. Do not listen to her, my friends!" Jamison shouted. The soldiers stomped the ground, but it was less violent, less resolute. *They are listening!*

Rosana laid a knife at her feet, and she said loudly, "Morality is the only thing that matters in war. It is the only thing that matters in life!" Now her voice sounded...young and innocent. The difference between the Sicarius Headmaster's voice and this voice could not have been more dramatic. She spoke with command but struggled to raise the volume of her voice to address the crowd. It didn't matter, as the crowd had silenced and was hanging on her every word. "I am Rose Regallo, and I am the reason soldiers fight in wars. I do not hold a sword or a knife. I do not question the morality of the army across a battlefield. I do not care about the problems of leaders." She looked across the soldiers, making eye-contact with each man, woman, son, or daughter. She said, "I am the innocence you lose when you take someone's life. I am the part of you that will never come back, even if you return from war. I am your joy of life. I am your wonder."

She slowly bent down and picked up her knife, becoming Rosana. She said, "If I needed to, I would do anything to protect what was most dear to me. I would hear the orders issued to me, but I would not fight because of them. I would fight so that others didn't need to, so that my husband, my son, or my unborn baby could grow up in a world in which they didn't have to make the sacrifices I have to make." Rosana tied her hair up, becoming Sana. "I will not be swayed by arguments of leaders with purposes different from my own. I will make my own choice." Sana pulled the Sicarius mask over her head, becoming the Headmaster. "I will do whatever it takes, because morality has no place in war...and it is the only thing worth fighting for."

The crowd remained silent long after the Sicarius Headmaster spoke her last words. Rainier held his tongue, knowing that the message Rosana had just delivered was far more powerful than anything he could add at this minute. Similarly, Jamison was bound by the rules of the debate to hold his tongue, so the silence stretched on until Sharan finally stepped forward and the Headmaster reclaimed her perch on the mizenmast.

"I have listened to both arguments within the pattern, and as the moderator, it falls upon me to make a decision."

She looked towards Jamison and said, "Our high priest has spoken eloquently regarding the morality of war, calling upon our most sacred tenants and evoking an emotional response from all of us. His speech is a masterpiece of patterned speech that should be written down and appreciated for generations to come."

Sharan then turned towards Rainier and said, "Your delegate offended everyone in attendance today by trampling upon our beliefs. Our high priest has labeled her a blasphemer, which makes her an enemy of Disentia."

Jamison smiled, but it was premature, as Sharan then said, "I also think that she has captured morality of war in a way that relates to every soldier that picks up a sword. It lacked the eloquence of Jamison's speech, but it captured the plight of a soldier leaving home and not knowing if she will return to her family, ordered away by someone she has never met and whose morality and sense of judgment she will never be able to question. I judge that there is a deep truth within her words..."

Jamison erupted, "She is a blasphemer and failed to use patterned speech. She should be labeled an enemy of the state and executed!"

Sharan stood toe-to-toe with Jamison and raised her voice, "I am the moderator, and the decision is mine! You have already labeled her a blasphemer, and the contest was not a contest in the use of patterned speech, it was an argument within the pattern. *A Life in the Pattern* was written before patterned speech became commonplace, so the use of patterned speech cannot be a requirement in a contest that invokes its name." Even Jamison failed to produce an argument against history, so Sharan backed away to address the soldiers. "Rosana delivered her message in a unique way, but by speaking from multiple perspectives, and even addressing us as multiple people, she has demonstrated her arguments in a way that brings new insight to the pattern and to ourselves. Rainier Tallow has won the argument within the pattern, and as such, Jamison is stripped of his duties as Rainier's Voice, as requested in the listing of grievances. I believe you had some other accusations that must be heard?"

Wait, did that just work? Did I rid myself of Jamison and gain control of the army? All Rainier had to do now was list the ways in which Jamison tried to kill him and had strayed from the enlightened path, and then rule against him during the listing of grievances.

"I do not accept the ruling. As the high priest of the Marked faction, I label Rainier Tallow a blasphemer and have removed him from his duties." Captains Tera and Filios drew their swords. Before his sword cleared his sheath, a throwing knife struck Captain Filios' helm in warning and bounced off. Tera cleared her sword from its sheath, but Sharan stepped forward and met her blade, protecting Rainier. "The next knife draws blood." The Oracle's Voice, Rosana Regallo, proclaimed from the mizenmast.

At the clash of swords, the soldiers below deck responded immediately. They turned from the quarter deck to face each other, with the third of soldiers under Sharan's command facing the remaining troops, weapons drawn.

Filios looked to Jamison, who nodded slightly, signaling him to stand down for the moment. Rainier tried not to laugh as Jamison ran his fingers through his hair and let them linger a moment or two where the throwing knife had struck Filios' helm. *It's good to know we can keep a healthy dose of fear in that fractal-forsaken bastard.*

Jamison recovered quickly and managed to keep his voice to a conversational volume as he hissed to Sharan, "You would dare defy me?"

Sharan responded loudly for all to hear, "I do not defy the priesthood. I choose not to follow a leader that I no longer trust or believe. I will follow Rainier, the oracle appointed by Julian the Immortal, and listen to his true Voice, and they will correct your wrongs and send us along the enlightened path. Let us hear what he has to say."

Don't overdo it, Sharan. I have enough people placing misguided trust in me. Don't turn me into a priest...control of the army will do just fine.

Having the odds even out a little freed Rainier's mind and loosened his tongue. Unfortunately, it did nothing to affect his ability to hold the enlightened path, which momentarily failed him. Left without the gift of foresight, Rainier stepped forward with the swagger of his upbringing and spoke without the pretenses of a title.

"I may not be practiced in the art of patterned speech, but I know you have ears. Hear what I have to say." Rainier said with an overly confident smile and speaking in a familial tone. *I'd bet my last dollar that they've never had a leader speak to them as if they were actual people.* "What a day! I woke up this morning locked away in my cabin while Lattimer sits in Ravinai, getting stronger every day. We should be working together, united and acting under Julian's directive to cleanse Malethya from his rule. And yet here we are, soldier facing soldier, countrymen facing countrymen, friend facing friend." He gestured to the soldiers below him. "And why? Our foe is not on this ship. We did not come here to kill each other as Jamison is so willing to do. We came here to end the threat of blood magic in Malethya."

Some of the soldiers below stomped their feet. *Some of them are listening, at least.*

"I could continue to list the wrongs that I place at Jamison's feet, but I don't think it will matter. I think there are those among you that choose to believe Jamison's message that was delivered so eloquently with the intent of ending my life. I believe others amongst you will contemplate the likelihood of the Inked Tides nearly capsizing on a night with calm seas."

Jamison started to protest, "I did not..."

But Rainier cut him off by saying, "...what you did is no longer relevant." He then looked across the soldiers and finished by staring straight at Jamison. "My proposal is simple. Let every soldier that follows you, follow you. Let every soldier that follows me, follow me. Let the soldiers use their own minds and follow their own hearts. We will not cross swords with each other until Julian arrives or Lattimer is dead. Agreed?"

Jamison looked out across the soldiers and Rainier knew he had the bastard cornered.

Jamison spoke loudly, trying to save face. "The people of Disentia have always served the pattern and that will not change. I welcome the opportunity for the Nameless Army to renew their vows of sacrifice in the name of the pattern. I accept your proposal."

The soldiers, who were willing to fight their brethren only moments before all sheathed the weapons. Rainier hadn't seen any way out of the situation that didn't involve bloodshed, but somehow, he managed.

Captain Sharan stepped forward and said, "Any soldier that wishes to follow Rainier shall board my smallboats and be transported to my ships or the *Remnant Awakens*. All others will remain here. Soldiers, fall out!"

Soldiers wishing to join Rainier began to filter towards the smallboats, and Rainier did some quick math. Only about a quarter of the soldiers moved to board the smallboats. *Not as many as I hoped, but at least I know they are loyal.*

Jamison said quietly to him, "You may have survived the day, Rainier Tallow, but it is I who will lead the forces that march on Ravinai, and it is I who will win the favor of Julian the Immortal. When you face his wrath, you will wish you had died here today."

Rainier didn't bother to respond. *You're right. I don't want to face Julian the Immortal if I fail. But at least now I have some troops I can point in his direction and a ship I can steal to head in the other direction if things go south quickly.*

Just then, Rainier noticed a small group of priests break away from the larger group, led by Kalana. Jamison noticed too, and said, "My own priests would break from the pattern?"

Kalana looked up and said, "The closest I've ever come to the pattern was before I started using wanderleaf. I want to see if I can relearn what has been lost, and so do they."

Jamison scowled and said with a sneer, "You can take the burnt-out ones anyway. They are worthless."

"They appear to believe otherwise." Rainier glanced over at the priests and noticed them still detaining Kalus. "I think it's time for you to let my Hand go now, don't you?"

Kalus gave Rainier a nod and a wink, one member of the Remnant appreciating the silver tongue of his brethren. He said, "I always knew you'd outwit this robed fool. He's two parts arrogance and one part ignorant." *Stop rubbing salt in his wounds, Kalus! People with as much pride as Jamison act unpredictably when you shake their pride too much.* Rainier shot Kalus a look of warning, but Kalus never did know when to stop. He said, "How does it feel to be played for a fool, Jamison?"

Hot anger on Jamison's face cooled into something even more dangerous. He looked over at Kalus and said, "Who him? You want me to let him go?"

Rainier recognized the treachery even as his best friend stood smiling stupidly, thinking that he had landed a solid parting shot at the high priest. *What is Jamison planning?*

Jamison said, "I stripped you of your title as oracle and we are standing on my ship. That means that man is not your Hand – he's just a criminal caught impersonating a priest. I'm afraid the evidence is overwhelming, and I have no choice in the matter." He looked over at the spiky haired priest and said casually, "There is no room for traitors on my ship...and no one plays me for a fool and lives."

Realization spread across Kalus' face just before the priest plunged a knife into Kalus' back.

"NOOO!!!" Rainier reached for his sword, but Lira grabbed his wrist.

"That's what he wants," she whispered urgently. "If you fight here, you will lose all honor, and no one will follow you. Stay your hand – you have won the day."

Rainier gripped the pommel of his sword, but his emotions failed to subside. It was only because of Lira's restraint that he didn't try to fight his way through anyone that stood in his way to open Jamison's throat.

The spiky-haired priest watched Rainier intently as he twisted the knife inside Kalus, opening the wound. He then laughed and tossed Kalus overboard, saying to Jamison, "The traitor is no longer on your ship, your Highness."

With his attention focused solely on his childhood friend, Rainier shrugged away from Lira. He sprinted across the quarter deck and jumped blindly overboard with thoughts of Kalus bleeding and drowning in the bay below.

The water rushed to meet Rainier and hit him with incredible force. Rainier's body failed to move for the first few milliseconds, but the adrenaline in his veins managed to kickstart his muscles and prevent him from passing out due to the impact. He kicked upwards and broke the surface of the water, gasping for air.

As soon as the salty air refilled his lungs, he swung his head from side to side, scanning frantically for Kalus. He didn't see a body, but an area of crimson colored water told him everything he needed to know. Rainier dove down, searching in the dark water for anything solid. Just as his lungs felt as if they would burst, his hand brushed Kalus' arm. Rainier grabbed ahold of his wrist and kicked upwards again.

Rainier soaked in the air while treading water and trying to hold his friend's head above water. The water turned a darker shade of red around them alarmingly quickly, and Kalus was not breathing. Rainier slapped his friend in the face, and when he still failed to wake, he put his arms around his chest and squeezed as tightly as he could. Water shot from Kalus' mouth, emptying his lungs, but even as his eyes opened and he coughed out the remaining water, Rainier knew that squeezing Kalus so tightly also forced the blood from his wound that much faster.

He looked around in time to see the Sicarius Headmaster dive into the water with a grace that had escaped Rainier and commandeer one of the smallboats. "Hold on Kalus. Help is on the way. We'll get you out of here."

Kalus' coughing slowed and then ceased, but the color also drained from his face, making Rainier even more worried. Kalus looked up at him with a gray pallor and said, "I always thought I'd die from a knife in the back." He coughed up some blood and said, "But I always thought it'd be the knife of a husband that just found out I had bedded his wife, or maybe Hanna would do it herself. Tell her she's a miserable cur of a woman to love...and that she's the best thing that ever happened to me."

"You aren't going to die. Sana is coming, and she can heal you, and you can tell Hanna how miserable she is yourself." The words sounded more like a plea than a promise, even to Rainier's ears.

Kalus continued as if Rainier hadn't even spoken. "Tell me you are going to kill that bastard Jamison. I don't even care about Lattimer anymore, just tell me you have some crazy plan to kill Jamison." He coughed again and Rainier shot a look towards the smallboat, willing it to hurry. "Tell me this is like the game of standing stones we played, and Jamison is going for the victory while you are just setting him up."

Rainier didn't know what to say, but he did what any respectable man of his upbringing would do in his situation. He lied. "Of course, brother. Jamison is doing exactly what I want him to do. He's a dead man."

A smile came to Kalus' colorless face and he mouthed, "Brother. I like the sound of that. Never forget your family..." His gaze turned distant as the smallboat arrived.

"Never forget the Remnant."

"Pull him in!" Sana commanded of the soldiers in the smallboat.

Rainier handed Kalus over to the strong arms of the soldiers reaching down from the boat. He pleaded, "Sana — he needs healing! He's lost a lot of blood."

Sana didn't waste time responding. Her focus was entirely on Kalus as she laid her hands on the wound in his back. By the time Rainier reached up and climbed into the boat, she was deep within her spell, probing the wounds of Kalus' body.

"Can you save him?" Rainier asked, but not expecting a response. "Will he make it?" Kalus lay unmoving on the bottom of the boat, and the blood trickled from his wound. Why wasn't Sana forcing his tissue to knit itself back together? Rainier looked up from Kalus to find Sana staring at him.

"I'm sorry, Rainier..." Rose placed her hand on Rainier's shoulder. Sana said, "I didn't get here fast enough. He lost too much blood and his heart stopped. Kalus is dead."

The last three words hit Rainier harder than a punch from Slate Severance. It wasn't that this was the first friend he had lost, or even the first good friend, but Kalus made all his scheming and swindling fun. He always gave a laugh when a scheme was at its thickest. There won't be as many laughs from here on out. *This isn't a child's game anymore.*

Rainier's thoughts kept circling between grief and reflection as he made the ride back to the Remnant Awakens. He couldn't shake the guilt and sense of responsibility for the death of Kalus, and he kept replaying his last conversation with his friend in his head. The words repeated over and over in broken, disjointed fragments. *Never forget your family...kill that bastard Jamison...Brother...* More than anything else though, the lie he told Kalus started to feel more like a promise. *Tell me this is like the game of standing stones...kill that bastard...Jamison is a dead man.*

On the silent ride, Kalus' words helped him formulate a plan. He said aloud to no one but the ghost of his dead friend, "I have a plan, Kalus. I've knocked my first standing stone. Jamison will go straight for the red mark, to Ravinai. He has the biggest army and the most direct route to victory, but I'm not done laying all my stones on the board. I'll need to set up my other pieces before he gets to Ravinai and claims victory. It'll be a race for the heart of Malethya, and if I don't hurry, all of my standing stones will fall flat."

⁂

REFLECTIONS

Rainier walked past the burning hot desert called the storage room with a smile on his face and without giving the poor bastards working in that searing heat a second thought. They dug tirelessly for objects they would never find, for a purpose they would never know. They were dutiful, for sure, and subjugation demanded loyalty, but there was no honor in digging holes for a madman. He had given up on honor long ago. That thought made Rainier's smile grow even larger. *Just look at the company I keep.*

Rainier started his descent down a long spiraling staircase, and even though he knew there was a hidden city buried in the depths below, the monotony of descending steps gave him time to reflect on the meaning of honor. Why did people try to live with honor? It was such an impossibility that society gave up and described people only with variations of the word. People could act honorably, but that only described a fleeting, singular act of honor. If a person strung together enough singular acts, society might call him or her honorable, but the very use of the word was an admission of failure. For every honorable act performed by people acting honorably, there were countless moments of dishonor in between.

Step after step, Rainier recounted all the times he had acted dishonorably, his memories as numerous as the endless stairs. The memories would have caused Slate grief and Sana immense inner turmoil, but Rainier owned each act. They were decisions he made, and damn the rest of them if they judged him for it.

While he was deep in thought, the stairs ended, and Rainier looked up, gazing upon the city beneath Minot for the first time. A bubble protected the people within the city, or perhaps more accurately, prevented them from getting out. Rainier knew their secret, and now the fate of Malethya rested upon the dishonorable shoulders of its least reliable and most morally ambivalent member. Who would he side with? Who would he save? Who would die from his schemes? Did he care if he saved anyone if he made it out alive?

I made the choices I needed to make to get this far. You can't play a game of standing stones without losing a few of your own. When they're gone, you don't keep thinking of them, you just figure out what to do with the stones still standing. I'm still standing. After the battle in Ravinai, that's more than I could have hoped for.

CHAPTER SEVEN

LAY THE FIRST STONE

"The prudent approach would be to let Jamison take the beachhead. He has more ships and can protect his troops with artillery." Captain Sharan discussed strategy with Rainier, Slate, Sana, Lira, and Hanna in the captain's quarters on the *Remnant Awakens*. After Kalus' death, she had inserted herself in their meetings, and Rainier didn't have the strength or energy to argue with a woman like Hanna. "I'm guessing you have a less prudent idea for the group?" Captain Sharan asked.

Does she know me that well already? Rainier pulled his thoughts away from his grief, aided by the necessity of the moment. The Remnant were preparing Kalus' funeral, using as many of the nomadic customs as they could on a ship. Despite his preference to sit alone and drown his emotions in alcohol, that wasn't an option. As the leader of the Remnant, Rainier would be expected to attend the funeral and to attend in a somewhat sober state. *Who says leaders get to do what they want?*

Rainier looked up from the map of Portswain and saw everyone staring at him. *Right...Sharan asked me a question.* He gave his winningest smile hoping that it covered the pain in his eyes and the moment of hesitancy. "Your tactics are sound, Captain Sharan, and I will need every bit of your advice and battle strategy when we abandon our vessels and sneak into Portswain under the cover of darkness."

Rainier expected an outburst of objections, but Hanna just observed as she had taken to doing in these meetings. *I never would have expected Hanna of all people to be the introspective type.* Then Rosana laughed and said, "You won't find an argument from me. I do my best work in the shadows."

Lira gave the practical argument and said, "Fully armored soldiers aren't great at sneaking anywhere."

"And the cannons on this ship are our biggest tactical advantage. Why would we abandon our ships?" Slate asked.

Slate smirked back at him. They'd been through enough together that Slate recognized his smile for what it was – a perilous plan in the making. He said, "Why don't you explain what's in that head of yours, Rainier, and maybe we can help out. We have some friends waiting for us once we get off this fractal-forsaken boat."

"Jamison agreed to let us go our own way, but that didn't change his hatred for us, and his goal is simple – take Portswain, defeat Lattimer, and claim all the credit and glory when Julian's ships arrive. If we land at Portswain first, how difficult would it be for him to explain to Julian that a renegade group splintered away from the main force?" Rainier looked around the room and saw affirmation in the eyes of his friends. "If we land in force, it would be pretty simple to direct a loyal ship to destroy the section of town wherever we landed and explain away our deaths as collateral damage."

"But if we let them land first, they'll capture Portswain and have the head start towards Ravinai." Sana argued logically.

"And if our forces aren't the army that captures Portswain or claims the honor of defeating Lattimer..." Rainier spoke his fears aloud.

"Julian will not be pleased." Lira said with enough finality that the consequences of failure were well-understood by the entire group.

"So, we need a quick, covert entrance...and a way to slow down Jamison's troops on their march to Lattimer," Slate said. "Villifor and Jak have been training citizens to fight against Lattimer. We call them the Underground. I'm sure they would serve as a harrying force for us against Jamison to buy us some time."

"This all makes sense, but these theoretical arguments are not actionable." Sharan observed. "What do we do with the army?"

"Sana is going to get along well with this one," Rosana laughed at the expense of her logic-driven personality while pointing at Captain Sharan.

"We know what Jamison will do. He has the tactical advantage, the most dominant military force, and he knows Lattimer is in Ravinai. He will march straight there and take on Lattimer in open battle, trying to go as quickly as possible so that his diminished supplies do not become a factor." Rainier looked around the room and said, "He has every advantage, except for one. He has become predictable, and there are few things as damning as becoming predictable. Before we can take advantage of it though, I need everyone to be aware of recent events in Malethya." He turned to Slate and Sana and said, "Would you share the story of Phoenix and explain why your arm looks like it's covered in the plague? Most importantly, share with the group anything that can help us against Lattimer or give us an edge in the race against Jamison."

The Sicarius Headmaster pulled out a knife as black as death and said, "The black spots on my arm are from holding this Blighted Knife. One touch of its blade will send the disease into your victim. If it cuts deep enough to enter the bloodstream, it is only a matter of time until it reaches your heart." She flipped the knife in the air and caught it by the hilt. "Phoenix was one of Lattimer's generals and that monstrosity found out about my knife the hard way. He also held a totem with Slate's blood inside of it, which helps him to control his Furies. For every totem we destroy, we weaken Lattimer's forces." She said, "If we want to kill Lattimer, we need to be able to get close enough to strike him. The only person that has been able to resist Lattimer's power is Slate. If we can destroy those totems, not only does Lattimer lose soldiers, but Slate can get close enough to kill him."

"How many more totems are there? What happens to Slate when he gets close to Lattimer now?" Rainier asked.

"Magnus holds the last totem that we know of, and he is in Minot." Slate then explained, "Lattimer tried to subjugate my mind, and he almost succeeded. If it weren't for Lucus' sacrifice and Sana's quick thinking in the catalpa grove, I'd be under Lattimer's control right now. When I get close to Lattimer, his subjugation spell grows stronger, and my head begins to hurt...at times it has been debilitating."

"So, we get to Minot, kill Magnus, and smash this blood totem. That will weaken Lattimer's control over Slate and reduce the control Lattimer has over all the troops under Magnus' command, correct?" Rainier asked. *And if I have the opportunity to get to Minot and destroy the blood mages beneath that city like Julian demanded, then I can be rid of another worry.*

Sana added some detail. "The trick will be to time everything. Jamison will be marching towards Lattimer and we'll need to reach Minot and get back to Ravinai for the main battle."

Sharan nodded as she processed the strategic information, but Lira had more questions about the fight with Phoenix. She asked, "How did you get the blade?"

"...And why doesn't the blade kill you?" Hanna finished the round of questions.

"Who said it wasn't killing me?" The Sicarius Headmaster answered without a trace of concern, even while Rose quietly worried. Sana continued logically, "As for the Blight, it is a disease that is spreading across Malethya that is caused by blood magic. This blade is made from catalpa wood, which can hold or contain blood magic, but if too much magic is held within it, the Blight leaks out. The Blighted blade kills me a little quicker every time I hold it, but Ibson has helped to slow the spread of the disease." The Sicarius Headmaster said, "So let's quit dawdling and kill people quicker than this thing kills me, huh?"

Rainier's ears perked up at the mention of Ibson. "I thought Ibson was rhyming himself silly in the Infirmary..."

"He was faking it to save his own skin, but he's helped us discover Lattimer's research in Minot and has atoned for his mistakes. We trust him," Slate said. *Would you trust him if you knew he was also Candor, the founder of blood magic?*

"What is Lattimer researching in Minot?" Sharan asked while looking down at her map of Malethya, trying to locate the tiny village north of Ravinai.

"We might need Ibson to explain that one a little bit better. He said something about a four-dimensional fractal that can be used to fold three-dimensional space." Slate said the words, but it was obvious they meant little to him. "All I know is that there is a tiny hut within Minot. It has a colossal library filled with books about blood magic that make Lattimer stronger every day, a storage room in the form of a vast desert, and a city covered by a magic bubble buried somewhere beneath it all with people walking around inside completely unaware of the outside world." He shook his head in disbelief. "Sana managed to pull the Blighted Knife from the sands of the storage room, and she barely escaped with her life."

"So, you've been busy." Lira said with a smile, and Rainier couldn't decide what astounded him more – the fact that Ibson was alive and well, that his friends had already located the hidden city that Julian had asked him to find and destroy, or the fact the Lira had made her first joke. He laughed despite himself and clasped Lira on the back.

"You could say that..." Rosana said, and Sana concluded, "...but I fail to see how our exploits are going to help our current situation. What will we do?"

Captain Sharan reiterated her earlier comments. "Yes, Rainier. While all of this is very interesting, you have not told us how you plan to get our army ashore ahead of

Jamison's attack."

Rainier kept a straight face while his mind was racing. The pieces of his plan were falling into place like a jigsaw puzzle. He couldn't see the whole picture yet, but no member of the Remnant needed the gift of foresight for a good scheme, and Rainier wasn't just anyone. He was their leader, and his schemes were legendary.

"Strip the soldiers of their armor and collect it. Gather me all the smallboats we have and prepare to honor our dead. Kalus' funeral will be worthy of song written by the bards."

The sun set on the horizon and Rainier looked out from the deck of the *Remnant Awakens*. An arrow shot into the distance, where the wrapped body of his dead friend lay atop a pyre of wood hastily constructed from broken barrels and other scraps salvaged from the hold below, piled as high as they could make it. Smallboats ringed the floating pyre a safe distance away, adorned with the brightly colored silks traditional to a nomadic funeral. With the setting sun casting colorful hues across the water and reflecting off the waves in a prismatic display of natural wonder, it was the most beautiful setting you could ask for to burn the corpse of your best friend.

Rainier steeled himself and turned back to address the members of the Remnant waiting to hear his words. He had sent away every soldier from Sharan's ships and even Slate and Sana, leaving only the Remnant to mourn his friend. He thought Kalus would have wanted it that way.

He looked into the eyes of his fellow nomads, and found his family waiting for his words. *What do I say about my best friend?* Rainier couldn't get the personal words to form in his head - they hurt too much - so instead he focused on his duties as a leader.

He raised his chin and spoke in a loud voice that hopefully masked his pain, "We have lived a difficult life. In Malethya, people called us tribesmen and we lived as nomads on the outskirts of society, watching the Malethyans from relative isolation."

"...And swindling them with every deal they dared make with us." Hanna called out to the enjoyment of the crowd, breaking the tension.

"Aye, we've made our share of favorable deals..." Rainier laughed with everyone else, and the words came a little easier. "...and taken a few fools for all their worth. During our exploits though, we hid our true purpose as the Remnant. While everyone forgot the lessons of the Twice-Broken Wars, we did not. While Malethyans let history turn into campfire stories and blood mages turn into myths, we did not. While our brethren returned to Disentia and carried on with their lives, we did not. WE DID OUR DUTY!"

The Remnant cheered, despite the somber reason for gathering. *No one knows what it is like to devote your life to a lie, all in the name of the greater good...only the people in front of me.* Rainier continued on, and the emotion he had bottled up came out, "Malethya may have secluded us. Disentia forgot us. They imprisoned us. They KILLED US!" Rainier extended his arm with his open palm towards Kalus' dead body atop the pyre. "I ask you..." he looked across the crowd, "...HAVE WE DONE OUR DUTY?"

There was shocked silence at the blasphemous words coming from their leader's mouth, but Rainier pressed on.

"Who do we owe? Our homeland? It spat us out faster than a blighted lemon. Jamison, our high priest?" He motioned again towards Kalus. "If this is holy, then I understand the fractal-forsaken pattern even less than I thought!"

"And you're a fractal-forsaken oracle!" someone yelled from the crowd to everyone's amusement.

"What about Julian the Immortal? Do we owe him anything? We stayed in Malethya after the Twice-Broken Wars, we waited until Lattimer rose to power and the threat of blood magic returned, and we reported back."

"We did our duty!" Hanna yelled. After she said the words, others let loose and created a chorus, yelling out their frustrations at a life of unappreciated servitude. *I understand their frustration. I've been carrying my own, ever since I was a child forced to choose a Teacher and knowing my lot in life had been decided without any input from me. That's why I chose Slate as my Teacher. I needed to break away, and I still feel like I'm caught in chains.* Rainier's emotions finally flowed freely, and he was able to speak about Kalus to the growing frenzy of the Remnant.

"I was the last person to speak with Kalus," Rainier said, and the crowd quieted to hear his words. "He did not speak of Malethya or Disentia, or the pattern or blood magic. He spoke of you." He let his words hang in the air. "He spoke of the Remnant. He spoke of his family." Each tribesman listened with rapt attention. "As of this moment, I declare that the Remnant has completed its duties. When we get to shore, you are all free to leave and make your lives wherever you see fit." *Julian may have other ideas, but hey, I'm on a roll.* "However, for those of you that stay, you'll get a chance at some payback. I'm going to kill Jamison, and I'm going to do it the way Kalus would have wanted. Jamison won't know he's in danger until his plans and strategies entangle and choke him tighter than the noose he tried to hang me from. When he dies, he'll know he's been swindled and strung up worse than a Malethyan making their first trade."

Whoops and hollers filled the air and for the first time in recent memory, Rainier felt like he had retaken some control of his life. Given that his life expectancy had felt extremely short as of late, even a moment of control felt good. A genuine smile spread across Rainier's face, and it felt completely foreign. He said, "If you are with me, we need to set Jamison up for a swindle that will live in infamy, and it all starts now."

Rainier gave a nod towards an archer, and she loosed a flaming arrow that struck the base of the floating pyre just as the last rays of sun dipped beyond the horizon.

The flames rose, but the Remnant wasted no time watching. They all went over the edge of the ship, lowering themselves into the water by ropes with the seriousness and silence of a funeral procession. Before he joined them, Rainier stopped Hanna, determined to have the conversation he had been putting off.

"Hanna, Kalus didn't just speak of the Remnant. He spoke of you. He wanted you to know he loved you with all his heart."

Hanna stood silent for a moment, gripping the axe she

had taken to carrying after Kalus' death. "Do you expect me to believe my Kalus said that? Do you think I'm some naïve village girl with flowers in her hair dreaming of a prince to sweep her off her feet? I chose Kalus, of all people, to be my man. Tell me what he really said."

Rainier breathed deep and uttered the words he had hoped not to repeat. "He said to tell you that you are a miserable cur of a woman to love…and that you are the best thing to ever happen to him."

Hanna's hand tightened around the handle of her axe, and Rainier was afraid she might take a swing at him, but then he realized she was gripping it for comfort as her eyes got wet, and she choked out between sobs, "That's the nicest thing he's ever said. Those bastards are going to pay for taking him from me." Then she grabbed a rope and swung over the side of the ship.

Strange woman, that one. I wouldn't want to cross her.

Rainier grabbed a rope to join them, reconcentrating his thoughts on the plan as he repelled downwards. *I lectured everyone that sound carries over water and that we are more likely to be heard than seen. This is not the time for a slip on the rope and an awkward fall after everyone else did it to perfection.* His hands didn't betray him though, and he slipped silently into the water. He let his body adjust to the temperature while the grey of dusk took over the night sky. The funeral had given Rainier an excuse to position the ship away from the rest of Jamison's fleet, and with a hand gesture, members of the Remnant started swimming towards the floating pyre. Rainier kept a methodical pace, making sure that his arms and legs didn't break the surface of the water. He kept his head low in the water and only raised up when he needed a breath, staying within the long shadows that the flaming pyre and the smallboats cast upon the water. They closed the distance excruciatingly slowly, but with each stroke, the distance got closer and the night got darker.

Rainier finally reached the smallboat that he had been stalking like a turtle all night and hung from the edge in quiet exhaustion. After his momentary respite, he investigated the shadows of the smallboats around him. Sana and Slate clung to the side of one smallboat. Sharan and Lira clung to another. They had been in the water with the boats since before the sun went down, hiding from Jamison's view on the sunny side of the boats. They were joined by a small contingent of Sharan's best paladins and the few priests and priestesses that joined Rainier's side on the *Inked Tides* hung from the hull of the smallboats as well. *I love it when a plan comes together.* Rainier flashed a smile, not daring to say a word, and slowly lifted himself to peak over the side of the smallboat. His smile got even wider at the sight.

Rainier caught Sharan's eye, and she nodded to acknowledge they would move to the next stage of the plan. Slate, Sana, and Lira broke away from the group and swam directly for the Portswain harbor, relying on the darkness to cover their swim. Rainier opened up his strokes and pushed for speed. The exertion he felt was counteracted by the warming of his muscles, and he propelled himself towards shore at a fast clip, not bothering to look behind for his friends. His time on a ship served him well, and he was soon swimming up to a pier. He waited a second, heard only silence, and climbed to the decking, crouching behind some abandoned crates that couldn't be loaded onto ships because of the ominous presence of the Disenite fleet in the harbor.

He took a moment to regain his land legs while Lira and Slate labored a fair distance back and Sana was just reaching the pier. While he waited, he took out the two knives he had tucked into his clothes and dried the blades. *I wish I had my short swords, but swords aren't made for swimming.* Sana climbed up the rigging of the pier and joined him on the deck.

"There's nothing like a midnight swim to get your heart racing," Rosana said.

"I kept imagining Jamison's face when he wakes up tomorrow and finds two abandoned ships in his fleet." They both staired out into the water, and the diminished flames from the long-burning pyre as it floated into the distance. Rainier imagined the long string of warriors clinging to boards or other items stolen from Sharan's ship that could float as they made the long swim through the water, following the light of the flaming pyre like a torch in a dark hallway. He couldn't see any of them in the dark of night, but he knew they were there.

"No one starts an attack by ordering an entire army to abandon their ship and swim through the night," Rosana said. "You'd have to be mad. Your troops would arrive without weapons or armor..." She smirked at him, knowing the answer.

"...unless you had enough smallboats to carry everything to shore, and a funeral procession to mask your intent." Rainier smiled back and said, "Even then, I might be mad." He thought of all the armor and weaponry hidden beneath the colorful silks being directed towards a beach south of the city by Sharan and her paladins. *It happens to be the beach that Captain Tera had so kindly pointed out on the map during a captain's meeting as a potential landing spot for her troops. If they decide to use it, I want a few surprises to be waiting for them. A couple well-placed exploding orbs will give them a rude awakening as well as whatever tricks Hanna cooked up for the Remnant to leave behind. Whatever she's come up with, I'm sure it will be clever as hell and as deadly as a woman scorned.*

Sana said, "It's brilliant," and Rainier took it as a high compliment, coming from Sana. "Our troops will take the beach away from the city with minimal casualties. We've arrived before Jamison's attack and will avoid any collateral damage that Jamison may attempt if we took the city. It's a good start."

Lira climbed up to the deck looking winded. She had wrapped her armor and sword in her cloak and had towed the whole package behind her by floating it on a piece of wood and tying it to her waste. She claimed that she would be dishonored if she arrived on Malethyan shores without her holy armor. Lira's legs wobbled as she stepped towards them and Rainier couldn't help but comment, despite the impressive feat of dragging along her weapons, "I guess there isn't much swimming in the mighty Nameless Army."

Rosana chuckled and Lira glared at him, giving a curt response, "No, there is not." She untied her bundled armor from the wood and looped the rope around her shoulders, creating a travel sack. A level of comfort settled in on her as the weight of the sword hung from its familiar spot on her hip.

Slate climbed up the pier after Lira and just laid on the decking. He said, "That is the last time I'm participating in any test or scheme that requires swimming. I love the land, and I am not leaving it." He spread his arms out as if he were embracing the pier.

"I'm sorry you had to swim. I know your Stonehand makes it especially difficult," Rose said empathetically.

Rainier wasn't having it. He said, "Look at the infamous Slate Severance, the most feared man in all of Malethya, has been brought to ruin by a simple evening swim."

Rosana laughed but the Sicarius Headmaster tired of the banter. The Headmaster said, "Get up. We only have a few hours of darkness left, and we need to be out of Portswain before Jamison attacks at sunrise."

Slate groaned but got up with a smile. All of them had been on a boat for too long. They were ready for a midnight mission. He said, "Lead the way, Headmaster. The night belongs to you."

The Headmaster didn't waste time. She darted down the pier, using the cargo boxes as cover, and worked her way towards the city of Portswain. Rainier held the enlightened path as he followed behind the Headmaster, but the path remained a soft light in all directions. *There is no place safer to be than in the dark and at the side of the Sicarius Headmaster.* They hid behind a pile of lobster boxes, and they didn't notice any movement, but one of the enlightened paths ended abruptly. He reached for the Headmaster to warn her, only to find the Headmaster had already risen above the boxes and sent a Guardswoman falling to the deck twenty yards away wearing the hilt of a throwing knife as a necklace. *Forsaken fractals, she's good.*

They raced ahead, not bothering to hide the body. In a few hours, the bodies in the city of Portswain would be piling up anyway. They dashed through the abandoned fish markets, where the smell of seafood permeated from the wooden structures despite the low supply of fish, which had dwindled with the fishing ships stuck in port and the blight starting to infest the fish that could be caught. The fish markets gave way to shops and the occasional inn trying to capitalize on sea views to entice customers and the Headmaster took to the alleyways. At one point, an innkeeper took a poorly timed trip from the kitchen of his inn and received a chop to the base of his neck and an unexpected nap for his troubles. Otherwise, the Headmaster navigated the alleyways with uncanny expertise that avoided all the patrols, even though they were on high alert with the Disenite ships in their harbor.

The buildings in Portswain rose in accordance with the prosperity of the inhabitants, and the Headmaster abandoned the alleyways in favor of the rooftops. Rainier, having some Sicarius training while living with Slate in Ravinai, managed to keep the Headmaster within eyesight, but Lira was not as fortunate. Slate stuck with Rainier's Hand and used his inhuman strength to help her cross the rooftops. *Compared to the soundless steps of the Headmaster, Lira might as well be shouting from the rooftops to announce our presence to the Guardsmen on patrol with her clumsy footfalls upon the rooftops.* Just when Rainier thought the Headmaster would lose them though, she would circle back, incapacitating any

Guardsmen within the area with an ease that defied logic. *She really is the Shadow in the Night. Out here, no one can compete with her.*

They continued this way until they reached the roof of a large inn on a hill, overlooking the harbor. At this point, Slate took the lead, jumping down to the balcony and bursting into the room. Rainier followed close behind, but the only threat was an old man sitting in a chair, completely unperturbed by the chain of events. Slate ignored him and cleared the room, while Sana said from the doorway, "Hello Ibson. It seems you have been awaiting our arrival."

"My defensive magic alerted me to your arrival from two buildings over." He smiled at Sana and said, "It isn't nice to wake an old man from his sleep."

Rainier was in shock. The last time he had seen Ibson, he was speaking in riddles with a clouded mind after a brutal head injury. He said, "I thought you were in the Infirmary." *And who else knows that you are the founder of blood magic, the infamous Candor?*

I sat and wait until Sana did break,
This wizard from his spell.
I acted too late and failed to abate,
The rise of Lattimer that befell.

Slate said, "In other words, he faked his head injury, Sana broke him out of the Infirmary, and he ended up helping us find Minot and stop Phoenix."

"Apparently he hasn't given up on the occasional riddle, though," Rosana commented.

"Yes, Ibson appears to be full of surprises," Rainier said. The words of Julian echoed in his head. *Find the blood mages that Candor has hidden and destroy them.* Rainier didn't feel any loyalty to the crusty old bastard, but he didn't feel much loyalty to Ibson either. *My loyalty is to myself. I'm done being tied to other people's plans.*

"Welcome back, Rainier. It seems you've brought some friends." He nodded towards the ships in the harbor and looked quizzically at Lira. "Will you introduce me to your friend and tell me what brings her to my room at this late hour?"

"Life is full of friends and enemies, and I fear I have brought some of both to our shores." Rainier introduced Lira by saying, "This is Lira. She falls into the friend category and serves as my Hand. She has vowed to protect me."

Lira nodded in acknowledgment and Ibson said, "I've always liked the silent types." Lira's face transformed into a glare that could melt stone, but the old man was unfazed. *I guess Ibson is still making unwanted advances on women with the unabashed enthusiasm that only the elderly can muster.*

Rosana jumped in before Lira turned violent and said, "As for the hour of the night, we need to get you out of here. Portswain will be overrun with Disenite soldiers in the morning, and they're the ones that don't fall into the friend category."

Ibson was never one for physical confrontation, so he stood up quickly and said, "When do we leave?"

"Right now. Slate will get you and Lira to the river. Rainier and I have a couple of stops to make. We'll meet you there."

Lira immediately objected, "I am Rainier's Hand. I belong at his side."

"I can get Ibson to the river safely," Rainier offered, seemingly to appease his Hand. *Not to mention that I'd love to have the opportunity to have a private conversation with Ibson. I have some rather difficult questions for him to answer.*

"I'll need you when we talk with Jak and Villifor." She pondered for a minute, and Slate solved the riddle. "I can get Ibson to the river. We'll take the alleyways and go slow. If there's fighting to be done, I can handle it." Rosana nodded begrudgingly, not wanting to send Slate into danger but acquiescing to Slate's plan because Sana agreed with its logic.

"Then it's settled. Ibson and I will meet you at the riverboat," Slate smirked and said, "Try to get there before the cannons start to fire."

They left, leaving Rosana, Lira, and Rainier in Ibson's room. Before they left, Rosana used some of Ibson's stationary to write a quick note. It said:

Sicarius Headmaster –

The raven returns to its unkindness in Ravinai and has need of its flock. Have our friend from the docks prepare for our safe arrival. I fly ahead of the Disenite jackals and the day will soon belong to Bellator. I hope the shadows have grown longer in the night during my absence. The night will always belong to Sicarius.

§

She folded up the note while Rainier asked, "Did you just write a note to yourself?" *I know Rosana is a complicated woman, but that seems crazy even for her.*

Rose laughed and said, "I gave control of Sicarius to Annarelle when I left Ravinai. She's recruiting new Sicarius members to the Guild and managing the Sicarius network, but...", the Sicarius Headmaster finished the statement, "I will always be the Sicarius Headmaster." She jumped out the window, caught the edge of the roofline, swung up above and out of sight using a move that Rainier couldn't replicate, and he seriously doubted if anyone else in Malethya could either.

"Yes, you will..." Rainier said, shaking his head in awe at the Headmaster. Then he looked to Lira and said, "We better get going. I don't think she's waiting for us."

Lira nodded determinedly and headed towards the window to scramble towards the rooftops. Rainier stopped her and said, "Save the rooftops for Sicarius." Rainier's partial training with Slate would help, and even he would have a difficult time. He said to Lira, "I'll climb up and direct you through the alleyways to avoid any Guardsmen on patrol. Watch for my hand signals."

Rainier noticed Lira give a slight exhale of relief, and she headed for the alleyways. Rainier climbed up to the rooftops, with infinitely less elegance than the Headmaster, and scanned the surrounding blocks using the enlightened path. Light jumped ahead of him, and his practiced eye quickly discerned the meaning of the separate streams. Several streams terminated near the docks, and a few seconds later, a group of Guardsmen came around the corner. Looking further into the city, he saw similar streams of light converging and terminating. *It doesn't take the wit of the Remnant to figure that one out. Avoid the converging streams of light and avoid the patrols.* Rainier refocused his attention on the rooftops and managed to pick up the Headmaster's silhouette jumping between buildings a few blocks away. *Forsaken fractals she's fast.* He looked down, saw Lira exit the building, and signaled her towards the alley in the direction of the Headmaster. He ran ahead, keeping one eye on the Headmaster and the other on the patrols as he directed Lira safely through the alley-filled depths of Portswain.

They continued onward, easily navigating around the orbs that sparsely illuminated Portswain's streets. Compared to the brightly lit opulence of Ravinai and the Regallo estate, the trek was devoid of danger. The bigger issue was keeping an eye on the Headmaster. She moved further and further ahead and no longer circled back to check how they were doing. Eventually, Rainier lost sight of her and being without any better options, navigated his way to the last location he had seen her. Then he signaled Lira to stop and gave the call of night owl, an old Sicarius trick for communicating in the darkness or from distance. From a block over, he heard the call return, but slower and deeper than his original call, which told Rainier to approach quietly.

He crossed the rooftop in a crouched position, taking care to keep the moonlight from showing his silhouette to any curious onlookers in the streets below. One final leap across an alleyway and a bellycrawl to the crest of the roof finally gave him a visual on the Headmaster. She lay flat on her stomach peering into the street below. She tapped her side, signaling for him to come by her without even bothering to turn around. When he wiggled his way down to her, he found himself looking upon a raucous tavern.

Rosana whispered to him, "Inside of that tavern, I have a drop box for my Sicarius information network. If I drop my letter there, an informant will relay the letter to Ravinai faster than we can travel."

"How?"

"Ravens – they are extremely smart birds and I have a number of them that can be dispatched between cities. Where's Lira?" Sana asked.

"She's in an alley waiting for my signal one block to the east. What's the plan?"

"Normally, I would just go to the drop box location, but that means I'd need to go inside without attracting too much attention. Unfortunately..." She motioned to her black wrappings adorned with various throwing knives, kunai, and other lethal weapons. "...it would be difficult for me to enter without undue attention." *And without leaving a pile of bodies in her wake.*

Rainier saw where this was going. "Lira isn't trained for this type of work, which leaves me right?" *At least the enlightened path is still working.* The soft glow of light was comforting on multiple levels.

"You got it." She handed him the letter. "Drop the letter between the crack in the floorboards near the back-right table as you enter. The location is marked with some nicks from the tip of a sword in this pattern." She demonstrated a cross hash with her fingers in the air. "I'll be out here in case things go south, but don't let that happen. The sun is closer to appearing with each passing minute."

Rainier put the letter in his pocket and scrambled down the side of the building into the alley. He brushed off his clothes a little to tidy up his appearance, but his damp clothes smelled like the fish markets, and he looked like he had the personal hygiene of a Fury after crawling across the rooftops of Portswain. *So much for blending in.* Instead, Rainier decided to use his current state to his advantage. He stumbled out of the alley like it was home and took a drunkenly round-about path to the door of the tavern, all the while checking the yellow paths emanating before him for danger and calculating his next move.

The hired hand at the doorway saw him coming and looked to bar his way by putting his hand out in front of him. He said, "You'll need to find somewhere else to drink tonight, friend." Rainier was deciding between fight and flight when a dart embedded in the big man's neck and he dropped in a heap of slumber. Rainier flashed a quick hand signal as a thank you to the Headmaster looking out for him up above.

As he entered the doorway, the harsh light of the tavern temporarily blinded him, but the warmth of the enlightened path and the feel of a knife hilt beneath his wet, dirty cloak comforted him. He stumbled to his left following the yellow stream of light as his eyes adjusted, and he narrowly avoided crashing into a wench with an armful of ale mugs for her thirsty patrons. With his normal vision returning, he scanned the room with a sweep of a single unfocused, drunken gaze. Rowdiness and carousing couples abounded, but the group of toughs in the rear, right table playing a game of Broken Fractal caught his attention more than anything else. *How am I supposed to deliver this letter to the drop box when it's beneath a group of people playing dice?*

Knowing that time was of the essence, he focused his abilities as an oracle on the floor beneath the table. Yellow streams faded away leaving a pathway that directed him right to the biggest, toughest looking man at the table. *Forward, forward, forward the path guides me. If the enlightened path hadn't saved my life a number of times already, I would think this was a fractal-forsaken trick.* He walked his way to the back table, trying to stumble with the appropriate level of drunkenness so that no one wanted to talk to him but not so drunk that someone stopped him. As he approached the table, someone alerted the big man, and he turned from his game of Broken Fractal.

He stood and said, with all the welcome of a door being shut in your face, "You look lost. Whatever you are looking for, you won't find it here."

Rainier couldn't agree more with the giant of a man standing in front of him, and he had to steady his hand to keep it from moving towards his sword hilt. As the man stood, however, he realized the enlightened path wasn't pointing towards the big man. The yellow stream of light was pointing towards his mug of ale on the table.

Rainier grabbed it from the table and slurred, "Here it is. I found what I was looking for!"

He lifted the mug to his lips and a drop of ale even

touched his tongue before the big man rammed a fist into his gut, doubling him over and dropping him to his knees. A swift kick toppled him to his side, he rolled beneath the table, and his head bounced off the floorboards. *Enlightened path, more like cursed path of pain. I'm never trusting that thing again.* Then he realized where he was.

Less than hands-breadth from the tip of his nose was a gap in the floorboards. A sword had cut a cross-hash pattern deeply into the grains of the wood. *The drop box.*

Strong hands grabbed the back of his cloak, and Rainier had just enough time to thank his Remnant luck, bless the enlightened path, and drop the letter between the floorboards before he was dragged out from beneath the table, carried by the big man out of the bar and thrown in the street.

Rainier started to pick himself up when the big man noticed the slumbering body of the hired door hand in the street. He said, "Did you do this?" with rising anger. Before he could act, Rainier heard a noise behind him.

"I did." The Sicarius Headmaster stood in the street with kunai at the ready, looking every bit as terrifying as the stories told about the masked shadow in the night.

The big man's face paled, going as white as Slate Severance. He began to stammer a reply, but the Headmaster beat him to it. She said, "Leave here. Tell your friends to get sober and find some swords. The Disenites will attack at sunup."

The man staggered backwards dumbly before turning and running back into the tavern as though his life depended upon it. It did.

"Did everything go according to plan? Did you make the

drop?" Sana asked him after the man left.

"It went according to the path, which wasn't necessarily my plan." Rainier grimaced and gingerly touched his stomach where he had been punched. He said, "But yes, I made the drop."

"Then let's collect Lira and get out of here. We have a mission to finish." The Headmaster turned and began running towards the alley where Lira was hiding. Rainier took a deep breath and ran after her, trying not to grimace at the pain from his bruised ribs where the big man landed a punch. *The Headmaster won't tolerate any of my complaints over something as small as a bruised rib. Best to get on with the mission.*

Lira saw them coming and stepped out to meet them. When she saw Rainier holding his side, she turned angry. "I am your Hand. It is my duty to protect you. You should not have fought without me by your side."

Rainier held out his hands in apology and gave his best Remnant grin, even though he knew she hated it, and said, "To be fair, I wasn't the one doing the fighting. I was more on the receiving end of the punching..."

"Fractal-forsaken fool!" Lira exclaimed. "You dishonor me with your actions."

I've never heard her swear. She must be taking a liking to me if she cares that much. Rainier chuckled on the inside because he knew if he chuckled out loud, he had a good chance of finding another fist buried in his stomach tonight.

"We don't have time for this. Jak and Villifor have a safehouse a few blocks from here. They are expecting us." The Headmaster stared them down from behind her unnerving mask, and Lira gave a reluctant nod.

"Lead the way, dear Headmaster." Rainier motioned ahead gracefully.

She took off down the street, not bothering to preserve the location of a safehouse that could become rubble after sunlight. She approached the back door of a market store that appeared dark and long past closed for the day and knocked four times.

"May the light blind you." A voice said from inside the door.

"And the shadows light your way." The Headmaster replied.

A heavy lock slid open, and someone in leather armor ushered them in. A windowless room of surprising size held a veritable armory of weapons, and at its center sat Jak, Villifor, and a beautiful woman that Rainier didn't recognize. The group studied over a table with a map of Portswain. *They look like the Disenite captains pouring over battle plans on the Inked Tides.* The two men looked up and smiled when they saw who their company was. The woman gave a discerning look, but clearly recognized Rosana.

"Rainier returns!" Villifor exclaimed and the former head of the Bellator Guild squeezed him entirely too tightly. "What do we need to know?"

"That we need to leave quickly. We'll have to save the reunion for another time." Rainier said. *Plus, I never really liked your peacocking, grandiose ways when you were the hero of the Twice Broken Wars, and that was before I found out you had betrayed Slate's father and taken his name for your own benefit. Slate may trust you, but I do not.*

Sana gave the report, "The Disenite soldiers will attack Portswain in a few hours. They will head straight for Ravinai to fight Lattimer and his Furies, but they are not under our command." Jak frowned. Inviting an army to your shores to fight your own army usually didn't end well, and he was a master tactician from his days at Bellator. "There are a number of Disenite soldiers loyal to Rainier, however. He is their oracle, although I am still learning the full meaning of that title, and they swam all night to this beach..." Sana pointed out the planned landing spot for the soldiers on their map. "...with their armor and weapons smuggled in smallboats under the guise of a funeral ceremony." Jak and Villifor both raised their eyebrows in appreciation of that bit of cleverness.

"What do you need from us?" Jak asked.

"First, I'll need my Stratego medallions. Do you all still have yours?" Jak and Villifor nodded seriously while Jak grabbed the Headmaster's Stratego box from storage. She left her halves of the Stratego medallions with Jak and Villifor after Rainier had broken his medallion to call for help. Now she gave Rainier a replacement medallion and moved to the next matter at hand. "We need you to activate the Underground and coordinate attacks, supply runs, harrying tactics, and any other tricks you have up your sleeve to slow the Disenite army as they march towards Ravinai. Do not engage the Nameless Army directly for any reason. They are too strong."

"We have been training for months. We can do more damage than you think." Villifor said.

"You can do less than you think, but I know you won't

believe me." She looked towards Lira and said, "Spar with Jak."

"Here?" Asked Jak and the beautiful woman simultaneously.

Lira responded with, "I do not take orders from you, shadow woman."

Rainier used his skills of persuasion and said, "Jak, I'll spar with you." He then turned towards Lira and said sweetly, "He's a much better fighter than me. Would you prefer to take my place so that I don't injure myself further than I already have tonight?"

Lira scowled at him, but she dropped her bundled armor in a corner along with her sword and found a practice blade to her liking from within the armory.

"Do you think you can take her or are you going to have whoever this is stand in your place?" Rainier asked Jak with a reference towards the beautiful woman on his arm.

The woman answered for Jak, saying "I am Lady Highsmith." She sauntered forward in a manner that accentuated all the right places. "And my skills lie in areas other than fighting." *I bet they do.* She picked up a wooden great sword and tossed it to Jak. "Jak, can you fight this woman? I tire of hearing this little man speak." *A woman with a sharp tongue. Maybe she's part Remnant?*

Jak caught the broadsword and swung his arms to loosen up before settling into a defensive form, giving Rainier a shrug as if to say "Women...what can you do?".

Villifor said, "It's been a while since I've seen Jak in a decent bout. Let's see it. Cross swords and begin."

Broadsword touched longsword with the customary sign of respect, and then the Underground safehouse turned into organized chaos. Swirling blades clashed, and the fighters circled in a dance of expert partners that had never danced before. Their techniques were different but perfectly matched, each one trading forms fluidly as the clashing of swords rang faster and faster. Jak's powerful swing was deflected perfectly while Lira's speed was counteracted by Jak's reach. After a minute or so, sweat poured from each fighter. After two minutes, their breath deepened, and their chests heaved. Jak swung a mighty blow that knocked Lira's sword from her hands, but she ducked and spun, pulling his arm down upon her shoulder. His grip released and the broadsword fell to the ground. Then they were in close hand fighting. Jak had the strength advantage, but Lira used his weight against him, bringing him to the ground. Then the two became untangled and Lady Highsmith had seen enough.

"Stop!"

Lira had her legs wrapped around Jak with her arm beneath his chin. Jak had both arms around her chest, preventing her from breathing. They slowly unwrapped from the intimately asphyxiating embrace and Lira said, "It has been too long since I've had a good scrap on the floor." She helped him up from the floor, and Jak nodded in appreciation for her skill.

Lady Highsmith didn't like the exchange and was about to let loose a string of biting responses sharper than either of the practice swords used in the match but Villifor beat her to the punch with hearty laughter that filled the room. He said, "I'm always up for a scrap on the floor if you need a partner next time!"

Sana couldn't stand the emotions clouding everyone's

mind and said, "That demonstration will suffice. Save some strength for the Disenites."

Lira walked past Villifor with a scowl to rejoin Rainier while Jak asked, "Are all the Disenites as skilled as Lira? I can see how formidable they would be."

Rainier said, "Lira is a member of their elite guard, but all the soldiers of the Nameless Army are skilled, even if they are not at her level. Even so, there is another reason not to engage them directly..." Rainier paused a moment for dramatic effect. He was still a member of the Remnant after all. He said, "...they fight with enchanted armor and weaponry. It makes them faster and stronger than normal soldiers. The Underground would be slaughtered."

"It can't be..." Villifor stammered as he saw months of preparation disappear in a heartbeat.

"It is." Rainier didn't sugarcoat his message. "But the Underground is still needed."

Jak took in the message quicker than Villifor and said, "We can do what you ask. We can slow them by blocking roadways, making midnight runs on their food supplies, and a host of other tricks." Villifor slowly nodded in agreement.

Sana, who shared no love loss with Villifor from her days as the head of the Sicarius Guild, didn't pass up on a chance to give her formal rival a command. "Jak, this won't be your job to tackle. This job will belong to Villifor."

"What will my job be then?"

"We'll tell you, but after Villifor leaves," Sana said.

Villifor turned instantly red, taking the dismissal as a lack of trust. He said, "I've proven my loyalty to Slate. How dare you..."

Rainier cut him off, "Stop Villifor. This has nothing to do with your loyalty." *Although your history of betrayal did have a big part in the role chosen for you.* "It is simply a precaution. If you get captured by Lattimer's Furies or Jamison's Disenite troops, you can't know our plans. If all goes well, we'll meet up with you in Ravinai. Tommy and Annarelle will know how to find us. Do you understand?"

Villifor stayed red but acquiesced to the logic of the plan. "I'll do this, and then you'll know. You'll know that I will stay true to my promise. I'm Slate's man, through and through." He marched towards the door. Rainier followed him out the door with his hand on Villifor's shoulder, in what he hoped was a reassuring gesture.

The door closed and Villifor growled, "Get your hand off me."

Rainier did. "I placed it there for the benefit of everyone inside. I wanted them to think I was comforting you."

"I don't need comforting."

"And I'd be the last one to offer it." Rainier acknowledged, "but I wanted to give you some additional information. I would suggest leaving a few surprises behind you as you leave the beach. Captain Tera fancied the beach as a landing spot, and with me out of the mix, it wouldn't surprise me if she decided to utilize it."

"Why couldn't you tell me that inside?" Villifor demanded.

Rainier smirked, "I may have agreed not to engage Jamison's troops until we reach Ravinai, but that doesn't mean you can't...I didn't think Lira would appreciate the nuance."

Villifor's anger turned into a grin as he said, "You may be figuring this war thing out. There aren't that many rules that are worth following." He thought for a minute and said, "We have some exploding orbs we can set and trigger remotely. That will give them a nice Malethyan welcome."

Rainier laughed and cusped him on the shoulder and turned to go back inside. He had thought long and hard about how to use Villifor and in the end, he decided on secrecy. *The only thing I trust Villifor to do is to remain untrustworthy. Hopefully by giving him a scheme to act out, I can at least keep him predictable and useful.* "Just make sure that all of my Disenite troops have cleared out before you set the traps. Don't be too eager."

When he reentered the building, Jak vouched for Villifor by saying, "He's turned into a good man, you know." Sana shrugged her indifference while Rose frowned.

Jak, having gotten no headway on the topic, switched to a more pertinent matter. He said, "What do you need from me?"

"I need you to smuggle the troops loyal to Rainier through the Malethyan countryside. You need to move fast, and you need to avoid Lattimer's troops. If he finds out we're coming, our mission will be forfeit. It depends entirely upon the element of surprise. We need this army to appear out of thin air."

Jak thought on it and said, "Moving that many people is not easy, but we know a good number of farmers between here and Ravinai. We can split the soldiers in groups, dress them in farmer's clothes, and spread their numbers out to avoid detection. It can be done."

Lady Highsmith piped in, "And I have my own contacts

that I've used to move people discreetly. There were times when patrons became too attached to a specific woman...or man...and I needed to get them away quietly. The ones that look like they could earn some coin can travel by coach as long as they are willing to dress the part." She looked Lira up and down skeptically. Lira scowled again.

"Good. You can both coordinate with Captain Sharan. She has a good tactical mind as well. There is still a problem with your plan though," Rainier said, "We aren't going to Ravinai."

"We're going to Minot." Rosana smiled and said, "We're going to hit hard and make it back to Ravinai before we miss all the fun between Jamison's troops and Lattimer's Furies."

Jak's eyes lit up at the prospect of the mission. He had missed out on the last battle in Minot when the Headmaster went in alone, and he had no intention of doing so again. "It's about time I saw some fractal-forsaken action in battle." He kicked aside the wooden practice sword he had dropped during his scuffle with Lira and pulled a gigantic sword from the weapons rack. Rainier wasn't sure he'd be able to lift it, much less swing it with any authority. Jak had no such issue. He smiled and said, "I'm ready."

"Good. Captain Sharan is awaiting your arrival north of this beach. She has orders to clear away from the beach as quickly as possible in case it is used as a landing for Jamison's troops." Sana pointed towards the location on the map again to make sure it was understood. "We will not be traveling with you. Please get her and her troops as close to Minot as possible without being detected. It is heavily wooded, so there should be plenty of hiding places as long as you arrive with enough supplies to feed everyone for a few days." Sana grabbed another Stratego medallion from the box and gave it to Jak. "This is for Sharan. Tell her I can coordinate the timing of our assault and locate her in Minot if she holds onto it."

"Where will you be going?" Jak asked.

Rose smiled apologetically and said, "I'm sorry Jak, but you don't need to know that." Sana had suggested the parsing out of only the most necessary info for their plan, and Rainier agreed with her plan quite quickly. *Does she have plans she hasn't told me? Does she realize I have plans that I haven't shared with her?*

Jak nodded, accepting his orders like a Bellator man should, and turned for the door. He commanded the Underground soldier stationed there to move the contents of the armory to a farm outside of the city as soon as Rainier left. Then he held the door for Lady Highsmith and said, "We'll see you in Minot."

Rainier looked to Sana and Lira. He said with his best smile, "The first steps of our plan are in motion. Nothing could possibly go wrong." *Nothing could go wrong other than Jamison beating us to Ravinai, or Lattimer discovering the attack on Minot, or being overrun by an army of Furies, or Ibson throwing a wrench in my plans, or Julian eating me as I drown in a whirlpool on a ship with a noose around my neck. It'll all go perfect.*

"You can drop the Remnant bravado. You don't need to persuade us of the infallibility of your plan. I always view the simplest plan as the best." Sana said, cutting through

Rainier's thoughts. "The fact that I agree with your plan at all should tell you that the situation is far from simple, and your plan is far from perfect."

Lira said, "Rainier has passed the Oracle Trials and leads us all along the pattern. Do not question him." She eyed a blade from the weapons stand and was ready to draw steel to defend Rainier's honor.

Rainier tried to diffuse the situation by explaining to Sana, "Lira is convinced that my abilities to see the enlightened path will eventually extend to the entire army beneath my command."

Rosana said, "That would be a valuable gift indeed, and I look forward to the day when I can trust your powers. Until then..." The Sicarius Headmaster restocked throwing knives into the folds of her outfit, motioned to the armory and said, "I suggest you find your favorite piece of steel. It's the only answer when a plan falls apart, and when the plan is complex, something always falls apart."

Rainier didn't hesitate to exchange his two knives for his preferred short swords and some padded leather armor that fit under his cloak.

Lira looked less impressed with the selection and said, "I have my sword, and I know what Rainier is capable of." She picked up her bundled armor and said to Rosana, "The oracle will lead us to victory when no one can see a path forward. I do not care if this plan is complex. It is the right path. It is the enlightened path."

It may have been the longest speech Lira had ever given, and Rainier found her loyalty both reassuring and misguided. *I have to remember to keep inspiring her with the occasional bout of prophetic wisdom. I can't afford for her loyalty towards me to slip.*

Rosana said to Rainier with feigned innocence and a heavy dose of sarcasm, "Well, Mr. Oracle, will you show me the enlightened path to the river? I could never find it by myself, so I'll blindly follow you, and my loyalty prevents me from having to think for myself." She looked pointedly at Lira.

Rainier didn't bother to respond, but Lira did. "Loyalty and sacrifice require more of a person than I would expect a Malethyan to understand, shadow woman."

Rainier turned and walked out the door, holding onto the warmth of the enlightened path to show him the way forward and to distance himself from the cold, hard feelings of the women trailing him. He was struck by the depth of the darkness at this hour, which signaled the imminent rise of the sun and the impending attack. *The night is always darkest before the light.*

He raced through the streets without an abundance of caution. At this hour, even the tavern regulars had finished their night, so the streets were empty, and Rainier had the path to guide him. *It doesn't hurt to have the best swordswoman in all Disentia and the Shadow of the Night on my heels either. It's amazing what those two can do for a guy's confidence.*

They approached the river, and Rainier's sense of smell warned him of danger before any prophetic powers.

"Smoke." Lira said. *I guess she has prophetic powers, too.*

They rounded the corner to see the cause. Slate Severance stood on the bow of a riverboat with his sword raised in the air. He yelled to a group of Guardsmen on the shore, "I am not here to fight you. Lay down your weapons and I will spare your lives. You'll need both when the Disenites attack!" Behind him, riverboats burned, leaving his message of peace to be less than convincing. His reputation as an enemy of the crown did nothing to help his cause.

"Get the Stonehands demon. Kill the Blightbringer!" Cries of blind anger shouted back from the shores. A spear flew towards Slate, and he caught it from the air, flipped it around and threw it with incredible force. It buried itself in the ground at the feet of the Guardsman as a warning.

"So much for a quiet escape from the city," Rainier said to no one in particular.

The Headmaster wasted no time talking. She sprinted ahead while throwing darts to thin the crowd with uncanny accuracy. She jumped onto the riverboat in closest proximity to her, and Sana cast a spell she knew from her days of traveling through the wilderness with Lucus. Her mentor had taught her the spell to ignite the kindling of a campfire, so that she would always have warmth upon her travels. Now she used the spell to ignite the decking of the ship upon which she stood.

"I guess it's our job to hold the docks with Slate while she finishes torching the boats," Rainier said to Lira, just as the frenzied Guardsmen mustered the courage for a charge.

Lira unsheathed her sword and said, "I have no reservations in killing the blasphemous." She smiled, but her joy didn't resonate with Rainier. *Blasphemous like me? I need to watch myself around that one if she ever sees through this oracle charade.*

With more religious zealotry than he felt, Rainier lifted his short sword and said, "For the pattern!"

Lira took the words as a rallying cry and charged towards the Guardsmen. The Guardsmen ran down the dock towards Slate. If Rainier were being honest, and he tried never to be completely honest, he knew that Slate could handle the overmatched Guardsmen by himself. At least that would be true if his friend were actually trying to kill the soldiers rushing at him. Instead, Slate dodged some spears, caught others, and tried his best to deter the oncoming Malethyans without killing them.

Lira held no such reservations. She strafed across the back of the group, bringing down a half dozen soldiers with quick, efficient, and deadly strikes before anyone even knew she was there.

Rainier ran behind her, just close enough to be a part of the charge, but far enough behind to remove himself from the immediate dangers.

Ahead, Slate danced between spears with fluid motions that belied logic. *Flash...flash-flash, flash...flash.* Whatever music he was dancing to was music only he could hear...and yet Rainier felt a connection to it. Watching Slate move in battle reminded him of fighting when he held the enlightened path. It was beautiful, and his dance only served to make the deep cuts dealt by Lira even more striking in contrast.

She struck mercilessly at unsuspecting victims and dispatched the Malethyan Guardsmen that realized the threat within their midst with powerful savagery. Rainier followed behind her and cleaned up her mess. Thankfully, his short swords were as quick as ever, and the work was efficient if not heroic. When he retold the tales of the Burning of Portswain, he'd have to remember to indulge a few areas.

The last few soldiers dropped their swords and ran. Lira threw her sword and impaled a woman in the back. She was still pulling it from the Guardswoman's dying body when Slate flashed down to them and said, "What are you doing? Those are Malethyans!"

Rainier looked down at the Guardswoman dressed in crimson. He should have felt remorse, or regret, or any number of other feelings, but Rainier had been betrayed too many times by too many people. The dead guardswoman wasn't Slate or Sana. She hadn't devoted her life to be a member of the Remnant. She wasn't Lira, misguided as she was in her zealotry, who at least knew what she wanted. She was just a corpse.

He looked down at her again and saw Kalus' dead face looking up at him. It carried meaning and purpose, but then it was gone, replaced by the meaningless, worthless face of a dead woman who swore her allegiance to a blood mage. *I promised Kalus I would kill Jamison. Short of that, I don't owe anyone anything.*

He looked up to Slate and stared his friend in the eyes. He said, "She serves Lattimer. They all did." *What other explanation do you need?*

Slate grabbed Rainier by the collar and screamed at him, "I could have handled them! They didn't stand a chance against me!!"

"They didn't stand a chance against us, either." Rainier said with more edge in his voice than he intended.

Lira crashed into them, sending the group sprawling.

Rainier knew she was just protecting her oracle from a perceived threat, but Slate didn't. He recovered quickly, but before he could respond, Rosana's voice cut through the early morning air from the boat that Slate had defended.

She said, "Save the tussling for me, Slate." Her comments gave Slate pause, but it wasn't enough to ease the tension in the group. "Besides, I only see one boat left that isn't burning, and I'm standing on it. Do you three want to join me and Ibson for a trip to Ravinai?" She tossed the stay lines from the boat, loosening the boat from the dock. The current immediately grabbed hold of the riverboat, and it started drifting away, leaving the group with little choice.

They abandoned their skirmish and jumped off the pier. Lira and Slate landed gracefully, clearing the railing with ease. Rainier smacked into the side of the ship but had just enough distance to grab the railing and haul himself over. *Bastards! I am not mentioning that when I tell the tale of the Burning of Portswain.*

He laid on the deck, waiting for the wind to reenter his chest, when Ibson walked by whistling. He said, without a care in the world, "When I tell the tale of this night, I believe your epic battle with the side of the ship will be the highlight." He chuckled. "The ship won in a landslide."

"I snuck half an army to the shores of Portswain under the guise of a funeral pyre, alerted the Resistance and the townsfolk to the impending attack by the Disenites, and THIS is what you plan to tell people?"

Ibson laughed even harder and kept walking away. *I hate that man.*

By the time Rainier had recovered his breath and his pride, Rosana already had the ship pointed upriver. He found that Ibson had joined Lira and Slate at the stern of the ship, looking back on the city. Riverboats burned in the foreground, eliminating the fastest way to move Disenite troops to Ravinai. *I wish I could see Jamison's face when he realizes he must march the whole way there.* The burning ships drew the attention of the eye, which made the subtle shapes of the buildings in Portswain against the early morning light almost an afterthought. They continued upriver while keeping their eyes to the city.

The boats burned brightly, as if the destruction they caused would never stop.

The sun crested the horizon, its rays reflecting off the smoke-filled air, creating a paradox of beauty and impending doom. Its rays gave hope to the simpletons and targets to the Nameless Army.

Cannons fired. Portswain crumbled.

CHAPTER 8

RIVERBOAT HARBINGERS

They moved upstream as quickly as the boat would take them, fighting the current and their own sense of urgency. Jamison trailed them, and every headwind diminished their chances of setting their plan in time. Ahead, Lattimer awaited, and yet within the confines of the riverboat, they were powerless against the forces of the river and hostages to the passing of time.

The gentle lapping of the hull against the waves made Rainier idly tap his fingers to the same rhythm, hoping that if he tapped faster the ship would respond in kind. Lira did her sword forms whenever she got anxious, which happened as frequently as the gusting winds changed their speed. Sunsets came and went, with the pastels wandering across the sky as aimlessly as Ibson pacing the decks.

During one particularly picturesque sunset, the group rested on the deck, but despite the relaxed setting, tension hung in the air. Slate had been distant ever since the attack on Portswain, and Rainier didn't feel like bridging the gap. *How many Malethyans has he killed? What does he expect from me, an apology for doing something he's done on countless occasions?* He looked back up to the setting sun. The color pallet upon the horizon reminded him of the smoke-filled sunrise marking the demise of Portswain that had been burned into his memory. He knew he should appreciate it anyway. *Who knows how many more sunsets I'll see? I'm one misstep from a Marked sword or a Fury's wrath. I've already lost one friend in Kalus. I called Kalus my Hand, and his passing really does feel like I'm missing a part of me.* He looked up at his other Hand, and she noticed his gaze. She said, "What do you see oracle? What is our path?"

"I can answer that one – upriver!" Ibson replied with a friendly laugh as he lounged on the decking, trying to avoid serious conversation. Rosana chuckled at Lira's expense.

"What is our destination? What do we do when we get there?" Lira persisted.

"Sometimes the journey is the destination." Rainier said, but his attempt to use common prophetic phrases as humor was lost on Lira. Instead, he said, "We are heading to Ravinai, and it will take about five days. It's the heart of Malethya and the heart of Lattimer's power. We have some more friends there that we will meet."

"I miss Annarelle and Tommy," Rose said.

Slate explained a bit further, "Annarelle has been recruiting for the Sicarius guild in Rosana's absence and Tommy leads the Resistance in Ravinai. Think of him like Jak's counterpart."

"I shall have to spar with him then." Lira smiled at the memory, and Rainier was glad that Lady Highsmith wasn't there to see it. Her smile disappeared when she looked back to Rainier and said, "You did not answer my question though. What does the pattern tell you?"

Rainier gave some background to his friends, which conveniently gave him more time to work around the question. "I see the Enlightened Path, which is kind of a misnomer, because it's really more like paths of light or possible outcomes rather than a straight and narrow path. When I'm holding it, I can see where to go to avoid trouble or when to duck from an arrow."

Sana asked, "When I first met you, you had claimed Slate as your Teacher. You said that he 'fought within the pattern.' Is that the same thing?"

"My father always looked for people that were close to the pattern for the role of Teacher. His hope was that we'd glean some greater understanding." Rainier thought for a moment and said to Slate, "Of course, there was also my desire to see something other than the back of a caravan for once in my life. I guess our raids of the Regallo estate and the Ispirtu towers will have to suffice."

Slate didn't respond to Rainier's attempt at levity and deadpanned, "I'm sorry my time as your Teacher didn't bring you anything more than that." Slate looked like someone had shot an Ispirtu fireball at his little puppy. *What is that look? Sadness? Oh curses, Slate isn't distant, he's depressed. How can someone who is half super-human be depressed? I can handle distant, but I need Slate to be functional when the ship reaches Ravinai. I guess I'll be mending fences sooner than I planned.*

"That's not quite true, Slate. I found a friend that I trust, and I seem to be short on those these days." Rainier said, thinking of Kalus and trying to fight back his own internal struggles to keep Slate sane. *I can still see the blood from Kalus' body mixing with the sea, expanding outward and fading faster than the color from his dead cheeks.* Rainier pulled himself from the edge of the grief that he was teetering over and said, "Besides, I still see something in you when you fight. Even back at the docks…" everyone looked towards Portswain without thinking "…you moved…differently…"

"Like a demon?" Ibson suggested.

"If he's a demon, at least he's a cute one." Rosana gave Slate a kiss. She also gave a wink to Rainier in appreciation of his kind words. *I guess I'm not the only one to try to keep Slate Severance from the depths of his own thoughts, but I don't want that full-time job. I'll give that one to Rosana.*

Rainier thought of how to describe Slate's movements while fighting. He finally decided on, "You fought like there was a song that only you could hear." Rainier paused and said, "Sometimes I feel that way when I'm holding the enlightened path." The pointed look from Lira told him that she was still awaiting an answer regarding his progress as an oracle. *I guess I'm not getting out of this then.* He looked back to her and said, "I can hold the enlightened path at will. I'm even holding it right now." *I don't even realize when I do it anymore. The soft light of the path is comforting, and it feels right to hold it.* Lira nodded in acknowledgment of his improvement. He said, "I still haven't found a way to transfer it to anyone but myself though." *If all it does is save my own neck, I'll be a happy man, even if I'm not the legendary general she expects me to be.*

"*A Life in the Pattern* will not discuss such things." Lira said and then sat in silence, thinking. Finally, she looked up and said, "Fight Slate."

"Excuse me?" Slate asked.

"Now?" Rainier asked. *How about never? What's the point of being on the same side as Slate 'Stonehands' Severance, the Blightbringer himself, if I still have to fight him?*

"You don't have anywhere else to go, do you?" Rosana quipped. Sana said, "It's a sound hypothesis, even if it doesn't work. Maybe Rainier can see the path better when he's fighting Slate." Rosana finished, "And maybe he'll hear that song he was describing. If nothing else, it'll give the two of you a chance to trade blows. The way you've been acting the last few days, maybe that will release some of the hard feelings from Portswain. You need to get over it. We have bigger enemies ahead of us."

"I am up for some evening entertainment. Impress me boys!" Ibson added to no one's benefit. *I need to get that man alone. Otherwise, all I'll get is lousy jokes out of him.*

Rainier got up and stretched, delaying the fight a few more seconds, while also throwing in a few side comments to his friend. "If it's entertainment you're looking for, maybe we should have Slate come out of the cabin, trip on his own two feet, and flip in the air with staff wielding flourish. The crowd loved that one."

Slate whirled his staff around, loosening his arms. "The crowd loved it almost as much as when I beat Magnus in record time. I managed not to trip over my feet in that bout. How did your second-round fight go?"

Sana cast a spell to dull their weapons, and the two settled into their favorite starting positions. They had trained against each other every night when they first started traveling together, and when Sana said, "Fight," it felt like old times.

They moved around the tiny riverboat deck with an easy familiarity. Rainier said, "Who was it that told you about Magnus' tendencies as a fighter?" He struck with two quick, successive blows that Slate deflected with ease.

Slate countered with a sweep of his staff that Rainier hopped over. Slate said, "I think your advice can be summed up by the words 'He's big.' I would have figured that one out." As the two sped up their movements the banter subsided in favor of concentration. Occasionally, Slate would sneak in a wrist flick with entirely too much power. When he did though, Rainier always saw it coming, seeing a change in the enlightened path, and responding to it. The longer they fought, the more Rainier depended upon the skill, because his reflexes couldn't keep up with Slate's speed. *Curses, Slate is fast.* Slate jumped to the side and struck, but Rainier sidestepped and was no longer where Slate expected him to be. Instead, Slate changed his attack in mid-air and flicked his wrist towards Rainier, who parried the blow with swords held at the perfect location. *I had no idea that was coming, but my swords were in the right place thanks to the path.* He kept following the path, jumping, diving, deflecting, and striking enough to keep Slate honest. Flash, fla flash, flash. Slate fought faster and struck harder with each blow. Flash, flash...flash. Rainier bent backwards as the staff whistled above his nose. *I don't want to think about what would happen if one of those blows hits me in the head.* Rainier moved straight into a roundhouse kick. Slate ducked beneath it to sweep Rainier's leg, only to find it was already gone.

"Stop!" Sana yelled.

Rainier dropped his swords in exhaustion. Slate flipped

backwards, smiling from ear-to-ear. *Maybe Rosana was right. Maybe the remedy for their friendship was banging some practice swords at each other mercilessly.* Slate said, "That was amazing! I haven't been able to spar with anyone like that in a long time. I always need to hold back, but you knew every move I was going to make!" *That's not what it felt like to me. It felt like I was fighting for my life.*

Rainier looked to the others and saw various expressions of incredulity spread across their faces. Surprisingly, Lira was the one to capture everyone's thoughts. She said, "I have never seen two people fight that way before." She nodded her head, almost in reverence, but she was still analyzing what she just witnessed.

Sana said, "I did not think that was possible." She shook her head and said, "If two skilled fighters choreographed and rehearsed their moves for ages, they still couldn't match Slate's speed and Rainier would have lost his head. The two of you...are remarkable." *You can add yourself to that list of remarkable people, Headmaster. I wouldn't want to meet you in a dark alley, and I certainly wouldn't want to taste the bite of that Blighted Knife.*

"Well, you certainly managed to entertain me. Good show boys!" Ibson laughed heartily, but Rainier didn't miss the discerning look hidden with the laugh. *What is he thinking?*

Slate patted him on the back and said, "We DEFINITELY need to do that again."

"I agree." Lira said, after thinking through the sparring session in her head and before Rainier could respond. "Rainier needs to improve."

Ibson laughed again and said, "Would you like to show him how it's done, my darling?"

"I am not your darling, and I am not the oracle." She looked to Slate and said, "I wish to train with you, but I do not use the strength of my armor during training. I could not do as Rainier just did." Slate nodded his acceptance of Lira's offer to spar in the future, and Lira turned to Rainier. "We should talk," she said as she marched into the cabin.

Rainier shrugged and said with a mischievous smile, "When a woman wants to get me alone in a cabin, I'm not one to argue."

"I am not your woman!" Lira yelled. Rainier smirked and was filled with memories of Kalus. *That one was for you, buddy. I think I'll stop before I end up curled on the ground and talking with the squeaky voice of a pubescent though.*

"You'll be lucky if you come back out in one piece with that one. I don't think she likes your comments, and she doesn't strike me as the type to suffer unwanted advances," Rosana said. The Headmaster added, "If she puts a knife in you, I want you to know you deserved it."

With those pleasant thoughts in his head, Rainier ducked into the dimly lit cabin and started by saying, "I'm sorry if I offended you..."

Lira looked up from the table in the room and said, "I don't have time for trivial comments. I especially don't have time for further conversations about past trivial comments. Sit down." Rainier did. Immediately. "You let that Malethyan attack you for the entire sparring session without a meaningful swing returned. Why did you not attack?"

Rainier was taken aback. "Did you see how fast he was moving? I did all I could just to keep up with him."

"I do not know what it means to be an oracle, but I do know how to analyze a fight." She pointed a finger in his chest. "You were timid. A great fighter must flow between offense and defense seamlessly. You did not. Why?"

Rainier was accustomed to direct questions from Lira, but this level of directness left him off balance. He responded using a technique he reserved for the direst of circumstances – the truth. "The path doesn't work that way. I could see where to put my swords so that his staff didn't crack my head in two, but that was it."

Lira nodded, as if his comments confirmed her thoughts. "There is more to the path, you just don't know how to use it yet. Think of the times you first held the Path. What do they all have in common?"

Someone slipped a noose around my neck, then some archers were shooting arrows at me, and I jumped into the sea. Then I met Jamison and my life turned into a constant battle to survive another day, another scheme, another plot. "People are always trying to kill me."

Lira nodded again. She said, "You are a soldier who has only practiced with a shield. You do not realize that your other hand holds the sword. This is why you will keep fighting Slate. You will hold the path differently. You will learn to attack!" She pounded the table and stared into his soul.

"Are you sure I'm the oracle? It might be you after all." Rainier grinned to diffuse the emotion and determination in her speech. He thought he heard her say something about 'trivial comments' under her breath.

That was how Rainier's training sessions with Slate became part of the daily routine. The pain Slate inflicted as Rainier attempted to use the pattern offensively was instant, but the bruises and sore muscles stayed with him all day. Ibson, an expert in the art of defensive magic, took pity on him and cast some protective spells on him for the training sessions. Ibson never cast a spell that completely protected him, though, because 'pain was a powerful teaching tool.' *Old bastard.*

Ibson did, however, heal the worst of his injuries right away, and that afforded Rainier some time alone with the wizard. Such was the occasion after a particularly poor display by Rainier in an early morning sparring session.

"Your head wouldn't be attached to your shoulders if I hadn't dulled the blades and protected you with hardened skin." Ibson commented as he laid his hands-on Rainier and cast a probing spell, searching out the damaged areas within Rainier's body.

Rainier didn't need the reminder. He had tried to lunge forward and catch Slate unaware, but the fractal-forsaken bastard jumped clear and delivered a double overhand blow to the base of his neck with his staff. He felt the tender spot on his neck and said, "Next time, you might want to consider armored skin, or stone skin, or something else a little stronger. Does that even exist? Could you turn my skin into armor?"

Ibson didn't answer the question, as he commonly chose to do. *Is he just absent-minded or is that part of his genius?* Instead, he moved his hands in a wizardly display, and a second or two later the pain in his neck subsided. Ibson, the other pain in his neck, was still right in front of him though, and Rainier was determined to get some answers out of him. He had tried for days to get him alone, but between Lira feeling it was her duty to be by his side constantly and Ibson being Ibson, it had proven difficult. With Lira taking her turn sparring with Slate after Rainier's humiliating performance, this was his chance. He tried a different tactic.

"Have you ever played standing stones?" Rainier asked.

Ibson frowned, "I know the basic rules of the game, but I have never studied the intricacies of the game. During my travels with Lucus..."

He was about to ramble on, so Rainier said, "I have a set. I'll grab it and we'll play." He clasped him on the shoulder and said, "It's not like we have anything better to do while we're stuck on this boat."

Rainier ran back to his bunk and rummaged through his travel sack until he found Kalus' set of standing stones. As he grabbed it, he thought of his friend's comments. "We should be living a life of ease after fulfilling our duty, and instead Julian threw us back into a deadly game where we don't understand the rules or the pieces. You will see us through, Rainier. Right now, you might still be understanding the lay of the board, but you will see the pieces soon enough. When you do, I know you'll tip things in our favor. You are the leader of the Remnant, and we are all behind you. We are family." *I don't know if I see all the pieces yet, my friend, but I've made my first moves. I've gotten ahead of Jamison, and I've hidden my strategy, but there are a lot of pieces left to set. I hope I have seen enough of the board to make this work.* He grabbed the set and ran back out to find Ibson.

Rainier spilled the stones onto the riverboat deck and started sorting them. Ibson commented, "Isn't standing stones a children's game? If we are looking for a game of strategy, there are many other examples. The game of chess, for instance was imported from..."

Rainier cut him off again by saying, "Do you have a chess set on this boat?"

Ibson startled a bit and said, "Well, no." He then picked up his grey stones and said, "Standing stones will be fine."

Rainier set the red stones between them and placed his first white stone on the deck. Ibson placed his first stone and as the game progressed, Ibson's attention became more focused on the matter at hand. After a few turns, Rainier looked up to watch Slate and Lira sparring. He said, "I'm glad we'll have the two of them on our side when the fighting starts in Minot."

Ibson didn't even divert his gaze from the board, saying, "Errm, yes, yes. We are extremely fortunate." He placed a stone, using a very conservative strategy of building his stones outward slowly from his starting point.

"I've never been to Minot, and from Sana's description, there's some weird stuff there. I feel like I should know some details before just showing up with a sword in my hand." Rainier placed a stone forward, pushing one side of his formation forward toward a red stone while playing defensively on the other side of his formation. "Lattimer has a base there, and they are protecting a hunter's cottage in the woods? It didn't sound like a hunter's cottage to me."

Ibson deliberated on the placement of his next stone and said, "Appearances can be deceiving. The hunter's cottage is the three-dimensional form of a four-dimensional fractal. It takes the form of a hunter's cottage, but inside, the four-dimensional fractal can be unfolded into infinite possibilities." *Of course, that was the obvious answer. What else could it be?* Ibson might as well have been speaking a different language, but at least he was speaking to him. Rainier played a few stones in silence and let Ibson keep rambling, since he was keeping on topic, "Inside the hunter's cottage, Sana found a library on spark-based magic, or blood magic as you describe it. Lattimer has a team of Ispirtu wizards combing through the library around the clock." *Great, so with each passing second, Lattimer is getting stronger and stronger. And here we are sitting on a riverboat playing a children's game.* "The damage that Lattimer can do with the knowledge in those books is astronomical. It's why I quit teaching him magic as a child. His predilection for spark-based magic troubled me, and I sent him back to his father." Ibson built his formation around the edges of the board, trying to surround the red stones and cut off Rainier.

"I wonder who made this hunter's cottage? If the books were so dangerous, why wouldn't the wizard that made the hunter's cottage just destroy them?" *I wonder why you didn't destroy those books when you imprisoned all your students, Candor.* Rainier placed another stone, pretending that he didn't know what Ibson was planning.

Ibson looked up at him curiously but shook his head slightly and said, "It may have been Candor himself. The founder of spark-based magic probably wanted to preserve the knowledge of his work, even if the practical use of it got twisted into something unimaginable. Who can say? History can capture events and actions, but rarely does it capture motivations." *Don't push too far too quickly. Get him focused on the game again to keep his guard down.* Rainier set up his stones for a big offensive push, but he tried to disguise it until the right moment.

After a few more turns, he asked Ibson, "What about this storage room? Sana pulled out a blighted knife from the sands of an expansive desert and used it to kill one of Lattimer's generals, and now it's killing her. That sounds like a campfire story to me."

Ibson smiled as he placed a stone. He said, "Yes, she was quite clever. She learned how to call forth the pattern of the knife from the sands using a probing spell. But not only that!" Ibson got excited about the subject and beamed at Sana, who was navigating the river from the back of the boat. "She also called forth a gateway to escape Lattimer and get to safety. It was truly remarkable." Ibson chuckled and said, "That storage area was a brilliant idea by whomever made the hunter's cottage. Lattimer could dig in those sands for centuries and never pull out any of the artifacts from the days of blood magic. He would never expect that you need to use pattern-based magic to retrieve the spark-based artifacts." Ibson placed another stone and in a few moves he'd encircle the red markers, winning the game before Rainier even attacked. *Now you compliment yourself on your own inventions, huh, Candor?*

Rainier placed his white stone and attacked with one of his formations. His stones fell one after the other until the trail of stones ended by knocking down a single, seemingly meaningless, grey stone in Ibson's defensive formation, turning it white. "How do you know so much about Minot and this hunter's cottage? Did you tell Sana how to retrieve the artifact before she infiltrated Lattimer's forces?"

"I could only tell her so much. I acted as a caretaker of sorts for the hunter's cottage, and I bound myself to silence until the secrets of the hunter's cottage were discovered. I did this so that I'd be immune to physical torture if I were ever forced to share its secrets. We both know I wouldn't withstand torture otherwise!" Ibson chuckled, and then continued, "She figured out how to use the storage facility on her own. Now that part of my bond is broken, and I am free to teach you the lessons of her discovery in all their detail!" Ibson placed another stone and said, "I think I'll be able to teach you a lesson in standing stones pretty soon as well." He smirked at his reference to his impending victory in the game before them. *Go ahead and smirk, you fractal-forsaken fraud. I know who you are.*

Rainier looked up and saw Lira take another beating from Slate. He took it easy on her but never let up to the point where she had a chance of winning. Judging by the sweat dripping from Lira's brow, the session would end soon. Rainier's time with Ibson was running out. He racked his brain, piecing together the information Ibson had shared.

Rainier placed a white stone and attacked with one of his smaller formations. It ended by knocking Ibson's leading part of his formation. When combined with the other stone Rainier had knocked down, the white stones formed a wall blocking half of Ibson's formations. He said,

"A wise man told me that appearances can be deceiving. Maybe this children's game is more difficult than you realized." He laughed, keeping the conversation light, and then said casually, "What is in the city beneath Minot? Why does Lattimer want to get into it?"

Ibson pondered his next move, but Rainier didn't care. The game was already won. Ibson just didn't realize it yet. He said, ""There are people walking around inside the city. Lattimer believes they are the blood mages of legend and wants access to the city to increase his power. I'm sure he has nefarious designs for them that I have not conceived of."

"How do you get into it? How is it destroyed?"

Ibson's eyes immediately glazed over and he answered, "My bonds prevent me from answering." His eyes refocused, and he frowned at the board as if nothing had even happened. Ibson asked, "Who's turn is it again?"

Slate and Lira were finishing their match. His time was running out. *Ibson had a powerful bond tying him to the hunter's cottage, and that bond is not completely broken yet. I bet that's why Ibson or Candor has spent so much time here. Julian said he could bend time, but he hasn't. He's stayed here, which probably means he's stuck here until the bond is broken.* Rainier was pulling pieces of information and trying to connect them, but this was a reach. In the end, he did what came most naturally to him, he took a gamble and squeezed the information to his advantage, just like any member of the Remnant would do. *The trick is to do it without giving away any of my own secrets. He doesn't need to know that I have Julian's memories in my head or that he gave me a separate mission to fulfill.*

"It's my turn, Ibson." Rainier placed a stone and attacked with another formation that blocked Ibson from the other direction, creating a corridor that led straight to the red markers that Ibson could not defend against. The game was his. He waited for the realization to hit Ibson, and when it showed on his face, he leaned across the board to knock down the red markers. Then he said quietly, for only Ibson to hear, "There is only one reason I can think of that you would know so much about that cottage. You've had many accomplishments in your life Candor, but I daresay that leaving that hunter's cottage behind is the single biggest mistake you've ever made." Shock spread across Ibson's face, and Rainier knew he had hit his mark. "I don't know what type of bond ties you to it, but it sounds like you can't share anything about your identity with anyone but me. If you want to break that bond before Lattimer figures out a way to enter that city to doom us all, I'm your only chance." *And you just gave away something you should have held very dear – leverage – especially when dealing with me.*

Ibson nearly jumped out of his skin to ask Rainier a question, but Slate walked up, and Ibson's eyes immediately glazed over again. Slate saw the look on Ibson's face and the standing stones outcome, and said, "You must not be used to losing, Ibson." He laughed, and said, "You're as pale as I am!"

Rainier laughed with him and said, "Standing stones can fool even the wisest of wizards, apparently. I've really enjoyed our game though. It was very enlightening." He looked across to Ibson and said, "Maybe you would want to play again and up the stakes a bit?"

Ibson recovered from his shock enough to say, "Yes, I daresay we have some wagers to discuss."

Slate shook his head and said, "Hasn't anyone ever told you about the Remnant? Never make a bet with them." *I'm sure Ibson completely agrees.*

Rainier knocked over the red stones and collected the set. He said, "I'm looking forward to our next game and our continued conversation."

Over the course of the trip upriver, several opportunities arose to play standing stones with Ibson, but Rainier always found ways to preoccupy himself. *The bait is out there waiting for him. It's best if I don't appear too eager. There's a fine line between eagerness and desperation when making a deal, and I need Ibson to realize I'm his only option.* Rainier would find Ibson giving him sideways glances throughout the day, but whenever he approached, Rainier would occupy himself by asking Sana about the intricacies of navigating the river or drop a line off the side to catch some fish, releasing all the blight-speckled ones, which were showing up with alarming frequency. If that didn't work, he'd pull out *A Life in the Pattern* and read it yet again or engage Lira in conversation about patterned speech and controlling the army. The only interaction he didn't avoid was healing after his sparring sessions with Slate, and even with those, he managed to stay close enough to others to avoid a private conversation. His stalling technique also had an added benefit – Ibson became less sparing in his use of defensive magic during the bouts and more generous with his healing spells following the matches. Rainier didn't acknowledge that he noticed the changes, even though his failure to improve his offensive techniques against Slate increased his appreciation for Ibson's efforts.

They continued this way until the open countryside turned to farmland speckled with houses. The houses became more numerous and turned into towns with small docks alongside the river. Their boat joined the bustling activity of commercial fishing boats and personal riverboats making up a floating caravan into Malethya's capital, and the nervous energy on the ship increased as the end of their journey neared. Finally, as dusk gave way to night and the lights of Ravinai came into view, Sana announced, "Our long trip upriver is almost at an end. Make any preparations you need to make. I want this ship to be quiet and dark within the next half hour. Annarelle has arranged for us to slip into the docks in the merchant's quarter, but that doesn't mean we need to announce our arrival either."

Lira immediately began to sharpen her blade, letting the ringing of the sharpening strokes echo beyond the boat before Sana's moratorium on noise began. Slate took the cue from her and performed a similar task on the Headmaster's collection of throwing knives. *That's not a bad move, Slate. A sharp set of throwing knives might be the fastest way to win the Headmaster's heart, if she has one.*

Rainier left them to their tasks and went into his cabin. He began to stow his gear, but that was just something to preoccupy his time until...

Knock. Knock. *The sound of an old man rapping on my door.* "Come in, Ibson."

Ibson came in hurriedly and asked, "How did you know it was me?"

Because you've been looking for an opportunity to talk with me for days, and I finally gave you what appears to be the perfect opportunity. That is, it would be the perfect opportunity for you if I weren't at the height of my negotiating leverage. "It was a lucky guess. Everyone else is busy making their pointy swords pointier. Have a seat." Rainier gestured politely to the chair in his cabin while he stayed on the bed, the picture of civility and friendship.

Ibson sat down and rubbed his hands back and forth nervously. "You called me Candor – I haven't been called that in a long time. I have gone by a few names since the days of the Golden Age. How did you know it was me?"

"You aren't the only immortal I've been in contact with recently. Although you are looking rather dapper and livelier than Julian these days. He gave me a history lesson and I put the pieces together." *He also gave me some fragmented memories, and it wasn't difficult to tell that the wizard who invited his followers of spark-based magic to his home so that he could poison them and put an end to blood magic looked identical to the man I knew as Ibson.*

Ibson's eyes widened a bit at the sound of Julian's name, but he recovered quickly and reset his face in a mask of feigned senility. Rainier didn't miss the momentary clenching of his jaw that hinted at Ibson's true emotions, though. *Anger? Hatred? ...Fear?* Ibson said, "So Julian is still alive then..."

"Yes. He looks like a walking corpse, but Julian the Immortal is the leader of Disentia, and he is on his way here with an army at his back."

Ibson's anger broke through his façade. "You don't know what you've done. This is your fault! You brought him here!"

Rainier controlled his emotions during the outburst and responded amicably, "I left Malethya to stop a blood mage. I didn't get the welcome home that I expected in Disentia, and Julian is not what I expected to find, but don't blame me. You sat hiding in an Infirmary, drooling on yourself and speaking in riddles. You still speak in riddles, with your 'bonds that can't be broken' and your secrets in the Hunter's Cottage. The fault is your own."

Ibson's shoulders sagged and the anger faded from his face. "You're right. I've made mistakes, but if we walk out of this room and you share everything you know with Slate and Sana and Lira, then more of my bonds will be broken, and I can help you stop Lattimer and Julian. Please, I'm begging you!" *Never plead in a negotiation.*

Rainier stared him straight in the eye, and any hint of friendliness dropped from his face. "You've had your chance to help, and you've messed it up at every turn. Now we do things my way." *I'm tired of everyone else pulling the strings. Never again will someone dictate to me how things need to be done.* "You seem to be fond of making bonds. Make one with me, so that you can't share the information we discuss with anyone else until I say so, or Lattimer and Julian lie dead and buried. I'll be a better caretaker of the information than you have been. These are my terms. Do you agree?"

Ibson tried to appeal to reason. "Let's tell Slate and the others. They can help us!"

Rainier was short on his supply of appeals or reason.

"Slate trusted Lattimer against my wishes and started this mess. Sana is a psychopath. Your deal is with me, and you will make it before we reach Ravinai or you can wallow in your bonds of silence until Julian comes and kills you." *The most important part of every negotiation is to close the deal.*

Ibson swallowed hard and nodded his head. "We have a deal."

"Make the bond."

Ibson furrowed his brow in concentration and started making some elaborate hand motions. Then he chanted softly, so that no one would hear outside the cabin, some words of intonement. "The strength of a man is in his words and deeds. By these words, I will bind myself and my deeds to a covenant with Rainier Tallow. Our conversation shall remain private, until Rainier terminates this consecration with his word, or our deeds terminate the lives of Lattimer and Julian." The hand motions finished in an elaborate flourish and a short period of silence. Ibson opened his eyes and said, "The bond is complete."

The whole show reminded Rainier of the fight between Julian and his high priest. Julian didn't require elaborate hand motions to cast a spell. *Am I really to expect that Candor, Julian's master, needed the hand motions?* Julian's memories broke into Rainier's thoughts. *Flash...Flash. Flash. Julian talks excitedly with Candor at a lab bench as he points down at a frog. Candor winks and the frog turns an iridescent blue. Flash, flash. Candor lectures his students on a lawn outside the university. A storm rolls in and Julian starts to pack his things to run inside. Candor says, "Don't rush off. I feel like being outside today, and it's a beautiful day." The clouds part above the group and warm sunlight shines upon them. Candor smiles at his students and they all laugh in wonder as the rain pours around them only an arm's length away. Flash. Flash...Flash.* Rainier collected himself from the jarring experience of sharing someone else's memories and looked up to Ibson.

His comment came out in a low growl. "If you're done with all the handwaving and fancy words, I'm ready to make the bond and finalize our deal." Ibson was unable to hide his surprise, and Rainier knew he had caught him in a lie. "And since you've already tried to renege on the deal once, let's add to it a bit. I've heard you like to jump between different times. I don't know how you do that or what is holding you here, but I want to make sure you stick around if our discussion allows you to take a vacation to a more peaceful time."

Ibson frowned and said with annoyance, "Fine. Hold out your hand." Rainier complied.

Ibson took out the small knife and drew blood from his own hand with a grimace and then gave Rainier a cut that was a little deeper than Rainier deemed necessary. While Rainier watched, the blood from Ibson's cut formed a perfectly round droplet and rose from the palm of his hand, hovering over it. It floated across to the palm of Rainier's hand. Ibson said with a gruffness that Rainier hadn't seen before, "With this blood, I bind myself to you. I shall not speak of our conversation until I am allowed, and I will follow any orders you give me that pertain to achieving our goal of killing that insolent punk named

Lattimer that fancies himself a blood mage and that bastard Julian, may he die a slow and terrible death." He looked to Rainier, "Close your hand around the blood and our bond will be sealed. Oh, and I won't cast magic that bends the space-time continuum."

Rainier looked at the drop of blood hovering above the palm of his hand. He said, "Is this blood magic?" *This is exactly what I warned Slate against doing.*

"It isn't a healing spell, boy. Think of it like the totems that Lattimer is using to control his armies, except when you close your hand it will become a part of you. There is no totem to break. It is an unbreakable spell that remains active as long as my blood flows through your veins." Rainier's apprehension must have been apparent, because Ibson said, "For goodness sake, I'm the founder of blood magic. You didn't think I knew how to use it? Close your hand if you want your bond."

Rainier deliberated, but not for long. *I'm tired of being in the dark. If I want to beat Lattimer and Julian, I need to see all the pieces on the board. I owe it to Kalus. I owe it to myself and everyone else in the Remnant who has devoted their lives to a cause they didn't ask for.* Rainier closed his hand. There weren't any tingling or magical feelings, just the touch of his fingertips against his open palm. He opened it up and the blood was gone, along with the cut and any indication that an unbreakable bond had just been forged. But Rainier knew that it had. *Ibson is mine.*

"I'll start talking about the night you poisoned your students. You can fill me in as your bonds get broken, especially when things pertain to Minot and your students that are stuck inside that bubble..."

CHAPTER 9

AN UNWELCOME WELCOME

"So now you know everything. You know who is in Minot and why they are there. You know what could happen if Lattimer or Julian control them." Ibson said. "The question is, what will you do with the information? I don't believe you have the altruistic heart of Slate, but I'm trusting that you'll do the right thing."

That's the thing about trust - people only use the word when they distrust you. Rainier looked earnestly at Ibson and said, "I'll do the right thing." *...for me. All the rest of you crusty old fools that got us into this mess can take a fractal-forsaken leap off a tall building.* Rainier didn't need to fake the conviction in his voice. He meant every word he said, and some that he didn't.

Ibson nodded in gratitude, and his shoulders sagged in relief. It was obvious that the secrets had weighed heavily on the wizard. *Don't worry, Ibson. You don't have to carry them any longer. Your secrets are mine. Now, I just need to see if you can follow a plan.* After hearing Ibson's tale, Rainier had given the old wizard a single order – do not break any bonds that you have already made.

A soft rap came on the door. Slate poked his head in and whispered, "It's time. Grab your gear."

Rainier stood up, strapped his short swords across his back, and grabbed his travel sack. He gave Slate a smile, the first genuine smile he had given in a long time, and said, "Let's get on with it then. I wouldn't want to be late to the party when Jamison's troops get to Ravinai, and there are a lot of pieces to this scheme to set in motion before then." *Now that I can finally see all the pieces on the board, I get to add a few of my own. If Slate and my other friends don't realize it, that's their problem.* He patted his friend on the shoulder and bounded onto the deck, constrained only by his need for silence and the stretch of water between the riverboat and the docks of Ravinai.

Lira stood at the bow of the ship, staring into the brightly lit city beyond the docks. Orbs lit the streets in a decadent blue, silhouetting and emphasizing the grandeur of the building at the city center. Rainier could pick out King Darik's palace, the mansions on Rue street, and of course the Ispirtu tower reaching upwards with condescending righteousness. Rainier pointed at it and said, "Lattimer's right up there. For all I know, he's watching us right now."

Lira's emotion gave way at the mention of Lattimer the blood mage. She hissed and said, "Let's go there now. I'll show him the strength of a paladin."

"He would light you on fire or keep the air from your lungs and suffocate you where you stand. If you want a crack at him, you'll have to follow the plan. We need Jamison and his troops to weaken Lattimer's forces and distract him. Then...maybe we'll have a chance for you to put that blue paladin sword in his back when he isn't looking." Rainier looked across the city at the blue light emitting from the orbs on the streets and in the homes of the rich and joked, "You might even blend in. This might be the only city in the world where you would, but that blue armor looks an awful lot like the orbs in Ravinai."

Lira didn't even spare him a glance as she continued to stare up at the tower. "My holy armor is of the pattern. Do not compare it to trinkets of the blasphemous." *Ok, point taken. I'll move along now.*

Rainier moved to the stern to talk with Sana, his good spirits not even slightly diminished. "Where are we docking this thing? How do we know there won't be a bunch of Crimson Guardsmen waiting to grab us?"

She scanned along the riverfront and then pointed. "Do you see the dock with the flickering light near shore? That is our sign from Annarelle. She'll have our passage planned out safely. Trust her." *There's that word again.* Rainier's hand went to the hilt of his short sword and his mind reached for the enlightened path. Its comforting light led towards the darkened dock with the flickering light. *At least there's one thing I can trust. The enlightened path hasn't led me astray yet. It hasn't always worked when I needed it, but hey, nothing's perfect.*

She navigated the riverboat over the darkness of the water in complete silence. As they approached the flickering light, they saw that the dock extended well into the darkness of the water and the light at the end of the dock was extinguished. She eased the riverboat next to the pilings and the waiting hands of two dock workers. The workers hesitated with their ropes when they saw Lira on the bow and froze completely at the sight of Slate Severance.

"Now would be when you tie the ship down, boys." Ibson reminded them quietly.

Their shock subsided even if their fear remained, and they tied down the riverboat. No sooner did the last knot get thrown than Slate and Lira jumped off, protecting the end of the dock like they were an invading army, and this was their beachhead. *I'm glad they're on my side.* The only other person on the dock was a fidgety man that continually wrung his hands against each other and looked to the corners for signs of danger. Lira frisked him quickly while Slate held his stonehand at the ready, but the only danger she found was the wet area in front of his pants where he wet himself at the sight of Slate.

Ibson and Rainier walked off when they got the all-clear sign from Lira. Rainier had to stop himself from unsheathing a blade. Blades caught the light, and he couldn't ask for better protection than Slate and Sana, so he settled his hand on the hilt and kept alert. The only action was of the two dockhands that started painting some numbers onto the side of the hull. *Curious, but not dangerous.*

The Headmaster jumped off last, wearing her Sicarius mask, and grabbed the piss-soaked man by the jaw, turning his face up towards hers to get a good look at him. The poor bastard looked like he was about to pass out, so the Headmaster hooked her finger under the corner of his jaw and pressed upward. His face lit up in pain as the pressure point was held, and the pain kept him from passing out immediately.

"I know you." She said in an eerily alternating voice. *Every time I hear that voice that goes from Magnus depths to schoolgirl squeals, it gives me the chills.* "The last time I saw you, you were eating in the Refined Palate. You made unwanted advances towards the serving girl."

"I'm sorry. I don't recall..." stammered the frightened man.

The Headmaster pressed harder, and he tried to scream, but the Headmaster delivered a quick blow to the gut. *You can't scream if you don't have any air. She knows her stuff.* She tilted his head back up and waited for his eyes to refocus their attention.

"Your name is Mr. Radcliff." Sana stated matter-of-factly and then Rosana said, "I heard that name a second time. An imprisoned man named Josef told me he had taken a less-than-legal delivery job from you. When he saw the deal going south, he fled. The next day, Guardsmen broke down his door and threw him in jail. You implicated that he had stolen the merchandise and killed the men at the scene. He was sentenced to die, but by the time he died by my hands, I'm sure that death was a relief compared to the nightmare he lived as one of Lattimer's Furies."

Recognition spread across Radcliff's face. He said excitedly, "I serve Sicarius now. I admit my crimes. Please, please, don't kill me. I smuggle in people and supplies for Sicarius using my former contacts." He pointed to the dockhands painting on the ship. "They are painting on a valid registration from a ship we sunk this morning. No one will ever know you were here."

"You deserve to die."

The fear of his impending death overwhelmed every other sensory input and Radcliff's eyes rolled backwards in his skull. He crumpled to the ground in a heap, which only became more undignified as the smell wafted from his body. Rainier waited for the Headmaster to put a knife in him and be done with it. *Passing out in your own piss and soiling yourself – I'd take the death of Kalus any day over that. What a sorry excuse of a man.*

The Headmaster's knives weren't put to use though, as Rose turned to the two deckhands and spoke. "This man will not die tonight, and neither will you, but I require something of the two of you after you finish your duties for the night." Rosana said, "Carry him somewhere public, preferably far from here in a place where the most beautiful young women of Ravinai are known to frequent and tie him to a park bench. The two of you seem to know your knots. Make them nice and sturdy. Leave him there in his own filth and come back for him late in the morning. When you untie him, tell him that if his usefulness to Sicarius ever wavers, I will find him and give him what he deserves. Can you do that for me?"

The first deckhand said, "Yes, sir...er, ma'am...err."

The second deckhand saved the first deckhand and his confusion on how to address the Headmaster by saying, "We'll get the job done."

Rosana nodded in satisfaction, and Slate led the way up the docks. He got to the shoreline and crouched in the shadows. He scanned the marketplace before them and said, "Something's wrong. There's no Guardsmen and the docks lack their normal...cast of characters."

Rainier couldn't disagree. At this time of night, the docks should have been the home of countless acts of illicit activities. *Where are the bandits, the gangs, and the cutpurses? Where are the shady business deals and ladies-of-the-night trying to turn some coin? At the very least, where are the city Guard and the groups of people dodging them?* Rainier scanned the city streets with the enlightened path without even thinking about it, but there was no immediate danger. The warm light flowed outwards in all direction past the square marking the boundaries of the dockyard.

"Annarelle must have planned a warm welcome for us." Ibson suggested, but there was little confidence in his tone.

Rainier said, "I don't see a threat." He walked ahead of the group, into the brightly lit dockyard, confident in his own safety. Lira followed dutifully and protectively behind him in full paladin armor. They didn't stand a chance of blending in, but there was no chance of convincing her to sneak into the city with a blood mage on the loose. Rainier wasn't surprised that Lira followed him so quickly, it was her job after all, but the others followed without even a hesitant step. *It's crazy how much I've begun to rely on the Path. It's even crazier that others are trusting in it as well, especially this group.*

Rainier continued towards the center of the dockyard, and it was impossible to miss how clean everything was. The streets were swept, the cargo from the riverboats was stacked with irregular precision, and everything sparkled with iridescent blue of the orbs lighting the square. The sterile cleanliness of the dockyard in Ravinai stood in stark contrast to the smelly squalor of Portswain. *I think I prefer the smell of fish guts in Portswain to this. It seems – unnatural. I'm the dirtiest, smelliest thing in this dockyard after spending so much time on the riverboat, and this place should be crawling with people that reek even worse than I do.*

"Lattimer's really cleaned up the place since we left." Slate said.

"He told me he wanted to return Malethya to the Golden Ages. It looks like he started in Ravinai." Rosana said.

Rainier stopped at the center of the courtyard and looked around. All the shops and markets were closed for the night, which wasn't unusual, and various supplies and equipment were stored in the alleyways, waiting to be pulled out at the start of business the next day. Nothing seemed amiss.

Thump.

An arrow landed twenty steps from his feet. Everyone drew their weapons while Rainier flinched and took cover behind Lira as panic struck him. *Where the hell did that come from? The path said I wasn't in danger! What's going on?* No one seemed to notice his cowering except Ibson, but the old bastard took an undue amount of pleasure in the sight. He laughed and said, "You didn't expect the Sicarius Guild to greet us with warm tea and biscuits, did you?"

Slate flashed forward and grabbed a note tied to the shaft of the arrow. Rainier pulled his sword out quickly and tried to reassert some manly authority by commanding Slate in a deeper than necessary tone. "Read it."

"It says, 'Welcome home, Headmaster. Follow me.'" Slate grinned at Rosana as the hooting of an owl drifted from the rooftops. They looked up to see a figure standing atop a building at the edge of the square, silhouetted by the moonlight.

"Annarelle." Rose gave a girlish smile at the sight of her friend and the Headmaster returned a hoot of acknowledgment. After the return call was given, two dozen figures stood up along the roofline. "And she's been recruiting."

Rainier never thought the sight of a bunch of masked members of the Sicarius guild would warm his heart, but it was nice to have some people on his side for once. *That's a lot better greeting than I received in Disentia, at least.* After the initial shock of the arrow, Rainier was beginning to relax again, knowing that they had dozens of Sicarius Guildsmen protecting them and the comforting rays of the enlightened path extending in all directions as far as...

Oh no.

The path extended outwards, but the rays stopped. They all stopped – in every direction. The Enlightened path constricted around him, and Rainier could almost feel the noose tightening around his neck again. Someone was coming for them and they were bringing a lot of death with them.

"It's a trap!" Rainier screamed. "They have us surrounded!"

Slate looked at him questioningly, and Rainier explained as quickly as possible. "People are coming from all directions, and they are only a few blocks away. We need to leave. Now!"

"If we go back to the boat..." Ibson started, but that's as far as he got.

"I'm not adding Annarelle's name to the list of dead Sicarius Headmasters tonight." Rose said with an authority she rarely used, leaving no debate for the group. "I won't leave her here to die."

"Then we'll punch through whoever is ahead of us," Slate said.

"And we'll cover you from the rooftops." Sana strategized as the Headmaster sprinted towards Annarelle. She jumped onto an awning of a storefront, grabbed a balustrade, and flipped herself gracefully onto the roof.

Slate, Lira, and Rainier held their weapons at the ready and moved towards the street nearest the Sicarius guild as fast as Ibson's old bones allowed. Slate and Lira took the front, while Rainier took the rear guard. *It's the easiest place to run away from if it comes to that.* He checked the Enlighted Path again, but unfortunately, there was no place to run to, even if he wanted.

The sound of marching boots came from ahead of them. *It truly is one of life's clearest and ominous noises. Once you've heard it once, you can never hear it again without a rush of adrenaline and an accompanying dread in the deepest parts of your being.*

The street turned, and they found themselves a block away from a full squadron of battle-hardened Bellator Guardsmen. These weren't some Portswain patrolmen that shook a few spears. These were armored men with full length shields and polearms in the front. The next rows of soldiers had long swords ready to jab between any gaps in the shield wall.

The captain raised his hand at the sight of them and the squadron spread out to block the street, setting their position. An archer launched a flaming arrow high into the night sky, marking their position for every Guardsman in the city.

"Lattimer sends his regards." The captain said with a smile. He yelled, "Kill them all!"

A second later, the Guardsmen moved forward, struggling to keep their lines tight because they fought the all-consuming instinct of a Fury – to rush ahead and kill without a second thought. These Furies were well-trained fighters and held some semblance of control. This wasn't going to be a fun fight. To make matters worse, Rainier could sense the other Guardsmen converging on their location. They'd have to fight, win, and do it quickly.

A volley of arrows came from the back row of soldiers, but they diverged around the group and skittered along the paving stones. Ibson winked, "Don't worry about the arrows. I'll handle those."

Wizards – just when you want to get rid of them, they go and do something useful.

An arc of electricity came from above and Rainier looked up to see Sana casting a spell. The electricity branched out from her fingertips in ever-expanding fractals, bringing the promise of death to the heavily armored men in the street. With that much armor, the electricity should have jumped between the soldiers with ease. Instead of turning them into a Bellator barbeque however, the electricity dissipated harmlessly against the armor of the Furies.

The captain said, "Lattimer modified our armor. He saw your tricks by watching you fight in Minot. You'll have to do better than that."

A second flurry of arrows, kunai, and knives rained from the rooftops, courtesy of the Sicarius Guild. The lightly armored archers in the Bellator ranks took heavy casualties beneath the deluge, but the heavy armor of the advancing Guardsmen absorbed the blows with little effect, with one exception. The Headmaster threw her knives with uncanny speed and precision, finding the gaps in the armor and the soft places around the joints and driving knives into flesh with impossible accuracy.

When one Guardsman went down, though, another stepped up to fill the hole in the shield wall and it continued its steady march towards them. Rainier consulted the enlightened path and it appeared that the Captain of the Guardsmen's signal was having its intended effect.

"We're running out of time. Reinforcements are coming." Rainier warned Slate and Lira, although he didn't have much of a solution.

"Then it's time for steel," Lira said as she rushed towards the shield wall in a blur of fluorescent blue armor.

Flash...fla – fla – flash. Slate joined the action, approaching the shield wall in a zig-zagging pattern that only he could see.

Well...they're dead. Rainier watched the two most skilled fighters he had ever met rush towards a heavily fortified, highly trained shield wall and assumed the worst. Rainier didn't need Julian's memories to know that was a bad idea, but that didn't stop a torrent of memories flooding into his head. *Flash...A gallant last charge into a shield wall by a cavalry unit ended in predictable fashion with courageously dead idiots and their poor horses that were too loyal to realize the mistake their masters were making. Flash. One creative soldier tried to jump the shield and half his torso cleared the shield wall before a spear*

met him in the face and his body was thrown backwards,
only to be trampled by the next foolish soldier in line. Flash.
A group of war-painted heathens rushed a shield wall and
got their feet tangled in the frenzied and uncoordinated
attack. Into the mud they went, and a few quick stabs from
behind the shield wall guaranteed they'd never leave. Then
a funny thing happened. Lira jumped, but her magically
enhanced armor carried her easily over the shield wall and
past the soldiers. Slate didn't trip like he did when he
entered the arena. He flashed to the edge of the street,
ran up the side of the building a step or two and then
slammed his stonehand into the face of the building. He
pulled himself up, planted his feet and flipped backwards
off the building, and his feet hit the ground less than a
stride away from Lira.

As dangerous as a shield wall is for those foolish
enough to charge into it, even highly trained Bellator
soldiers don't expect their enemies to magically appear
behind them. The heavy armor that protected them
became their downfall, as Slate crunched helmets with his
stonehand and swept feet with his staff before the soldiers
could even turn around. Lira smashed forward with her
shield and sent soldiers sprawling right before a sweeping
cut from her blue sword cleared away anyone unfortunate
enough to still be standing.

The rest of the shield wall began to turn towards the
new threat, and Rainier found his courage. He rushed in
and stabbed his short swords into the weak spots of the
armored men with their backs turned to him, running on
to find another victim before anyone knew he was there.
Never turn your back on the Remnant. He took out a few

more soldiers that hadn't been taught that vital lesson during their time in Bellator, while Slate and Lira dished out their own lessons in mortality.

As soon as the last shield fell to the ground, Ibson was hobbling through the wreckage as fast as his old legs would take him. "It took you long enough."

"I said we'd punch through." Slate tapped his stonehand and waved the old man past. He nursed a gash in his arm from an errant sword, but the open wound produced only a trickle of blood – another gift of Lattimer from when they stormed the Ispirtu tower and killed Brannon. Slate shrugged off the wound and said, "I have a heck of a punch."

Rainier reached out with the enlightened path, but he didn't need to warn his companions of approaching danger. The Sicarius scouts on the rooftops could now see them coming. "We've got Guardsmen coming from all sides. They are in an all-out sprint and have red eyes. Ispirtu wizards are trailing in support. We need to leave now!"

Ibson didn't need to be told twice, but the old-man's dead sprint slowed the entire group. They raced through the streets of Ravinai at the direction of the Sicarius guild above, ducking through alleyways and trying to find every advantage they could to stay ahead of the Furies at their back.

After a few side streets though, it became apparent to Rainier that this was a race they were destined to lose. Ibson was too slow, and there were too many Furies. Even if they had eluded the main force, the death driven Furies filled every street and alleyway in their search for victims.

Once they were discovered and the sounds of fighting filled the streets, they'd be descended upon.

Sana apparently reached the same conclusion, because she motioned the group into an alley while Annarelle and the rest of the Sicarius Guild continued along the direction they had been running from the rooftops, hoping to bait the Furies into following them. *If that's where the Sicarius Headmaster wants us to go, then that's where we'll go. No one knows the city like the Sicarius Headmaster. Ravinai is her city, and I'm sure she has a few tricks up her sleeve.* Rainier nearly shoved Ibson into the darkened alleyway, driven by the sounds of trampling footsteps behind him.

"Move those crates — quickly and quietly," the Headmaster demanded. Rainier obeyed immediately, leaving Lira and Slate to guard the alleyway entrance and exit. The crates were set atop a wooden pallet.

"This is the start of an old cleansing run. If Annarelle has maintained it in my absence, this should lift us up to the rooftop and get us off the street. Climb aboard."

Ibson climbed on first and asked, "You said, 'if she maintains it.' What happens if she let it fall into disrepair?"

"Then a rope breaks and we all fall to our deaths."

Rainier didn't get to hear Ibson's response, because a group of Furies decided to peel away from the main group in the street and come down the alley. Lira met them with a shield, but they grabbed ahold of it and started tearing it away, even while Lira plunged her blue blade into the soldiers. The lethal wounds would undoubtedly kill the Furies from blood loss, but a Fury doesn't stop fighting, even if it is dying. The red-eyed monsters let out a cry and lifted swords against Lira as she struggled for control of her shield.

Slate flashed to her aid and smashed the chest plate of the Fury holding her shield, stopping his heart. As the Fury fell to the ground, Slate grabbed the sword from his hand and sliced through the neck of the snarling Fury beside him. "Take their heads off. It's the quickest way," he told Lira.

The enchanted blue sword turned into a scythe that cut through the remaining Furies faster than their heads could roll away. Slate laughed and said, "I think you are getting the hang of this. That's some good work."

"That's some loud work." The Headmaster scolded. "Get over here now!"

Lira and Slate ran back towards the group, not needing to argue the Headmaster's point. As they neared the pallet, a much larger group of Furies sprinted into the alleyway with swords raised. The instant Lira and Slate stepped onto the pallet, the Headmaster cut a rope attached to the wall, and the pallet shot into the air, barely avoiding the Furies' swords below. One Fury jumped up to try to grab the ascending pallet, but Lira met his outstretched arm with a blue blade and removed it for him.

Rainier looked up just in time to see a second pallet plummet from the heights above. It smashed into the Furies below as they reached the rooftop. The Headmaster didn't need to tell them to jump off, and Rainier encouraged Ibson with another push in the back to make sure he made it. *I still need him, even if he has told me his secrets. If anything, I need him even more now that I know the secrets he holds.*

Sana said, "Guard the stairwell." She pointed towards the roof access a short distance away. "They'll find their way up here eventually, and I have to see how we're getting down from here."

Slate and Lira scoped out the access point, and Rainier knew they could hold that choke point almost indefinitely. In that confined space, the number of soldiers coming at them wouldn't help much. Against Slate's speed and power and Lira's armor, the bodies would pile up quickly.

Ibson had other thoughts on his mind. He said, "You brought us up here without having a way to get down?" Rainier looked around and realized that the tall building they were on gave them a great defense against the soldiers below them, but it towered above the adjacent buildings. *I guess we aren't running across the rooftops then.*

Sana ran to a corner of the roof and began to uncover some hidden mechanism. "This is a cleansing run. I only designed it for one person, namely me." She pointed to a harness stowed on the rooftop. "I planned to zipline to safety with this harness using that line over there." Rainier looked, saw nothing, and then looked again. A black cable ran to a clock tower in the park a block away. In the nighttime, it was almost invisible even when Rainier tried to find it. "I didn't plan on having an elderly wizard, two grown men, and a heavily armored Disenite traveling with me. I'll need some time to modify it."

The sound of footsteps rushing up the stairs made Rainier look down. Soldiers swarmed around the building, and they were pushing inside with the eagerness of ants finding a piece of fruit on the ground after a picnic. *The only difference is that this isn't a picnic, and I don't like being the piece of fruit in that analogy.* The sound of a Fury's cry of rage and the clash of steel indicated that the first soldiers had ascended the stairs and met Slate and Lira. "Whatever you are planning on doing, you can start anytime."

Sana said impatiently as she took the harness off the rigging, "Get that pallet we used as a lift off the cable and bring it over here."

Rainier set to work on the pallet with Ibson, and they just got it unlatched from the rope and dragged it onto the roof when an amplified voice yelled from the street below.

"Look what we have here!" Boomed a deep voice that Rainier instantly recognized as belonging to Magnus Pudriuz, one of Lattimer's generals. He peered over the edge and saw Magnus, who was every bit as formidable as ever. He looked the part of a hero of legend, towering over everyone around him with shining armor and a massive double-bladed battle axe strapped to his back. His deep voice dripped with authority and contempt. "I sent my army out tonight to sweep the streets of vermin, and what do I find? Slate 'Stonehands' Severance and the rest of his traitorous friends have been chased up a building. What's the matter? Nowhere to run?"

Slate continued to fight soldiers at the roof access, but he still managed to yell down between blows. "I'm up here Magnus, and all of your soldiers are a nice warmup. I'm almost starting to break a sweat."

Rosana looked over and saw that Slate was heavily engaged with the soldiers, so she said to Rainier. "Get over there and talk to Magnus. Use that silver Remnant tongue to stall while I get this rigging attached to the pallet."

Rainier stepped up onto the ledge of the building with trepidation. The enlightened path had turned from a comforting light that expanded in all directions into a demoralizing pinprick devoid of hope. *There's no way out, unless I can buy Sana the time she needs. Don't fail me now, tongue.*

He called out, "Is that Magnus Pudriuz I hear?" Rainier started clapping loudly in mock awe. "I was told they are making statues of you in Minot. Is that true?"

"Rainier Tallow, I'm so glad you could join us. I haven't heard your name in some time, although I must admit, no one really talks about people that fall in the first round of the tournament. That would be like discussing a servant — you know they are there, but there isn't any point in talking to them unless you need something, and it's hardly worth even knowing their names."

"But you do know my name!" Rainier exclaimed with great animation. "The great hero that helped take down Brannon Regallo, scourge of the Ispirtu Tower, actually knows my name. I am so fortunate to be recognized by someone that is so high above me that a statue has been erected in his honor in the great city of Minot, one of the most remote villages in all of Malethya! I bet your likeness has been gazed upon by tens and tens of people!" Rainier snuck a quick look back at his companions while Magnus processed the blatant sarcasm laced within his words.

Lira and Slate fought rhythmically at the stairwell, with Lira's blue shield as steady as a fortified wall and Slate's speed and power that made him the deadliest man in Malethya. *Slate has earned the fear in people's eyes when they speak his name, but if he learns to fight this way with Lira, he might be unstoppable.* Watching Lira, he was struck by how complimentary her skills were to Slate, but he knew this alliance was temporary. She was too devout to the pattern to team up with a blasphemer like Slate on a consistent basis. *She is so grounded in her attacks — calm, steady, immovable. She's an impenetrable blue wall that Slate can operate behind. Is it my imagination, or is that blue armor more dim than when the battle started?*

Sana and Ibson, meanwhile, tied knots as quickly as they could, weaving the ropes through the pallet and tying them to the rigging to form a cradle that would suspend from the cable. As fast as they worked, they still needed more time. *Keep talking. Keep stalling.*

Magnus collected his wits, or the wits available to him, and yelled up to Rainier. "There are statues in other places!"

"Good, maybe after tonight, you can add to your fame by telling your tens and tens of fans how you sent soldier upon soldier to their deaths while you sat in the street and tried not to cut yourself with your axe." Rainier then delivered a low blow, a verbal attack right to the manhood of the testosterone fueled Bellator man on the streets below. "Or maybe you already are injured? Did you accidentally cut off your fractal-forsaken balls? Is that why you sit down there doing as little as a castrated bull in a cow pasture? I thought you were a general! Your master plan was to have your soldiers killed one by one in a stairwell?"

Magnus was silent for some time. *Did I go too far? What is he thinking?* Finally, he said, "You talk too much little man." He motioned behind him, and three Ispirtu wizards stepped forward to join him. "We have you trapped. I tire of your yapping mouth, and you underestimate me. You think you can provoke me into coming up there to fight you? I grew up on these streets, and my survival was based on my ability to fight in the underground pits. I learned many things, but above all, I learned that there is no honorable way to kill a man, and survival means more than glory." He smiled up at Rainier and said, "I don't need to fight you. You have nowhere to go. I can just watch you burn a slow and painful death."

The three Ispirtu wizards made some hand motions, and a few seconds later, fireballs materialized in the air. The fireballs shot forward, hitting several of the lower levels of the building and lighting it ablaze. *I went too far.* If there was one thing Rainier knew from prior experiences with Ispirtu wizards, it was that wizard fire burned *everything*. The base of the building was instantly ablaze.

Magnus' tactic killed dozens of his own soldiers, but Rainier couldn't argue with its effectiveness. Smoke already rose to their location on the rooftop, burning his eyes and clouding his vision. He ran over towards Rosana to check on their progress and his chances for escape.

"I said to keep him talking, not to provoke him into burning the building!" Rosana screamed at him.

"Be more specific next time." Rainier said with some attempted Remnant charm, but his heart wasn't in it with fire beneath his feet and smoke in his eyes. "How are the knots coming?"

"Almost there. As long as the roof doesn't cave in first." Ibson answered as he threw another knot and cinched it tight. The two of them grabbed ropes on either side of the pallet and lifted their contraption into the air to carry it over to the zipline.

Across the roof, smoke poured out of the stairwell, forcing Slate and Lira away so that they wouldn't get overcome. As they pulled back into the cleaner air, they lost their hold on the chokepoint in the stairwell and a stream of Bellator Furies came rushing out with singed faces and soot covered armor. The flames in the floors below them only further encouraged the Furies that survived the initial fireballs to climb faster and higher.

Slate and Lira fell back towards Rainier, Sana, and Ibson, but they fought a losing battle without the stairwell to focus their attack. *Curses. I'm going to have to go help. And what's up with Lira?* Lira's armor and shield had dimmed to a dull blue glow and she was moving noticeably slower than she had at the start of the battle.

Rainier unsheathed his short swords and started to run towards his Hand when a creaking sound stopped him in his tracks. A split second later, an entire section of roof collapsed to his right, making him stumble and regather his footing.

Flames shot out of the collapsed roof, with the open air feeding the fire to burn even faster. *Great. As if we didn't have enough to worry about right now.* Then a flaming arm reached upward, and, to Rainier's horror, a Bellator Fury pulled herself onto the roof, burning with a hatred that matched the fire in her eyes.

Rainier had no choice but to fight the flaming monstrosity, and he counted his blessings for the enlightened path. *Duck.* The flaming Fury swung her sword in a sweeping arc, trying to decapitate Rainier in a single blow, but he followed the path and slipped beneath it. As it passed overhead, the threat of the sword disappeared, but the smell of burnt flesh lingered. He delivered a hard blow to her knee and rolled away. The blow would have crippled a normal person, but the Fury continued to attack while dragging her maimed leg behind her.

She came at him again. The heated metal plates of her armor had already become one with her charred skin, but the edges of the armor cut into her flesh with every movement. They cut and instantly cauterized the wound with each step, making her advance in a grotesque combination of hissing movements and rising flames. The only thing that didn't change was the fire in her red eyes. The hatred remained even as her skin melted away and her face blackened, driving her to kill Rainier with every ounce of her being.

The path took a hard jump to the left. Rainier sidestepped as the flaming Fury thrusted her sword forward, connecting with nothing but smoked-filled air. Rainier brought his short sword down on her outstretched arm, making her drop her weapon. He cut down across her other leg, and she finally fell to the ground. She turned her melted face upwards and stared at him with pure hatred as her remaining arm clawed forward. *Die already, you fractal-forsaken abomination!* Rainier chopped his short sword through her neck and put an end to her misery.

"Get over here now!"

Rainier looked through the smoke to see Slate and Lira battling a host of Furies. They gave ground constantly, jumping across a rooftop that buckled in some places and blistered from the rising heat in others. At Sana's word, they abandoned the fight and dashed across the treacherous terrain.

Rainier turned and ran towards Sana and Ibson as well. He could see Ibson sitting on the pallet, which was now suspended beneath the zipline, motioning for Rainier to hurry. Sana held the rigging in place so that the pallet wouldn't move until the others got there. Slate flashed to the pallet with his inhuman speed and climbed aboard, easily beating Rainier to safety despite the longer distance he had to traverse. Lira, in her dimly lit armor, took a mighty leap over a hole in the roof and beat Rainier to the pallet. When it was his turn, he ungracefully dove headfirst into the group, forcing his way aboard while trying his best to avoid skewering himself on the pointy bits of his friends' weaponry. The second he was aboard, the Sicarius Headmaster pushed off the side of the building while holding onto the rigging above and the whole pallet slid down the black cable.

Rainier looked back to see one of the large blisters in the roof give way and a huge flame erupt from the building. The blast backlit the figures of a host of Bellator Furies rushing after them and diving from the roof towards the escaping pallet. Some of them fell to their death but others managed to grab the cable. It shook the pallet as the rigging moved up and down along the cable and Sana gave a worried look.

"Relax, Sana. Even if a couple of Furies manage to follow us down the cable, we can handle them." Rainier said with a smile. They whisked away from danger at an incredibly satisfying pace, descending towards the park with ever-increasing speed.

"That's not why I'm worried. I designed this zipline for one person. I always account for a lot of extra weight, so I wasn't too worried about all of us going down on the pallets, but those Furies jumping onto the cable add a lot of weight..."

The cable bobbed up and down worryingly, and then, as they entered the park, it gave way. The crew entered a freefall and the pallet smashed to the ground with a violent combination of crunching armor and rolling bodies. Rainier's sword smashed into his side as he tumbled away from the wreckage. He looked down and saw that it wasn't his sword hilt pressing into his side, but the blade itself, but it didn't cut him.

Ibson said with a groan, "I dulled the blades when the cable started to wobble. You're welcome." He got onto his knees and moved his limbs slowly, testing their abilities.

Everyone else did the same, and despite some obvious pains, they all survived the fall relatively intact.

"Still alive," Rainier said.

"As the pattern wills," Lira added, touching her holy armor, even though its blue luster was nearly completely gone. *I'll have to ask her about that later.*

"I think the Sicarius Headmaster, your shield, and my fist had more to do with it than the pattern." Slate said. *I couldn't agree more. I'll take Slate's fist by my side rather than pattern-based fervor any day.*

Lira spit on the ground. "You disgrace yourself with such comments."

"We can debate later. Magnus will be sending his troops in this direction. We need to disappear." Rosana said.

"I couldn't agree more." A voice came from the outskirts of the park. Everyone found their weapons, but Annarelle emerged before any of the Headmaster's knives were thrown in her direction. The blades disappeared and Rosana gave her a hug. "I saw the battle forming on the rooftops and I've arranged for a little surprise a few blocks from here. Can you make it that far?" Everyone looked to Ibson.

He gave a smoke-filled cough and said, "I'll make it if it gets me away from those flaming Furies I saw up there. Let's go." He started limping in the direction Annarelle had indicated.

Everyone else did their best to shake off their own injuries and follow Annarelle's lead. Slate put Ibson's arm around his shoulder to support his weight and hurry him along while Rainier took up the other side and did the same. *With Magnus here, I'm going to need Ibson more than ever. I may never trust him, but I need him, and if I hold his secrets, he needs me. Besides, Slate trusted a lot of people, and look where that got him. He can keep his trust. I'll settle for being useful, especially if it means that Ibson keeps using his defensive magic to keep me alive.*

The group struggled through the park, pushing towards a narrow side street. Rainier kept picturing the army of Furies running after them and gaining on them with each slow, belabored step from Ibson. When they reached the side street, they had a welcome surprise. Tommy stood at the front of a group of fighters from the Underground.

They wore a mixture of mismatched armor set against determined faces. *I wonder if that determination will turn to fear when they see a bunch of Furies running their way. Either way, I'm glad to put them between me and Magnus.* "It's good to see you Tommy!" Rainier said, and meant every word of it.

Tommy acknowledged Rainier's welcome, but the real greeting was given to Slate, who had helped him survive the halls of Ispirtu when he had minimal spark and became a target for any wizard needing one to boost their own morale. Tommy and Annarelle had bonded in those trying Ispirtu halls, and the help that Slate provided would not be forgotten. Tommy's embrace with Slate oozed of loyalty and devotion.

"I'm so glad you're back!" Tommy nearly crushed Slate in his excitement. "I wish you returned without so much fanfare though. Annarelle had the Underground on notice for tonight, but we didn't really expect you would need us."

"We planned on a nice quiet entrance into Ravinai, but one burning building and way-too-much fighting later, here we are." Slate quipped. "What do you have in store for us?"

"A safe exit from the fighting. You've had enough of it for the time being."

"You can't possibly expect to fight that many Furies without us..."

"I don't - so get out of here. You can watch from atop that hill if you'd like. We'll be fine." Tommy nearly shoved Slate through the line of men, and Rainier and the others followed. *You don't have to tell me twice. I'm happy to have a line of men between me and those crazy, red-eyed bastards.*

Annarelle stayed with Tommy and said, "I have a big part to play in the surprise. Where should I meet you afterwards?"

"The raven's nest that burned to the ground." Sana said, in reference to her childhood home.

"We'll see you there."

Then the group of wary warriors started traipsing up the hill. About halfway up, they heard a bunch of footsteps round the street corner and Magnus' amplified voice boomed through the streets.

"Look what we've found here — it's an Ispirtu wizard pretending to be a Bellator man and a girl playing dress-up as the Sicarius Headmaster. More traitors have come out to play." He laughed and held up his fist, stopping his army of Furies from rushing ahead. "Do you have any last words before we run through that collection of farm boys behind you?"

"Just this! I am the Sicarius Headmaster!" Annarelle stepped forward and hurled a throwing knife with a small blue orb in the hilt. It arced clumsily through the air and skittered across the road, well shy of the first line of Furies. Magnus rolled with laughter.

"You call that a knife throw. I once saw the Sicarius Headmaster throw a knife from a mountain ridge with enough accuracy to pin my foot to the ground. That was pathetic!" He laughed from the deepest of depths.

Annarelle yelled back, "You're right. I'm not any good at throwing knives." Annarelle threw her arms out wide and released the spell she had been holding. The blue orb on the hilt of the throwing knife exploded, triggering caches of exploding orbs hidden in surrounding crates and adjacent buildings. The exploding orbs created a deafening boom, and the chorus of destruction spread outwards at unbelievable speed. The buildings collapsed in an impressive display of rubble. By the time the explosions ended, an entire line of buildings collapsed, separating the two forces with a mountain of stone and dust.

Tommy yelled to his Underground troops, "Disband immediately. Find cover and blend into the city! Go now!" They all ran away, throwing cloaks over their armor as they ran towards wherever their favorite hiding place was located. Within seconds, Tommy stood alone with Annarelle as she screamed across the rubble.

"You and Lattimer will never win, Magnus! After one Sicarius Headmaster comes another, and we will never stop. Whether our knives fly true through the night or explode in the face of our enemies, they will always pack a punch. There will always be Sicarius!"

CHAPTER TEN

SCHEMES WITHIN SCHEMES

The warm rays of the morning sun failed to bring warmth to the cold remains of the Regallo estate. The night-cooled stones matched the melancholy mood of Sana and her lifetime of troubled memories from her childhood home. Rainier didn't dare try to cheer her up, and no one else had the courage to try either.

Rainier picked his way through the ruined estate, needing some meaningless activity to take his mind off the evening's events. He overturned some rubble and found a charred serving spoon. The metal was dented in obtuse angles from the falling rock walls and the handle had been burned away in the fire. He held it up to the group and asked, "Why did we meet here?"

"It's the last place in Malethya that Lattimer would expect me to go, so it's the best place for us to hide and make a plan." She shrugged, but it was the shrug of someone carrying a tremendous burden. Rainier didn't know what memories were weighing on her, but in some ways he didn't really care. He needed her to think straight and help figure this situation out. Thankfully, she shook her head to clear her thoughts and looked around at the group, which now included Tommy and Annarelle. When she spoke, it was the clear, logical brain of Sana that addressed them. "Let's start by finding out where everyone is and deciding how much time we have before we get smashed between two armies."

Sana unpacked a wooden box from her travel kit, opened the top to reveal a map with a bunch of pins and some Stratego medallions. She explained to the group, "Each of these Stratego medallions is one half of an entangled pair. Our friends carry the other Stratego medallion, and by casting a spell on the medallion I hold, I can sense where the paired medallion is within Malethya." She kept explaining but Rainier tuned her out. *Just let me know when you've figured out where everyone is.*

Rainier tossed a few smaller stones aside and discovered various other treasures beneath – a smashed jewelry box, a clock without a face, and a letter opener that was bent to the point of being almost unrecognizable. Then, beneath the rubble he thought he saw something. *Is that a soft glow under that pile of stones?*

Sana finished casting a spell and said to the group, "I can't see Jamison's army, but we know they are coming to Ravinai. Villifor is leading the Underground efforts to slow their progress. Meanwhile, Captain Sharan is leading Rainier's forces to Minot, who are being shepherded through the countryside by Jak and Lady Highsmith using contacts from the Underground. I can see Captain Sharan will arrive at Minot shortly, but Jak is halfway between here and Portswain. I can only surmise that he is bringing up the rear as Captain Sharan prepares her forces in Minot to attack Magnus and break the last totem carrying Slate's blood." She paused, before commenting, "Now we know Magnus is in Ravinai and our army is pointed the wrong way. On top of that, Lattimer knows we are here and has an army of Furies trying to flush us out."

You could just sum it up by saying we're screwed. Rainier kicked a rock, and the faint light became a dim glow. He turned over a few more stones and saw the source of the light. An exploding orb lay beneath the rubble, but the blue light swirling inside of it was a fraction of itself. Rainier thought back to his arrival in Ravinai when he joked that Ravinai, with its orbs lighting the streets, would be the only place Lira would be able to blend in with her holy armor. Then she fought, and the glow of her armor dimmed, to the point where it looked a lot like the orb in his hand. Rainier pocketed the dim orb and headed back to the group.

Slate was saying, "We had a good plan. Rainier tried to point Jamison's army at Lattimer's army and let them fight each other, leaving us to mop up the rest. We couldn't have known that Magnus had joined Lattimer in Ravinai."

Slate's comment triggered some dormant memory from Julian's past that pulled him from his thoughts about Lira and her armor. *Flash, flash...fl-flash. A defeated king looked to Julian right before he signed the treaty papers to end the fighting, giving over his country's land, wealth, and people to the conquering Disenites. He said, "Our generals had a great plan." Flash, fla flash.* Rainier chuckled at the fractured memories that broke into his mind and gave Julian's response to the group. "Everyone has a great plan. Then the fighting starts."

Ibson laughed, and soon everyone else did as well. If ever there was a group that appreciated some good gallows humor, it was a group of people that allowed a blood mage to take power and now found themselves stuck between two armies with their only allies pointing in

282 J. Lloren Quill

the wrong direction.

"Our names didn't join the dead last night. That's good enough for me." Annarelle said and Rainier could see Rosana silently mouthing a lengthy list that had no meaning to Rainier.

"So, what do we do?" Tommy asked.

Silence lingered like the morning chill, and Rainier let his mind wander. He found himself playing out scenarios as if it were a game of standing stones. *Jamison is pointed at Lattimer. Lattimer looks for us, but his attention will be diverted when Jamison arrives. At least there are two parts of the board where the pieces are clear. Then there's our little group. Slate and Sana are determined in their efforts to kill Magnus and destroy the totem. They control the Underground and the Sicarius Guild, and yet they have been hesitant to use them. Then there is Ibson and his secrets in Minot, powerful secrets that could alter the course of the war. Secrets that I now control.* Rainier glanced at Ibson to find the wizard staring, pleading with him to tell the group everything he knew. *I could tell them now, old man, and I'm sure that's what you would do. But secrets are like a game of standing stones. Once they are played, they are there for everyone to see. If I make my best move now, Lattimer and Jamison will have time to respond, and that's before Julian even entered the game.* Rainier gave Ibson a wink and shook his head no. Ibson snorted, threw his hands up in disgust, and walked away from the group, confusing the others that had missed the exchange. *Let him be mad. He's bound to me and the choice is mine.* To the group, though, Rainier played the peacemaker by saying, "I'll go see what's wrong."

He ran to catch up with Ibson, who had stalked into the grounds of the estate behind the mansion. When he heard Rainier approaching, he turned and lectured, "You should have told your friends my secret. They are grasping for hope, and you are playing games."

"Do you remember who won our game of standing stones?" Rainier asked, but didn't wait for a response. "I did, and I was toying with you. I happen to be fairly good at games, and I've spent my entire life trying to fool the people around me into thinking I'm someone I'm not." A little bit of anger slipped into his tone and he said, "More importantly, you made a deal with me. You may question whether you should have made the deal, or you may regret it entirely, but you made an unbreakable bond, and I expect you to play along with all my schemes until I see fit to share your secrets. Do I make myself clear, or do we have a problem? If we do, then you can sit and stew in silence while your secrets die with me and live in the hope that someone, someday, will be able to break your bonds to Minot."

Rainier glared at Ibson, daring him to play his bluff, and the old wizard wilted under his stare. He said with contempt, "I'll follow your schemes, but watch your back when the bond is finally broken. I'm not someone who is used to being played." *Get used to it. You made a deal with the Remnant and sealed it with magic.*

"When we survive this mess, the Disenites have been pushed off our shores, and Lattimer is dead, then we'll see if your hatred for me still burns that deep. Personally, I'd prefer a thank you." *What's with these crusty old bastards always thinking they have some type of ownership over me. Forsake that.*

"Humph." Ibson crossed his arms across his chest. "What's the next part in your brilliant scheme, oh wise oracle?"

"I'm glad you asked." Rainier took the dim orb out of his pocket and tossed it to Ibson. "I found this in the wreckage of the Regallo estate."

"It's a burnt-out orb. What of it?"

"Did you see Lira's armor fade while she was fighting? It looked like this orb."

"It must have been losing its enchantment." Ibson stated, as if speaking to a child.

"Can an orb be refilled? Do you know how to do it? Could you recharge Lira's armor?"

Ibson frowned and said, "Since I don't think you are asking a question so much as telling me to do it, then the answer is yes, I can refill an orb. As for Lira's armor...I don't know. I never got into making enchanted artifacts. I was always more on the theoretical side of magic rather than practical side, but I may be able to recharge one if I had a source to draw from."

Rainier laughed and said, "You're holding it. Now hide it and follow my lead when we talk to Lira." He patted Ibson on the back and said, "We'll teach you to swindle with the grace of the Remnant yet."

Ibson didn't grin. *Fine, don't take my compliment. You could live forever and never learn the skills I've honed. But if you're willing to take orders from me, at least you'll stay useful.*

Rainier led Ibson back to the group with a cheerful whistle, just to drive home the point to Ibson that his causing a scene had led to this point – with Rainier getting exactly what he wanted. While he whistled, he pondered his bigger problem, which involved two armies large enough to crush them even if he managed to get Sharan's troops from Minot down to Ravinai before Jamison showed up. By the time they reached the group, Rainier reached a conclusion that he didn't enjoy.

"We need to make contact with Lattimer." Rainier announced. He didn't know all the answers, but he needed an avenue to influence the blood mage.

"Are you crazy!?" Annarelle asked, and now it was Tommy's turn to snort and throw up his hands in disgust.

"You wish to speak to the Blasphemer?" Lira spat on the ground.

"You should know better than to trust him, Rainier. I've already made that mistake." Slate said with the deepest of regret.

"I am the leader of the Remnant. I don't trust anyone."

Only Sana, with a cold and calculating tone, asked, "Why do you want to speak with him?"

"Because fooling him is our best chance of surviving." Rainier said, only realizing the truth to his words after he had spoken them aloud. "Once we survive, then we can set about our business of killing him again. Besides, Slate needs to be close to him to kill him, right? How else do you plan to get close when he has an army in front of him? Wouldn't it be easier if you were standing by his side?"

"How do you plan to fool him?"

Good question. Ibson answered on his behalf, from firsthand experience. "You find leverage." *Maybe the old wizard can learn a new trick or two.*

Rainier expanded on Ibson's answer by saying, "...which we don't have, so we need to convince him that we have something he wants. Rosana, didn't you say that he has tried to get you and Slate to lead his army?"

"Yes, but that bridge is burned. I killed Phoenix and vowed to stop him. He won't believe we want to help him now."

"We know he wanted it at one point, so that's the best lead we have." Rainier was thinking out loud. "We could help our chances if we manage to kill Magnus and make it look like Jamison did it. Then we would increase our leverage by knocking out another totem. Lattimer would have a harder time controlling his army and have a bigger need for us." *It also keeps Slate and Sana fully committed. They get what they want – a dead Magnus. And I get what I want – Jamison and Lattimer squaring off against each other and thinning out their forces without committing my own.*

"Then I'd be free to go after Lattimer again." Slate said anxiously.

Sana took a while longer to think about it, but she finally said, "I may have a way to get in contact with Lattimer...we could use my mother." Rainier thought he saw Rose cringe, but it was obvious she had already agreed with Sana's reasoning in principle and acquiesced to the decision. "She dines at the Refined Palate regularly, and I have an arrangement with the manager. She doesn't know Lattimer is a blood mage and wouldn't believe me if I told her, but I think she would still deliver a message if she knew it was from me."

"Why would your own mother not recognize you?" Lira

asked.

"She thinks I'm dead. I'll have to show her that I'm not." Even though Sana delivered the message, she couldn't hide Rose's exuberance at the news. "I'll get to talk with my mother for the first time since I left Ispirtu!"

"I better go with to stand guard while they talk." Slate said.

"I guess Rosana is finally bringing you home to meet her parents, huh, Slate? At least that is as close as you are going to get under the current circumstances." Rainier laughed and added to Rosana, "You better give him a good disguise. You wouldn't want to give your mom a heart attack when she finds out that her long-lost, presumed-dead daughter is dating the man that Caitlyn believes is half demon. Even I would have a hard time talking myself out of that one."

Slate stammered, "Umm...yeah...that might be a good idea. She might need to warm up to me."

"So, what do we put in the note?" Tommy asked, bringing them back to the matter at hand.

The group deliberated for some time, and they ended up with a cryptic but clear message of support.

Dear Brother,

Our last few encounters were heavy on throwing knives and fireballs. I'm hoping that the next time we meet, it will be on a battlefield with dead Disenites at our feet, and we have time for words rather than weapons.

The Disenite army is marching to your doorstep. They are led by a high priest named Jamison, and he has an army of paladins driven forward by religious fervor and protected by enchanted armor. They can move with extraordinary strength and speed.

I realize that you have little reason to believe me but keep an eye open in battle. When the tide turns unexpectedly, look closely, and you may find me and my friends there. Hopefully, this act will prove my intentions. I may not believe in the Malethya you rule, but I don't believe in handing over my country to crazed Disenite zealots either. We need to act for the good of all Malethya.

Your sister,

P.S. Their weapons and armor shine bright blue and their power is somehow connected to the orbs. Consider that piece of information free, and if you know one thing about your sister, it's that I value information above all else. Use it wisely.

"What do you think?" Annarelle asked Tommy.

"I'm sure he expects a trap, but maybe the concept will intrigue him enough for us to say a few words instead of just killing us outright."

"With any luck, it will at least make him concentrate his efforts in the coming days on preparing for battle rather than hunting us down. That would be a win, too." Slate said.

"There's no harm in sending it. If it creates even a moment of hesitation when we meet him next, it may be the moment we need to kill him," said the Sicarius Headmaster.

"It is not honorable...but it has some advantages." Lira conceded.

Ibson still tried to kill Rainier with a withering stare, but Rainier would have none of it. The old man would have to keep his secrets a bit longer. Rainier smiled with a little extra exuberance, just to rub it in the old wizard's face a little more and said cheerfully, "Well, that's good enough for me. Why don't the two of you prepare for your visit to the Refined Palate, and we'll keep strategizing."

Rosana looked up at the sun, judged the time, and said, "Yes, we'll need to hurry if we are going to get disguises and get to the Refined Palate. My mother has always been a creature of habit, and according to her normal schedule, she'll be arriving at the restaurant in a little over an hour. Annarelle, do you still have the safe house down in the market?"

"Of course. It's fully stocked with clothes, make-up, wigs, and a host of weapons."

"You're the best. Be safe and keep your name off the list of past Sicarius Headmasters." Rosana gave her a parting hug as she and Slate turned to leave the group.

"I'll be fine — I had a better teacher than they did." Annarelle shouted after her.

They watched them walk away in relative silence. Slate and Sana were the two people that tied all of them together, in one way or the other. Without them, it felt less like a group. *That suits me just fine. I don't want to be tied to anyone but myself.* Rainier looked at Ibson, who he was tied to with an unbreakable bond, and Lira in her dulled armor that had devoted her life to protecting him. *I guess that makes me a hypocrite.* The sight of Lira brought a question to mind that had been bothering him, though, and this seemed as good a time as any to ask.

"Lira, your armor dimmed during battle. What happened?"

Lira's fingertips danced across her armor, caressing the intricate patterns of the Marked faction on its surface. "The priests and priestesses fractal-bless our armor before battle, and their prayers help us maintain strength while we fight. I am a long way from our priests, and I don't think anyone will be coming to bless my armor. I'm afraid my skills as your Hand have been greatly diminished."

"Can an oracle fractal-bless your armor?"

Lira snorted. She said, "You have proven that the pattern has blessed you with gifts, but I don't think this is one of them."

I couldn't bless a meal without an extra serving of hot air dished up alongside it. The chances of me enchanting someone's armor are worse than the odds that I strike a fair deal out of the kindness of my heart. Thankfully, Lira doesn't need to know that, and I've got an endless supply of white lies at my disposal. "Why don't you let me give it a shot? It's not like we have anything to lose, and we have some time before Slate and Rosana return." Rainier reached out for her armor with an open hand.

Lira hesitated, not wishing to part with her holy armor, but in the end, she passed it over to Rainier with a heavy dose of skepticism mixed with the slightest hint of hope. "You may try."

Rainier took the armor with gentle hands and placed it across his lap while sneaking a slight nod towards Ibson, who joined him by his side. Then he rubbed his hands over the armor in elaborate fashion, knocking a spaulder over the edge of his legs to dangle. Out of the corner of his eye, Rainier saw Ibson reach out and touch the dangling spaulder with one hand, while the other hand remained in the pocket containing the dimmed orb.

Once Ibson touched the armor, Rainier said in his holiest voice, "I bless this armor with the pattern." He finished his hand motions with a flourish and the armor did...nothing. *Come on, Ibson! This is the part where you make this light up.* Rainier squinted his eyes in feigned concentration, leaving just enough of a slit in his vision to see if the armor was doing anything. *Any time, Ibson! His arms started to tremble and just when he was running out of gimmicky magical movements to try out, it happened.*

The Marked faction tracings turned a brilliant blue, creating a beautiful pattern of fenestrated lines etched across the surface of the armor.

Lira gasped.

Then, the brilliant blue stopped abruptly, and the color diffused into the armor until it reached a dull steadiness. After all the theatrics, Rainier found the dull metal result rather anti-climactic.

Lira had other thoughts. She grabbed her armor and exclaimed, "You did it! You blessed my armor!" She gave Rainier a hug and tears streamed down her eyes. "You have no idea what this means to me!" She let go of him, looked down at her armor, and said, "Do it again! I'll stay here all day if it means my armor will be whole again."

Rainier coughed to buy himself time while concocting his next lie. He took Lira by the shoulders and said, "As you said, I have been blessed by the pattern, but I am no priest."

She looked confused, and Rainier rushed on before it turned to skepticism.

"I could not simply bless your armor. I needed to transfer the energy from a blessed object into it, instead." He motioned to Ibson, who revealed the orb from his pocket, now completely devoid of color.

Ibson said, "This orb used to be blessed."

Rainier said, "Do you remember the blue orbs your priests create for your cannons? They are blessed, and the orbs in Ravinai are remarkably similar. I think I can restore your armor, but I'll need more blessed orbs to do it."

The confused look didn't really disappear, but Lira said, "If I find some more of these orbs, you can restore my armor?"

"Yes. I think I can." Rainier deflected his head downwards with a solemnness that reflected the seriousness in Lira's face.

"Then I'll go collect some orbs and bring them back to you."

Ibson offered, "I can go with you. Some of these orbs do different things like taking an image of your face, alerting Lattimer's forces, or exploding." He smirked and said, "I wouldn't want a pretty thing like you to find one that explodes."

Lira's face hardened and she said, "Keep those comments to yourself. I left the last person that spoke to me that way curled up on the deck of the *Remnant Awakens* clutching his manhood and swallowing his pride."

"Point taken!" Ibson enthused. He slapped her on the back and said, "Let's go find some orbs!"

Lira shrugged his hand off her shoulder and walked away, with Ibson hustling to keep up.

Rainier watched the odd couple walk off and then turned his attention to Tommy and Annarelle, only to find Tommy already looking at him.

He said, "I don't remember you doing any magic back when we assaulted the Ispirtu tower. What was that? I may not have the strongest spark, but I know magic when I see it."

How to explain the lie they just saw? I could just ignore them, but that was a test of sorts, and now that I know the outcome, I have to win these two over. Don't fail me now, Remnant charm. Rainier flashed a grin and said, "You caught me. But I wasn't the one doing magic. Ibson did it."

"Why would you pretend to 'bless' her armor instead of just telling her that Ibson could cast a spell to recharge it?" Annarelle asked.

"Lira is a Disenite, and our form of magic is nearly blasphemous in their eyes. Even wizards like Ibson use some spark to cast their spells, and that is frowned upon by their priests, who are taught to hold the pattern above all else. If she knew that Ibson was responsible for recharging her armor..."

"...she wouldn't have allowed it." Annarelle finished. "She needed her armor 'blessed' and not recharged."

"And you thought it was better to lie to her and have her armor powered up than it was to tell the truth?" Tommy asked. "She's your friend."

Rainier shook his head. "She's my Hand — my bodyguard, but even more than that. She has devoted her life to protecting me. With two armies bearing down on us, she needs every advantage she can get if I'm going to keep her alive through all of this. Would you rather I told the truth and have her die the next time Lattimer's troops find us?"

Tommy gave in and said, "I suppose not..."

"I understand." Annarelle said. "As the Sicarius Headmaster, I've had to do things I'm not proud of, but they were always necessary." *That's good, but there is a difference between you and me. I don't regret the lie I just told, and I won't regret manipulating you now.*

Rainier stared earnestly at Annarelle and said, "You see the difficult situation I'm in. It's even more difficult because Slate is blinded with altruism and Rosana is blinded by love."

"Slate always tries to do the right thing!" Tommy defended his friend vehemently.

Rainier put up his hands, "I know. I know. That's my point." He said, "Slate will run through a brick wall if he thinks it's the right thing to do, but he won't stop to see if there's a door to walk through. Think of the assault on Ispirtu. He trusted his friends to a fault, and Lattimer played him like a fractal-forsaken fool. He knew that if he could convince Slate that Brannon was the blood mage, then Slate wouldn't stop until he was dead."

"He got fooled. It could have happened to any of us..."

"But maybe it's up to us to make sure it doesn't happen to him again."

Tommy went silent and Annarelle raised her own objection. "Rosana isn't blinded by love. She has Sana to balance out her emotion with strategy and logic. She tied up Slate and went on a suicide mission at Minot just because she thought that sacrificing herself and keeping Slate alive was our best chance of success against Lattimer."

Rainier nodded, but looked at her and chuckled softly. "You're right. Sana isn't blinded by Rosana's love for Slate. She's blinded by you."

Annarelle gaped at him. "What do you mean?"

"She is so afraid of you adding your name to the list of dead Sicarius Headmaster's that she will do anything to protect you. Ask yourself this — how many missions have you gone on? Have you gone on any, or have you just been the recruitment specialist for the Guild?"

Annarelle frowned. "The Guild needed to be rebuilt. I did what needed to be done, like every Sicarius Headmaster has done."

Rainier nodded. "It was an extremely important role, and we owe you our lives. I don't think any of us would have made it away from Magnus and his Furies last night if it weren't for you both and the people you've trained." He put his hands up in a placating manner and continued, "But aren't there nights when you are racing across the rooftops, you see one of Lattimer's officers, and wish you could have taken him out, but you stayed your hand? Do you think you could have done more than building the Sicarius Guild if you had the freedom to act on your own instincts?" *I'm taking a chance on this one, but Annarelle must have had moments of frustration as she stayed in Ravinai rebuilding what Sana had lost.*

Annarelle frowned deeper, and she hesitated as she spoke. "I would never disobey Rosana. She has given me everything."

She hesitated, so at least she's listening, but I can't push too hard. "I would never ask you to disobey Rosana. She has your best intentions in mind." He looked over to Tommy to make sure he included him in the conversation. "Our troops are spread across Malethya and heading the wrong way. What do you think Slate and Sana will ask you to do when they get back?"

Tommy pondered for a second and said, "We'll need to aid the movements of our troops through the Underground and coordinate our efforts using the Sicarius network." Annarelle nodded, but Rainier could tell her mind was drifting towards the unstated question in her mind. *I'll state it for her.*

"That would bring you within spitting distance of the biggest army to invade our shores since the Twice-Broken Wars. What if you could accomplish the mission that Sana gives you and still have an opportunity to cripple Jamison's forces before they arrive here?" Rainier held his breath, because the next response would determine if his efforts had been in vain.

The moment strung out, with Tommy looking at Annarelle, having an unspoken conversation that only lovers can have. Tommy didn't take his eyes off Annarelle as he said, "If we completed our mission first, we owe it to everyone to do what we can to hamper Jamison, right?" *I have Tommy convinced, but he was never the one I worried about.*

Annarelle's frown deepened, but she said, "How would we hurt Jamison?" *I have them!* Rainier exhaled in a controlled manner, careful to not let them see his relief. Inside though, he had the same thrill he felt with every negotiation won and every deal successfully swindled.

"Jamison's army has cannons and other weapons powered by their priests. I don't know how they make them, but they create orbs, distribute them to the paladins in their army, and use them while casting spells. If someone with the right skills can find where they keep the orbs and destroy them, the whole army will be affected."

Annarelle said, "You mean someone with the skills of Sicarius to infiltrate their army that also has a natural talent for triggering explosive orbs?"

Rainier smirked and said, "You wouldn't happen to know anyone like that, would you? Just imagine the damage you could cause if you snuck an exploding orb into their storage facility and triggered it..."

Annarelle finally smiled. She said, "That would be a story worth telling."

"I'm not going to tell you what you should or shouldn't do. You'll make that choice on your own, with your own hearts, to do what's best for Malethya." Rainier spread his arms out wide to emphasize the obvious choice. "Slate and Sana will be back in a few hours, and you'll know your primary mission. Maybe you should spend this time in preparation for any secondary endeavors that your heart will guide you in?" *Just keep thinking about that story they'll tell about you after your victory against the Disenites.* Rainier gave a Remnant smile.

Annarelle said, "Our primary mission will always come first, but if we can help more after we complete our mission, then we'll do what we can to help Malethya. We all need to do our part." Tommy nodded in agreement and said, "We'll make some preparations and give you a final answer after we meet up later and receive our primary mission."

They turned to leave, and Rainier said to their backs as they walked away, "You are a testament to what is good in Malethya. Fractal's blessings to you both." *Did I really just say that? I sound like one of those Marked priests, the pompous bastards. Oh well, if it convinces them to do what I need them to do, then I'll be as pompous and righteous as I need to be.*

He watched them walk away and realized that he was alone for the first time since being locked away in a Disenite jail cell. No priests, no paladins, no Hand sleeping in his cabin. He exhaled deeply and took a moment to appreciate being alive. The pattern knew there had been plenty of times in the past few months when survival had been anything but assured. As strange as it sounds, the rocks strewn about the Regallo estate were the closest thing to safety and comfort he had felt in some time. He sat down and leaned against a rock that overlooked the city. The sun was rising, birds were singing, and he had just manipulated all his friends into doing exactly what he wanted them to do. *What could be better?* He let his eyes close with a smile on his face as he drifted to sleep. *Maybe things will turn out ok after all...*

Rainier stood before the Nameless Army in a field of battle, where Lattimer's troops lay in ruin. The army banged their shields in appreciation of their oracle, and he heard himself give a victory speech. "Today, you fought a foe that held no regard for the pattern. You have returned their blasphemous bodies to the ground and stopped their treacherous ways. You have fulfilled your bonds of service to the Nameless Army with honor and helped restore the pattern!" More banging of shields and shaking of swords filled the air. "May you all leave this battle with your hearts filled for restoring honor to the land of Malethya, but before you go, Julian the Immortal would like to say a few words."

The stomping stopped immediately out of respect for the Immortal and Rainier turned his head, noticing for the first time that he stood beside Lira and Julian. Julian announced to the crowd, "As Rainier Tallow has said, you all deserve to be congratulated on this day, but let's not forget the man that led you to victory, your oracle!" Thunderous approval pounded into the ground with stomping feet. "As many of you return to Disentia, this land will need a leader that can teach the ways of the pattern to its wayward people. I can think of no one better than Rainier Tallow, who I name as Regent over all of Malethya, serving in my place as I return home."

Rainier gazed over the adoring masses as they banged their shields and raised their swords. Then, before his eyes, the undulating motions of the crowd took on the shape of a face – a crusty face that belonged to Rainier's least favorite Immortal. The crowd moved, forming a mouth that opened and closed. When he spoke, the words reverberated within his body. "The rewards for those that serve me are great." The strength of the words bouncing around his head forced him to close his eyes. When he reopened them, the face was gone, and the Nameless Army stood shaking their swords again.

Before he could breathe a sigh of relief though, Julian addressed the crowd from his side. "You have persevered

in your fight against blood magic in Malethya, despite the
failings of Rainier Tallow, who once held the title of oracle,
but has failed to utilize the gifts given to him in the name
of the pattern. Rainier Tallow, I sentence you to death."
Rainier looked down to see that he was on his knees. He
frantically looked around and then up, only to see Lira
standing above him with her sword aimed down at his
neck. She didn't say a word. She just pushed his head
towards his knees and plunged her sword into the base of
his neck. The pain was blinding, and when the pain was at
its peak, he heard Julian's voice again, bouncing around in
his skull. "The price for those that fail me is grave. Have
you found the blood mages and eliminated them yet?"

"I have found them. I have found them."

"Then kill them. DO. NOT. FAIL. ME. Your time grows
short."

Rainier awoke in a fright and sat straight up. His hand
shot to the back of his neck as he frantically looked for the
entrance wound that took his life. Only when he
repeatedly felt smooth, uninterrupted skin after patting
his neck repeatedly did he realize that he had just received
another message from Julian in his dreams.

He looked around to see the remains of the Regallo
estate, and he began to regain his senses. Then he noticed
that Ibson and Lira had returned and were laying out orbs
next to her armor. *How long have I been out?*

Lira looked at him and asked, "Are you all right? It looks
like you've seen a ghost."

Rainier tried to give a light-hearted chuckle as he said,
"I just received a message from Julian the Immortal again."

Lira beamed. "What did his holiness say? You are so

blessed!"

Blessed — that's not the first word that comes to mind. "He sends his encouragement and promises that he is coming soon to grace us with his presence." *Hopefully, I can keep my head attached to my body after he reaches our shores. So much for feeling good about things.*

"Excellent! We found some orbs that you can use to bless my armor. Will you perform the blessing?"

Why not? I can waive my hands around with the best of them. "Of course, Lira."

Rainier walked over to where they had prepared the armor. He waved his arms in various gesticulations while Ibson cast the spell and then held a look of intense concentration as the armor began to shine. First, the markings lit up, and then slowly, ever so slowly, the metal began to regain its blue hue. *This is taking forever! What's wrong with Ibson.* Rainier strained his voice and asked Lira, "Does it take the priests this much effort to bless your armor?"

"When the priests bless our armor, it regains its holiness immediately."

Rainier looked to Ibson and found the old man with sweat on his brow, trying not to look fatigued from overexertion. He said to Rainier, "Your method of blessing must not be as efficient as what the priests do. Maybe we should stop?"

Rainier nodded, and Ibson's shoulders sagged in exhaustion. Through his efforts though, the armor took on a bright blue coloring. Lira was beyond grateful and gave Rainier a hug, much to the chagrin of Ibson, who was never opposed to a hug from an attractive female.

Rainier looked down at the pile of orbs they had gathered and saw that most of them had dimmed. He recalled the orbs on the ship. He said, "Lira, when you witnessed the army firing the cannons at sea, how many orbs did they use?"

She said, "Each cannon had a single orb, but they didn't replace it after firing. It was still brightly lit."

Ibson commented, gesturing to the pile of dimmed orbs. "I guess you aren't as holy as you think you are."

"It's worked for now. Lira's armor is blessed. Maybe you should work through a few forms to make sure everything is working normally?" he asked Lira and she complied immediately, eager to use her holy armor again. "Just don't use up too much of your blessing!" He yelled after her as she ran to the grounds in the rear of the estate to get in some practice swings.

He then looked at the pile of orbs and pointed to the few remaining lit orbs. "Ibson, can you grab those few remaining orbs and keep them in your pocket? We don't know when we'll need them next." Ibson started to pick them up, and Rainier couldn't help but ask, "What happened back there? Why didn't that work the way we thought."

An exhausted Ibson spat back, "I told you I never spent time learning to enchant artifacts. Some of my students, like Julian for example, had a natural inclination towards that type of spellcasting. Apparently, he's improved his techniques substantially since going to Disentia. Just be grateful I was able to recharge her at all, you ungrateful little twit."

"This ungrateful little twit is going to remove an

unbreakable bond that you placed on yourself, you old fool. Don't condemn me for your past failures." *And keep doing what I say, or you'll be bound to your mistakes forever.*

What was bound to be an uncomfortable silence was broken before it began, as Slate and Sana approached from one end of the street, and Tommy and Annarelle came from the other. When they all met Ibson and Rainier, Slate looked over towards Lira and said, "You've got her armor juiced up again. That's good — that shield of hers was a big help against all those Furies. How'd you do it?"

"Rainier blessed her armor." Ibson said with a heavy dose of sarcasm.

Before they dove too far into the subject, Rainier asked Rosana, "How did it go with Caitlyn? Will your mother help us?"

Rose beamed and said, "We snuck her into the manager's office, and I revealed who I was. When she realized that I was her daughter, and I wasn't making it up, she cried tears of joy and gave me a huge hug. I haven't been hugged by mother since I was a little child." Tears welled up in her own eyes as she told the story, but then Rosana took over for Rose so that she wouldn't be overwhelmed. "Caitlyn implored us to come with her back to the castle. She thought Lattimer would be ecstatic to find his long-lost sister again, and she spoke glowingly of her only son who had garnered King Darik's favor even after the indiscretions of Brannon." Rosana spoke in a tone that left no doubts regarding her opinion of her mother's comments. Caitlyn would not be convinced that Lattimer was anything but benevolent. "Naturally, I told her I wished I could, but circumstances would not allow it. I gave her the note and said the main reason I contacted her was so that she could give a message to my brother. I told her I wanted to help him in the coming war with the Disenites, and that family is stronger than any bond. Tell him that I'll be there for him, and that the details are in the note."

"Lattimer won't believe that." Annarelle said.

"No, he won't, but it was what a mother wanted to hear from her long-lost daughter. She wants her son and daughter to work together and bring honor to the family name. It will be enough for her to give the message to Lattimer. That's the best I was hoping for..."

"You did great, Rosana." Slate put his arm around her and gave a comforting squeeze. "And I'm happy you were able to see your mother again." Then he looked over to Tommy and Annarelle and asked, "What were you two up to?"

Annarelle answered for them both, "With the two of you being gone, we took the opportunity to check on the Underground and the Sicarius network. We managed to survive the night with minimal Underground casualties. The blast provided sufficient cover for the resistance fighters to escape. In the Sicarius Guild, we weren't as lucky. We lost several Guildsmen last night as we fought from the rooftops." Her voice cracked a little at the end, and Rosana gave her a hug.

"It's never easy to see one of our shadows in the night turn dark forever."

"Did Caitlyn mention any of Lattimer's plans? Was there any other useful information that came from your conversation?" Tommy asked Slate so that Rosana and Annarelle could have a moment.

"The only thing she mentioned in conversation was that King Darik would be leading the army onto the field and that she was so proud to know her son was at his right hand."

Tommy laughed. "...at his right-hand whispering commands. We all know who rules Malethya now, even if Darik wears the crown. The populace may be ignorant, but we were there when Lattimer subjugated King Darik's mind."

"Yes, but it is still significant. If Darik is leading the army to the field, then it will be easier for us to track his movements. He lives in the palace and will be marching with an army. That's a lot easier task than trying to keep up with a blood mage and whatever spells are at his disposal."

Tommy nodded in agreement with Slate while Rainier saw that the ladies had finished their little moment of Sicarius time. "Well, if we're done talking about our days, let's figure out how to win the fight in front of us." *And since I've already set them down the path, I'll let them reach the conclusion on their own.*

Annarelle and Rosana looked hurt, but Sana said, "I couldn't agree more."

"My army is spread out and we'll need them for the battle." *Although I'm hoping to avoid sending them into the worst of the fighting anyways.* "I need to get to Minot and bring Captain Sharan back as quickly as possible, but Jamison's forces are coming too quickly. I won't make it back here in time."

"And word needs to be given to Jak and Lady Highsmith to stop shuttling people to Minot and redirect them to Ravinai." Sana looked to Annarelle and asked, "Could you and Tommy do that and meet back up with us? It sounds like we'll need to plan a few surprises outside of Ravinai to slow down Jamison's forces and buy Rainier some time. I think Slate and I can manage that, and it will give me a chance to track the movements of Lattimer's army. I'm not sure what the main battle will bring, so I want to have as much information as possible."

"Of course, Headmaster." Annarelle said. "We'll plan to use the Stratego medallions to meet up with Jak and Lady Highsmith and redirect them to Ravinai." Sana nodded, but Rainier kept his eyes on Annarelle. He could see her head spinning with possibilities, and Rainier had already planted the seed of the idea he wanted her to land on. *She's sending you away from the action again, protecting you from danger when you know you can help more. You can DO more, if Rosana would let you. You could do something like...triggering a few exploding orbs and destroying the supply of orbs that power the invading army...* Annarelle's face set determinedly, and she looked directly into Rainier's eyes.

She nodded.

Rainier kept his smile hidden as he turned back to the group, afraid that Rosana would read his face and know something was up. He managed to stay impassive as the group discussed the details of their plans, listening but not really caring. As only the absolute best swindlers in the Remnant could do, he had managed to win the argument before it took place, and now he had what he wanted without saying a thing.

When they finished discussing, Rainier said to the group, "Ibson, Lira and I better get going. We'll be slowed on our way back from Minot, so we better leave at once. Thank you all for your efforts. I didn't realize when I left Malethya that I'd be bringing someone like Jamison back."

Rose stopped him and said, "You left to get help. Without you, we would be fighting Lattimer by ourselves, and we know he is too strong for that."

Slate agreed by saying, "It takes an army to fight an army, and you've provided that. We'll prep everything we can for when you get back, but none of us have experience leading an army. We'll need you when the battle begins."

Rainier nodded, pretending to gather his confidence when he just wanted them to realize how much they needed him. He said, "Thank you. We won't let Lattimer or the Disenites have Malethya. This is our home, and we'll win it back." *And I will twist whatever needs to be twisted, turn whatever needs to be turned, and manipulate whoever I need to manipulate to make sure that Julian, Lattimer, and Jamison die for what they've done. I won't let them hurt anyone again. I owe it to Kalus and to my family. I owe it to the Remnant.*

CHAPTER ELEVEN

WHY DO WE ALWAYS END UP IN MINOT?

The wind blew through Rainier's hair as he flew across the plains of Malethya, carrying with it a joy that he hadn't felt in far too long. The horse beneath him strove ahead, reaching for the horizon at his urging, and working up a happy lather. Each bounce of the saddle reminded him of his childhood. Each gust of wind reminded him of his nomadic youth.

With each hoof that landed, the horse carried Rainier one step further from Lattimer and his Furies, one step further from Jamison and his Marked priests, and one step further from Julian and his haunting dreams. *Could I just keep riding? Could I go straight past Minot, into the mountains, and keep going until no one found me?* The fantasy held some appeal, but Rainier wasn't prone to fantasies. He knew that with each pounding of the hoof, he'd remember riding with Kalus and the rest of the Remnant. Every night he stopped to build a fire, and his only company would be of his dead friend. Every step would fill him with regret. *I made a promise, Kalus, and I'll try to see it through.*

So instead, Rainier urged his horse towards Minot and rode as quickly as his company could keep up. They spoke little, and Rainier had no desire to break the silence. A hard ride required concentration. Any misstep could be a broken leg for his horse, and then he'd really be in trouble, so he focused on the trail and pounded ahead. It wasn't until they reached the woods surrounding Minot that the group slowed down, and only then because the trail demanded it.

They winded through the woods towards the location that the Stratego medallion had indicated. They passed through a blight-infested patch of forest where the trees rotted, the leaves wilted, and maggots feasted. The wind that had just felt so good as he rode across the plains now carried away diseased leaves. *As if we don't have enough to worry about right now. If we survive this war, the blight might kill us anyway.* They passed through the diseased forest and slowed their speed, knowing that they were nearing Sharan and not wanting to startle whoever they rode upon. Rainier continued to check the enlightened path as they approached and didn't sense any immediate danger.

"Stop where you are!" A voice called from a tree. Rainier looked up to find a man with a bow-and-arrow pointed at his chest. *So much for not sensing any danger. I'm either losing my touch or this guy isn't a real threat.*

"I hope you are under the command of Captain Sharan!" Rainier called back as he slowed his horse to a stop. "Otherwise, I've made a terrible mistake."

Once they stopped, a number of other soldiers stepped out of the woods, both ahead and behind them. "Who are you and what is your purpose in these woods?"

"I'm Rainier Tallow, the esteemed Oracle of the Nameless Army, come to talk with Captain Sharan, who leads my forces in my absence." Questioning looks between the soldiers told Rainier they were less than convinced. "You may not recognize me when I'm not wearing those robes that Jamison insisted upon, but at the very least, you have to admit we probably didn't come from Lattimer's forces in Minot." He motioned towards Lira, "After all, you don't see fully armored paladins in Malethya very often."

More questioning looks, but the soft, comforting light of the enlightened path never wavered. The man in the tree kept his head and said, "We'll escort you to Captain Sharan. If any of you make any noise or sudden movements, you'll be dead."

Rainier knew from his time with Lira that seriousness was a trait inherent to the job, and so the group walked in silence until they came into a small clearing in the woods, where a temporary base had been built. There were no tents or other structures associated with a large army, but there was clearly order and professionalism in the setup of the camp.

They headed towards the very center of camp, which had some logs arranged in a circle. Rainier saw Captain Sharan engrossed in conversation with her high-ranking officers around a map spread across the level ground. She looked up upon their arrival, and she smiled for the first time Rainier could remember.

"Welcome, Rainier!"

"Could you tell them we're welcome?" Rainier asked, referring to the armed men and women surrounding him. "I don't want to get poked with anything sharp today."

"Lower your weapons and get back to your posts!" She

ordered and then turned back to Rainier. "I have to admit that I expected you to show up with a few more friends. What's going on?"

"Captain Sharan, you already know my Hand, but you haven't met Ibson yet. He's a crotchety old wizard that should have died years ago." Ibson shot him a glare, and Rainier had to laugh. *I always love the jokes that are funny because of their improbable but accurate truths, especially when no one else knows the sincerity behind the statement.* "As for my other friends, they are still in Ravinai, where we'll be heading very soon."

"Ravinai? I thought we planned to attack Minot first."

"We did. But the main reason for attacking Minot is to kill Magnus and destroy the totem he carries, which would weaken Lattimer's forces during the main battle. Now we know that Magnus isn't here. We had a run-in with him and know that he is already in Ravinai, so we've had to change our plans. We rode here as fast as we could to give you the news, and we'll need to move out as quickly as possible to make sure we reach Ravinai in time to influence the outcome of the battle."

Sharan said, "My troops are still arriving here. We're spread out across half of Malethya."

"I know. We've sent some friends to carry a message to Jak, Lady Highsmith, and Hanna. They'll be finding their way to Ravinai as well."

Sharan took the news, processed it, and acted immediately, just like a brilliant Captain should do. She ordered her officers, "We leave in two hours. Pack light and carry your own rations. We need to get to Ravinai and be ready to fight. No supply carts or anything else that will slow us down!" She ran down the line, rousing her troops who sprang into action like the well-trained army they were.

Ibson looked down at the map of Minot, with its battle plans laid in exhausting detail. Each patrol had been timed and listed with the most frequent locations. Potential entry points were marked with the estimated number of troops needed at each site. If Rainier had any concerns with the professionalism of Captain Sharan, this map put them to rest. Ibson also looked at the map and shook his head. He said, "We're in Minot with an army. We should attack."

Lira said, "You heard Rainier. Magnus isn't here, so there is no reason to attack."

Ibson snorted and said, "Do you believe everything that comes out of the holy mouth of our esteemed oracle?"

"What Ibson is trying to say is that he has his own reasons for being here." Rainier responded innocently, knowing that Ibson's bonds prevented him from saying too much. "Would you care to share with Lira what is so important to you in Minot?"

Ibson glared at Rainier, but he tried to explain anyway. "Within Minot, there is a hunter's cottage that was created in the days of blood magic to house important books, artifacts, and..." Ibson's face scrunched up as he tried but failed to get out the words. Instead, he said, "and there is a shielded city that Lattimer desperately wants to have access to."

"Why does he want access to it?" Lira asked. *Yes, why don't you tell her, Ibson?*

"Because Mi..." A blank look came over Ibson's face and

he said, "I can't say." Then he looked back down at the map, realized what his bonds made him momentarily forget, and yelled, "Minot is IMPORTANT. We need to ATTACK!"

I'm all for some fun, but I can't have the old man make a scene like this. "Calm down before one of these soldiers decides to do the job for you." Rainier grabbed the old man by the arm and whispered in his ear. "We have two hours before we leave. If you are fractal-bent on discussing this, let's do it in private."

Ibson continued to steam, but the comment at least quieted him enough to not draw the attention of everyone in camp. Rainier looked to Lira and said, "We're going scouting. I take it you are joining us?"

"I am your Hand. It is my duty to protect you." Lira said. *I know. I'm counting on it.*

He led the way through camp, only pausing to tell Captain Sharan of his plans to go scout Minot. After her initial objections, she pointed them in the right direction and assigned one of her scouts to guide them. "You won't be able to get very close. The town is heavily fortified."

"Is there somewhere we can get a good view of it. We don't need to be too close."

Sharan nodded. "How do you think we made the maps?"

They wandered through the forest on saddle-sore legs, following the Disenite scout on a circuitous path that had undoubtedly been designed to avoid the painstakingly mapped patrol routes. *I'm glad Sharan sent a scout with us. Even with the enlightened path emitting its soft glow around me, I still feel comforted by having someone lead the way who has done this before.* They picked their way through underbrush and skirted around the open areas with rocky terrain that would leave them more visible to anyone that cared to look. Each step took them closer to Minot and higher in elevation at the same time. Rainier looked over at Ibson to see the wizard glistening in sweat. *Don't die on me because of a simple climb, old man.* After what seemed like ages, they reached a small outcropping high above the surrounding area.

The scout said, "Belly crawl past that ridge, and the city will be beneath you. Stay within the shadow of that rock." He pointed at a particularly large boulder that cast a shadow over the rest of the outcropping. "It will keep you out of sight of the lookouts they have placed there and there." He pointed out two other outcroppings that were disconcertingly close. "Come back down the trail when you are ready to leave." Then he disappeared into the woods without another word.

Rainier said to Lira, "Can you take a spot close by and stand guard? That guy seems competent, but I'd much rather have you close by in case a Guardsman patrols by to find me lying flat on my belly and looking the wrong way." *Then I'll give Ibson a chance to say his piece in private as well.*

"You'll be safe. Just stay in the shadows." Lira said. *No problem there. I don't want a host of Lattimer's men chasing me again. I had enough of that in Ravinai.* Then Lira found a spot close by the trail that gave her good visibility to anyone approaching.

"Well, that's about as safe as we're going to get. Time to slither up to that rock." Rainier said.

Ibson dropped down and started crawling up the hill, but Rainier heard him mutter under his breath, "Slithering should be something you're pretty good at you little snake."

Rainier smiled and said, "You shouldn't say such things about me. Calling me a snake is an insult to snakes everywhere."

Ibson continued his mutterings at an even lower volume as he worked his way up the hill. Rainier crested the final rise of rocks first, which gave him a moment to gather himself before speaking. Ibson followed him and had no such advantage. His mutterings stopped with a satisfying little gasp.

Beneath them was a veritable compound. A stronghold of Ispirtu and Bellator Guardsmen that rivaled the strength of the Ispirtu tower. The biggest difference was that Ispirtu was made to be a place of learning, and Minot held no such pretenses. Guardsmen protected Minot as if it were King Darik's palace and given that King Darik was nothing more than Lattimer's puppet at this point, maybe more so.

"Captain Sharan's map doesn't do this place justice." Ibson said in dismay.

"Do you still think we should attack immediately?" Rainier managed to ask without the smugness he felt sneaking into his tone.

Ibson didn't bother responding to the question, and instead pointed to a small structure that had escaped Rainier's initial notice. "There's the hunter's cottage."

A tiny shack stood a short walk from Minot. It was insignificant in every way, except that it was very clearly significant. The guards surrounding its entrance made it clear. The stumps of trees chopped and burned to the ground created clear sightlines in every direction. Walls were being erected at the edges of the killing field to further fortify the position and laborers were hard at work clearing even more trees beyond the wall. No shack in the history of hunting had been so well protected.

"We need to get in there." Ibson said with conviction. Being alone with Rainier, his words were no longer limited by the bond he had spoken so many years before. "The artifacts all of my students created during the Golden Ages and the days of blood magic are in storage in that shack. They would help us win this war. Even more importantly, my students are held beneath the city, and they have knowledge of magic that goes beyond any in Malethya. We need their help."

"They are blood mages." Rainier stated the obvious and let it linger in the air.

Ibson waved his hand as if it were inconsequential. "They spoke an unbreakable bond. The only magic they can do is magic that I allow."

"And if they have been under that dome plotting against you and finding ways out of their bond?"

Ibson said, "Then they would have taken down the dome and killed me by now." *Fair point.* "If that dome is still up, it means that they are still under the unbreakable bond and haven't accomplished what I required of them."

"Which was what, exactly?" Rainier asked.

"My students meant everything to me. I never had children, but I can only imagine the responsibility a parent feels for a child. During the Golden Ages, when our cities prospered and our people flourished, I was filled with pride. Then their lust for power and their insatiable greed turned the Golden Ages into something...horrifying..." Ibson shook his head and shaded his eyes from the sun despite being in a shadow. *Is he tearing up? Don't start crying. I don't want to deal with that.* Ibson composed himself enough to say, "I did what any parent would do with petulant children – I punished them for their behavior. I set that wall up so that it would only disappear at the hand of a Perceptor or when the people inside had atoned for their actions. Then I made an unbreakable bond that prevented me from speaking of the hunting shack, my students, or the bond. They can't come out until they have created something that balances out the atrocities committed by their hands, and they can't access the spark without my approval." Ibson wiped his eye with his sleeve. *Ugh. Old man tears.* "They are in that bubble with only the trickle of spark I allow them to have. I didn't think they'd be in there this long..."

"I understand why it's so important for you to see your students released." *You didn't have the nerve to kill them like you should have done and your sense of responsibility and guilt linger the longer that dome stays up. Too bad.* Rainier patted Ibson on the shoulder in what he hoped was a comforting gesture. "But step back and think for a moment. What would happen if we took all the soldiers I command, crashed through this heavily fortified compound, and managed to release your students?"

Ibson, ever the academic, couldn't pull himself away from a good thought exercise. He said, "We'd lose most of our forces in the assault. If it allowed us to free my students, we'd have a huge advantage. With Jamison fighting Lattimer, we'd probably have enough power to finish off whoever won."

"But that isn't enough, is it? Slate and Sana may be focused on killing Lattimer, but you know better. You know who's coming next."

"Julian."

"He's coming, and he's bringing with the other factions. Jamison commands the Marked faction, but Julian will bring the Scorched, Frozen, and Charged factions." Rainier thought of an analogy that he hoped would drive home his point, and he hoped the old wizard was fond of chess, even though standing stones was obviously the better game. "Have you ever tried to play a chess match with just a king and a queen?" Rainier asked. "They are the most important pieces on the board, but they are worthless without pawns, bishops, and rooks around them."

Ibson was still in denial. He said, "Julian was a good student. It can't be as bad as you say. Besides, my student Koch was always his equal. Koch would know how to stop Julian. Together, we can fix this mess." The last words were said with a deluded comfort level that could only come from a clouded mind. *Well, I'm done trying to use logic on him. I guess I'll have to use a decidedly less honorable tract — guilt and shame weren't his preferred methods of manipulation, but he wasn't above using them in the right situation. This was the right situation.*

Rainier didn't try to hide the edge in his voice as he asked, "Why did you use an unbreakable bond on yourself?"

Ibson recoiled slightly at the question, but said, "It was the best way to help Malethya."

Rainier said, with brutal honesty, "That's not the reason. If you wanted to do what was best for Malethya, you would have killed your students on the spot. No one in our history has done more damage to Malethya and victimized its people more than your students. You could have killed them and felt completely justified in your actions. The Sicarius Headmaster would have killed them. I would have killed them…but you didn't. Instead, you spared their lives, locked them away from the world, banished Julian to a foreign land, and prevented yourself from ever changing your mind. I'll ask you again, why did you use the unbreakable bond on yourself?"

Ibson said nothing but Rainier could see his mind wrestling with a response. *I won't give him the option.*

"You did it because you made horrible mistakes and are largely responsible for the genocide your students caused in Malethya. You may have a brilliant mind, but you are a terrible judge of character, and you didn't trust yourself to make the right decision in the future. That realization was probably the only good decision you made." Ibson crumpled in defeat, shoulders shaking as he heard the words said aloud that he had carried inside his own head for years. Rainier didn't have time for pity. "You should have killed them. Think of what your choices have cost us. Look around and see what they are still costing us."

Ibson had buried his head in his hands in shame, but he picked his head up and looked out at Minot through teary eyes. Rainier said, "This whole army is here because you failed Malethya by burying your students in a shroud of magic, and then you didn't even have enough common sense to keep it hidden. Instead, you taught Brannon and took on Lattimer at a young age. When you found he had an affinity for spark-based magic, you stopped teaching him, but the damage was already done. He knew of Minot, and he knew it held more secrets. Now he rules Malethya from the shadow of King Darik and the biggest army Malethya has ever seen is about to lay ruin to our land and our people. No one could have prevented this from happening – no one but you."

The tears flowed freely now, but Rainier didn't care. *The old man needs to realize the extent of his failures. He needs to realize that he can't save Malethya.* "You aren't the person to lead us against Lattimer or Jamison or Julian. If the decision were yours, you'd throw the forces we do have at our command to free your handful of students, and then we'd do just enough damage to hand our country to Julian, and they'd all turn into nameless soldiers listening to fake patterns of speech." Rainier paused to let that sink in, and then he said, "And that's why you're going to go along with my plans and agree with everything I say."

Ibson turned his puffy eyes and tear-streaked cheeks towards Rainier. He said, "You can't possibly expect me to do that. I don't even know what plans you have." *He's fighting it, but he didn't refuse. He just questioned what my expectations are for him. Well, he's about to find out how serious I am.*

"You don't need to know my plans. What you need to know is that I'm trying to clean up your mess. I want to cleanse Malethya of Lattimer and his mindless subjugation of our people. I want to avenge my friend Kalus and wet my sword with the blood of Jamison and his followers, and I certainly don't want Julian to rule either. If I can do all three of those things and your students never leave their bubble, then so be it. All I know is that right now, if we use all the forces at our disposal to free them, we can't do any of those things. We aren't going to free your students right now, and I'm not telling anyone your secrets so that no one else is tempted to make the same mistake as you. Am I clear?"

Ibson frowned deeply, but tears on his cheeks were a fresh reminder of his failures. He stared at Rainier for a long time, and he finally said, "You are cunning, ruthless, immoral and I'm not sure you are any better than Lattimer, Julian, or Koch. You probably deserve to meet the same fate as anyone on that list." He thought for another second and said, "Given that we're outnumbered and overmatched in every sense of the word, you might be our only hope. I'll go along with your scheme, but only because this is my mess. I did make it, and I need to clean it up."

You also don't have much of a choice, but if it makes you feel better to pretend the choice was yours to make, then that's fine with me.

Ibson exhaled deeply and continued, "I've already agreed to play my part to take down Lattimer and the Disenites, so why don't you tell me more about what is in that scheming, manipulative head of yours? It might inspire a little more trust."

Rainier smiled his best Remnant smile and said, "That's the thing. I don't care if you trust me. You trusted your students. Slate trusted Lattimer. That's where trust has gotten us." *I won't trust anyone, and I will break from all these strings that people keep tying to me. I'll beat*

Lattimer, kill Jamison, and get Julian out of my fractal-forsaken head. "If I told you what I planned to do right now, you wouldn't even believe me. We're going to ride back to Ravinai to find a battle starting, and I'm going to do things that would make Slate's altruistic, bleeding heart stop dead in his pale white chest. I will manipulate whoever I need to manipulate, trick people to the point of treachery, stick a sword in any enemy with their back to me, and you will help me do it. You'll do it so that we leave this battle with enough forces, and more importantly, enough leverage, to get your students and fight Julian. You'll do it because I'm the fractal-forsaken leader of the Remnant, and I don't need some enlightened path or someone with Immortal as a title to tell me what to do."

Rainier thought back to his game of standing stones with Kalus and his friend's words to him. *"You see things differently than those around you. Anyone else would have been fixated on the red marks, but you saw the whole board and won the match by using my own stones against me. You will see us through, Rainier. Right now, you might still be understanding the lay of the board, but you will see the pieces soon enough. When you do, I know you'll tip things in our favor. You are the leader of the Remnant, and we are all behind you. We are family."* He couldn't help but think that this might be a little different. *I finally see the board, my friend, and to win this game, I'm going to have to use all my stones, except this time the stones are my friends, the troops under my command, and even my enemies.*

He looked back at Ibson and felt no pity for the old man. He might as well have been a standing stone, waiting for Rainier to place him on the board. "Wipe those tears from your face and quit looking at me with murder in your eyes. Save the judgment for when this is over. Until then, wrap me in some defensive spells and do as I say. We're going back to Ravinai. We have a battle to win."

CHAPTER TWELVE

THERE CAN BE ONLY ONE VICTOR

Rainier sat upon his horse and moved with agonizing slowness towards Ravinai. He sat atop an animal just waiting for the signal to catch the wind and fly ahead, but Rainier couldn't give the order. He was stuck matching the pace of the soldiers marching double time, and it took all his restraint to keep from digging his heels into horse and racing ahead, even though he didn't know what would be waiting for him when he arrived. *Did Villifor slow Jamison's troops enough to delay the battle? Did Annarelle and Tommy find Jak and redirect his troops? Did they succeed in infiltrating Jamison's camp and destroying the orbs that powered his forces? My thoughts make for poor company. I can't think of any company that could be worse.*

The silence of Lira and the non-stop glowering of Ibson changed his mind. *I'll keep company with my thoughts for now.* Unfortunately, his companions had other ideas.

Lira said, "The two of you have been at odds ever since Minot. What happened?"

Rainier smiled and said, "Oh, nothing. Ibson just realized the best way for him to help Malethya and is still coming to grips with it."

Lira said, "There is honor in knowing your role and excelling in it." Then she looked at Ibson's withering stare and said, "But some lessons take time to sink in."

"It's funny to hear you speak of honor when you serve

someone who knows so little about it."

Lira's hand went to her hilt as she started to unsheathe her sword. The late afternoon sun glinted off the exposed metal, but Rainier's hand stopped her motion with no more than a few inches unsheathed. He laughed and said, "There's no need for that, my Hand. We all have a role to play in the pattern, and Ibson's is a complicated one. His past failures make his tongue wag too often and his opinion moot. Despite that, he is still a useful failure, aren't you Ibson?"

Ibson stared at Rainier for a long time, but in the end, it was Ibson that looked away first. He hung his head and rode on in brooding silence.

Rainier spotted Captain Sharan ahead and headed in that direction to give Ibson some time to lick his wounds and come to grips with his new lot in life. As he cantered up to Sharan, Lira commented, "That was a little rough, don't you think."

Rainier shrugged. "I need him now as we go into battle, and I couldn't leave any doubt about my expectations for him. He might hate me, but he'll do what I need him to do."

Lira looked back at Ibson, and Rainier tried to guess what she thought of the wizard. Rainier knew he was Candor, the most accomplished wizard in the history of Malethya, but Lira didn't know that. And not knowing that, he just looked old, frail, and beaten down. She asked, "Do you really need him?"

"More than anyone knows."

Sharan saw them coming and greeted him with her fist to her palm as she said, "My oracle."

"How long until we reach Ravinai? Have we had any word regarding the battle? Are we going to arrive in time?" Rainier couldn't help but blurt out all his questions at once.

"I've been sending scouts in advance of our march, but so far I have no news. We will arrive in Ravinai at dusk. Do you have any insight into which direction we should approach from or how we should enter the city when we arrive?" She asked her supposed prophet.

Rainier held the enlightened path, and it streamed out in every direction, telling him that he was perfectly safe in the middle of the army he commanded but utterly useless for the question posed to him. He tried to focus on Captain Sharan, thinking that if he could focus on just her future paths, then he'd have a better chance of protecting the forces at his command, but he couldn't see her enlightened path any more than he could see over the horizon. *I guess I get to speak in generalities again and hope some of our friends see us coming.* He said, "Our path will be determined before our arrival and through the words of someone besides me."

Lira gave him a sidelong look, and it worried Rainier. *That girl is around me way too much. She's starting to be able to read through my lies despite my lifetime of practice.*

Thankfully, Sharan didn't question the comment, and she moved on to other matters. She said, "Our troops will be arriving in Ravinai after a long march and heading straight into battle against Lattimer's forces. They will be at a disadvantage."

"They've been training their entire lives to fight a blood

mage. They'll be so excited to swing their blue swords that this march will be nothing more than a warmup. It gives the troops a chance to break a sweat and work themselves up a good lather before facing some real competition, right?"

"The Nameless Army will fight with the passion and duty the pattern demands." Then Sharan said, "But I worry about a long, drawn-out battle."

Rainier recalled Lira and how her armor dimmed as she fought. He looked around and saw Kalana and the few other priest and priestesses that had decided to join them. "You don't have enough priests to bless your armor, do you?"

Sharan grimaced, but didn't deny the fact. "It's worse than that. The priests and priestesses that have joined us are...not highly ranked within the faction."

"They were burnt out on wanderleaf."

Sharan nodded. "Most of the journey to Minot, they spent sweating and shaking. It's not a group I would expect much out of in a battle." *That's because their bodies didn't know how to function without the drug. They've spent too much time under its smoky haze.*

Lira said, "Without priestesses to bless our armor, we'll be limited to quick strike maneuvers. Our battle tactics will be extremely limited."

Memories from battles long past came unbidden from the depths of his brain, or from Julian's, depending on how you wanted to think of it. *Flash, fl-flash. Armored soldiers rushed a heavily fortified position, using their enhanced armor to jump over the enemy lines. Wave after wave of the Nameless Army jumped to random positions within the* enemy's ranks. *From this vantage point, it almost looked like fish swimming upstream while a bear waited to catch them from the air. Some of the soldiers died as they landed in the enemy ranks, but others survived. In the ensuing chaos, the enemy's army broke rank and the whole battlefield devolved to individual battles. Flash. Three cannons were decimating the Nameless Army and the general ordered a quick strike to neutralize the targets. Groups of soldiers zig-zagged across the battlefield, seemingly at random, forcing the enemy to maintain ranks and not reinforce any strategic positions. Then, as they approached the enemy, their random movements turned into three attacks, focused on the cannons. The soldiers overwhelmed the defenses and brought down the cannons before the soldiers flanked them and converged on their positions. The soldiers accomplished their mission and destroyed the cannons, but none of them survived to lift a mug of ale in victory. Fl-flash, flash.*

"Yeah, that would limit our options. I'll have a talk with Kalana and see if I can understand what we can count on them for. Where can I find her?"

Sharan gestured behind them and said, "The priests and priestesses of the Marked faction are used to traveling under their own banner. There aren't enough banners in camp, but they have stuck to the practice anyway. You'll find our holy partners in the rear of the army."

Rainier nodded thoughtfully and turned his horse around. *Maybe this will be an activity I can have our downtrodden wizard help me with? I can send our beaten-down failure of a wizard to work with the burnt-out failures of the Marked faction priesthood. What could go wrong?* He said, "Lira, can you tell Ibson I'm in need of his aid? He'd probably respond better to you than me right now."

Lira said, "I'll drag him by his robes if I have to." Then she went off to fetch him, and Rainier half-hoped to see him dragged through the mud by his robes, but the man had seen his substantial ego bruised badly. Now that he was clear on his place, it was time to build him up and make him feel important again, so that Rainier could get some actual use out of him.

He kept working his way through the ranks of the army, nodding at soldiers as he passed. He was greeted by a pounding of a shield or some other such greeting he had become accustomed to from the Nameless Army. *Hey, it's better than when they were trying to kill you. At least the banging noises are a greeting instead of a death sentence like they were aboard the Inked Tides.* Rainier muttered phrases like "for the pattern" and "duty above self" as he pushed against the flow of marching soldiers. By the time he saw a group of huddled priests and priestesses in the rear of the army, he was relieved to be done with all the leadership platitudes his army expected out of him.

Then he realized who he was talking to, exhaled deeply, and prepared a bunch of hopefully prophetic nonsense.

Kalana saw him approach, and she bowed in formal greeting along with the small contingent of wanderleaf junkies that had chosen to follow him. Rainier said, "Greetings. I hope the pattern finds you well."

Kalana said, "The pattern is what a priestess of the Marked faction always seeks. It is why we followed you." She paused and fought against the frustration that was evident on her face. "So far we haven't found the pattern."

One of the priests behind her muttered, "We haven't seen much of our oracle either."

"Yes, I've heard that your journey has been a difficult one." *And apparently even the holiest of junkies still gets irritable when you take away their wanderleaf.* "I applaud your courage in making the decision to follow me and to reconnect with the pattern. The decision must have been incredibly difficult. You left everything you knew in the hopes of reconnecting with the pattern, but I never said this would be an easy journey. The right choice is rarely the easy choice." Rainier looked at all of them. Kalana held his stare, but the others wilted and diverted their gaze like a pack of abused puppies. *At least Kalana still has some steel in her.* He said, "Kalana, can you tell me what this has been like for you since arriving in Portswain?"

"We hit the beach and recovered from our swim as Captain Sharan secured our position. It wasn't long until Jak and Lady Highsmith arrived. They told us we had a long march ahead of us, and that we would be moved in small groups. They sent us first, and sometime during the first day's march, the headaches began. They got worse and worse to the point where the very light hurt my eyes. I started sweating. The sweating turned into nausea, and when I wasn't throwing up, I was shaking so hard I could hardly stand. Jak ended up hiding us in some wagons and covering us with blight-ridden straw." She paused and composed herself, fighting back the tears that threatened to form at the memories. "I don't remember most of the days that followed, and the parts I do remember, I wish I could forget." She stopped her description of the journey and jumped ahead in her story. "I started feeling better once we reached Minot. Some of us recovered more quickly, but others are still dealing with the last of their tremors."

"And the pattern? Have you been able to reach out and find it again?" Rainier asked as Lira and Ibson approached the group.

Kalana grimaced and shook her head. "I've tried so many times. I try so often that I forget my meals unless someone reminds me to eat, but it hasn't worked." A glimmer of hope entered her voice as she said, "Now you're here, though, so you can show us the path."

Captain Sharan was right. The priests in our army can't help us during battle, at least not in their current state. "I start by calming myself and sensing the world around me. Its only when I feel the pattern that I can call upon its power. I know from my own experience learning to use the enlightened path that it doesn't work if I try to control it. I'm only sensing it and reading what it tells me." Rainier tried his best to explain the use of magic without mentioning the spark and relating it to the beliefs of the Marked faction. "It's taken me quite a while to learn these lessons on my own, and unfortunately, I don't believe I will be a good teacher to you all."

The priest that muttered irritably before voiced his displeasure more audibly by saying, "We left our faction for you to teach us how to reach the pattern. I couldn't reach it before, but at least Jamison gave me a bed to sleep in and enough leaf to forget my failures. What have you given us besides empty promises? Where have you been?!?"

I've been trying to keep us all alive long enough that we don't get caught between Jamison's army and Lattimer's Furies. I've had my dreams invaded by the scariest wizard I have ever met. I've been chased through the streets of Ravinai by Magnus, and I've somehow managed to not only stay alive, but to keep my army and priests out of harm's way as well. That's where I've been while you've been shaking under blight-infested straw accomplishing nothing, you ungrateful waste of time. That's what Rainier wanted to say, but instead, he said, "You've made huge sacrifices to join us, and you've put a lot of trust in me. You're right to say that I haven't been there for you, but you are mistaken if you think I haven't been trying to help you."

Rainier tried to give his most earnest and trust-worthy look, which admittedly wasn't his strong suit even though he had plenty of practice faking it. "When you joined my side, I knew I would need help to guide you back to the pattern. While I was away, I traveled to find Ibson, a highly esteemed member of the Remnant." Rainier motioned towards Ibson and nodded his head with deep respect. Ibson startled but covered his initial reaction while he tried to figure out what lie Rainier expected him to play along with this time. Rainier continued, "He chose to stay behind rather than take the voyage to Disentia because of his advanced age, but Ibson has traveled with the Remnant and helped us to understand the pattern around us when everyone assumed we were just a band of nomadic tribesman. He taught me, and he can teach you, can't you Ibson?"

Ibson puffed out his chest as he slipped into the comfortable role of teaching magic. He began, "Provided they all have…"

Rainier jumped in and cut him off before he could mention the spark and the priests labeled him a blasphemer. "…been blessed by the pattern. Yes, yes, they have all passed the first Oracle Trial and are blessed by the pattern." Rainier smiled at the priests and waved his arm out before him, as though welcoming them into an exclusive club.

"Er…yes. Blessed by the pattern." Ibson recovered and said, "Since you are all blessed by the pattern, there are many things that I can teach you, and I'm confident I can lead you back to the pattern you have lost."

Kalana looked relieved while the other priests and priestesses were somewhere between hopeful and skeptical. She said, "We have waited long enough. Please begin your lesson."

Rainier jumped in again, by saying, "Before the lesson begins, you will each need a blue orb that your faction uses to bless your cannons and the armor of your paladins."

Kalana's brows furrowed. She said, "The orbs are our most sacred artifact. They concentrate the blessings of many into one."

"I can't think of any purpose more holy or noble than bringing priests and priestesses back into the pattern, can you?" Silence met his request, which he took as acceptance. "How many do you have with you?"

"Precious few." She glanced back at a cart with a chest in it. "We'll stop and get them out, disperse them among

334 J. Lloren Quill

the priests here, and then the lesson will begin."

At her words, the cart stopped, and she dismounted from her horse. While the other priests joined her and waited for their orb to be handed out, Rainier motioned for Ibson to come over.

"What scheme do you have going this time?" Ibson asked. "I played along, but I want to know what..."

Rainier cut him off with a terse whisper, "We need these priests and priestesses to bless our army's weapons and armor during battle, or we are walking into a slaughter. What type of scheme am I running? I'm running the scheme that will save our lives." He kept going before Ibson could flap his lips with any other complaints. "I need you to teach these people to power up armor using the orbs, and I need you to do it without mentioning that they are casting a spell. Don't mention wizards or magic and certainly don't mention the spark or they might kill you where you stand. Do you understand me?"

"You tell me to teach novices a complex spell, and then you tell me to do it without the proper instructions. Are you going to tie one hand behind my back next?" Ibson retorted.

Rainier tried another argument. "You've spent years in isolation protecting something that you thought could help Malethya. I may not agree with the decisions you've made, but I know you've always tried to do the right thing, am I correct?"

Ibson said nothing but Rainier could tell he was listening. "If you really want to help Malethya. This is a place to start. These soldiers will help in the fight against Lattimer, but they can't go up against Furies without their armor powered up. You're the only person that can make that happen. You may not have time to teach these priests and priestesses everything you know about magic, but they have done it. They've just forgotten how. You can remind them of how to do it and teach them a single spell on the way to Ravinai. You are the most accomplished wizard in history. I know you can. The only question is...will you do it?"

Ibson shook his head and muttered, "There isn't much time until Ravinai..."

Rainier could see that he had already decided to help though. Rainier had appealed to Ibson sense of self-importance and righteousness and then given him a challenge to test his claims as the greatest wizard in the history of Malethya.

"I'll do it," Ibson said.

Rainier bowed his head in feigned gratitude. *Of course, you will.*

Ibson left to join the group of priests and priestesses as they tried to catch up with the rest of the army. His lips moved and his arms flapped in excited instruction as he took on his most challenging pupils of his life. "The pattern is more than something for you to worship. The pattern is all around you. In your search for the pattern, you have forgotten that it lies within all of us and in everything around us. Take this fire for instance..." Ibson cast a spell and a small flame danced around his hand. "It is more than a flame. If you really get to know it, you know that it is always hungry, always searching for something more. It feeds off the air and..."

Rainier smirked, knowing that the priests were in good

hands. *He might even pull it off. He definitely has a talent for teaching.* Rainier looked back up and the smirk disappeared from his face.

Lira was glaring at him. She had heard everything.

"You deceived the most holy people in our faction, just as Jamison deceived you. You are no better than him." Lira had always been a hard woman, but now her face seemed etched in stone and her will made of steel. "You are a fraud."

Rainier, for once in his life, had nothing to say. *She was bound to find out sooner or later. At least she didn't draw her sword and cut me down. That's more than I could have hoped for.* He turned his horse and started marching with the army, not wanting to make a terrible situation worse. Lira took up her customary position at his side, but the lines on her face stayed creased. To ride ahead and find Sharan felt like he would be running from the situation, so Rainier stayed silent in her void of discomforting quiet.

As the horse hooves shortened the distance to Ravinai, Rainier caught pieces of Ibson's lecture. He talked about "holding the pattern and reaching out to explore the pattern around you." To Rainier's ears, it sounded an awful lot like a probing spell, which was used as the basis for most spells. A little while later, he discussed "pouring in your own pattern to fill the gaps in your understanding of the pattern around you." *I have to hand it to Ibson. That's a clever way to teach someone how to use the spark without discussing spark-based magic.* Then Rainier looked back over at the stone-faced woman riding next to him, the woman he hoped would still protect him in battle and decided his livelihood may depend on saying the right words to her at this very moment.

"You say I am a fraud. If that means that I don't meet your expectations of an oracle, or that I don't fit what *A Life in the Pattern* describes as a pious servant of the pattern, then I can't argue with you. That's not me."

Rainier fought to find the words, which was a problem he wasn't accustomed to dealing with. He tried to explain by saying, "I learned to lead Kalus and the rest of the Remnant in the heart of Malethya, and I know more about the country I was spying on than I knew of the country I was spying for. Growing up here, I learned that things aren't black and white in Malethya, and I guess I'm not either. I believe that Lattimer needs to be stopped and the only way that will happen is if my troops have their holy armor shining nice and bright in the battle to come."

Rainier searched for any hint of understanding from the master swordswoman at his side but found none. *Maybe I shouldn't have spoken from the context of my own history, which is as alien to her as Disentia is to me.* He said, "You and the rest of the Nameless Army have trained and devoted your entire lives to this moment. Most of them don't understand the people they plan to fight any better than I understand patterned speech. They only understand swords and where their commander tells them to point them. Right or wrong, I am the commander of this army. I've been blessed by the pattern and appointed by Julian, and the paladins of the Nameless Army under my command will go into battle where I tell them to go. I need to do everything in my power to protect them, even if it means deceiving a couple of priests and priestesses." *In this battle, there can be only one victor, and I intend for it to be me. I'll protect my friends and the Remnant if I can, but I will keep Ibson's secrets from them if it gives me leverage for what I need to do. I won't hesitate to send Annarelle and Tommy into danger without telling Slate or Sana if it gives me a better chance of beating Jamison. I'll do whatever it takes. I'll lie, cheat, and swindle my way to victory, just like I grew up. I'll win the Remnant way.*

Lira inserted herself into the silence of Rainier's thoughts. She said, "You have lied to our priests, and I don't know what you have said to Ibson, but I have rarely seen a person harbor such contempt for a fellow human being as I see when he looks at you. You are not a person that can be trusted."

That would hurt my feelings if I hadn't already seen the damage that trust can cause. I won't fall into that altruistic trap. Rainier said, "Then why do you still ride by my side?"

Lira almost spat her answer, "Because I know what it means to do my duty. I am bound as your Hand, and I will honor the commitment I made. To do less would be to dishonor myself as you have done."

Rainier rode ahead quietly, hoping he could count on Lira in the battle to come. *She still didn't draw steel against me. I guess that's something.*

Rainier's thoughts were interrupted by a shout of unbridled emotion. Rainier spun around in his saddle and reached for his short sword, despite the warm glow of the enlightened path ensuring him that he wasn't in any danger. Lira had moved even quicker and had her sword drawn by the time Rainier processed the scene before him.

Kalana raised a small dagger straight in the air in

triumph. It held the faintest blue light.

Ibson clapped his hands in excitement and the other priests and priestesses stared at her in awe. Kalana found Rainier and yelled, "I did it! I found the pattern!"

"Fractal's blessings!" Rainier yelled back, "There's a dozen or so of your fellow priests and priestesses that could use your help learning to do the same."

Kalana nodded emphatically and started discussing her techniques and methods with her fellow priests. Rainier gave a knowing smile of genuine appreciation to Ibson and then turned back around in his saddle.

"I may not be a person you trust but remember why your armor doesn't lose its power in the middle of battle. My little lie gave purpose to Ibson, all of those priests and priestesses, and gave everyone in this army a better chance of surviving this fight." Rainier said without bothering to look at Lira. *I know she won't respond anyway.*

The rest of the ride to Ravinai took place with increasingly frequent shouts of joy. With each priest that rediscovered how to cast a spell, the mood of the entire group lifted, and more and more people found what they had lost.

Rainier didn't say a word. Neither did Lira, but she would alternatively turn her head to look at the priests and priestesses celebrating their successes and look towards Rainier with a furrowed brow. *I wish I knew what was going on in that head of yours.* Rainier had been around Lira long enough to know that the best way to reach her was to leave her with her own thoughts, though, so he let the shouts of joy perform a second type of magic

– persuading Lira.

The litany of magical successes was interrupted by a horse and rider coming to find them. Upon spotting them, he shouted, "Captain Sharan sends word for you to come at once. Villifor rode out to meet us. Jamison has reached Ravinai."

CHAPTER THIRTEEN

WHEN A SWINDLER LAUGHS

It took every ounce of self-control for Rainier not to tell Captain Sharan to get the lead plating out of her armor and hurry up, in his most prophetic voice, of course. All the seeds of his schemes were coming together in one battlefield, and he wasn't there to manipulate the outcome. *I'll be starting out this battle with one hand tied behind my back.* For the thousandth time, he looked over at Sharan and screamed within his own head. *Get your fractal-forsaken troops to Ravinai! I don't care how you do it, get there now!* Even though the fragmented memories in his head reminded him of the value of showing up to a fight fresh, he couldn't help it, he wasn't Sana. It drove him crazy to know that the battle had started, and all he had for a distraction was a bodyguard that refused to speak to him while she decided whether or not to kill him and a man he trusted about as far as he could throw. Rainier took one look at Lira, saw the stony response, and decided Villifor was the best option.

"What's happening in Ravinai, Villifor? What information do you have about Jamison's army?" Rainier asked the former Bellator Headmaster as they entered the outskirts of Malethya's capitol. He also impersonated a famous war hero during the Twice Broken Wars, betrayed his own people, and lived a life of luxury while they were exiled to Pillar. Somehow, he stayed in the good graces of

Slate and had managed not to get himself killed, even when the truth came out. All in all, someone with those skills could find a home with the Remnant.

"I mobilized the Underground forces between Portswain and Ravinai. We created roadblocks where we could, engaged in late-night raids of their supply carts, and did everything we could to slow them down." Villifor grimaced, "I can't say it did much. Their enchanted armor cleared the roadways quick enough and the supply carts were heavily guarded. That army knows the business of war."

Villifor didn't let details like failing to do his job get him down though. He laughed and clapped Rainier across the back. He said, "At least they'll give Lattimer a run for his money though, huh?"

If that were my only concern, I'd be sitting pretty. Unfortunately, a clear victory by Jamison means certain death for those under my command. More importantly, it would mean certain death for me, either by Jamison's hand or by Julian's. Maybe the bastards can draw straws for the honor of decapitating me? We should be marching faster.

Now that Villifor had the excuse to start talking, he didn't stop. "I did bring some valuable information back with me though. While tracking Jamison's troops, it became apparent that they have only the most basic information regarding the terrain of Malethya. They tried to bring their cannons with them on the march, but they were too heavy and cumbersome for the trip. They left the cannons in Portswain and took a direct path to Ravinai. We may be able to use the land to our benefit."

Rainier frowned. "That isn't valuable. I've seen all their

maps when I was aboard the Inked Tides. What else do you know?" *They left their cannons with their ships. That takes away one of their best advantages. Jamison must have been worried I'd reach Lattimer first and steal his victory...or he's afraid of Julian's response if he doesn't produce results. I won't tell Villifor, but it is helpful to know Jamison is in such a rush to defeat Lattimer that he's willing to leave his cannons behind.*

Villifor leaned over and whispered conspiratorially, "I know that you sent Tommy and Annarelle on a raid of their own. It didn't go well."

"What do you mean?" Rainier asked.

"Those two lovers found me using the Stratego medallion and said they had a secret mission. I managed to pry out of them that it was you that sent them there in exchange for my help. My suggestion was to leave well enough alone. The army's camp was too well-guarded to infiltrate. They had guards patrolling with their priests, which I've come to understand have some spellcasting capabilities." Villifor looked to Rainier for confirmation, but Rainier just nodded for him to continue with the story. "Anyway, they are young and brave and stupid, so they didn't take my advice. I watched them go into the camp under the cover of darkness...they didn't come back out."

Curses. Hopefully, they were able to destroy a few orbs before then, at least. "That's really disheartening. Tommy and Annarelle are two of our best. I don't know why they'd say I gave them a mission though. Annarelle takes her orders from Sana."

Villifor looked skeptical and said nothing.

Rainier argued, "If you don't believe me, ask Lira. She

has been by my side since we landed in Portswain. Lira, did I ever have time to give out secret missions to people?"

Lira said, "I did not see Rainier do such a thing." Rainier's expression didn't change, but he smiled on the inside. *She's completely wrong, but that's beside the point. She wasn't there when I convinced Tommy and Annarelle to take on the mission, so she can answer truthfully. Always trust the honesty of honest people – it makes for the best lies.*

"I see." Villifor said, and he didn't press the issue further.

"Where did they enter the city? Where will Lattimer's forces meet them?" Rainier tried to change the subject.

"Jamison came from the south and entered the city without any opposition. I would have thought Lattimer would ride out of the city to meet them, but Jamison entered the heart of the city and aimed his troops towards King Darik's palace." Villifor gestured towards the outline of the city ahead of them, narrating the position of Jamison's troops as he replayed their march to the capitol. "Lattimer must have something up his sleeve."

Just then, Rainier felt the wind go still. At first, he thought nothing changed, but his attention kept being drawn back to the city. It almost seemed too bright, like the surface of every building was a mirror.

"What is happening?" Captain Sharan asked. "Is that some trick of the eyes?"

Then the mirror effect lifted into the air and surrounded Ravinai in a reflective dome. The buildings disappeared in a bubble of light. The army stopped in their tracks and stared in awe...or terror...at the sight.

"Did Lattimer just hide the entire city of Ravinai? Why would he do that?" Sharan asked. "And how?"

"Blood magic." Lira said and spat on the ground.

Ibson cantered up to the group as Rainier said, "I don't think he's trying to hide the city. That spell reflects light..."

"...meaning that everything inside is dark as the darkest night." Ibson finished Rainier's thought and a silence fell over the group as they tried to understand what was happening inside the dome.

"Lattimer is a blood mage. As far as we know, the only limit to his power is his own imagination. With months to prepare for this fight, he had plenty of time to concoct a spell that would throw the battlefield into darkness."

Lira said, "Our armor produces its own light."

"And will make every paladin in Jamison's army an easy target. We might as well have targets on our backs." Captain Sharan observed.

Rainier nodded in agreement. "The Nameless Army came to fight the demons of a blood mage. Now the only thing they'll see is the red eyes of a Fury jumping out of the darkness and trying to bury a blade in their neck." Silence followed while everyone pictured a battle in which you couldn't see your opponents until they were right on top of you. Red-eyed monsters would jump at you from every direction with no warning except where the pale light of your own armor reached. Unseen wizards would launch volleys of fireballs into your ranks. Formations would crack and fear would reign. "A battlefield is never a pretty place, but that would be hell."

Villifor said, "If Jamison came to fight demons, it looks like Lattimer plans to grant him his wish."

"We need to know what is going on in there." Captain Sharan said. *Thanks for stating the obvious.* "There's no telling what other tricks Lattimer has up his sleeve. We are fortunate that our oracle has guided us down a path to avoid this trap. What else does the enlightened path tell you?"

What does the pattern tell me? It tells me to take a fractal-forsaken dive into some shallow water from a tall cliff. It tells me to take a long drop from a short rope. At least that might as well be what the enlightened path is telling me for all the good it's doing right now. This yellow light all around me only tells me that no one is about to put a knife in my back, but it doesn't tell me a forsaken thing about what's going on in Ravinai.

Rainier said with prophetic remorse, "The enlightened path can't see into the city any better than the sunlight around us."

Ibson conjectured around his lie, either taking it for truth or fulfilling his promise to play along with Rainier's schemes. He said, "If the enlightened light of the pattern can't penetrate Lattimer's spell, then we'll need to get you inside. If the spell only reflects light, I believe your abilities will function normally again once we pass into the city. Any light that hits the dome cannot enter, but once inside the dome, light should behave normally."

"Are you sure of that?" Villifor asked.

"I am making an educated guess based on the observations placed before me."

"You aren't sure then. Great." Villifor scoffed.

Rainier said, "That's even more reason to sneak inside and see what's happening before the rest of the army marches in. Villifor, I take it you know how to meet up with Slate and Sana. Can we get into the city without any issues?"

"Everyone's attention is focused on the battle. I didn't have any problems when I left and, yes, I can get you to the others."

Rainier looked around at the others, and it was Sharan that asked, "What would you have us do? What do you command of your army?"

When you get to Ravinai, stay between me and anyone with red eyes. "Continue marching towards Ravinai as fast as you can. I'll ride ahead with Villifor and Ibson. I'll have the answers I need before you arrive." Rainier thought for a moment and then said, "In the meantime, have your soldiers blacken their blades and do their best to hide their armor."

"A paladin's weapon is holy. It should not be befouled by blackening the blade." Lira said.

Flash fl-flash, flash. Rainier crouched in a dark forest, peering into an encampment of soldiers. He counted thirty patrols, and who knew how many soldiers slept inside the tents, but his attention kept being drawn to a giant of a man speaking boisterously at a fire while drinking his mead and playing with a battle axe. Rainier looked to his left and right and counted his men. It took less time than he would have liked, which meant they were vastly outnumbered. The soldier to his right whispered, "Julian, what do you want to do?" Rainier heard himself reply, "Blacken your blades and cover your armor. The man by that fire dared to raid a village under my protection. He will not survive the night." The men nodded and greased their blades. Then they smeared mud on their armor and waited for the signal. In the darkest hour of night, Rainier gave the hand signal and the men creeped forward, dispatching guards in silence. When one soldier failed to land a killing blow on the first swing, a cry went up, and the alarm was raised. Rainier readied his spell, and when he saw which tent the first soldiers began to pour out of, unleashed a gigantic fireball. It hit the tent, and every soldier that didn't die immediately ran around the camp alit with wizard fire. Chaos erupted, and with the element of surprise evening the odds, Rainier had the battle axe of their leader in his hands before the first ray of sunlight crossed the horizon. He was spinning the great weapon in his hands, when one of his soldiers said, "Congratulations Julian, you've done it again. People will be singing the praises of the midnight raid of Erimer for years." Flash...fl-flash.

Rainier recollected his thoughts and looked to Lira. "Julian ordered the blades of his troops blackened during the midnight raid of Erimer. If he didn't have a problem with it, why do you?"

Lira looked confused, and it was Sharan that said, "I have heard of the midnight raid of Erimer, but only in my days as a student while learning battle strategy. It was a small but important battle that took place while Julian was still establishing his rightful place as the leader of Disentia. Very few people know the name of that battle much less the tactics they employed, but I happen to be one of them. He speaks the truth."

Frackin' memories. What good is having the memories of an Immortal if no one knows what I'm talking about? I got lucky that Captain Sharan knows her military history, but I better keep my mouth shut in the future.

Sharan said, "We will order the blades blackened, and we will cover our armor in any fabric available. If we can't find fabric, we'll use mud." She shouted the command to her lieutenants and said, "Prepare for a midnight raid. Prepare to fight in the dark." She looked back to Rainier and said, "Is there anything else?"

Rainier said, "Some of your priests have regained the ability to bless a paladin's armor. Ibson, how are they getting along?"

"Most have done it, but to varying levels of efficiency. Kalana has the priests and priestesses that have worked it out helping to teach the ones that are struggling. They will be ready." Sharan looked visibly relieved while Lira said nothing as she looked to Rainier with an icy stare. "Now, the only thing we need is..."

"...to get going!" Rainier interjected before Ibson could mention their shortage of orbs. *That's another problem I'll have to figure out. Maybe the army can steal some as we go through Ravinai, but there's no point in worrying Sharan unnecessarily. If I send her troops into battle, I want their morale up, with all of them expecting to have some priests to back them up.*

Rainier dug his heels into his horse as he yelled, "Ibson and Villifor, you're with me." Then he looked at Lira and said, "Are you coming?"

She dug her heels into her horse and said, "It is my duty."

Rainier shot ahead of the army, happy to let his horse run free and feel the wind against his face. He was even happier that the wind rushing past him prevented conversation of any sort, especially with Lira. Rainier couldn't help but feel as if he were running away from one problem and right into another, but it didn't diminish the sense of freedom that this momentary respite provided.

The countryside turned from farmland to villages of ever-increasing size, and Rainier raced through the inconsequential plots of land that they were. As the villages got bigger though, it was harder to ignore the townspeople that left their homes and stared in wide-eyed wonder at the reflective surface in the location Ravinai used to be. Rainier saw people scratch their heads, bewilderment on every face, and above all, an intense feeling of fear. Each person he rode by served as a reminder of the dangers in front of him. *I've been running in so many dangerous circles lately, that I hardly even notice the sense of pending doom all around me.* The thought grew as they approached the mirrored dome. It stretched before them and everyone naturally slowed as they approached. Rainier looked at that dome and realized all his plans were about to play out, and he had no idea which way the stones would fall. *I wonder what Kalus would think of all this. It's the highest stakes game of standing stones that anyone in the Remnant has ever played.*

Rainier couldn't have said why he thought of Kalus at that moment, but the absurdity of relating his current situation to a childhood game combined with Kalus' ability to always lighten the mood made Rainier laugh out loud.

"Why are you laughing like a fractal-forsaken fool?" Ibson asked. The horses stopped before the reflective surface of their own accord and refused to go any further.

Everyone dismounted and turned their attention to Rainier after staring at the display of magic in front of them.

"Have you lost your mind?" Lira asked, and it wasn't a rhetorical question.

Have I lost my mind? I don't even know anymore. I know I'm fed up with people threatening me, using me, and manipulating me.

That's supposed to be my job.

Now that all my plans lay before me, I find that I care a lot less about the outcome than I thought I would. Malethya? Disentia? Blood mages? Marked priests and paladins? They are just stones standing on a battlefield being pushed around by people playing a game. Julian made the mistake of giving me a spot in the game, but he failed to realize something particularly important.

Never wager against the Remnant. Never wager against me. I always win.

Rainier laughed again and plastered a Remnant smile on his face. He said, "Everyone has their armies pointed at each other. Jamison is marching towards his pre-ordained victory, and Lattimer has hidden his tricks under the cover of darkness. There's only one thing they didn't account for – ME."

Rainier felt the comforting light of the enlightened path before him, drew his short sword, and ran ahead. He heard Villifor laughing maniacally, and he gave a Bellator shout of approval. Then Rainier plunged through the reflective surface of Lattimer's dome. He left behind his fear, his doubts, and his caution as he entered a world of darkness created by blood magic to instill fear in anyone that entered. *Your plan failed Lattimer because I don't fear anything in the battle ahead. I don't fear you or that bastard Jamison. It's all just a game.* "It's time to play."

CHAPTER FOURTEEN

PALADIN'S BLESSINGS MEET RED-EYED FURY

The darkness disoriented Rainier as he ran into the dome, but disorientation isn't the same thing as fear. Rainier had the warm glow of the enlightened path around him, and he knew he was safe despite his lack of visibility. He took a moment to analyze the pathways of light streaming away from him and found he was so used to reading the paths that he could make out the roadways and structures around him. Some paths carried straight ahead, which was obviously the road, while others took an abrupt turn upwards, indicating he would have to climb a wall or scale a building. The combined streams of light formed a soft, glowing map of the city he knew so well, and he ran ahead only to be stopped by the sounds of dismay coming from behind him.

"It's black as night. I can't even see my hands in front of my face." Villifor grumbled. There was a distant blue glow emanating from somewhere in the city, but it was far ahead and didn't help them see their immediate surroundings.

"It will be impossible to find our way through this." Lira said pragmatically.

"There should be orbs lighting the city streets. Lattimer has taken them all down." Ibson said, then tried to solve the problem as one would expect of a wizard. "I could cast a spell that…"

"No." Rainier said immediately. "Do you really want to draw attention to us in a city full of Furies told to attack anything that's lit up?"

"Then how will we find our way? If we walked towards the blue light, I bet we'd find the battle, but do we really want to dive straight into that without knowing what's going on?" Ibson asked.

Rainier didn't bother trying to explain how he read the enlightened paths. He just needed to know where to go. He asked, "Villifor, where are we meeting Slate and Sana? I can get us there."

"My favorite place – the Royal Boar. Maybe I can steal a mug of ale before I have to swing my sword." Villifor said hopefully. "But how do you plan to get us there?"

"Place your hand on my shoulder. Lira, place yours on Villifor, and Ibson…put your hand on Lira's shoulder." Rainier debated but felt an extra warning was necessary. He was about to say something when Lira beat him to it.

"If I feel your hand anywhere besides my shoulder, I'll cut it off."

Rainier felt Villifor's hand clasp his shoulder and some vague mutterings from Ibson of mock offense that she could think so lowly of him. Rainier started moving slowly, picking up the pace as fast as his train of followers could keep up. The darkness, and their own fear of smacking into a building at a full sprint, prevented them from taking off too quickly. Rainier could read the path around him, though, and guided them down the middle of a broad street. After a few blocks, the group lost some of their fear, and they were only limited by the speed of Ibson's elderly gate.

"How are you doing this?" Lira asked.

"Because I'm the fractal-forsaken oracle. Did you forget?" *I might lie, trick, and use who I need to use, but don't forget who I am and what I'm capable of.* "My prophetic wisdom suggests everyone keep their voices down too. The Furies might not see us in the dark, but the last time I checked, their hearing works fine."

On cue, a shrieking cry rose from a short distance away, and Rainier read the enlightened paths to identify the source as an alleyway. He pushed Villifor's hand off his shoulder, drew his blade and said, "Wait here."

The sound of the Fury's scream headed straight for him. With Rainier's view of the darkened world, the Fury appeared as a void in the enlightened paths, running with her arm raised and a sword in her hand. Thankfully, she was running too quickly to be wearing armor, and her slight build eliminated any previous training in Bellator. Rainier stepped ahead to meet the charge of the Fury. As she swung a wild overhand blow with all her hate fueled might, Rainier read the paths and stepped to the side, easily avoiding the clumsy, untrained swing. She ran by and Rainier brought his short swords against the base of her neck. Her head rolled and Rainier rejoined the group.

"What happened?" Villifor whispered urgently.

"He fought with the enlightened path." Lira said quietly, and if he wasn't mistaken, there may have even been some respect in her voice. *Is her icy demeanor towards me starting to thaw? Maybe some Remnant embellishment could help. I fought a peasant woman in the dark that was just as likely to trip on her sword as hit me with it, but it's too dark for them to know that.*

"I had to take care of a Bellator Fury. She was highly trained, and if you keep talking, there may be more of them, so shut your fractal-forsaken mouths before anyone else shows up." Rainier slapped Villifor's hand back onto his shoulder and said, "Now follow behind me, and try not to make me turn from an oracle into a hand. I don't want to have to be your protector again."

The group moved on in silence after that, with Rainier navigating the barren city streets towards the Bellator Guild and The Royal Boar that specialized in service to its Guildsmen. Villifor had been treated as a hero every time he walked into that tavern, and apparently it still held a soft spot in his heart. Rainier slowed on his approach, knowing the tavern's location well enough. He had even impersonated a waiter back in the days when he first met Slate, but he didn't know the restaurant well enough to recognize the front door based off a few streams of light. "Describe the Royal Boar to me," Rainier said quietly to Villifor.

"It's the place where heroes are celebrated, and legends are made. The ale flows freely and the women flock to be with a ..."

"I need a description of the building, not a tale of your exploits," Rainier snapped.

"Um...long flat building with a big patio."

"You're an architectural genius, aren't you? I can almost commission some drawings from Darik's royal builders with a description like that." Rainier looked at the long vertical streams of light in front of him that marked the edge of the building, searching for some point of reference. Halfway down, one of the recesses in the wall had something sticking out from the building near the roofline. "The Royal Boar – does it have a sign above the door?"

"Yes, it has a boar drinking from a crown painted on it. Everyone knows that." Villifor scoffed.

Rainier walked beneath the overhanging sign and felt around the surface of the building like a lucky adolescent, fumbling with equal parts eagerness and complete cluelessness. Finally, his hands wrapped around the door handle, and he pulled it open slowly, trying to stay quiet.

A single candle came into view, and a throwing knife embedded in the doorframe.

An eerie voice said with alternating pitch, "Show yourself or your next breath will be your last."

Rainier had no reason to push his luck. He opened the door and said, "It's Rainier. Keep your knives in your pants!"

Slate flashed from a darkened corner so fast that he startled Rainier even while he held the enlightened path, but the sudden rush resulted in something only as dangerous as a hug. He ushered everyone in and motioned towards the table, which no one cared to sit in. He said, "We've been waiting for you and almost gave up. Do you know how hard it is to sit in the dark when a battle is about to begin?"

Villifor was already behind the bar filling his cup. He took a swig, smacked his lips in satisfaction and said, "It couldn't have been that hard."

Sana said, "Where's your army? It's great to see you,

but I'll be honest, I was expecting some reinforcements before we entered the fray."

"They're marching double time to get here. We rode ahead to meet you," Rainier said. "What do you know of the battle? Where is it taking place?"

Slate shrugged incredulously and said, "Jamison went unchallenged through all of Ravinai until he reached King Darik's palace. Darik stands surrounded by the might of the Bellator army, challenging and cursing the Disenites with every fractal-forsaken insult he can muster. Jamison wanted to know where Lattimer was, but he never showed. We had to leave at that point to meet up with you, and it's a good thing too, because it would have been hard to find the Royal Boar after the light left."

Rosana scoffed, "You belong to Sicarius. The night is our home. We would have been fine."

"I think we'll need to put that presumption to the test. Do you think a Sicarius escort could be arranged?" Rainier said. "My troops will be stumbling around with their hands in front of them if they don't wear their armor and will be a blue-lit beacon for any Fury in the city if they do. If you have any caches of orbs tucked away, we could use them too. The priests use them to recharge the armor of Sharan's paladins."

Rosana frowned and said, "Of course, Annarelle has an affinity for exploding orbs, so we've accumulated as many as possible, but it will be a little complicated. Annarelle would normally lead the mission, but she never returned from their trip to locate Villifor and Jak. Tommy hasn't returned either."

Rainier nodded in feigned sorrow. "Villifor informed me

on the way here. I'm sorry for your loss. Is there someone else that could be trusted?"

"They aren't dead. They're with the Disenite army." Rosana tapped her box for tracking the Stratego medallions and said, "I haven't been able to get close enough to track her exact location, but she's alive." Rainier didn't have the heart to crush the small hope that Rosana clung to. *She went on a mission to sabotage Jamison, and she got caught. I don't expect much leniency from that guy.*

Rosana continued, "The Sicarius Guild will get your troops through the city and your priests will have their supply of orbs refilled. We are Sicarius. We do what needs to be done." The statement seemed to bring the resolve back into Rosana's voice. "As for the covering the armor, we can help with that too. We have plenty of storerooms full of costumes and disguises. We should be able to manage some charcoal for blackening and cloaks for covering armor. If we're short supplies, we'll have to make up for it with mud. It wouldn't be the first time some mud has made the difference between life and death in a Sicarius mission."

Slate said, "Jak has the rest of your troops hidden in Bellator with the Underground."

"Bellator?" Rainier didn't try to hide his surprise.

Villifor smiled and said, "Nobody knows that place better than me, and it has as many secrets as the Sicarius Guild. Lattimer may have taken over command, but he doesn't know half the secrets of that place."

Slate nodded. "With the battle coming up, we knew we couldn't just hide in the city any longer. We needed a place to stage our troops. Lattimer sent every Guardsman in the city to Darik's palace several days ago to meet the Disenite forces, so we took some liberties with the empty guild house."

"Didn't they leave anyone behind?" Ibson asked.

"There was a skeleton crew." Villifor said and then smiled wolfishly. "Now they are all skeletons and not so much of a crew. We got it cleared out before I left to find you."

"You didn't bother to mention any of this to me when I was with my army? Don't you think that would have been useful information?" Rainier asked with a scowl.

Villifor's smile got even bigger as he said, "I'm sure it would have been useful, but as you once demonstrated to me, not everyone needs to know everything."

Rainier thought back to his time in Portswain when he had sent Villifor away without telling him that Jak was directing troops to Minot. This wasn't nearly the same thing, but obviously Villifor had taken it as more than a small slight to his pride. *Fractal-forsaken Villifor! That bastard is a wild card. Lucky for him, a wild card can come in handy when playing a game, and I'll need every piece on the board. I better keep him close for now, though, I can't give him the space for any of his own plans.*

Sana interjected, "We are about to go into battle, and we are trying to coordinate across a city, in the dark, with a scattered army that is less than half the size of Lattimer's or Jamison's troops. Now is not the time for petty games."

Rainier played the game by placating the situation despite wanting to give Villifor a tongue-lashing worth of the Remnant. "Thanks for arranging a place for us to stage our troops." He thought for a minute and then said, "I'm assuming the Bellator secrets you mentioned require that you show us in a secret door or something? You'd better come with us to make sure we don't take a misstep."

"Of course!" Villifor smiled warmly and patted Rainier on the back, resuming his normally boisterous personality. "I'd be delighted to accompany you to Bellator and see what's going on during the battle. Who is coming with us?"

"I am the Hand of the Oracle. I go where he goes." Lira stated without any room for argument.

"That's fine by me. I'd like to have your shield by my side the next time I face an army of Furies." Slate said, referencing the rooftop fight on their race through Ravinai.

Sana said, "I'll need to coordinate the Sicarius escort, but I can meet you there." She gave her own wolfish grin and said, "No one keeps secrets from the Sicarius Headmaster." She stood, grabbed her supplies, and disappeared into the night.

"Well, that settles it. We're all going. I'm not exactly excited to head into a battle, but I don't want to sit in the dark by myself, and the prospect of making two more trips through that darkened city isn't any more appetizing. Let's go to Bellator."

With that ringing endorsement from Ibson, the group set out as they had done before, with Rainier in the lead. It was a short distance to Bellator, which was a necessity for The Royal Boar to lay claim as Villifor's favorite drinking establishment, and the eerie walk was uneventful for the silent group. As they approached, Rainier realized that there were lights coming from the windows. He was becoming so accustomed to the faint light of the enlightened path that he hadn't noticed the Bellator compound was lit up.

"Where's this secret door?" Rainier whispered as they approached.

"There isn't one. I lied." Rainier could almost see the smirk on the bastard's face. "We took over the East tower. I'm sure Lattimer will try to reclaim it after the battle, but he's been too preoccupied to evict us. It's a good thing we don't plan to be permanent residents. Just look out for any pointy swords as you enter the door."

Damn Villifor. Rainier led the group to the east tower and said, "Here's the door. I'll let you lead the way from here just in case some overeager Guardsman decides to turn you into a pin-cushion."

Villifor had been reaching to pull the door open but stopped, turned his hand into a fist and pounded on the door instead, bellowing, "The Underground is underground no more. This is Villifor. Open up!"

They could hear footsteps on the other side of the door and shrieks from Furies in the city around them. Rainier counted a half dozen of them using the enlightened path, and they'd be on them in seconds.

"You fool!" Rainier hissed. "The Furies are coming!"

"I don't feel like getting skewered by walking in uninvited."

Villifor kept pounding on the door, and Rainier watched the voids in the enlightened path get closer. He drew his sword and turned to face them, but then the pounding stopped and the faint paths around him coalesced into a bright stream heading straight for the door. Rainier jumped through the doorway, crashing into everyone that had similar thoughts of escape into the Bellator compound. The door slammed shut just before a mass of Furious flesh tried to break it down like a human battering ram. Thankfully, Bellator was called a compound for a reason, and no Fury was going to break down its doors.

Rainier removed a sword hilt from his side and untangled himself from Lira, who he had flattened in his rush to get inside.

"I am your Hand, not your pillow. Get off me." Lira said.

"You're made of tougher stuff than a pillow. I'd rather sleep on a stone slab." Rainier said truthfully. Strangely, he thought Lira took it as a compliment.

Villifor, having been the first person through the door, recovered first, and demanded of the guard that opened the door, "Show us to Jak."

"I need to guard the door. What if someone else comes?" the poor guard reasoned.

Villifor talked right over him. "We're the only ones out there without red eyes, and if it came to a fight between you and those Furies, let's just say I'd rather wager on the strength of that door. Show us to Jak."

"Er...yessir." The boy guarding the door looked ten sizes smaller after the rebuke and took off quickly.

"What about Rosana? There won't be anyone to let her in the door." Ibson asked.

"When have you ever known the Sicarius Headmaster to need a door? She'll be fine."

They passed through a large hall, where paladins mixed with the ragtag soldiers of the Underground in their mismatched armor. Despite their appearance, Rainier noticed they kept their blades sharp and held them like they knew how to use them. "You have been training them. Good work, Villifor." Rainier only got a grunt in response.

Everyone hushed as the group went past and recognition spread through the soldiers. One of the paladins pounded his spear on the ground in rapid succession. Within seconds, the paladins rushed into formation in an impressive display of military discipline and training. They all faced him in rows of shining blue armor and stared at him expectantly. *I'm going to have to say something. Don't fail me now tongue.*

"You've all traveled a long way to get here and have been through so much." He looked over the soldiers. "I cannot articulate the sacrifices you have made as eloquently as Jamison or as earnestly as the Sicarius Headmaster, so I will just say thank you. Thank you for placing your trust in me and choosing to follow me." *I am thankful for the choice you all made to follow me, but I'll never understand it. Why would anyone blindly follow someone else? Half the time I don't even trust my own decisions and for some reason these soldiers think I'm some prophetic oracle with wisdom that will save their lives. They couldn't be more wrong.* "You have devoted your lives to the pattern, training and preparing in case a blood mage once again rose to power. That time is now. You are ready. By the time this battle is done, we will kill Lattimer or die trying."

His eyes slid past the soldiers towards the ragtag army calling themselves the Underground. To his surprise, he spotted Hanna in their ranks and then recognized Luca Graxis, Lara Bodier, and everyone else from the Remnant within their ranks.

Hanna saw his surprised expression and yelled up as means of explanation, "They've spent months in hiding. We've spent our whole lives in hiding. It turns out we have a few things in common." A cheer went up from those around her, and it encouraged Hanna to continue speaking. "Like our desire to live without someone controlling or manipulating us from the shadows." An even bigger cry went up. Then Hanna, rolling with the tide and speaking too freely, yelled, "We want to carve up some Furies and stand over their dead carcasses. The blood dripping off our weapons will be the last thing they see before they die. I'll kill the bastards that gutted my Kalus and threw him into the ocean like chum for the sharks. I'll cut them into pieces so small that the fish wouldn't even eat them!"

Silence filled the room as everyone looked at Hanna. Those closest to her took a step away, and the crazed look on her face turned red with embarrassment as she realized she had gone too far with her speech.

"Thanks Hanna...for...whatever that was. Why don't you come with us as we discuss a few things?" *Besides, I don't think any of your new friends in the Underground will be enjoying the presence of your company after that speech.* Rainier shook his head, trying to clear the image of Hanna feeding the cut-up pieces of her enemies to the fishes from his memory.

He looked back to the group, knowing whatever chance he had to rile the troops was gone after that gruesome comment. "We're going to discuss our plans for the battle ahead while we await the arrival of the rest of the forces under my command. Fight hard everyone, and let's make it through this thing." *Let's make it through this thing? I'm the silver-tongued leader of the Remnant, and the best I can come up with is 'Let's make it through this thing?' Somewhere, Kalus is doubled over with laughter after that pitiful display.*

Rainier motioned for the boy that had been guarding the door to continue leading them towards Jak. They passed through the meeting room and into a stairwell, where they climbed all the way to the top of the East tower. They emerged from the stairwell to see the outlines of a small group, silhouetted by the only light within the city, a faint blue produced by Jamison's army. One figure towered over the others and stood next to a silhouette that was decidedly feminine, even in the dim light.

"You chose a good spot to meet, Jak." Rainier said. The Bellator complex was near King Darik's palace, so that he could call upon their service at a moment's notice, if needed. The east tower not only provided a place to stage their troops, but it also provided a clear view of the battlefield a short distance away.

"That doesn't surprise me one bit," Slate said. "Jak always had the best tactical mind in Bellator." He then inclined his head to the feminine figure at Jak's side and said, "Lady Highsmith, it's good to see you again."

"Yes, yes, everyone knows each other here." Villifor cut through the greetings. "Has the fighting started yet? It's still really quiet."

Jak stepped to the side and waved his arm, saying, "See what you make of it."

Rainier had been imagining the battlefield and

comparing it to the memories in his head countless times on the trip from Minot. Now he understood what a pointless exercise that really was. Before him was a battlefield unlike any he had seen before. By the lack of disjointed memories forcing their way into his mind, he took it that Julian hadn't seen anything like it either.

Through the darkness stood row upon row of highly regimented paladins, adorned in holy armor, and shining with so much pattern-filled righteousness that they literally brought light to the battlefield. The might of the Nameless Army was awe-inspiring to anyone that looked upon it. Rainier could pick out the banners of Captain Tera and Captain Filios, but Rainier's attention was drawn toward the rear of the army. Jamison stood atop what could only be described as a dais or a moving throne, wearing immaculate robes inscribed with the intricate patterns of the Marked faction flowing outwards in resplendent blue markings. He looked every bit a king rather than a priest, or maybe a false god was a more befitting description.

Rainier wanted nothing more than to stick a sword in the man, but instead he watched as Jamison raised an outstretched hand and yelled in an amplified voice, "Show yourself, Lattimer! You have befouled the pattern, and you will answer for your crimes. Today is your day of reckoning!" *I can't stand that guy. Even listening to him speak drives me crazy. Befouled? Who says that stuff? Arrogant, self-righteous priests of the Marked faction, that's who.*

The other sycophantic priests of the order rode atop similar, but less extravagant, daises interspersed between the troops of Filios and Tera to provide support during the battle. Even Rainier, who had seen several demonstrations in Disentia and aboard the *Inked Tides*, had to begrudgingly admit that seeing the Nameless Army spread out across a battlefield was beyond impressive.

The sight of the priests and paladins momentarily distracted Rainier from everything else on the battlefield, including the most prominent, living symbol of Malethyan power. King Darik stood alone and defiant on the top step of his palace, lit only by the might of his enemies. Two golden lions snarled ferociously in their timeless pose with deadly paws raised to swat back any pesky invaders. King Darik snarled back in his own amplified voice that mimicked the lions by his side, "You have invaded Malethya for the last time! You are cut off from your ships, you are low on supplies, and you will die a lonely death on a foreign soil. Cherish your last breaths!"

"They've been talking back and forth like this since everything went dark. I don't think Jamison knows where to attack. He expected to fight his way into the city and crush any resistance he found. Instead, he was welcomed in, only to find himself on a battlefield where he can't even find his enemy." Jak said, "I've never seen or heard anything like it."

Slate said, "I don't think this is Lattimer's last trick of the day. He is a blood mage and a darn clever one. We have no idea what he'll do next." *That may be true, but by the time we're done playing this game, we'll find out who the clever one really is.*

Ibson scanned the battlefield as well, and Rainier wondered what it looked like from the eyes of the person that discovered spark-based magic. The old wizard looked haunted by his memories and said, "Lattimer's power has grown considerably. Let's hope that he hasn't mastered too many other disciplines of magic or a dark battlefield will be the least of all our concerns. This place will run with blood."

"That's what typically happens during battle." Villifor said with a laugh. No one joined him.

Lira looked tactically at the formations of the Nameless Army. She offered her analysis to the group, saying, "Jamison has his troops set in an aggressive formation that we call Heated Needle, but it is only for appearances. That particular formation can be changed quickly to Ink Well by drawing troops into the center of the ranks and reinforcing them." Rainier had a flood of memories enter his head at the mention of the formations, and he knew she was right. He was still shaking off the uneasy experience of sharing Julian's memories when she said to Jak, "I believe your assessment of the situation is correct. Lattimer has Jamison on the defensive."

"A sword hasn't even been swung yet. You can't possibly know all that already." Lady Highsmith inserted herself into the conversation. By her immediate dismissal of Lira, Rainier guessed that she still held a grudge over her sparring match with Jak in Portswain that ended with the two of them rolling on the ground.

"I know what I know." Lira snapped.

The group was saved from Lady Highsmith's jealousy and any other biting remarks between the two by the verbal feud on the battlefield.

Jamison's amplified voice yelled, "Show yourself

blasphemer! The pattern has come for vengeance! Where are you?"

Darik yelled back, "You are a dead man. You don't know where to point your sword. We could sit here for weeks and watch your men starve while they sat in the dark." He paused to let that reality set in. Then he said, "But letting you starve is far from our only option. You asked where Lattimer is?"

King Darik started laughing maniacally, but his amplified voice was drowned out along with everything else by a voice that shook Rainier to his core. It rattled his bones with the power of its simple message.

"I AM EVERYWHERE."

A volley of fireballs rocketed across the darkened sky of the city of Ravinai and raced towards the saintly blue aura of the Nameless Army. Moments before colliding with the army and incinerating the troops, the fireballs dissolved as quickly as they had appeared, snuffing out in the air above the paladins.

"Jamison has defensive magic." Ibson said to clarify the obvious to anyone that had seen it.

Arrows fell from the sky, passing through whatever magical barrier Jamison had at his disposal, but they hit and fell away from the paladin's holy armor without damage. A small number of unlucky soldiers had an arrow drop between the soft spots of their armor and embed deeply into flesh. Cries came up from the army as Lattimer's troops drew first blood. The paladins recovered quickly by gathering and raising their shields towards the sky for protection, but as soon as they lifted their shields up, Furies attacked from the darkness.

Filios and Tera barked their orders across the field of battle and the soldiers changed formations while swinging blue blades at the exposed necks of the Furies and smashing their enchanted shields into the oncoming masses.

"Those Furies aren't trained by Bellator." Jak stated, as he watched their movements. "They barely pass for angry peasants."

The soldiers fought their way into a rough circle, which must have been the Ink Well formation Lira had mentioned. During their movement though, they were momentarily exposed, and Lattimer didn't waste the opportunity. A squadron of soldiers led by Cirata Lorassa charged in from the darkness. Whereas the previous attack by the Furies had come from every direction in an uncoordinated manner, this assault was as deadly and focused as a spear tip. Cirata wasn't some angry peasant. She was a fully trained Bellator Guardsman that volunteered to follow Lattimer in exchange for the physical gifts he bestowed. She drove her swords into the unsuspecting paladins as they were already engaged with the first round of Furies. Paladins fell as Cirata and her soldiers carved a path deeper into the army. When she reached a priest and ended his pattern-filled life, a cry of outrage went up from the paladins around her.

They rallied and drove back Cirata and her Furies with the strength of their enchanted armor and blades that refused to turn when the Guardsmen raised shields to block. Filios saw the attack and ordered reinforcements. With their enchanted armor, they could redeploy and change their positions at an incredible rate. They launched themselves into the air, jumping over their fellow soldiers and enemies alike to reach Cirata.

Cirata didn't wait for the reinforcements to arrive. The second the paladins turned to fully engage her squadron; she sounded the retreat. Untrained Furies flooded in to become fodder for the paladin swords while Cirata escaped into the night.

The remaining Furies got slaughtered like mindless animals, and the Nameless Army stood encircled in a ring of bodies and blood.

"Lattimer was just testing them." Slate observed.

"He wanted to know how Jamison would respond before he launched a real assault." Rainier shook his head in appreciation as memories of past battles crashed through his brain. "That's a difficult tactic to pull off, because once you commit to battle, it's hard to pull back. Lattimer can do it because Jamison doesn't know where to attack next, he's stuck where he is." *Smart move, Lattimer. No wonder you were able to trick my overly trusting friend Slate into helping you seize power.*

"Then I guess I didn't get all the brains in the Regallo family after all." A dark figure flipped onto the east tower and landed on one knee. She smiled and said to Rainier, "I've arranged an escort for your army through the city, courtesy of the Sicarius Guild. Your troops will be here within the hour."

"The question is, what do you plan to do with them once they arrive?" Slate asked. "I can't go in there and give them all a beating by myself. There are too many people and too much magic floating around." Slate gave Rainier a mischievous smirk that reminded Rainier of the time they scammed their way into the Regallo estate. "I'm ready for one of your crazy schemes. How can you make use of a half-demon, bloodless ghost whose very name strikes fear into everyone that hears it?" *Except your head probably feels like it's ready to explode being this close to Lattimer, who tries to take over your mind whenever you are close to him, and it will only get worse unless we find Magnus and destroy that totem with your blood in it.*

"For now, we wait." Rainier said.

"What are you saying? That sounds like the words of a coward or a fractal-forsaken fool!" Hanna shouted as she shook her axe. "Blood has been drawn. Let's get out there!"

"You of all people know that Rainier isn't a fool." Slate said, coming to his friend's defense. "He's led the Remnant since his father's death, hidden it from everyone close to him, and showed up with an army at his back when my mistakes got us in this mess in the first place."

The grief in his voice was palpable, and Rosana finished his thought before his emotions pulled him into a dark place. They couldn't afford for him to do that now. She said, "Why are we waiting? What are you waiting for?"

I'm not sure. Rainier tried to explain. "Right now, it's a battle between Jamison and Lattimer. While they fight, they are both getting weaker, which makes us stronger. They both have their own plans and strategies, and we don't know what surprises they have in store. I guess I'm waiting for an opening. I'm waiting for one of them to make a mistake." He looked around and saw slow nods from everyone around them. "But that doesn't mean we need to be idle. Jak, the Furies led by Cirata wore Bellator armor. How much of it can we round up?"

Jak said, "We've already gotten that underway. Bellator always prides itself on giving its fighters their choice of weaponry and armor, so even with the troops engaged in battle, the famous Bellator armory still had plenty to choose from."

"Great. Can you and Hanna oversee the distribution? I want every person in the Remnant or the Underground to be indistinguishable from Lattimer and his troops." Rainier asked Jak, who was above all a faithful soldier. He knew how to follow orders and left immediately, with Lady Highsmith in tow. Hanna followed afterwards.

Next, Rainier looked to Slate and Sana. "You want to reach Lattimer, but we have no way of knowing where he is right now. Until he shows up, you'll have to hold off on that mission."

In the distance, the shouting between King Darik and Jamison continued with Lattimer holding his silence, letting unease turn to fear within the ranks of Jamison's troops. Slate and Sana surveyed the battlefield again and gave Rainier nods of agreement. Slate said, "We know that Magnus isn't really an option right now, but if the opportunity comes up, we plan to take it." Slate unintentionally rubbed his forehead, making it completely unnecessary for Rainier to ask if the proximity to Lattimer was having any effects. Slate needed to break Magnus' totem if he wanted to get closer to Lattimer.

"Why don't you check the Stratego medallions again? I can tell that the disappearance of Annarelle and Tommy is weighing heavily on you both. It might clear your minds a little bit, and maybe it will give us some new information."

It also buys me a little more time.

Sana pulled out and started consulting her Stratego box wile Darik yelled another insult, comparing the likeness of the Marked Priest to a pair of old boots. *Not the cleverest line, but hey, not everyone can have the wit of the Remnant.*

That left Rainier alone with Ibson, Lira, and Villifor, the three people in his party that he trusted the least. He walked to the edge of the tower, creating some privacy from Slate and Sana while he considered what he would say next. *Lira is duty-bound to protect me, but she knows I've lied to her priests and don't live up to my title as oracle. I hold Ibson's secrets, so he needs me until they are revealed. Then there's Villifor...what to make of that bastard...*

He looked out on the battlefield and said, "My plan hinges on the three of you." *Pattern help me.*

"Is this a prophecy?" Lira asked hopefully.

Rainier had been holding the enlightened path, but as always, he failed to use it for anyone but himself. He considered lying, but Lira already knew the truth. "You know it's not. This is a plan. Maybe a scheme is a better word, and for it to work, I need all of you."

"That's the first honest thing you've said in a long time." Lira noted.

"I'll try not to make a habit of it." Rainier joked, even knowing that Lira would find no humor in it. *Old habits die hard.* "I need you to place your duty as my Hand above all else. Don't question who I am fighting or why I am fighting them until the battle ends. For this to work, I'll need to play both sides."

"You would have me fight Jamison's troops?" Lira asked with a clenched jaw. "Those are my countrymen and you agreed to a truce with Jamison until Lattimer is dead. If you attack them, the entire Nameless Army will turn on you."

"Do you remember what Jamison did right after agreeing to that truce? He had Kalus stabbed in the stomach and thrown into the sea to die." Mentioning it brought the memory crashing into his head and the pain of his friend's death gripped him anew. He said with all the hatred he could muster, "I will see a knife in Jamison's belly by the end of the battle. If you are my Hand and doing your duty, you will need to fight paladins and priests. Will you do it?"

"Jamison's failures do not excuse your own." Her eyes bore into him and after an eternity her stony face moved a fraction of an inch. "I will protect you. My duty to you requires it." *Well, that's about the best I can get.*

Rainier turned to Villifor next and said, "I assume you have some troops within the Underground that are more loyal to you than they are to the cause?"

Villifor smirked at him and said, "Rainier, I'm offended that you would suggest such a thing." The mock offense was all the confirmation Rainier needed.

"That's all I need to know. I just ask that you stick close to me, since I may need some people with ...flexible... allegiances that are more concerned with surviving this battle than defending a cause. Can you do that?" Rainier asked.

"I'll stick close to you. I thought the leader of the Remnant might value some ...flexibility."

Lira snorted in disgust and spat on the ground, but Villifor ignored her.

"That leaves you, Ibson." Rainier looked at the old wizard who didn't bother to hide the hatred on his face. "I don't expect you to like me, especially not after our previous conversations. I just need to know that you will honor our agreement. Will you play along with my schemes?"

Ibson said, "You know how to break the bonds that bind me. I have no other choice." *Perfect.* Villifor raised his eyebrows and looked like he wanted to ask some questions, but activity on the battleground drew their attention.

Below them, Jamison shifted formations again, going back to Heated Needle, with the head of his formation pointed at Darik. He yelled into the darkness, "If you will hide behind your king, then we will take your king. Then we will kill the next person you hide behind, and the next, and the next, until we free this land from blood magic."

King Darik stepped forward and roared in defiance, paying homage to the lions at his side. "Let's see your blue armor run red!"

Slate and Sana hurried over to join them. "The rhetoric is really heating up."

"Yeah, I think the real battle is about to begin. Let's get Jak up here." Rainier then asked, "What did the Stratego medallions tell you?"

Sana pointed out on the battlefield. "It doesn't make any sense. The other half of Annarelle's Stratego medallion is coming from there." She pointed directly at Jamison as he stood atop his elevated dais. Low-level priests wheeled him around the battlefield, pushing the gigantic enclosure that he stood upon to survey the battlefield and sling insults at the Malethyan king.

"It must be some kind of trick." Slate added. "Could he have altered the medallion somehow?"

Villifor snorted and said, "He could have modified the medallion based on magic he doesn't understand...or he just killed her and took her medallion. It's a dead end. Forget about it." Then the snort turned into a sneer. "Forget about Tommy and Annarelle. If your head isn't in the battle, you're going to find a sword in your side."

That's some sound advice, even if I think he's wrong. Rainier had been contemplating the mission he sent Tommy and Annarelle on ever since Villifor said they disappeared. This helped confirm his suspicions. *You may have done more for me by failing in your mission than you would have if you succeeded. Thank you, Tommy. Thank you, Annarelle.*

Jak and Hanna appeared from the stairwell. "The Bellator armor is divided up. What's happening out there?"

"Darik is picking a fight with the whole fractal-forsaken army, and it looks like he might finally get it."

Darik yelled in his amplified voice, "If you think you can take me, then come get me!" At those words, soldiers poured from the palace and down the steps. Archers took up positions at every elevated position. Ispirtu wizards found locations out of direct conflict, and Darik laughed again as one more person joined the party.

Lattimer exited the palace in long flowing robes, holding the scepter of his dead father in his right hand and exuding power with every step. Their bones shook once more as Lattimer spoke. He thundered, "I stand behind no one. I hide from no one. Come get me!"

"There he is! It's the blasphemer himself! ATTACK! ATTACK!" Jamison screamed. Filios and Tera gave the orders and the Nameless Army darted forward, the tip of the Heated Needle driving towards Lattimer and burning into the Bellator troops like the start of a tattoo as the needle touches flesh. The Marked faction drove forward in practiced fashion. The paladins smashed their shields into the Bellator Furies and then deflected them to the side. As the shields turned the swords of the soldiers, the next group of paladins were drawn forward like ink from a needle, leading with their swords and cutting further into the Malethyan defenses.

All the while, Darik provided insults, his main contribution to the defense of his kingdom. "Drive back those pattern-worshipping ink guzzlers! Carve 'em up into so many pieces you can't tell where one tattoo ends and the other begins!"

Lattimer stood defiantly, even as the Disenite forces advanced with practiced precision. Enchanted shields overcame the mindless anger of the Furies. Each body redirected created room for swords to advance and the Nameless Army pushed swiftly towards their nemesis.

Then Darik pulled a trigger orb from his pocket and without even a single insult, jammed his belt knife deep within the swirling blue. Explosions rocked the grounds in front of the palace as soil spewed upwards, clouding the battlefield in earth. Through it all, the radiant blue of the paladins and Marked priests shined, but as the soil returned to its home, Rainier noticed a change in the Nameless Army.

Their armor dimmed. The wrath of the Furies suddenly overpowered the paladins, and pockets of the Nameless Army began to fall. Bellator Furies, no longer at a disadvantage of facing enchanted armor and weapons, let their skills show. Battle axes cleaved the dimmed helms of the Nameless Army and the dimmed blades no longer turned aside every thrust. The Nameless Army maintained their formations as years of training held their lines and prevented the battle from breaking into individual skirmishes, but the battle was no longer one-sided.

Then the priests raised their arms in unison, and the radiance returned to the Nameless Army. Any thoughts of a quick rout for Lattimer died in a brilliant blue glow.

Darik, seeing the recovery, screamed, "Archers, fire! Wizards, cast! Burn the bastards!" On his command, flaming arrows arced across the night sky. Fireballs shot towards the soldiers only to have the priests dissipate the flames before they had any effect. Wizards cast spells that heaved huge sections of earth, sending waves of soil at the army, only to have the priests push their hands out, stopping the earth like a wave against the breakers.

"The priests are counteracting every spell sent at them. It's incredible!" Ibson exclaimed to no one's delight. *I'd like it if they weren't quite so good at staying alive.*

"It does affect them though. Their armor dims momentarily every time they stop a wave of fireballs." Sana observed. "They must be incredibly strong wizards to fend off all of Ispirtu. They are completely outnumbered."

"They are not wizards. They are priests of the Marked

faction, and they call upon the power of the pattern to aid the Nameless Army. Do not assume your wizard rules apply." Lira corrected Sana and spat in disgust. *She isn't ready for the truth yet. Will she see it before this battle is done?*

"Well, however they are doing it, they aren't just managing to fend off Lattimer's forces. Look at them advance. They are almost to the palace gates." Slate commented.

Lattimer had joined King Darik on top of the steps, and Jamison yelled up to him as his robes shook in holy righteousness, "The might of the Marked faction is at your doorstep. Enjoy your last breaths before the pattern leaves you!"

Lattimer remained quiet, holding his scepter high, choosing to let Darik speak. The king yelled back, "You stumble through the dark like a lost child! Do you think we fear you?" He let loose another maniacal laugh, enraging Jamison even further.

Stumble through the dark? How can he be so confident when Jamison is advancing on him so quickly? Rainier had been so engrossed with the battle before his eyes, he had forgotten to read the enlightened path. He had kept holding it, but with the fireballs and blue radiance, the faint light had gone forgotten.

Yellow streams of light covered the surfaces of the buildings around him, stopping occasionally where a Fury roamed the city streets. He looked further towards the palace, and his heart nearly stopped. There were two gigantic voids on either flank of the Nameless Army, out of sight, but clear as day to Rainier.

"We need to move! Send word to the army." The suddenness of his order surprised everyone in the group, himself included.

"What have you seen? Is it a prophecy?" Lira asked. Rainier tried not to laugh. *Despite all the tricks and cons and schemes that she has seen me run, she still thinks I have some crazy power to see the future. Julian really has brainwashed these people.*

"Lattimer isn't losing this battle. He's drawing Jamison's forces exactly where he wants them, and he'll pinch them off like a vice."

"That doesn't make any sense. He's using himself as bait?" Slate asked.

"We said he'd have some tricks up his sleeve. I don't know what this one is, but it's the opening I've been waiting for. We need to approach Jamison's troops from the back of the Heated Needle formation, and we need to do it quickly, so that we can support Jamison."

"You want to support Jamison?" Hanna sneered as she raised an eyebrow.

Rainier shook his head in disagreement and said, "I want to see him dead just as much as you but going in head-on is the wrong approach."

"Captain Sharan and the rest of your troops should be arriving shortly. Should we wait for them to join us?"

Rainier smiled and said, "No. They have their own role to play."

"He has a plan," Slate said with a smile, "and I'm guessing it isn't the type of plan you can find in Jamison's memories or Jak's textbooks on military strategy."

"Are you willing to try something less...direct? Do you

trust me?" *Funny how I end up asking for everyone's trust when even I know I don't deserve it. I'm probably going to get half these people killed, and if I need to sacrifice them all to save my own neck, I won't hesitate to do it.*

Hanna said, "The Remnant followed you across the sea and back. You know we'll do whatever you need. Just point my axes where you want me to bury them, as long as one of these blades ends up in that bastard Jamison." *I'm starting to see what Kalus saw in this girl. She's as crazy as he ever was.*

"The Underground will fight where you need them. I've already decided that marching them into battle against either of those forces without the support of your Disenite troops is a suicide mission, so the Underground is at your command." Jak proclaimed and Rainier nodded appreciatively for the show of support.

Villifor leaned casually against the wall of the east tower and nodded in agreement but made no commitments to anything. *It's just as well. Even if Villifor did promise his support, I wouldn't believe him anyway.* Rainier glanced at Ibson and Lira, but he already knew where they stood. The last person left was the Shadow in the Night.

Rosana walked forward with the grace of a lioness on the hunt. She unwrapped a few pieces of cloth from her Sicarius outfit and exposed the skin of her arm. Black tendrils of blight snaked beneath her skin, poisoning her from the inside out. "As for me, I've never been great at following orders. I've been able to solve most of my problems with a sharp knife or a visit in the night, but that hasn't worked so far. Lattimer is stronger than ever." The

Sicarius Headmaster flipped a blade of pure darkness through the air and caught it. "Let's see what this Blighted Knife can do before this fractal-forsaken disease takes my life. What's your plan?"

"I want to kill Lattimer. That fractal-forsaken bastard of a blood mage needs to die, but that's not enough. Jamison killed Kalus, and for that, I want to watch Jamison hold his insides in shock as he dumbly tries to put them back into his body." He saw nods across the group, and then he said what he had known ever since his plan started to come together on the deck of the *Remnant Awakens* as he prepared for his friend's funeral to start this whole mess. "I can't promise you vengeance today, at least not in the way vengeance plays out in your dreams." Rainier thought back to all the deals he made as a Tribesman, to a type of victory he knew better than anyone, when he cut a deal and left his mark smiling, knowing that it would take him days to finally realize he had been fleeced. "Today isn't the day of vengeance, it's the day of the deal. It's the type of deal the Remnant is famous for, and I can promise you that it will taste sweet. We will have our vengeance, and so much more..."

Slate laughed and said, "Never deal with the Remnant!" *You're frackin' right.*

"I'll tell you the details on the way. Let's march."

CHAPTER FIFTEEN

ENTERING THE FRAY

Fear. Excitement. Trepidation. Nervousness. It felt like Rainier's emotions changed with each step through the darkened streets of Ravinai. The litany of soldiers marching in time behind him propelled him forward as he walked alongside Slate, Sana, and the other leaders of their eclectic army. *All my plans lead up to this moment, and now that it's here, it feels so surreal. I gave most of my orders to everyone in advance, so why am I worrying so much? I just need to hope that I read my opponent's plans correctly, let the game play out, and be flexible.* Rainier tried to shake the nerves before battle, so that he was calm and could react quickly, almost like he did in preparation for his tournament matches in the arena.

Sana had her own ritualistic preparations for missions, and it involved reciting each person's role repeatedly to make sure no one made a mistake. After Rainier's poor attempt to give a morale-boosting speech to the troops at Bellator, he was happy to let her do some talking. It was a short walk to the palace, and he wanted to be alone with his thoughts for a moment. He tuned out Sana and the others, confident that he had been clear in his orders, and that Sharan would receive hers and do her part as well. He was too busy cycling through different scenarios in his head to worry about orders he had already given. While his head spun with different possibilities and replayed different battles from Julian's memories, they rounded a corner and suddenly appeared at the edge of the palace grounds. *And just like that, we're here.*

Rainier checked the enlightened path to find the two voids signifying Lattimer's forces approaching the sides of Jamison's Heated Needle formation, but they had not yet engaged. Meanwhile, Jamison's troops had made short work of the palace gates. They lay battered and broken and tossed to the side as foreign troops drove into the heart of Malethya.

The Nameless Army advanced up the steps of the palace towards King Darik and Lattimer Regallo, and the outcome appeared inevitable. Jamison yelled to his troops, "Push through! Kill the king and the great blasphemer! End this!"

His troops fought with renewed vigor and broke through, leaving only the king's honor guard as a defense. Lattimer raised his scepter but said nothing. King Darik roared his defiance, "For Malethya!" *I would be impressed by his bravery if his mind hadn't been subjugated by Lattimer. Lattimer commands Darik to be brave, so Darik has no choice but to let loose a blood-curdling scream even when he is facing imminent death.*

The king and his honor guard charged down the steps to meet the Disenite army. Darik fought with all the passion and rage of a Fury, but with the skill of a king that had been too long removed from the battlefield. His honor guard fought valiantly to protect him, but his old arms lost their strength after a few minutes of battle, and he was a second too late in raising his shield. A blue sword cut clean through Darik's neck, and the defiant king's head rolled down the steps. The crown he wore upon his head bounced away and lay as useless and lifeless as the man who had worn it.

The priests cried out in anticipation of victory as the Nameless Army surged forward, with each paladin racing for the right to bury their sword in the blood mage at the top of the steps. Rainier kept waiting for Lattimer to cast a spell or set a trap or something, but he just stood there. He didn't move a muscle or rustle his splendidly flowing robes as the onslaught of paladins came up the steps. He didn't flinch as a blue sword slashed downward. In the moment before the blade entered his shoulder, he stood stoically observing the battlefield below him.

The blade sliced through Lattimer, crossed his chest, and exited his hip. A second later, another paladin's sword landed another lethal wound. Then another.

Still Lattimer stood, unflinching.

Slate was the first to understand what was happening. "It's not him. He used an orb to create an image of himself. It's like the warriors in the Ispirtu halls that recreate famous battles."

Jamison was a little slower in realizing he had been tricked. He yelled out, "What trickery is this? Where are you?!?"

The deep voice that reverberated throughout their bodies came from the darkness, "Hahahaaa. Darik told you that you were stumbling in the dark like a child and rushed forward blindly. You make this too easy for me, Jamison. You are a dead man."

"Clever." Villifor said. "Brannon once used the same trick in the Twice Broken Wars to make his numbers appear greater than they were. It's what caused me to switch sides. I wonder why he sacrificed Darik though?"

"Darik has been a puppet, and Lattimer needed someone with enough authority to make his ruse believable. Darik served his purpose perfectly." Rosana said as Rainier looked at the crown lying on the steps. *One more person used in the name of someone's schemes. I can't fault him for that. I can't count the number of people that will die when we enter the battle, and most of them don't even know my real plans.*

Jamison looked around anxiously as Filios and Tera tried to draw their formations into Ink Well, but the palace steps were long and narrow, preventing them from creating a defensive formation as they had done in the open space of the grounds.

In the enlightened path, Rainier saw the voids of light start to advance and Lattimer's voice shook the battlefield as he said, "Your death comes!"

"Charge!" Rainier commanded, "We need to get to Jamison before Lattimer's troops arrive. I don't want to have to fight through them! Hurry!"

Jak had prepared their army for the sudden advance, and they executed it in impressive fashion. The Disenite troops had the discipline to advance quickly while still maintaining their order, and the rest of the troops had enough training to follow their example and not trample each other. They raced across the field as Jamison gave an order to his priests.

Jamison looked frantically around, trying to locate his enemies, unable to see past the blue aura of his own army. Then he reached within his robe and pulled out an orb, holding it above his head and said, "By the power of the pattern, I bathe this field in holy light!"

The orb shot into the air. The soft blue didn't provide enough light to brighten the city, but it transformed the city from pure darkness to dark grey blues. Jamison's priests followed his lead, and more orbs joined Jamison's in emitting a soft light, revealing a battlefield that had been visible to only Rainier and the enlightened path. *I bet Jamison didn't want to have to use his orbs for something as trivial as light. Any orb hovering over the battlefield is one less orb that can bless the armor of paladins, and it is one more spell he has to hold active in the middle of battle as Ispirtu wizards launch fireballs at him. Jamison is making tradeoffs he won't want to make. He's getting desperate.*

The mindless Furies loose in the city attacked at random, from any angle, but the hovering orbs revealed Lattimer's troops closing the distance from both sides of the Nameless Army. Their dim light gave Filios and Tera enough time to bark orders and have their paladins meet the oncoming onslaught with shields in place. The mass of soldiers hitting the paladin defenses would have overrun any conventional line of soldiers, but the strength of the paladin shields didn't crumble beneath the weight of the charge.

"I can't believe those paladins held their lines," Slate said incredulously as they ran forward to join the fray. "We better hope that Jamison realizes we are here for support. I wouldn't want to run into a shield wall like that."

"That's why we waited until now. Jamison knows he needs help." Rainier turned to Ibson and said, "Amplify my voice."

The old wizard concentrated as he ran ahead, trying to keep up with everyone else. He nodded that the spell was prepared, and Rainier yelled, "Blood magic has no place in Malethya! We will defeat your army and find you wherever you are hiding, Lattimer!"

The Nameless Army under Jamison's command pounded their shields at the sound of his voice as it carried across the battlefield, thankful for the support. Rainier doubted that Jamison had the same level of appreciation, but you can't be too picky when your enemies are attacking from all sides.

"Won't Lattimer just attack us, too? Why are we proclaiming our support for Jamison?" Ibson asked. "I thought you wanted to be a wild card."

"The best way to play both sides is to make everyone think you are on their side. We already sent a note to Lattimer from Sana. He could just ignore it and fight us, as you said, but we told him about the blue armor. He believed enough of what was in his sister's letter to take advantage of our advice, and now he's seen the Nameless Army in action and knows they pose a real threat. Why would he risk the lives of his own troops when he knows Julian is coming, and we said we'd betray Jamison? Judging by the lack of fireballs coming our way, he at least intends to find out if we live up to our word." Rainier gave his best Remnant grin and said, "Besides, I have another message for Lattimer arriving shortly."

The first lines of Rainier's army hit the backs of the mindless Furies attacking the Nameless Army. These Furies weren't highly trained Bellator soldiers, but peasants from

Ravinai who had the misfortune of being recruited for battle. Their minds had only one thought, and that was to kill the soldiers in front of them. They didn't notice a throwing knife from the Sicarius Headmaster flying through the air with deadly accuracy. They didn't turn around when Slate Severance flashed ahead and dented a few skulls with his Stonehands. Even the Furies that remained standing continued to bang on the paladin shields in front of them as Rainier's troops started removing heads from shoulders.

After making short work of the mindless Furies, they met the glowing shields of the Marked faction's rear guard. Cordial nods of appreciation were shared from Disenite to Disenite, it was all the greeting a battle allowed. The Underground and the Remnant were largely ignored.

A messenger found her way through the scrum of soldiers to find Rainier. She recited her message from memory, stating, "Jamison commands you to split your forces and fortify our flanks. The rear guard will remain under the command of Captains Tera and Filios. You are to remain in reserve if Lattimer should appear."

He wants to use us as fodder where the heaviest fighting is expected, but he wants to make sure his troops are the ones that kill Lattimer. I guess he isn't entirely desperate now that we've shown up. There's no way I'm letting him give me orders though. "Tell Jamison that I've never taken orders from him, and I'm certainly not going to start today."

The messenger started giving all sorts of demands and issuing statements about the organizational hierarchy within the Nameless Army. Rainier ignored her and consulted the enlightened path. What he saw stopped any other thoughts from entering his head. He interrupted the messenger and said, "We won't be going anywhere. Don't you see Lattimer's troops advancing?"

At the far reaches of the blue ambient light, a huge collection of Furies appeared and charged towards them. They raised their swords and released guttural screams of anger. They pushed each other as they jockeyed for position to reach their enemies first. They sprinted forward despite their full armor, hatred propelling the dark figures towards Rainier's troops.

"Hold your lines! Shields up!" Jak shouted and his commands were carried down the line.

"Look at all those Furies! Lattimer must be sending everyone!" Rosana exclaimed.

Slate ran over to the messenger and picked her up with ease, staring straight at her with his red, half-demon eyes and screamed. "You go tell Jamison that Tera and Filios better hold their lines." He clenched his jaw in determination and said, "We'll hold the rear guard." He dropped the messenger and screamed across the ranks of Disenite soldiers, "We'll hold the rear guard. Do you hear me Malethyans? WE WILL HOLD."

Whether it was the sight of the Furies running towards them or being lifted in the air by the scariest man in Malethya, the messenger didn't waste time leaving. Her feet were running towards Jamison the second they hit the ground, and she didn't look back. The soldiers in the Nameless Army took Slate's command as an order, assuming it came at the behest of Jamison since his own messenger was leading the way.

Ahead, the Furies were almost upon them. Rainier unsheathed his sword, singled out one of the Furies running at him and crouched behind the shield wall. A tall Fury in dirty, darkened armor raised her sword and crashed into the wall with a twisted scream of rage. Rainier lunged forward with a guttural scream of his own. She parried his thrust and Rainier found himself in close quarters with the blackened Fury, just as he had planned.

"You smell like mud, pig manure, or both, but your timing is impeccable." Rainier said. Through the enlightened path, the Furies in front of him didn't show up as a void. They weren't the darkened shape of enemies. They were as bright as a summer day and more welcome than a bed after a long day of work. They had been marching hard since Minot, and they had finally arrived with blackened blades and dressed as Furies, courtesy of the Sicarius Guild. "It's so good to see you...Captain Sharan."

"I'm glad those Sicarius friends of yours were able to guide us through the city or we never would have made it." She swung a clumsy overhead blow that Rainier easily blocked. Then she yelled down the line, "Make it look real people! Some of you savages have to take a fall."

The fake Furies fell with screams that could only be caused by a deep wound or some bad acting. The next Disenite soldiers stepped into place to have mock battle with the rest of Rainier's forces in their gleaming Bellator armor.

"Be careful not to trample anyone!" Sharan barked as the fallen soldiers lay helpless on the ground. Then she said to Rainier as they traded blockable blows, "We received your orders, but I don't pretend to understand them. I'm assuming this scheme is as crazy and as brilliant as Kalus' funeral? What do you need us to do now?"

"Lattimer thinks we will betray Jamison. This charade allows us to get close so that he doesn't have time to respond when we all disengage and attack as one unit."

"Was this a prophecy?" Captain Sharan asked. *Half-truths and lies — now is when I'll need my silver tongue.*

"The enlightened path has shown me the way of the pattern. This is the only way. Jamison won't defeat Lattimer on his own. It's up to us."

Lira grunted by his side and gave an unnecessarily hard blow to a fake Fury she was battling. *Duty or not, that one may put a sword in my side yet.*

Sharan on the other hand, lit up with pride. She said, "I knew you saw the pattern differently when I first met you on the *Inked Tides*. It's an honor to serve with you, my oracle. What do you need us to do?"

"Make it look like we're locked in battle. As a group, I want you to drive my men back into the Disenite formation, getting us closer to Lattimer's troops." *It'll get us closer to Jamison as well.* "Above all, make sure we avoid casualties. We'll need everyone. When I give the order, you and Jak will lead your forces against Lattimer's troops. Do you understand?"

"We are the Nameless Army. We will do as the pattern wills. Lead us to victory, my oracle."

Rainier gave her a determined stare that he hoped inspired confidence and disengaged from the line of Furies, searching out Slate and Sana, but Lira found him first.

"You just lied to the commander of your own troops. You did not have a prophecy. This is just one of your schemes. Why did you lie to her?"

Rainier didn't have time for an argument, and he certainly didn't want his troops to see his Hand confronting him on the battlefield. He grabbed her by the arm and pulled her close, whispering, "I told her what she needed to hear to do her job. She came here to fight a blood mage, and I'm going to try to give her that chance. If she fights a little harder or it inspires her troops to think that they are a part of some pre-ordained mission, then that's what I'm going to tell her. Do you understand me?"

Lira said, "She trusts you and deserves better."

"Maybe she does," Rainier snapped, "Let's see if the pattern wills it. Until then, me and my schemes are the best bet you, Sharan, and everyone else have for coming out of this mess alive."

Lira shook his hand from her shoulder. Rainier couldn't help but notice her hand tighten its grip on her sword again, but a voice filled the battlefield with an intensity that interrupted any other thoughts.

"MORE OF MY ENEMIES COME TO DIE HERE TODAY! FEEL THE WRATH OF MY FURIES, SLATE SEVERANCE!"

Lira asked, "Why would he say that? He must know that Captain Sharan's troops aren't real Furies."

"He's playing along." Rainier smiled and said, "We need to find Sana." He scanned the battlefield and saw Ibson and Villifor standing by Jak away from the front lines. Thinking they'd know where Sana and Slate were, he rushed over.

"Good, you're here Rainier. You need to see this." Jak pointed across the battlefield where Lattimer's troops were engaged with Jamison's along the flanks. In the time it had taken to fake an assault from Sharan, the two sides had spilled a lot of blood. "Jamison's troops are still holding their own, but they are losing the battle of numbers. Lattimer's troops will overrun them soon."

Rainier could see the accuracy of Jak's assessment. From Julian's memories, he knew when a line was about to break, and the radiant blue of the Nameless Army couldn't stop all the Furies coming at them. He consulted the enlightened path again and saw a void approaching from behind Lattimer's troops. "Someone's coming to support Lattimer."

A colossal figure carrying a battle axe exited the darkness of the city and jogged towards battle under the eerie blue light of the hovering orbs, picking up speed as he came. Magnus Pudriuz, a snarling hulk of muscle and violence, was dressed in pure black armor that seemed to draw in the light, almost like a Sicarius mask. At his side were similarly dressed warriors carrying their weapons of choice, and there was no question that they knew how to use them.

"They're going to break through the line!" Rainier exclaimed.

Ahead of Magnus' charge, the Ispirtu wizards concentrated their spells on the point of impact. Fireball followed fireball in an awesome display of magic. The concentrated spells dissipated right before they hit the lines of Furies battling across the paladin shield wall, but that didn't stop the onslaught of spells. Boom! B-boom!

Boom! Wave after wave of spells kept coming. The blue armor of the paladins started to dim as the priest needed to concentrate his attention on defending against the incoming fireballs.

"It takes an incredibly powerful wizard to defend against that many fireballs. I am a master of defensive magic, and I don't know if I could do that." Ibson said in awe.

"Except we know they aren't. Half of their priests can't get out of bed before smoking wanderleaf." Rainier said. "They get their power from orbs. Lira saw some priests place them in the cannons of their ships during a demonstration of their power. They must have a stash of them that they draw upon during battle, but you'd need too many orbs to carry by yourself in a battle. Where are they?" *I've known since I set eyes on the battlefield, but everyone was looking at the battlefield with the eyes of a soldier and didn't see the deception right in front of them.*

Villifor rubbed his chin and said, "You mean like a gigantic, wheeled chest that your fellow priests push you around on?" *That bastard does think like the Remnant. He deserves more credit than I give him.*

"I thought it was just to give them a better view of the battlefield." Jak said, shaking his head.

"If that entire dais is filled with orbs, that would be a tremendous source of power." Ibson confirmed. "I think you are right, Rainier." *Of course, I am.*

The priest defending against the incoming fireballs fell to his knees atop his dais. His hands stayed extended, warding off the onslaught of spells even though he was too weak to stand.

Then he collapsed. Wizard fire enveloped Fury and paladin alike, indiscriminately burning everything it touched. Jamison extended his hands and dissipated the remaining fireballs before they landed, but the damage had been done. The fireball created a gaping hole in the middle of the Disenite lines.

It was the only opening Magnus needed.

He crashed through the charred remains with a great swing of his battle axe. The blade buried in the chest of a paladin, whose dimmed armor couldn't turn a direct blow from Magnus. Without hesitating, he flowed into another form that removed the axe from the dead paladin while simultaneously swiping at the feet of three more. The Furies fighting with Magnus finished off the fallen paladins and jumped ahead, working in pairs. They fought with the aggression of a Fury but the skill of a Guardsman, with no fear and inhuman strength.

Slate and Sana found them, and Slate said, "Magnus is on the field. Now is our chance!"

"Watch him fight first and learn his weaknesses. This won't be like fighting him in the arena, and that armor gives him strength, as if he needed any more." Rainier commented.

The Headmaster flipped the Blighted Knife in the air. "We aren't kids banging sticks in the arena anymore. Let's see how he fares against us instead of some powered-down pattern lovers," she said as they watched Magnus and his crew carve a path into the Nameless Army while Furies flooded the space left in their wake.

Jamison yelled across the battlefield, "I bless these servants of the pattern in holy light!" He outstretched his hands and the armor of every paladin burst with the intricate patterns of the Marked faction, instantly rejuvenating the soldiers on the field. He yelled to Lattimer, "We do not hide in the shadows. We are the light that will never be extinguished!"

The Nameless Army moved quickly under the command of Filios and Tera to support the break in their lines. The rejuvenated soldiers launched into the air, landing near Magnus and his crew to support their fellow paladins.

Then Lattimer stepped from the shadows for the first time, gazing down on the battlefield from a tower in the palace grounds. At the sight of Lattimer, Rainier immediately looked to Slate to judge his reaction, knowing that he fought a battle in his head that none of them could see. To his relief, even though Slate had a pinched look of concentration on his face, he looked to be far enough away from Lattimer that he wasn't left in a debilitating puddle of uselessness. With Lattimer in a tower, hopefully it would stay that way.

Lattimer boomed across the palace grounds, "I will hide no longer, while my troops will hide in plain sight. See how much your holy light helps you when you can't tell friend from foe."

Lattimer raised his scepter and turned the battlefield awash in blue light. As the wave of light passed by, everyone's armor turned the same radiant blue of the Nameless Army.

"Brilliant," Villifor said. "Magnus and his Furies are within the ranks of Nameless Army and now they can wreak havoc from all sides."

Lattimer yelled, "Your troops thrive on discipline and

400	J. Lloren Quill

order. What will they do when they can't tell who their enemy is? What will they do when they are forced to fight in chaos?" He laughed and said, "Chaos is the home of a Fury. Your paladins are not prepared for this. You traveled across the sea to die at my hand."

As Lattimer spoke the words, another portion of the shield wall broke and the battlefield began to devolve into pockets of fighting.

"What should we do?" Jak asked.

"We take advantage of the chaos." Rainier said, and the Sicarius Headmaster smiled. If there was one person here who thrived in chaos, it was her, and it was more than a little disconcerting to see her smile. Rose smiled at the most innocent of times. Rosana had a smile that could win over a room, and she smiled whenever it suited her purpose. Sana smiled on the rare occasion that her analytical mind allowed her to, but the Headmaster didn't smile.

Rainier gave her orders first so that he didn't have to look at her hideously upturned lips any longer.

"Go fight Magnus but bring Sharan and her troops with you. They have been waiting for the word from their oracle to enter the fight. Tell them the time is now."

Slate flexed his stonehand and stared at his friend with blood-red eyes. The blue light made his ghostly complexion even more disturbing, and he said, "We'll get Magnus. The rest is up to you." He smiled as he left with the Headmaster. The pale smile from Slate the Bloodless reminded Rainier of Kalus as the blood drained from his body and slipped into death. "We trust you."

That's your mistake. You should have learned your

lesson in the Ispirtu tower. Don't trust anyone.

Rainier turned his attention to the next fool to trust in him. "Jak, I need you to lead the Underground reserve unit. Hold the rear guard and support anyone that looks like they need it. I know it isn't the role you'd like to take on, but I need someone that can read a battlefield. Will you do it?"

"If you need us, we'll be there." Jak confirmed.

"Good then, go coordinate your troops. Things will be happening fast now." Jak ran off, leaving Rainier with Ibson, the wizard who despised him, Lira, the soldier who despised him, Hanna, the crazed girlfriend wielding Kalus' axe, and Villifor, the man with allegiances even more questionable than his own.

"That leaves us to do the dirty work," Rainier said. Lira glared, Ibson looked down at his feet, Hanna tested the sharpness of her axe, and Villifor smiled like a madman.

"What do you have in mind?" Villifor asked.

"We're going to need those soldiers with...flexible...morals." Rainier said. "We're going after Jamison, and any other priest of the Marked faction we can kill along the way."

Lira erupted, "You cannot do this! No one in the Nameless Army will follow you if you attack their priests and priestesses. Sharan will turn on you immediately!"

"That's why I sent them ahead to attack Magnus. They won't see a thing, until it's too late."

"If you do kill Jamison, then what? You'll be surrounded by troops and no one will give you the chance to use that silver tongue of yours before they slip a sword into you." *I don't exactly need the reminder. All I need to do is look at the enlightened path. All those comforting yellow streams of light aren't extending outwards very far anymore. If I'm going to make it out of here, it will need to be by the strength of my wits.*

Hanna interrupted Lira and said, "Haven't you learned by now who you are dealing with? This is Rainier Tallow, the fractal-forsaken leader of the Remnant. You don't think he knows the situation we're in? I don't know what he plans to do, but I know he'll be two steps ahead of anyone else out there, and a good dozen more steps ahead of you, little lady." She cut the edge of her thumb against the sharp edge of her blade and looked at it approvingly. "Now are you going to do your duty and go kill some priests or are we going to stand here looking at each other? My axe wants to see more blood than just my own, and Jamison is only spitting distance away. I'll grab the Remnant. We'll kill some priests for you. Maybe I can even find that spiky haired one that stuck a knife in my Kalus." She shrugged. "If not, someone else in Marked robes will have to do."

Surprisingly, Lira held her tongue. Rainier guessed that she didn't know what to make of Hanna, which was fine by him.

Rainier talked with Villifor, anxious to get moving. "Can you talk to those in the Underground that are loyal to you? Send them out in groups and give them each a different priest as a target. Try to sneak up on them and make quiet work of it. Whatever you do, don't damage those rolling thrones they're standing on. If they're filled with orbs like we think they are, the explosion could kill all of us." *I can't believe I'm entrusting this part of the plan to Villifor's loyalists, but Sharan won't attack her priests when Lattimer is still alive, and the Underground was recruited to stop Lattimer. I have no idea if they would follow through on an order to attack the priests of the army fighting him. The only people left are the people without any loyalty whatsoever. Fractal's curses! I can almost feel those yellow streams of light getting shorter.*

"It is a special person who does not balk at an order to kill a priest, and that goes for priests of any order." Then he smiled and said, "I have just the people in mind." He left to consort with his loyalists, and Rainier wished he could be on his way. *I'm still going to wait for Villifor though. I don't trust him to be loose on the battlefield.*

He asked Ibson, "Do you still have me protected with your defensive magic?"

"I do. I need to keep you alive long enough to free me from my bonds." *And probably not a moment longer, if I'm not mistaken.*

Lattimer laughed from his tower and yelled, "Blue fighting blue! I don't care if it's just an illusion, the sight brings joy to my heart. I wonder how many paladins have fallen. It's impossible to count in this beautiful chaos."

"That man sounds as crazy as they come." Hanna commented, which meant something coming from her. "Just so I'm clear, are we trying to kill him or help him?"

"He's clever and he's playing the part of the crazed blood mage to strike fear into the paladins below. Don't underestimate him."

"And the killing part?"

"Yes, we want to kill him. We just can't do it yet, because he's the only one with an army big enough to fight Julian when he comes," Rainier clarified for Hanna.

"Sounds complicated. Just find me some priests. I like to keep it simple." *Simple is a luxury I haven't been able to afford in a long time.*

Rainier saw Sharan advancing her troops towards Magnus, their armor awash in the blue light of Lattimer's magic. As always, she had tight command of her troops and moved out immediately. As the only coordinated force left on the battlefield, they were able to overwhelm anyone with crazy red eyes while recruiting members of the Nameless Army into their ranks as they swept past. Their numbers grew and Jamison saw their approach from the top of his dais as it was wheeled towards Magnus, Lattimer's champion on the battlefield.

He yelled to the Marked faction, "Do not be discouraged by the lies of the great Blasphemer! Even now, the pattern provides us with support! Reinforcements are on the way. Stay strong, my paladins!"

The Remnant and the rest of Rainier's group set off in the direction of Slate and Sana as soon as Villifor reappeared. Rainier didn't need the enlightened path to know that the safest place on the battlefield was following in the wake of the two most dangerous people on his side of the fight, but it had saved his life many times, and he consulted it out of habit. The problem was that he didn't like what he saw. *There certainly isn't any comfort in seeing all the yellow streams leading towards Magnus end rather abruptly. The paths leading to Jamison don't look any longer. I guess I will have to find a way to change my fate.* Any member of the Remnant knew the best way to tilt the odds in their favor, and Rainier knew how to lie, cheat, and steal with the best of them.

Their progress slowed as they encountered the inevitable skirmishes with both Furies and pockets of paladins that confused them for Furies. The chaos of the battlefield allowed Rainier to disguise his movements to some degree, but it came with a cost as they had to fight anyone that sought to occupy the empty space on the battlefield behind Sharan's troops as they marched through. While the Remnant knew their way around a sword, they weren't the lifelong soldiers of the Nameless Army, and they didn't have Slate and Sana in their group either.

Watching those two fight was a thing of beauty, or terror, depending on your perspective. Slate had experience fighting beside Lira, and it taught him the benefits of a paladin's shield. He flashed between the shields, punching, stabbing, and killing with inhuman speed and then retreating before he got pinned down in any one location. He was a terror on the battlefield, appearing to sow death to all those in his way and then disappearing just as quickly.

The only thing more terrifying was the sight of the Sicarius Headmaster. She threw a flurry of throwing knives that always found their mark, finding the soft spots in armor and victimizing any exposed skin. None of her impressive skills inspired the fear of the Blighted Knife though. Everything it touched turned black as Blight. Furies that had once fought through indescribable pain now fell with the most minor of wounds. If she couldn't find exposed skin, she'd slash at a shield or a piece of armor, turning it brittle and black so that it wouldn't survive the next blow from one of Sharan's paladins. Everywhere she went, she left a trail of blackened, Blight-riddled corpses with looks of agony etched on their lifeless faces.

As they carved their way towards Magnus, Rainier marched comfortably in the middle of the Remnant, as far away from the fighting as possible. Soft yellow streams of light emanated a short distance away from him, and although he held his short swords at the ready, he had no problem letting others be on the front lines. His part of the fighting would come soon enough, whether he wanted it to or not.

"Are you marking the progress of your men?" Rainier asked Villifor, who had the height of a war hero, even if he had stolen the title. Rainier's diminutive stature came with some limitations on a battlefield.

"I see several of those rolling thrones standing empty. My men have knocked out a few of the targets. There appears to be fighting at a few more." He then paused and said, "Look at Jamison up ahead. He appears to have taken up the responsibilities of defending against the Ispirtu attacks."

"Then we're having the desired effect. If we're forcing Jamison to get his hands dirty, then we're straining their priests. What about Magnus and his Furies? Are they still advancing?"

"It looks to be at an impasse now that Jamison powered up his paladins again. Slate and Sana will get there shortly."

Lira said, "Your need for revenge against the Marked priests will prevent them from blessing their paladin's armor. You not only threaten the lives of the Nameless

Army, but of your own troops as well, who are marching in to fight him. You even threaten the lives of the people you claim as your friends."

She's right, but every scheme has a cost, and I'm giving them what they wanted, the chance to fight some Furies. "You talk as if there is an outcome of this battle in which we win. I promised that we would get vengeance, but I've already told you that today is not that day. We'll have to make some sacrifices, and some will be bigger than others."

As he spoke, the armor of the paladins dimmed from radiant to shining, signaling the change that was to come. Jamison noticed it too, as he scanned the battlefield. He yelled, "Tera, Lattimer is attacking the priests! Reinforce their positions now and leave Filios to hold against the Furies until Sharan arrives!"

Tera responded immediately, barking orders that sent her paladins jumping towards the rolling thrones of the remaining priests spread across the battlefield. Filios, on the other hand, felt the loss of Tera's troops as the strength of Magnus' forces pressed against Filios' paladins, causing their armor to lose power even more quickly.

Sharan arrived like a Disenite hero worthy of the storybooks, attacking Furies with the preordained, pattern-filled righteousness of a paladin army sent on a prophetic mission. Her forces hit like a holy hammer, a lifetime of training and waiting unleashed on some unlucky bastards that had the misfortune of losing control of their minds to a blood mage. The Furies were put out of their single-minded hatred with merciless blows from Sharan's troops.

Jamison rejoiced in their downfall, yelling, "You can't fight the strength of the pattern!" His dais rolled closer to the action by Magnus, where he could protect his troops centered at the most important part of the battle. As he scanned the battlefield, he saw Rainier for the first time and said, "Every Disenite despises blood magic from the depths of their soul. We will band together and stop you!"

Rainier nodded his agreement back to the bastard on his rolling throne of hypocrisy. He tried to look as earnest as possible as he yelled, "I honor my commitments when we agreed to fight Lattimer. We stand with Disentia. We stand for the pattern!" *What's one more lie?*

A roar went up from Jamison and Sharan's troops alike, but it was the grunt of disapproval from Lira that Rainier felt the most strongly. *It's too late to worry about her feelings. This is a game, and I'm going to win.* Rainier's thoughts conflicted strongly with the streams of yellow light that failed to reach any further than Magnus or Jamison, but there was never a choice to be made. Slate and Sana made it their mission to kill Magnus, but Jamison was responsible for Kalus' death. The bastard needed to die, but Rainier knew this wasn't the time. *Play the game and strike when the timing is right.*

"Won't that anger Lattimer? I thought you were trying to make him think you were on his side." Ibson commented.

Lattimer's voice rattled through his bones as he yelled, "MY ENEMIES HAVE ALL SHOWN THEIR TRUE COLORS. NOW YOU WILL ALL FACE THE CONSEQUENCES OF YOUR BETRAYALS."

Rainier smiled and Villifor said, "I don't know what

you're planning, but the wizard is right. You just blew your cover." Villifor's comment was followed shortly by a new barrage of fireballs sent by the angered blood mage himself, casting from his tower and no longer caring if his own troops suffered damages in the chaos below him. Jamison raised his hands in defiance, dissolving the onslaught.

"There's always a time when you need to make your move. Just keep working our way closer to Jamison." Rainier smiled even bigger as Lattimer renewed his volley of fireballs aimed at Jamison, his inner Remnant shining through. He said, "I plan to win. It just won't be in the way any of you are thinking, which is why it will work. Jamison and Lattimer are preoccupied with each other, and that gives us an opportunity, and Slate and Sana are going to take advantage of it. Now, watch the two scariest people I've ever met do their thing."

There wasn't any further explanation needed as everyone looked towards Slate and Sana. They still fought with the paladin's shields, but now they had Magnus in their sights. They slaughtered with purpose, slicing Blight into soldiers, crushing armor with impunity, and carving their way to Magnus and the elite Bellator Furies at his command.

Magnus saw Slate coming, and he let out a roar while decapitating a paladin in front of him. The other Furies under his command took his place on the front lines of fighting as Magnus turned and raised his axe in the air. "I've waited a long time for this, Slate Severance."

Slate flashed around a blow from a Fury and delivered a backhand with the force of a boulder to the base of his neck. The Fury collapsed to the ground and Slate yelled back, "I hear you are a war hero now. The statues are impressive...I bet most people have already forgotten that you lost to me in the arena in record time." He gave his best crazed grin that made his demonic eyes stand out even more against his ashen skin. "Care to see if I can set a new record? This time I'm not alone."

A throwing knife cut through the air with the speed of bird of prey on the hunt, but it stopped just short of Magnus, halting in midair before dropping to the ground. He laughed and said, "Your tricks won't help you this time Headmaster. Lattimer saw you fight in Minot, and he's provided us with armor that is protected from your projectiles and your electric spells." He kicked the knife on the ground and said, "You won't be putting one of those things through my foot like you did in Pillar. Come see how you fare against my axe." Then Magnus motioned forward, sending his teams of elite Furies towards Slate and Sana. "That is, if you can even handle this lot."

The Furies came forward fighting in pairs of two, but before they reached Slate, Captain Sharan stepped in front of him. She said, "We'll keep them engaged." Her best paladins formed a small shield wall, protecting Slate and Sana from the advancing teams, absorbing the attack.

Slate clasped Sharan on the shoulder and said, "Then we'll get Magnus, right Headmaster?"

She smirked and flipped the Blighted knife in the air. "He may be protected against projectiles, but I don't think he'll be protected against this. Just get me to him."

Slate threw the Headmaster over his shoulder, ran up the back of Sharan, and launched himself over the entangled paladins and Furies. He tossed the Headmaster in midair, and she landed in a roll off to Magnus' side. Slate flashed to the side the second he landed, narrowly avoiding an axe blade that bit into the ground. The Headmaster came out of her roll as Slate sprung forward to attack Magnus. The armor Lattimer provided increased Magnus' speed though, and Slate needed to dive under a gauntleted fist aimed at his face, delivered even as Magnus freed his axe from the ground with his other hand. Slate avoided a direct blow, but Magnus caught his shoulder, and it was only when the razor-sharp spikes sliced into his flesh that Slate realized the dangerous addition to Magnus' gauntlet. He screamed in pain as the Headmaster darted forward, trying to land a slice with her knife, but the axe of Magnus kept her at bay as it flowed into a sweeping arc that the Headmaster couldn't penetrate.

Magnus jumped back with the aid of his armor, keeping Slate and the Headmaster in front of him. He laughed as he yelled, "Already I hear the screams of Slate the Bloodless! You may not bleed like a normal man, but I can hear your pain. It's only just beginning."

Rainier thought Magnus may be right. *He may be the only person alive who can match Slate and Sana in a fight, and it takes enchanted armor to make it even.* Rainier pulled his attention from the fight to look up at Jamison. The head of the Marked faction had dropped any regal pretenses and was fully engaged in battle, simultaneously fending off Lattimer's fireballs while blessing the armor of his paladins in an impressive display of magic. Beads of sweat glistened on his forehead and he no longer flung insults at Lattimer.

Low ranking priests pushed Jamison's rolling throne ever closer. Coupled with Rainier's own efforts to position the Remnant, he could now see that some of the priests were tasked with transferring orbs from the rolling dais onto a basin at Jamison's feet. Ibson saw Rainier's gaze and said, "Direct contact makes every spell easier. He's standing in the orbs. It doesn't get any simpler or more effective than that."

"There is nothing simple about the display Slate, Sana, and Magnus are putting on." Lira said in awe. "I have never seen movements so quick, so powerful, and so deadly."

"Don't forget your duties." Rainier reprimanded, but he couldn't blame her. Rainier had trouble pulling his own eyes away from the beauty of their battle.

The Headmaster flipped and slashed while Slate flashed in and out of range of Magnus' axe. Magnus bull-rushed Slate, trying to corner him, but even with enchanted armor, he couldn't pin Slate down. It was one big whirlwind of spinning blades, inhuman speed, and extreme skill.

All the while, Lattimer kept sending volley after volley of fireballs at Jamison. The air smelled of smoke and crackled with electricity as Jamison dispersed the magical energy of the fireballs. Rainier wasn't a Perceptor like Slate with the ability to feel magic that was done to him, but it was impossible not to notice the pure energy in the air. It felt thick enough to taste and volatile enough to explode.

Sweat poured down Jamison's face now and his attention was entirely focused on defending his troops against Lattimer. The armor of his paladins dimmed to dull blue, and Rainier saw his chance. He said to Hanna, "We make our move now! Go! Kill that bastard while his paladins are weak!"

The Remnant turned from the Furies and charged at Jamison. The distance was short, and the paladins were weak, but the Remnant are not paladins. The Remnant had the element of surprise, but they shed a lot of blood in overpowering the unsuspecting paladins with their sheer numbers, bursting into the area reserved for the Marked faction's priests.

They were so close to killing Jamison, but Rainier saw things through a different lens. He had the enchanted path, and the enchanted path didn't leave this clearing. *I'm a dead man.* Rainier pushed through the Remnant with his swords drawn with Lira and Villifor at his side. Ibson followed behind as quickly as his old legs would take him, searching for the safest spot on the battlefield.

Jamison looked down, saw the blood of his paladins staining the ground and Rainier rushing forward with swords drawn. He shot one hand out, sending a fireball of his own at Rainier as he yelled in an amplified voice across the battlefield, "Rainier Tallow has betrayed us! Paladins, to me!!!"

The fireball dissolved in front of him and Rainier ran through a wave of heat where the fireball once flew. *Thank you Ibson.* Then the ground around him erupted in wizard's fire as one of Lattimer's fireballs finally slipped through Jamison's defenses. When Jamison attacked Rainier, it distracted him enough that he failed to disperse one of the incoming fireballs from Lattimer's deluge.

Jamison recovered quickly and resumed his duties, but the damage had been done.

Dozens of paladins and Furies alike burned in the insatiable heat that melted armor and charred exposed flesh. Screams of agony slipped from the silent lips of the Nameless Army, their pain overcoming their quiet vows to the pattern. Furies continued their guttural screams of hatred, as even burning flesh could not stop their desire for paladin blood. They fought and clawed and bit until their own lives ended in ashes. Rainier and everyone with him were only saved by the defensive magic of Ibson and Jamison's own protective spells, which created an island of safety within the ring of charred earth and writhing bodies. *I guess I owe Jamison a debt of gratitude for saving me from a death like that. I'll try to remember to thank him before I put my sword through him.*

Rainier's feelings of gratitude ended quickly as he consulted the enlightened path. The streams of light were hardly a flicker ahead of him, lasting no longer than the open space between him and Jamison. Without any other options, he concentrated on the longest stream and hoped for some Remnant luck. He ducked a few weapons aimed his way as he ran, leaving it to Lira or Villifor to land more meaningful blows and trying to close the distance on Jamison as quickly as possible. Halfway across the opening, the enlightened path shifted sharply to the left. Rainier reacted without thinking, throwing himself into a roll. When he came out of it, he found a paladin barring his way. Having heard Jamison's call, she had jumped to his aid. *If one paladin came at his call for aid, then I'm sure more will be on the way. I'll need to make quick work of this one.* The paladin lunged at Rainier with blessed speed, trying to drive her blue sword into his blasphemous soul, but Rainier still held onto the enlightened path, and he had already shifted to the side, blocking the blow with one sword, and slashing at the throat of the nameless warrior in front of him, but she raised her shield in time to block the blow.

Then her eyes went wide as she stilled, falling to her knees to reveal Villifor standing behind her. He smiled and said, "Haven't you figured out yet that it's a lot easier to kill people from behind?"

"Honor means nothing to you." Lira snapped as she spit on the ground. Rainier couldn't tell if the comment was directed at Villifor or himself. *She's not wrong either way. Villifor laughed even louder. This is Malethya. We do what needs to be done.*

Then two more paladins landed in the clearing.

Members of the Remnant descended on them as soon as they landed, overwhelming the powerful warriors with their numbers. Somewhere from within the mess of humanity, he heard Hanna scream, "I gave my life to you fractal-forsaken bastards! Is it too much to ask for some gratitude and a bed to roll around in with my Kalus for my troubles?" The sound of an axe blade into flesh interrupted her rant. Then she yelled, "Instead you send us back to fight some more and kill the only decent man I've ever met. Well, you wanted us to fight. How am I doing?" More squishing sounds from her axe were the only answer anyone needed.

Rainier rushed ahead while Hanna served up some more lessons in gratitude to the Disenite paladins. He glanced up at Jamison and saw him locked in battle with Lattimer and his Ispirtu wizards, not even bothering to look down at Rainier, knowing the cost of his previous misstep. Rainier darted between the two paladins that were under siege from the Remnant, following the enlightened path to its frighteningly short end. He was only a few short paces away from Jamison and his priests. *Maybe this next step won't be my last?*

Thump.

Captain Sharan landed on one knee, blocking his way. A split second later, the other members of her elite paladins joined her. Rainier's heart sank. *I wish the enlightened path didn't have to be right ALL the time. I'm six steps away from Jamison!*   Enlightened path or not, Rainier raised his swords and charged onward.

Sharan blocked his swords with ease, raising her blessed shield and absorbing the blows. "You betrayed me after all of this?" She asked incredulously, delivering a powerful thrust that Rainier only avoided because of the enlightened path. *This may be the patch of ground I die on, but I'm not giving it up without a fight.* "There probably wasn't any prophecy either, was there?"

"I told you what you needed to hear. You needed to hear a prophecy from an oracle, so I gave you one." Rainier admitted. "You weren't ready to hear the truth. Jamison deceived you, but it's nothing compared to the lies that Julian has told. Your whole way of life is a lie. I couldn't tell you if I didn't get proof."

"More lies!" Sharan shouted as she slashed her sword into open air. While holding the enlightened path, Rainier knew where she would swing before she did.

Jamison shouted from the top of his dais, "Enough messing around. Grab him before he ruins your hearts with his lies. I want everyone to see his death by my hands." He then redirected his message to the elite guards behind Sharan. "There is no need to protect me from anyone but Rainier. Attack!"

Rainier didn't know what he was talking about until he looked back and saw Villifor smiling at him. The troops loyal to Villifor turned and defended against the Remnant, preventing any help from reaching him. Lira was fighting bravely to break through and the look on Ibson's face was filled with sorrow, although it was probably just the knowledge that his secrets would die with Rainier. Villifor said, "It's nothing personal, Rainier. If it looked like you were going to pull this scheme off, I would have stayed right by your side the whole time."

The elite paladin under Sharan's command joined her side, and Rainier was out of options. He dodged, parried, stepped through blows, rolled around attacks, but there were just too many. Four paladins converging on him in the middle of a battlefield, and he had nowhere to run.

Villifor explained, "When Tommy and Annarelle snuck into the Disenite camp on that mission you sent them on, I decided to go with them. I wanted to see what we were up against and to see if there was any information that would be valuable to me." He shrugged and said, "We got caught and brought to Jamison. It turns out that he's a man that knows the value of a deal, so I made one with him. Tommy and Annarelle's loyalties were...not as flexible." He smiled and said, "My loyalty has always been flexible."

Fractal-forsaken bastard! Rainier had always thought

that Villifor may betray him, but he hadn't counted on his timing being so good. Just then, Lira broke through the line of Villifor's men and crashed shield first into Sharan, clearing some room and joining the fight. Rainier could have wept for joy, and any sadness he should have felt knowing that Lira had thrown her life away by joining him was balanced out by his selfish satisfaction to know he wasn't dying alone.

Rainier followed the enlightened path, short though it may be, and started backing towards Lira, his Hand, the woman who committed her life to protecting him. Rainier had never felt what it was like to trust your life to someone, but he found comfort in that trust. As he parried blows from the paladins in front of him, he backed up towards Lira, guided by the soft stream of yellow light signifying the enlightened path. I should have always trusted her. *I should have known that her sense of purpose and duty would never let her betray me. I should have known that she would be here, protecting me until my last breath...*

A strong arm reached around him, and a sword pressed against his neck.

Lira shouted, "Jamison, I have captured Rainier Tallow and await your judgment!"

Curses! Lira, too? I had assumed Villifor would have some tricks up his sleeve, but Lira? The shock of her betrayal left Rainier frozen as Jamison looked down from on high to deliver his death sentence.

Jamison amplified his voice and said with entirely too much satisfaction for Rainier's tastes, "Rainier Tallow has been captured by his own Hand, who has born witness to his treachery. Disarm him and bring him up here. The whole Disenite army deserves to see his death, carried out by his Hand." The entire time he spoke, his arms remained outward, defending his troops from Lattimer the blood mage, robe's flowing, dripping self-righteous beads of sweat with every spell he cast.

Rainier felt sick. *Someone's going to make a statue out of that guy. Sorry Kalus. I failed you.*

CHAPTER SIXTEEN

ONE ARMY TOO MANY

Sharan took his swords and walked him the six short steps to Jamison. Lira leapt to the top, aided by her enchanted armor, while Rainier was handed over to the priests at the bottom. The spiky haired priest that put a knife in Kalus met him. He lifted Rainier atop the rolling throne, and Rainier smelled the reek of wanderleaf drifting from his breath as he said, "I got to gut your friend. I wish I could wet my blade with you, but I guess that honor goes to the traitor that swore to protect you."

"I guess you'll have to stand in line." Rainier said, as he reached the top. Lira pushed him to his knees before Jamison and stood behind him, sword raised. The only thing that remained was the order to finish him off, but Jamison wouldn't have brought him up here if he didn't intend to make it a spectacle.

Before Jamison could speak, Lattimer's voice rumbled across the battlefield, "MY ENEMIES KILL EACH OTHER AS I GET TO SIT AND WATCH. ENJOY YOUR MOMENT, JAMISON. YOU. SHALL. MEET. THE. SAME. FATE." Lattimer punctuated each word by launching a fireball towards Jamison, demanding his attention to fend off the onslaught.

The brief respite gave Rainier a chance to look over the fallen soldiers and charred earth of the battlefield, but in his head, he couldn't think beyond his own fate. *I'm a dead man. There isn't a single fractal-forsaken stream of light within the enchanted path. That yellow light used to give me comfort. Now it's a damning two-foot circle of faint light around me. This bloody battlefield may be the last thing I ever see. I might as well get a good look at where my scheming has led me.*

He saw the still-burning soldiers and Furies that were unfortunately getting a first-hand lesson in the dangers of wizard fire, courtesy of Lattimer Regallo. He looked up the stair to the palace, and the swirling mass of armor and blades boiled with fury and skill. Somewhere buried beneath the soldiers was the trampled crown of Malethya, separated from the head of King Darik, who was given as much respect as the body of any other dead soldier - none.

The air crackled with magical energy as the Ispirtu wizards and Marked priests battled in the skies above the darkened city of Ravinai. The abyssal darkness that Lattimer created in Ravinai had turned into a haunting blue from the Disenite orbs hovering above the battlefield as they cast dancing shadows on the soldiers below. The screams of the dying mixed with the smells of charred flesh in a combination that required an equal mix of adrenaline and fear to keep his senses from being overwhelmed, but even amid all these distractions, his eyes remained transfixed. He couldn't take his eyes away.

Slate and Sana battled Magnus and his Furies in their enchanted armor and their movements made everyone else on the battlefield look like they were moving in slow motion. With Sharan coming to Jamison's aid, Magnus' troops had rejoined him in battle, leaving Slate and Sana badly outnumbered.

Slate flashed in, out, and around the soldiers with inhuman speed. Magnus and his men worked in groups to try to contain Slate, but even with their armor, they couldn't match the speed and changing directions of Slate Severance. He eluded them with every step, but Slate's main weapon against the enchanted armor was his fist, and he had trouble getting close enough to use it against Magnus or his men. On his own, he would have darted in and out until he made a mistake and an enchanted blade cut a little too deep.

The Headmaster was known as the Shadow in the Night and could put a throwing knife in your throat from three rooftops away, but she didn't have Slate's inhuman strength or speed, and she didn't have enchanted armor like her opponents. All she had was her skill and one nasty knife. On her own, she would have taken out a few of Magnus' men, but they would have overwhelmed her.

Slate and Sana didn't fight alone – they fought together – and they littered the ground with corpses.

Slate grabbed the Headmaster by the waist and flashed backwards to gain room, always staying out of range of Magnus until they could eliminate some of his Furies. Sana saw an opening and planted her feet against Slate's stomach, launching forward and extending the Blighted knife with an outstretched arm as if she were a spear and the knife the spear tip. She thrust the knife into the armpit of one of Magnus' men, and he dropped his weapon. Her forward momentum stopped as Slate grabbed her ankle and pulled her back towards him. She swung an arm around his neck as he flashed again, leaving the Blight to spread within the injured soldier. Sana flipped onto Slate's shoulders and jumped through the air as Slate flashed forward, sending her hurtling through the air at breakneck speeds. She turned head over feet and landed a thin cut into the neck of a soldier whose extensive training had never accounted for midair knife attacks from someone flying like a poisoned dart through the air. Slate flashed across the blood-soaked ground and by the time he caught the Headmaster, the two soldiers were blackened, blighted husks on the battlefield. Only Magnus remained.

The mountain of humanity stepped over his dead companions, grace and skill wrapped in scorn and malice. He waved his heavy battle axe with a single hand and sneered in challenge to Slate and Sana. They came at him as one, flashing left and right while Sana looked for her opening with the Blighted Knife, but Magnus kept her at bay because of the reach of his battle axe. If she timed an attack to miss the blade, he had his spiked gauntlet at the ready. They circled and tested each other in a deadly stalemate, but Slate didn't get close enough for Magnus to hit, and they couldn't break Magnus' guard.

At least Slate and Sana are holding their own. Maybe they'll be able to kill Magnus, destroy that totem and disappear into the darkened city of Ravinai. If anybody can escape this fight, it's Slate and Sana. Maybe some good could still come out of my schemes. It's easy to look for platitudes and rationales of self-worth when you're on your knees with a sword above your neck.

Jamison had fended off Lattimer's latest onslaught, so all that was left was for the bastard to give Lira the execution order. Of course, Jamison couldn't do that without a speech. *I bet listening to Jamison will hurt my head worse than losing it entirely. At least Lira's sword will be quick.*

"Rainier Tallow failed in his duties as an oracle. He gave false prophecies that kept the Nameless Army from glory, forcing us to wait on our ships while our supplies ran low. He then sent his Hand to spy on members of the priesthood, and I was forced to assume command of the army in his place. Despite all these warnings, some of you chose to continue following this false prophet." He lowered his head in sympathy, as if he were theatrically forgiving his lost flock. "Today, his true nature has been revealed as he attacked me and broke the covenant we forged on the *Inked Tides*. Like all Malethyans, he cares more for his own ideals than he does for the teachings of the pattern."

The fighting continued as Jamison spoke, his words carrying over soldiers too busy with the immediacy of battle to stop and listen. At the mention of other Malethyans, Rainier looked down at the Remnant below him. They struggled against Villifor's men, but they didn't have the skill or numbers to break through and save him. Behind them, Jak led a charge to reach him, but they wouldn't get here in time. It had all happened too quickly. Rainier felt a pair of eyes staring up at him and noticed Ibson locked in a gaze of contempt. Rainier could only imagine the thoughts running through the old man's head. *He must hate me more than anyone. I could have freed his bonds, and instead I used it as leverage, and the only thing I have to show for it is a sword in my neck. I'm going to take your secrets to the grave. Sorry old man. That's some tough luck.*

Then, he saw Villifor standing casually behind his lines of men, and in the good graces of Jamison's troops on account of his betrayal. He looked up while chewing on a fingernail, watching Jamison's spectacle as if it were a troupe performing a play for his personal enjoyment. *I'd be angry with that bastard if I weren't so impressed. He has the heart of the Remnant.*

Jamison proclaimed to the masses, "For your crimes against the pattern, I sentence you to death at the hands of your own Hand, Rainier Tallow. She will list your treachery in her own words as she executes the sentence."

Rainier glanced up at the stony face of Lira standing above him. She kept her eyes on the base of his neck, sword at the ready in case he tried to run. She said, "Rainier Tallow became an oracle because of his ability to see the enlightened path, but he has used his ability to swindle, deceive, and corrupt everything he touches." She lifted her arms above her head, ready to plunge the blade and Rainier looked out on the battlefield once more, searching for Slate and Sana. *At least I might be able to see Magnus lose his head before I lose mine.*

Slate circled Magnus as Sana tested his defenses. She lunged forward only to have Slate pull her back before a sweeping arc from his battle axe could cut her in two. As soon as her feet hit the ground, Slate made his move. Slate flashed forward ducking beneath Magnus' blade to deliver a blow with his stonehand. Magnus was ready and struck Slate a direct blow to his chest with the spiked gauntlet that sent him flying. Rainier hung his head and closed his eyes. Taking a blow from Magnus was like being hit with a sledgehammer. Even if Slate survived, the injury would

426 J. Lloren Quill

cripple him, and Magnus could finish him off at his leisure. As for the Headmaster, as talented as she was, she was outmatched in a direct fight with Magnus. *They are as dead as I am. Kill me before I have time to realize how big of a failure I am.*

Lira announced, "As his Hand, I have witnessed his deception. Every truth he speaks hides a lie." *Here it comes. Will it hurt or will I just go black?* Rainier braced himself for the cold steel to end his life. He felt Lira's muscles tense in anger and anticipation of the execution.

"...but every lie he speaks carries a pattern of truth. He is my oracle, and I will follow him!" A whoosh of the blade. Rainier waited for the searing pain, but it never came.

Rainier snapped his eyes open to pure chaos.

Lira had buried her blessed blade in Jamison, and his holy robes burst into crimson. His outstretched arms weakly fumbled for the hilt protruding from his chest, his dying mind trying to process what had happened behind a face filled with self-righteous sanctity. Rainier could see all the thoughts that had been tumbling through his own head now crashing through Jamison's in a torrent of shock, confusion, and mind-numbing pain. Watching Jamison claw at the blade in his chest while his own blood leaked out of him a minute after the bastard ordered Rainier's execution was more satisfying than Rainier cared to admit, even if he couldn't hide from his own thoughts.

I hope he soils himself – one final act to humiliate that self-righteous prick. Now that would be something worthy of a statue. If I get out of here, I'll commission it and dedicate it to Kalus. I wonder what I should call it. "Death of a fractal-forsaken-jerk-that-kept-trying-to-kill-me" has a nice ring to it.

Jamison was so shocked by the blade in his chest that the smug smile never dropped from his face, even as he lost the concentration needed to fend off Lattimer's attacks. Without Jamison's magic, fireballs landed randomly across the battlefield, causing untold damage to Disenite soldiers and Furies alike. Rainier didn't have time to process it though, as yellow streams of light urged him to roll forward from his kneeling position along the enlightened path.

The spikey-haired priest jumped onto the dais with his knives at the ready. After his tuck-and-roll, Rainier found himself at the feet of Jamison, and the yellow streams directed him towards Jamison's chest. Having learned not to question the enlightened path, Rainier reached up, grabbed Jamison's robes, and pulled down hard. The dying man toppled over him just as the spikey-haired priest thrust his knives forward. They buried into Jamison's back and although using the dead body as a meat shield protected him from the knives, Rainier was assaulted by something foul. Being in this close of proximity to Jamison's corpse, there could be no question. The bastard died in his own filth.

Then Lira was there. With one kick from her enchanted armor, the priest went flying to the ground. He was met with a chop of an axe. Hanna pulled it out of his stomach, licked the blood from her blade and said, "That one's for Kalus."

Rainier removed himself from beneath Jamison's stench to find the Remnant eagerly disposing of Jamison's priests. Sharan and her troops were kept at bay by more members of the Remnant, and surprisingly, Villifor's men. Rainier looked to him, and he shrugged as he said, "Like I said, it was never personal, and Jamison seems to have gotten the sharp end of the stick. Besides, I always liked you better than the smug bastard anyway." Then he gave him his most winning grin, a grin worthy of the Remnant.

Beside him, Ibson extended his arms in concentration and thrust them towards the sky. He caught and dispersed the fireballs coming onto the battlefield and said urgently, "I won't be able to do this for long! I don't have Jamison's supply of orbs at my disposal to draw from like he did. If you have a way to end this, do it now!"

Rainier didn't need to be told twice. He said, "Amplify my voice!" Beads of sweat formed on Ibson's face, but he nodded, and Rainier yelled across the battlefield.

"Jamison is dead! Without him, we do not have the defenses necessary to withstand Lattimer and his Ispirtu wizards' attacks. All troops that serve me are ordered to maintain defensive formations only and to stop all attacks."

Rainier looked up to Lattimer in his tower. "I wish to negotiate the terms of our surrender."

"TERMS?" an incredulous Lattimer shouted across the battlefield. "YOU ARE DEFEATED. YOU WILL AGREE TO WHATEVER TERMS I ASK."

There's always something to negotiate when there is leverage involved, and I have more than he knows, even if I had been hoping for more. Rainier glanced over to where Magnus had punched Slate, expecting to see the hulk carving his way towards him with one swing of his axe at a time. Instead, he saw Sana supporting a gravely injured

Slate Severance. Her foot stood atop Magnus' blackened and blighted body. When Rainier saw her, she thrust her fist in the air, and blood flowed from her hand and down her wrist. *I don't know how she did it, but she destroyed the last totem. That gives me all the leverage I need if I can just stay alive long enough to use it.*

Rainier answered with more confidence than any leader of a defeated army should possess. "You misunderstand the situation. Your army of Furies have won the day, but how many of your people have died at the hands of the Nameless Army?" Rainier paused for dramatic effect. "The man who leads the Disenites goes by the name of Julian the Immortal and this..." Rainier swept his hand across the dead paladins. "...was simply an overeager landing force that should have stayed with their ships in Portswain."

Lattimer contemplated the information and finally said, "You lie, Rainier Tallow."

"All the time, but not right now, and the lies I tell pale in comparison to the lies that have been told to the Nameless Army. Once they realize the depths of Julian's lies, they will join me, and I will join you. Let me prove it to you!"

The onslaught of fireballs ceased, giving Rainier a temporary respite to win over the Nameless Army.

Ibson exhaled a breath of relief and lowered his arms, exhausted from his spellcasting. Rainier hopped down from the dais and told Lira, "Find Kalana. I need her here...now!"

"I saw her supporting the troops near Slate and Sana. I can have her here shortly." She turned back before leaving and warned, "You better be able to win over the Nameless

Army. You better have a plan that's better than just giving up."

Rainier gave her his best Remnant smile and winked, saying, "You know I have a plan." *I just hope it works.* "Oh, and help Slate and Sana back here too, will you?"

She left to fetch everyone, and Rainier turned to Ibson, "This is the part where I need you. Will you honor our agreement?"

"I don't have a choice." Ibson said, and Rainier smiled. *I can't think of a better answer.*

"When everyone gets here, just play along and amplify their voices as they speak."

Ibson nodded and said, "I'll make sure everyone is heard. I'm not that tired yet."

Rainier hopped back up on the dais so everyone could hear him. He yelled across the battlefield, speaking to the Nameless Army, "You have been told a lie, and there are few people in Malethya that understand the intricacies of a good lie as well as me. Some lies are innocent. We tell our wives or husbands how good their cooking is because we want them to feel good, and it saves us from having to do the cooking ourselves." Slate looked down to see that Lira had found Kalana and was starting to work her way back to him. "Other lies are less innocent, and while no one gets hurt, we tell them for our own personal benefit. Then there are the lies we tell that swindle someone out of their purses or coerce someone into our beds, and we rationalize our reasons for doing it so that we don't have to admit to our own wickedness. I've told plenty of these lies in my lifetime as well." He looked down and saw Lira leading Kalana, Sana, and a seriously injured Slate towards

Ibson. "None of these lies can compare to the lie you have lived. It's a lie so profound and so broad that it affects every single one of you, and it's a lie that Julian the Immortal has fostered and grown for years upon years."

Rainier looked from the burning dais to Kalana and asked, "You were a burnt-out priestess when you joined us, right Kalana?"

She nodded and Ibson amplified her voice as she said, "I was addicted to wanderleaf and could no longer touch the pattern."

"What did you learn from me and Ibson since joining us?"

"I can now touch the pattern again and bless the armor of our paladins." She said with obvious pride.

Rainier crushed her hopes. "You haven't blessed anything. We taught you magic. Ibson, what is the name of the spell you taught them and how does it work?"

"Let's start..." Ibson began before being interrupted.

Captain Tera stood atop a dais across the battlefield, and shouted, "Don't listen to this Blasphemer! If you die here today, at least you will die serving the pattern. Do not..." A series of fireballs launched from Lattimer's hands. The remaining priests dispersed the first few coming towards Tera, but the priests weren't Jamison, and they didn't stand a chance against Lattimer. Wizard fire engulfed the dais and everyone around it, silencing her.

"MY PATIENCE IS WEARING THIN, RAINIER. PROVE YOUR USEFULNESS, OR THE SAME FATE AWAITS YOU."
Hurry it up – got it.

Ibson spoke up, saying, "I taught them a spell of dispersive energy transference. The orbs contain a condensed source of energy that we..."

Rainier summarized for him, "You took the energy of the orbs and used it to power up their armor, right?"

"Right." Ibson nodded and Kalana looked confused or betrayed. *Those feelings are just beginning.*

"Everything you've witnessed here today has been a battle between wizards, you just call them priests. Wizards darkened the sky and priests set the blue orbs hovering over the battlefield. Wizards cast fireballs while priests dispersed them. It's all the same."

"Blood magic is evil!" Sharan shouted.

"Blood magic is evil – I couldn't agree more." Rainier paused for effect, and then shouted with all the anger that had pent up inside him since landing in Disentia and discovering the truth. "It's too bad Jamison and all your other priests practice blood magic. I'm standing on the proof. Would you please open up the dais, Captain Sharan?"

She stepped forward numbly, no longer sure of her own convictions and completely unsure of what she would find in the dais. She wedged her shield into a seam in the sealed dais and pried it open. The dais swung open, and her mouth dropped.

"What do you see, Captain Sharan?"

She couldn't say a word, so Rainier waited for Villifor to reach in and give Tommy a hand. He walked out dumbly, mute, and oblivious to the world around him. Next came Annarelle, and Rosana gasped. "What have they done to you?"

Rainier answered for her since Annarelle no longer had the desire to speak. Rainier's suspicions started when Lira discovered the priests using orbs to power their cannons. They grew when Ibson was able to recharge Lira's armor using magic, but he didn't really know until the Stratego medallions pointed him towards Jamison.

"Your priests subjugate the minds of anyone that has the spark, burning out their minds with blood magic and giving them a single purpose in life. If they pass the first Oracle Trial and fail the next, they are turned into mindless producers of orbs, concentrating magic for priests to use. Julian concealed the truth from all of you through the Oracle Trials. He uses the trials to farm magic, and he has every mother and father in Disentia eager to send their kids to him in the hopes that they'll be the next great oracle. Did you ever wonder why so few make it through the trials? They aren't intended to! Why else would he send me away the second I passed the Oracle Trials without any training? He only wants to feed his priests with more orbs and to keep you oblivious so that you fight his enemies when he calls on you. He doesn't want to kill Lattimer because he offends the pattern by using blood magic. He wants to eliminate his competition." The battlefield went silent. "If you don't believe me, tear into any rolling dais around you, and see for yourself."

The screams of priests followed as paladins of the Nameless Army broke into the rolling thrones and drew their own conclusions about Rainier's story. He yelled to the paladins, "You can die here today fighting a blood mage, or you can live, and get revenge against the blood mage that turned your lives into a lie. It might not be a holy prophecy from your oracle, but you'll get the chance to find out how immortal Julian really is."

"MY MEN WILL HALT THEIR ATTACK." Lattimer boomed from the tower, "COME HERE, RAINIER. IT APPEARS WE HAVE MUCH TO DISCUSS."

Rainier smiled, even though he was still contemplating how his head remained attached to his neck. *We do have much to discuss, Lattimer, and you are going to regret this day even more than Jamison, because you will carry it with you far longer. You'll regret the day you agreed to negotiate with the Remnant.*

CHAPTER SEVENTEEN

ONE ARMY

Villifor waited for him as he stepped down onto the battlefield and offered his hand. "You're the only one that could have pulled this off." He winked and said, "I never doubted you for a second."

Rainier looked at the arm in front of him, contemplating the man extending it towards him. Slate would have judged him too quickly, deciding on whether he was good or bad with his stonehand. Sana would have put a knife in his throat the second he betrayed her. Rainier shook it and clasped the man on the back. He thought he would have need of a man that knew how to navigate a situation without the burden of morals. Rainier smirked and said, "I never doubted you, either. You timed your move beautifully. I could use someone like that...why don't you stick with me?"

Villifor smiled back, and said, "I'd be honored to..."

Before he could say more, Rainier dropped the smile, saying, "Good. You're my new Hand. I'd ask Ibson to perform the ceremony, but neither one of us would put any worth in it anyway." Rainier swept past Villifor, forcing him to turn and keep stride with Lira as he followed. He then motioned to Lira and said to her, "If you ever get the scent of betrayal wafting from Villifor again, you have my permission to stick a sword in him, understood?"

Lira's chiseled jawline barely moved as she said, "With

pleasure, my oracle."

"You had me convinced that you were going to bury a sword in me back there. What made you do it?" Rainier couldn't help but ask.

"I wasn't convinced that I wouldn't. I thought about it all the way from Minot. I almost did as we walked through the darkened city of Ravinai. It would have felt good." Lira admitted. "Then we saw the battlefield for the first time when we stood on the Bellator tower. You threatened me and Ibson and Villifor and it would have felt so good to slip a blade between your ribs..."

"Ok, you didn't like me very much. You don't have to tell me about every time you wanted to kill me. I get the idea. Why didn't you do it?" *I would have appreciated a little less...enthusiasm at the prospect, but hey, I'm still here.*

"Duty prevented it. Then you lied to Sharan and attacked the Marked priests, and I stopped thinking about duty. I thought of the deception you sowed, the trust you violated, and that I had never known a man more deserving of death than you." She paused and said, "Then I saw you fight Sharan. You fought with the pattern, and it was beautiful. It was pure and true and everything you are not. I didn't understand how a man such as you could coexist with something so beautiful. I didn't want the fight to end. I wanted to watch it forever. I couldn't let you die, but I couldn't save you with my sword either. There were too many of them. I tried to do what my oracle would do. I acted with deceit. I lied and dishonored myself, and it was the right thing to do."

For once in his life Rainier didn't know what to say.

Flattered and offended, he stammered, "So I guess you don't want to kill me anymore?"

"Did I say that?" Lira smiled her stony smile. "You are my oracle, and I will follow you. Just make sure the beauty inside you never gets lost in your slimy exterior or I may need to reconsider."

I have two Hands again, protecting me, unless they decide not to. Some things never change.

Ahead of him, Ibson examined Slate's wounds while Sana probed Annarelle's mind. Slate's prognosis was much better.

"Magnus gave you some deep wounds, with damage to your liver, kidneys, and a laceration that cuts through your diaphragm, connecting your mediastinum to your intestinal cavity. By all accounts you should be dead. Your body's ability to minimize blood loss has given you some extra time to get treated. I'll be able to close up the worst of them now." A look of concentration came over the wizard's face as he cast his spell, and the pain etched across Slate's face lessened in kind. Rainier wondered how the old wizard was holding up after so much spellcasting, but then he noticed Ibson's free hand holding an object concealed beneath his robes. It created a bulge that was decidedly orb shaped and Rainier smiled. *The old man is picking up a few tricks as well. There's still hope for that one to learn the ways of the Remnant.*

Sana, on the other hand, looked perplexed, and Rose was completely despondent. "I can't find what to repair. I can sense the damage, but there isn't enough healthy surrounding tissue for me to sense the pattern of her mind and repair it. It's all just...burnt out."

Ibson finished closing the worst of Slate's wounds and stepped forward to check Tommy, who didn't even respond to his touch. He said, "This is what subjugation does. His mind is gone. I can't bring him back."

"I'm sure Jamison got some sick pleasure out of subjugating our friends and using their spark against us." Slate added with a shake of his head. He looked exhausted, but exhausted is a big step up from being on death's door.

A tear formed on Rose's cheek as Slate spoke, but the Sicarius Headmaster was all action. She pulled out one of her throwing knives and sliced it cleanly through Annarelle's throat. Annarelle fell to her knees, and by the time her face hit the dirt, Tommy had met the same fate.

Sana said coldly, "It's better this way." Rosana seconded the sentiment, but with a lot more warmth, saying, "The Tommy and Annarelle we knew and loved are already gone. I'll miss them terribly." No one argued, and Rainier could hear the Headmaster silently reciting a list of names and adding Annarelle's at the end.

Rainier didn't want to dwell on the deaths of Tommy and Annarelle or know what list Sana was reciting. *I knew coming into this that not everyone would be walking out. Magnus and Jamison got what they deserved, but I don't even know the extent of our own casualties yet, and I'm darn lucky that I wasn't one of them. How many of the Remnant died? Or the Underground? How many of Sharan's troops that fought for me and thought I betrayed them when I went after Jamison?* It was no time to count the dead now, not with Lattimer waiting for them. Besides, you can't play standing stones without losing a few pieces.

I can weigh the blood on my hands later. I promised Kalus I'd win. He remembered seeing his dying friend's eyes sparkle when he promised to get revenge, even as the spark of life left his body. *I'm almost there, my friend. All the pieces are on the board, and now I need to outwit Lattimer.*

He marched ahead purposefully, followed by Lira and Villifor, who seemed amused to be given the title of Hand, although a man that can bite his fingernails in the middle of a battle probably finds amusement in odd places. Slate, Sana, and Ibson came next, and the Headmaster had wiped away all signs of Rose's momentary grief, replacing it with the seriousness of a Sicarius Guardsman on a mission. Jak made it through the ranks and was joined by Hanna and, surprisingly, Captains Sharan and Filios.

What a delegation we make. We have a war hero and the most dangerous man in Malethya along with a Disenite captain and the wizard that discovered spark-based magic. That ought to be enough to scare the average soldier.

Rainier's thoughts proved accurate, as Lattimer's soldiers and the Nameless Army both made room for them on their passage to Lattimer's tower. While they walked, Rainier saw Hanna looking at him, so he asked, "Did your axe find enough blood to satisfy it?"

"Not even close." Hanna cackled crazily, "but you've done your part to wet its appetite. I owe you a debt of gratitude, Rainier Tallow."

Rainier accepted the praise but warned her not to go swinging it at Lattimer when they met. *The last thing I need is Hanna picking a fight in front of a blood mage.* "Will you follow my lead, even if the terms don't make sense to you?"

"Don't worry about me, Rainier. I'm Remnant. I'm family." *I guess Hanna is the crazy in my family. Every family has one, and the Remnant is no different.* Hanna's comment was made with a meaningful look towards Captain Sharan.

Rainier took the hint. "What about you, Sharan? Why did you join our party?"

"You lied to me." Anger twisted her face, which looked out of place in someone wearing holy armor etched in the exquisitely intricate patterns of the Marked faction. Her face twisted even more as she said, "You exposed an even bigger lie that effects not just me but everyone under my command. I still can't comprehend it all, but I thought someone should represent the Nameless Army in these negotiations, so I am here." She paused for a minute and then said, "What I think you really mean to ask is whether I will try to finish our fight in the middle of negotiations. I will not. I don't know what to think of you Rainier, but after watching you sneak into Portswain under the guise of a funeral procession and deftly trick Jamison by having my forces pretend to be Furies, I expect you have a few tricks left for Lattimer. I'll let you play them, but they better be good. No one in the Nameless Army will want to surrender to a blood mage, and all of them are as conflicted as I am right now. I almost wish I had died an honorable death in battle before I opened that dais, and my life got turned upside down."

"Life's more interesting when things get a little out of order. I just embrace it more than most. You should give it a try...I think you'll like it." He gave her a Remnant grin and for once it hit the mark. Her face untwisted in anger and contorted in confusion at the curious remark. Rainier said, "As for Lattimer, I have plenty of surprises for him, but today will be a difficult day. We lost the battle, and I can't negotiate out of that."

"You said we wouldn't get vengeance from the battle, but we would finish satisfied. Are we still going to win the game?" Slate asked. Slate and Sana had done their part. They got to Magnus and broke the totem containing Slate's blood, freeing him further from Lattimer's clutches. *Now it's up to me.*

"I think we're about to find out."

Lattimer emerged from the base of his tower. He waved a robed arm to the left as if he were flicking a crumb off the table. A wall of air hit the slowly parting soldiers between Rainier and Lattimer, smashing them aside. Then he flicked his scepter to the right, sending more soldiers flying. Nothing remained between them but trampled grass and blood-stained soil.

"How's the head?" Rainier whispered to Slate.

"I can resist him, but I can't cover that much ground. He'll have time to stop me."

"Don't bother trying. I just don't want him turning you into a Fury halfway through the negotiations."

Slate nodded in acknowledgment while Ibson stared daggers at him. Rainier didn't have time to argue so he just held Ibson's gaze until the old man looked at his feet in submission. He would play his part, and his was the biggest part to play.

A delegation of dangerous people joined Lattimer. The Bellator trained Furies stood on edge, sensing a trap. They wielded savage weaponry and made sure it was on full display, as proud as peacocks of their victory. Their Ispirtu brethren lacked the savage style of the Furies, but their simple robes and staffs were scary enough when they looked at you with red eyes. Of all the dangerous people, Rainier could only recognize Cirata Lorassa prowling about, but that was it. *That's an intimidating group, but they look less intimidating without Magnus and Phoenix standing in their ranks. Lattimer's taken losses, too. He's not infallible, even if he is impossibly powerful. I can beat him.*

Lattimer said, "I can't say I expected to be speaking with you, Rainier. I saw Slate's strength and respected the many talents of my sister, but I must say I underestimated you. During those conversations in the Infirmary, I never gave you a second thought." He raised his arms wide, let some fireballs dance around his extended hands and gave a maniacal laugh. "Congratulations. You have my attention."

"ME? You underestimated ME? It's not because I'm short, is it? That's too cliché even for a guy that turns his soldiers into mindless replicas. Have some creativity! I'm the fractal-forsaken Oracle of the Nameless Army, viewer of the enlightened path, and blessed with the gift of foresight! I can see all combinations of future probabilities and guide my army to victory, just as I've done here today. I'm standing right where I want to be." *So, what if I can't actually lead my army the way an oracle is supposed to? Lattimer doesn't know that and he doesn't need to.* "Now, if you're done celebrating your power by turning yourself into a birthday cake, maybe Cirata can blow out those candles flickering around your hands so that we can get to talking?" Cirata spit on the ground and Rainier said, "Oh, is that job beneath you, Cirata? I could ask Magnus to do it. Where is he?" She screamed in anger and looked ready to charge him, but the other Guardsmen held her back.

Lattimer let a fireball grow in his hand and said, "If your goal is to anger me, this will be a short negotiation." He then stopped his casting and dropped his arms back to his side. "Why don't you tell me how you can be useful to me, and I'll decide if I let you live."

Rainier pushed Lattimer a little more, saying, "I'll admit that death can be highly persuasive, but it's a card you can only play once. If you play it now, you'll lose a general for your armies with the gift of foresight, and if I'm not mistaken, there's been a recent vacancy of that position. I can't carry Magnus' axe, but no one can direct your army against Julian better than me." Rainier took a bow. *And if the only battle training I have is in the form of shattered memories from the man we'll be fighting, then that's one more thing Lattimer doesn't need to know.*

"This isn't an interview for a job, and while you may possess some unique gifts, your claim of victory on the battlefield is absurd. You are beaten."

"Jamison is dead, and as I already mentioned, I am standing right where I want to be. We wouldn't have sent you that note if we didn't plan this all along." Rainier paused and let the silence concede his point. "You'll lose the blood of the one man that can keep your Furies from completely losing their minds." Rainier motioned towards Slate. "You'll lose the Shadow of the Night, the surviving paladins in my command, and the wizardry of Ibson."

Lattimer interrupted him, "All of you have been a thorn

in my side since I took control of Malethya. The offer of surrender and subjugation is an offer of respect but make no mistake — I would be just as happy to see you die here today."

"Subjugation? I think not. I came here to negotiate the terms of surrender, but there will be no subjugation. We'll work with you to defeat Julian, but the idea of working with a blood mage is less than appealing to us." Rainier said, "But I know what is coming. You need us when Julian the Immortal arrives. In fact, you need more than just us...you need all the secrets buried in Minot..."

Lattimer's eyes turned sharp. "What do you know of Minot?"

The Sicarius Headmaster stepped forward. "I know how to pull more than just sand from that desert you've been digging in." She flipped the blighted knife in the air, letting its black edges soak in the light ominously. Any evidence that Lattimer needed for the deadly effectiveness of that knife lay in the blackened husks of bodies that littered the battlefield, including that of Magnus.

Rainier waited for Lattimer's calculating eyes to come back to him. Rainier's years swindling people of their wares left him keenly aware of when he had hooked a mark. He smiled, knowing that Lattimer was interested. Now he just had to reel him in. He said, "And let's not forget about the true treasure buried in Minot. Have you had any luck with that bubble covering the town or do you just keep sending more Ispirtu wizards to their death? Have you discovered what lies within it?"

Lattimer stayed silent, unwilling to divulge what he knew or how much progress he had made. Rainier didn't care, he already knew the answer and gave a slight nod to Ibson. *Now's your time. Play your part, old man.*

"I know what Minot is. Minot is the folding of a four-dimensional fractal, built by Candor, the founder of spark-based magic. It houses the most extensive library of spark-based magic ever assembled, and if I'm not mistaken, you've immersed yourself in that knowledge. Your growth as a wizard is impressive." Ibson gave a scholarly bow of appreciation to his former student. "It also houses a repository of spark-based artifacts, which your sister deciphered and extracted two artifacts as you watched, I am told."

"Quit telling me what I already know, Ibson. Save the lectures for your students."

Ibson bobbed his head like a reprimanded child and pushed forward. "Then you must know what's in the city. Candor built the hunter's shed in Minot, and he built it as a prison for his former students. You know them as the blood mages from history. I am the caretaker of the cottage. I know...how..." Ibson couldn't finish the sentence, so Rainier explained.

"As the caretaker of the cottage, Ibson is bound by an unbreakable bond to not divulge its secrets unless they are already known. I know them, and Ibson has spoken openly with me in private. I know how to open the city. I know how to release the blood mages, and most importantly, I know how to make them serve you."

The weight of the statement hung over the group, and Rainier could almost hear Lattimer salivating at the thought. *His interest is piqued. Close the deal.*

"I will serve as your general. You will spare anyone that

agrees to fight under my command. In return for sparing our lives today, we will help defend Malethya, and we'll go to Minot to open its secrets to you. We'll give you the books, but we'll take the artifacts. We aren't Furies, and we'll need them to even the playing field against Julian's armies. You will also have the most powerful wizards in the history of Malethya under your command. Do we have a deal?"

Filios jumped in. "My men will not serve under Rainier Tallow. I demand that I retain command..."

Captain Sharan ended his demands with a sword thrust. He doubled over, and Captain Sharan said, "The Nameless Army will serve under Rainier Tallow. Our only condition is that no one be forced into servitude."

Lattimer said, "Servitude doesn't have to be a choice."

Sharan shook her head, "We have dedicated our whole lives to servitude. They don't deserve subjugation. Let this be the one choice the Nameless Army makes. They can hold to their ideals and die a swift, honorable death, or they can join me." She looked at Rainier, "I choose to do the unthinkable. I will serve you. I will do it for the small chance that I am the lucky paladin who gets to slip her blade into Julian's immortal heart."

"Your captain is a cold and decisive woman. I like her." Lattimer mused, but he contemplated the offer and made his decision. "I will spare your lives and grant a swift death to anyone who desires it. You may serve as my general and command your forces, but you will not be my only general. Cirata Lorassa will assume Magnus' post and command my Furies. My terms are non-negotiable, and I will need some assurance that our agreement be honored. Forgive me, but your reputation requires more than just your word."

"I take it as a compliment. Us Remnant have a hard-earned reputation for one-sided deals. Besides, you just saw me back out of a deal with Jamison. Only a fool would not want some assurances. What do you have in mind?"

Lattimer laughed and said, "This isn't a problem I normally have to deal with. If I need assurances, I take it in the form of complete control and devotion. I take minds."

"I may have a solution. What about an unbreakable bond?" Ibson offered. "I am familiar with the technique, and it would seal the agreement until Julian's death." *Well done, Ibson. Your timing is perfect.*

"I don't know if I'm comfortable with that..." Rainier feigned worry.

"That is my condition. I will agree to your terms but require them sealed in an unbreakable bond. Do you agree?" Lattimer demanded the bond even if he posed it in the form of a question.

Rainier looked down at his feet and scratched the back of his head worriedly, but inside he was all smiles. "I guess I agree. Let's get this magic bond over with then." He walked forward with Ibson to meet Lattimer.

Ibson pulled out a knife and made two small cuts on each palm. A drop of blood turned into a sphere on their upturned palms and began to hover. The spherelets of blood switched places under the direction of Ibson's spell, hovering above their open wounds while Ibson completed his spell. Ibson said, "With this blood, I forge an unbreakable bond between Rainier Tallow and Lattimer Regallo. All members of the Nameless Army that choose not to serve under Rainier's command shall be granted a quick death. Lattimer shall not harm or subjugate Rainier or anyone under his command. Rainier will free the blood mages from the city in Minot, and they will serve under Lattimer's command. This bond will remain in effect until the death of Julian the Immortal. Do you both agree to these terms?"

"Yes." Both Rainier and Lattimer said without breaking eye contact with each other.

"Close your hands." Rainier did, mixing Lattimer's blood with his own. "The bond is sealed. Only Julian's death can break it." Ibson removed his hands and Lattimer said, "You are mine, Rainier Tallow."

Rainier gripped Lattimer's hand and dropped to his knees. He turned Lattimer's hand over, exposing a large, jeweled ring with a raven embossed on it. Rainier kissed the raven. Doing so made his stomach churn, but it was nothing compared to the excitement in his gut. *I can't believe that worked!* Rainier put on his best Remnant smile and said, "I, and everyone under my command, are at your disposal. What is your first command?"

"My men can sort through the loyalty of the Nameless Army. Bring Slate and the others. You have some blood mages to release."

It would be my pleasure.

REFLECTIONS

"Get on with it. Open it up!" Lattimer stood at Rainier's left shoulder, anxious for his prize.

Rainier looked up at the swirling blue bubble that protected the blood mages within the city. It had withstood an onslaught of spells from Ispirtu's best wizards, storing the energy and sending it back from where it came. The people within the city had never paid any attention to the attempts, but they seemed to know the importance of the moment, and they began to gather in the street. How did they know? There was some jostling of people in the crowd and seven robed figures made their way to the front. At first, Rainier thought that they all stared straight at him, and it took a moment for his eyes to adjust to the swirling blue of the wall to realize it wasn't him they were staring at.

Ibson stood at Rainier's right shoulder, and the blood mages stared at the man that entrapped them. They didn't know the name Ibson, but they would never forget the face of Candor.

"We're here and you've made a bond. You are duty-bound to open it. What are you waiting for?" Lattimer was unaccustomed to waiting for the things he asked for. Absolute power has a way of conflicting with the virtue of patience.

My only duty is to myself, and I made that bond using

exactly the language I intended. Rainier said, "The wall responds to the pattern, shifting and absorbing the energy of spells. You don't take down the wall, you feel its pattern and move it."

"There is no spell that allows someone to feel the pattern." Lattimer objected.

"You'd need to be a Perceptor." Slate said with a sigh, and he stepped forward, as the pieces fell into place for Lattimer.

"Candor was a Perceptor, and so he made a wall that only a Perceptor could take down...brilliant." Lattimer admitted. With his attention drawn on the swirling blue wall, he didn't see Ibson hiding a smile. *If the old man blows his cover now, it's too late for Lattimer to do anything about it. The bond is in place, but I hope Ibson doesn't give it away and lets Lattimer realize his mistake. It's so much more fun if it happens later.*

"I can't cast any magic, though. What do I do?" Slate asked.

Ibson started saying, "You don't need to be the one to cast..." and then he trailed off, forgetting what he had planned to say. His bond still held his lips, but Rainier knew his secrets, and he could finally share them.

"You'll have to manipulate someone else's spell. Sana, would you help Slate? You used a probing spell to summon the Blighted Knife in the storage room. If you use that same technique and probe the entire wall at once, Slate should be able to manipulate the spell."

Sana reached her hand out until it touched the wall and sent a probing spell. Since she wasn't trying to change anything about the wall or its pattern, it continued to swirl as it always had, and it didn't turn Sana into another crispy wizard.

Then Slate stepped forward and put his hand on the wall. At first nothing happened, but with his secret told, Ibson could provide more direction. "Feel the pattern. Try to manipulate the swirls so that they come apart where you want them to separate and together where you want them to fold." *Ibson could do this in his sleep, but where would the fun be in that?*

The swirls in the wall became less random as Slate tried to do what Ibson counseled. They stopped turning over themselves and concentrated in certain spots. A thick vertical line of blue swirls formed in front of Slate. As the thickened line formed, some areas of the wall thinned. They continued to thin and when they disappeared completely, the wall folded inward along the vertical line. It swung open, freeing the city's inhabitants.

"He made a door." Lattimer said with a smile that couldn't hide the hunger in his eyes. The most powerful wizards in the history of Malethya were freed. He announced, "I am Lattimer Regallo, Ruler of Malethya, and practitioner of spark-based magic, like you. We have need of your service, blood mages. Please, come here! I am ever so excited to meet you."

The seven wizards walked through the doorway as one. The one in the middle said, "My name is Koch, and I was once considered to be Candor's top student in the arts of spark-based magic. I helped bring about the Golden Age before I became responsible for the deaths of so many Malethyans. Those wars earned me, and all my fellow students the title of the blood mages."

He looked to Ibson curiously but turned back to Lattimer. "For our crimes, Candor locked us away. We could not be freed from the city, until he let us out or we had atoned for our crimes by researching and studying fractal-based magic. We could only get out if we learned to do magic without the spark. We have not practiced magic in years. You call us blood mages? We call ourselves the Fractal Forsaken."

Koch's eyes kept darting to Ibson, even as he continued to speak to Lattimer. "We learned that fractal-based magic is a fallacy, a flawed concept. Even with the repeating patterns of fractals, magic always required some amount of spark. We've studied fractals and every other self-similar subsets of Euclidean space that we could study. It doesn't work."

Now he did look to Ibson and addressed him directly. "Did you know that when you locked us away forever, Candor? Did you know you sentenced your immortal students to an impossible task?"

Confusion stretched across everyone's faces, and Rainier loved it. His favorite part of a scheme was when his mark finally started to realize he had been played. Lattimer wasn't quite there yet. He still thought he was in control of the situation.

Lattimer tried to reassert his authority by inserting himself into the conversation. "You are free now, and I have no need for fractal-based magic or Ibson or Candor or whoever he wants to call himself. A Disenite army is coming to invade Malethya. We need to defend our home. I need the might of the Fractal Forsaken to serve me."

Koch laughed from somewhere in the depths of his

soul. "You expect me to serve you? That will never happen. I'm not yet free of all my bonds, and if I were, I wouldn't serve you. You've learned a few tricks from the books in our library, I assume. Who do you think wrote those books?"

Now Lattimer turned red with anger, and he turned towards Rainier. "You said you could make them serve me. We sealed it with an unbreakable bond! What trickery is this?" *There it is. He starting to realize our agreement wasn't quite what he had in mind.*

Rainier smiled his best Remnant smile and said, "I can deliver everything I promised. If I couldn't, I never could have made the bond with you."

"You said you could release them and make them serve me!" Spittle flew from Lattimer's mouth as he spat the words.

"He already does serve you. They will serve you in the war to come, they just don't know it yet. You have the Fractal Forsaken, the most powerful wizards in the history of Malethya, at your disposal." Rainier saw Ibson smirking. Slate, Sana, Villifor, Lira, and everyone else in his delegation were grinning like idiots. *They're enjoying this as much as I am, but this is just the beginning. He's still realizing what he has agreed to. I love this part.*

"What are you talking about?!?" Lattimer squawked, losing his air of authority.

Rainier turned to Ibson. "Would you care to explain? I believe your tongue should have loosened up by now, right?"

Ibson smiled and said, "I've waited a long time. I'd be happy to explain. Koch says they can't serve you, because

454 J. Lloren Quill

they already spoke an unbreakable bond to serve me, before I imprisoned them here. Isn't that right, my students?"

They all nodded, and Koch said, "We could speak the bond, or we could die. None of us were powerful enough to get away, except Julian, and even he didn't escape unscathed."

"Yes, Julian has been a problem ever since that night, and while I couldn't control him, I did manage to banish him from Malethya. He can't set foot on our soil unless spark-based magic is being practiced. Since I locked away every other blood mage and forced myself to speak a bond that prevented me from practicing it myself, we should have been safe." Ibson looked to Lattimer, "You've allowed him to come back."

Rainier tried to move Ibson's story along before he got into the annals of Malethyan history. "So, the Fractal Forsaken serve you, until you release them from their bond?"

"Yes."

"Then release them." Lattimer demanded. "I command Rainier and you serve him, so release them now."

"Release us." Koch echoed the demand. "We have been punished long enough."

"I can't." Ibson smirked and now everyone not named Lattimer or Koch was smiling openly. *Lattimer can't do anything about us now anyway. He spoke a bond that prevents him from hurting any of us.* "That would go against the bond I made with Rainier and he commanded that I honor all of the bonds I already created. It isn't released until you and Jamison are dead." Lattimer looked like he was ready to explode. "He ordered me not to release the blood mages from their bond until our bond was broken. There's nothing I can do. I'm duty-bound."

Rainier jumped in now that Ibson had warmed Lattimer up. He gave his best smile and wrapped his arm around Lattimer's shoulder like they were old pals, confident that Lattimer couldn't attack him. He said, "I don't know what you are so worked up about. You are getting exactly what you wanted. The Fractal Forsaken serve Ibson. Ibson serves me, and I serve you. That means you control the Fractal Forsaken until Julian dies."

"And if we can kill him?" Lattimer pondered out loud, grasping to put the pieces together.

Sana figured it out first and let out a gasp. *Is that respect or surprise? I'm good with either.* Villifor, Lira, and Sharan were next. Villifor spit out the nail he had been chewing. Sharan and Lira looked at each other and Rainier knew he, the most disloyal person in Malethya, had just earned their loyalty.

Lattimer figured it out before Slate and the others. His eyes widened, and Rainier jumped in before he could say anything. He had waited too long to say these words to let Lattimer stammer through them in his state of shock. "If Julian dies, I no longer need to serve you, but the bonds to Ibson and the Fractal Forsaken will remain intact. They will serve me until you die."

"You dishonorable, untrustworthy, disloyal, Remnant bastard!" *If you can't handle losing, don't bother to play the game, and now we've swung the tables enough to keep playing. That one's for you Kalus. Nah, forget that. I have no use for honor and my loyalty is to myself. That one's for me.*

From somewhere near the back of the delegation, Hanna yelled out. Rainier couldn't have said it better. She cackled crazily, "Never make a deal with the Remnant!"

ACKNOWLEDGMENTS

Remnant Awakens presented new challenges for me as a writer. As you've probably noticed by now, I switch main characters for each of my books, and it's only when I start writing as that character that I really get a grasp of the complexities and challenges that someone like Rainier faces. Rainier was fun to write because he takes some of the parts of his character and leans into them to turn them to his advantage, even if they are characteristics or traits that most people would see as negative or amoral.

Thinking that way goes against my own nature, and it made me think about things from a different perspective, which is always a good thing, especially in 2020 when so many people feel so strongly with such deeply divided emotions. Sometimes I wish everyone had the experience of trying to write as someone vastly different than who they are. It's taught me a lot about having empathy and understanding the problems of others from their perspective instead of viewing them from my own.

Like all my books, I've relied on a lot of friends and interested readers to help me. Thank you to Julie, Dannah, and Josh for being early readers and providing some developmental feedback. Thank you to Katie and Devon for doing the final editing and proofing. Abby always does an amazing job with the cover art and seeing what she comes up with is one of my favorite parts of publishing. Most importantly, I'd like to thank my family for supporting me as I sneak out to the garage to write in the middle of the night or before the sun comes up!

I also hope you've enjoyed my books so far. I always try to make each book stand on its own merits and have its own conclusion, but this book had to set the table for the final book in the series, *Blood Reigns*. I hope this book gave you a few twists and turns at the end and leaves you anxious for the big finale. Please enjoy the sample chapter of *Blood Reigns* and check back at facebook.com\jllorenquill to track my progress. As always, if you enjoy my work, please share my work with others, either by lending the book, writing a review, giving a recommendation, or by following me on social media and sharing your favorite posts. I can't wait to share the rest of the story with you!

OTHER BOOKS BY J. LLOREN QUILL

Severance Lost – Fractal Forsaken Book 1

Shadow Cursed – Fractal Forsaken Book 2

Coming Soon, The Final Book in the Fractal Forsaken
Series!
Blood Reigns – Fractal Forsaken Book 4

Please enjoy a sample of the prologue and first chapter
from Blood Reigns

PROLOGUE

Power. Everyone wants it. Children push the boundaries of their parents, striving for more freedom and the power to live their own life as they see fit. The less fortunate look to the affluent and dream of what they would do with their power and influence. The affluent look at nobility and pine after the power given to them by birthright. They're all wrong, useless whiners grasping at the droppings of power that fall to them. None of them deserve to wield any true power.

Lattimer had a taste of power as a child when he cast his first spell. It was a small spell, an insignificant push of a fork across the dinner table at the prompting and coaching of his father, Brannon. Lattimer didn't remember the words that his father told him on that day. He remembered the look of pride since they were so few and far between. What he remembered most, though, was how the servants treated him after that day. He was no longer Little Lattimer or The Boy. Now they addressed him as Master Lattimer, avoided him when they could, and deferred to him when they couldn't.

A taste of power is just that, though. It's a taste. Some people are satisfied with a little taste. Some wizards strut around in their robes casting rudimentary spells, happy with their status in society and content in life. Lattimer didn't understand those wizards any better than they could understand someone like him. Power isn't something you want. Power is something you take.

Lattimer had taken power. He plotted in the shadows to deceive his father and his friends. He grew his secret army of Furies and subjugated the minds of those that opposed him. When the time came, he didn't hesitate to launch a fireball at his father and kill him where he stood. When Jamison invaded his shores, Lattimer was the only person with the strength to oppose him. With Julian and the Disenite army coming, there was only one choice – take more power. There was only one person with the strength to do it. Lattimer didn't have a choice.

CHAPTER ONE

LONG LIVE KING LATTIMER

"The time of the Lion is past. Today, we celebrate the strength of the Raven!" A crier with a magically amplified voice yelled to the masses from the steps of Darik's former palace. Raucous cheers returned from the masses standing upon the rebuilt grounds, easily overpowering the volume of the crier, and preventing her from continuing her oration.

Lattimer waited in the palace for his introduction, which was to include trumpets and all sorts of fanfare, but hearing the cries of the people, he knew the time was now. *The people love me, and why wouldn't they? I've cleaned up the streets of Ravinai, brought prosperity to the people and turned away the Nameless Army. Besides, I'm Lattimer Regallo. I'm not going to let a few trumpets stop me from doing what I want.*

Lattimer grabbed the crown off a fancy pillow meant for some other part of the extravagant ceremony and stepped out of the darkened palace. The morning sunbathed his fellow Malethyans in the light of a new day as they stood upon the immaculate palace grounds. One of his advisors, if you could call a palace clerk an advisor, had suggested setting the ceremony at dawn so that masses would relate the new day with the ushering in of a new era. *I must admit, the morning light creates quite the setting for my coronation. It's a shame that clerk demanded my coronation take place after the burial of King Darik. I told him what I thought of his arguments of history, decorum, and precedence. The stubborn idiot continued pressing his opinions, and I could tell he was convinced that he was in the right, right up until I wiped his mind and silenced any more objections. If he would have shut his mouth, he would have ended up with a commendation and a cushy job.*

Upon seeing him emerge from the palace, the crowd whipped into a frenzy. The crier tried her best to announce him, yelling "...I give you the savior of The Battle for Ravinai, your next king, Lattimer Regallo!" The trumpets recovered a second later and blasted their horns in celebration. Bellator soldiers stood at attention in full armor and Ispirtu wizards remained stoically detached and deferential towards their leader, maintaining their mysticism in front of the masses. Banners were released from the palace walls, unfurling to reveal the Regallo Raven, the new symbol of Malethya.

Lattimer strode to the top of the steps, drew a trickle of spark from his vast reserves, and amplified his voice above the crowd, drowning them out along with the crier and the blaring trumpets.

"Less than one week ago, the grounds that you stand upon were torn asunder, trampled by the Nameless Army. They forced your Ispirtu wizards to desecrate this land with wizard fire and roiling earth, but we turned them back. We defeated an army bent on destroying us. We defended Malethya from unprovoked aggression by the Disenites. Look at it now!" Lattimer spread his arms out wide to encompass the magically repaired and manicured palace grounds, drawing another round of applause from the crowd.

"The very steps upon which I stand is where our brave King Darik fought the Nameless Army with his own personal guard. He used himself as bait to lure their army up these steps, exposing their flanks, and giving the Bellator soldiers the advantage they needed to turn the tide of battle. Because of his leadership, I was able to assume command and finish the battle, but it cost our King his life." The crowd quieted in respect of their fallen king.

"I walked these steps after the Battle of Ravinai and found his crown crumpled beneath the wreckage. It was cracked and dented. I was told that it had been damaged and contorted beyond repair. It did not represent the country I know. We are Malethyans. We don't crack, dent, or fall into disrepair. No matter what happens to us, we persevere. We do what must be done!" The crowd quieted further as Lattimer played with the crown in his hands. "I thought about what it would take to reforge this crown and to reforge our kingdom. It will take the leadership and bravery that King Darik exhibited in the battle of Ravinai, so I took his old crown in my hands and melted it with wizard fire." Lattimer spoke a little louder. "It will take the strength to do what needs to be done and the POWER to see it through, so I took my father's scepter and melted it, letting the gold of House Regallo mix with the white gold of Malethya's king. Finally, I stripped away all the ornamentation in Darik's crown, choosing to set only the jeweled orb from my father's scepter. THIS is the crown that could not be repaired. It is no longer what it once was. It is something new, stronger and more powerful than before." He lifted the smooth, simple crown in the air, but the simplicity of the metalwork only served to emphasize the depths of the swirling orb that it held. Screams of excitement and celebration thundered through crowd as Lattimer held it aloft and said, "I will wear this crown as your king..." Lattimer lowered the crown onto his head, another thing that mangy clerk said was impossible. *Who would set it upon my head? There's no one here worthy of the honor. I am the king, and I will crown myself.* The applause became deafening as he removed his hands from the crown to let it rest upon his head. He yelled, "...and I will reign with the strength and power that Malethya needs. As your king, I will do what needs to be done, regardless of the cost!"

Lattimer waited for the applause to die down while shooting a quick glance of warning towards the crier who looked like she was ready to jump in with some of her nonsense. She withered at the quick look in her direction. *I wonder what would happen to that poor woman if I stared her down? She wouldn't be able to see anything but the tops of her shoes for a week.* The crowd quieted and Lattimer moved onto the next part of his speech.

"I will be the king you need, but in return, I expect you to be what Malethya needs." The crowd stirred at the curious comment, waiting to understand. He said, "Our shores are not safe. Our land is not safe. The Nameless Army is coming to invade us even as I speak." A gasp went up from the crowd that thought they had just won the war with Disentia. "The army that is coming will be bigger than the last, and they will not make the same mistakes as Jamison. We can't meet them as a broken, battered country in disrepair. We need to meet them as something new." He looked through the ranks of Bellator fighters, found his general and said, "Cirata, come here."

Cirata Lorassa stepped forward in black armor that soaked in the light, giving it the look of perpetual shadow. The shadowy armor masked her lithe, predatory movements as she stalked towards her King. When she reached him, she bowed to one knee, and asked, "How can I serve you King Lattimer?"

"By showing everyone what you have become." Lattimer waved his hand towards the palace door and ghastly pale figure with scars crisscrossing his torso and devilish red eyes emerged. Lattimer announced to the crowd, "You all know Slate 'Stonehands' Severance, although you may call him Slate the Bloodless or a host of other names when you are telling stories about him to frighten your children at the campfire. I assure you the stories are true, and he possess abilities beyond any normal man. Cirata will fight him."

Malethyans will show up for a coronation, but no one anticipated a fight between one of Lattimer's generals and the most notorious criminal in all Malethya. The crowd went wild, and Lattimer didn't bother with any more pleasantries. He let Cirata and Slate circle each other in front of the crowd like the dangerous people they were.

After a few feints to feel each other out, Lattimer tired of waiting for the spectacle to begin. He filtered between the spells he held active in his mind, finding the stream of consciousness that aligned with Cirata, and overwhelmed the part of her brain that stimulated aggression without pushing too hard and turning her into a mindless Fury. It was a fine line that Lattimer had extensive experience in.

Cirata's eyes turned red, and she lunged forward, moving with the grace of someone uninhibited by fear and the speed of someone wearing enchanted armor. Any fighter would have fallen to her blade in seconds, but Slate wasn't any fighter, and after the Battle of Ravinai, he was accustomed to fighting enemies with enchanted armor. He darted backwards, propelling himself with inhuman strength and easily creating the separation necessary to avoid her thrust. As he flew backwards, he flicked his wrist with the strength of a full swing and smacked his staff against Cirata's wrist, making her drop her blade.

Cirata rolled and caught her blade before it hit the ground. Slate planted his feet and lunged forward, aiming his staff at her exposed armpit, but she was able to turn her shoulder in time, sending the staff glancing away harmlessly. She finished her roll and swung her legs upwards, trying to catch Slate as he flew overhead. Instead, he kicked out, sending her spinning on the ground like a top. He jumped up, flipped, and drove his staff straight towards her spinning body. Cirata pushed hard off the ground with her enchanted gauntlet, which launched her into the air. Slate didn't anticipate that she could close the distance between them that quickly, so his strike with his staff was premature, and the two collided in the air while his staff was still raised above his head. Slate pushed back with his left hand, trying to gain space, while Cirata pulled him close where her enchanted armor had the advantage. They hit the ground in an awkward embrace, and the impact was just enough for Slate to free his stonehand.

"Stop!" Lattimer commanded before Slate could land a punch that left permanent damage. *I should have known better than to expect him or any of his friends to follow a simple order. Slate was supposed to throw the match.* Lattimer recovered quickly, though, and turned his command into a slow clap at the performance, which the crowd eagerly joined. Slate took an extra second or two longer than he really needed to untangle from Cirata. There was no love lost between those two, but in the end, they separated and stood to accept the praise of the crowd.

Lattimer urged them on, yelling to the crowd, "Yes, give these two champions the honor they deserve. Cirata has fought valiantly in the Battle for Ravinai. Her sword ran red with the blood of our enemies. She was joined on that battlefield by Slate Severance. You may know him as a notorious criminal, but when Malethya was invaded, he was the first to answer my call." The crowd continued their applause with fervor, but Lattimer spoke over them. He said, "Look at their power! Look at their speed!"

Cirata took her pre-arranged cue and stepped forward to speak to the masses. Lattimer cast a spell to amplify her voice with as little effort as a thought, and she said, "Very few people have met Slate Severance in battle and lived to tell the tale. The armor I wear gives me the speed and strength to match Slate, a living legend of death. You, too, can have this power. You can join Lattimer's army, put on this armor, and become a legend."

Now it's your turn, Slate. Stick to the script. Lattimer amplified Slate's voice and held his breath. Slate said, "Very few people answer when they are called to serve.

This is your call. Defend Malethya and let your enemies tell stories of you at campfires to frighten their children...stories that are true." The crowd erupted with murderous intent as they imagined themselves saving Malethya from the Disenite hordes.

Slate fought to keep from curling his lip in contempt, and it didn't make the smile on Lattimer's face drop even an inch. Slate, the most famous fighter in Malethya, had just extended the opportunity to become a hero. The populace would stir in excitement, every young boy or girl would dream of becoming him, and his army would overflow with recruits.

Lattimer raised his own voice to seal the deal. He yelled, "Be what Malethya needs. Join us. Defend your family from the Disenites. Show them what it means to be a Malethyan! Your King commands it!"

The crowd lost their mind in excitement, and Lattimer turned around, swirling his regal robes in a flourish of authority, and stalking back to the palace. As he walked past, Cirata and Slate fell in line beside him.

Cirata said simply, "Congratulation my king."

Slate offered no such statements of support. *Why would he? He knows I made an unbreakable bond with Rainier that won't let me hurt him. He needs to follow orders from me until Julian dies and then Rainier, Slate, and my sister are going to turn on me faster than a gambler with pocket aces.* Instead, as they walked towards the palace, Slate said, "That's the first and last time I will ever throw a fight."

"You did a piss-poor job of it. If I hadn't stopped the fight, Cirata's head would be a decidedly different shape right now."

"It was all part of the show. Next time, put me up against someone with some skill, and I can make it look more realistic."

"You got lucky," Cirata fired back.

Everyone there knew otherwise. Slate decided to make the point clear. "You can call it what you'd like. I'm sure Magnus had the same thought running through his head when he took his dying breath."

Cirata tensed at the mention of her dead boyfriend, and Lattimer eagerly reached for the palace door their pretend match turned into a real fight. He opened them to see the smiling face of Rainier Tallow, flanked by his sister Rose, Captain Sharan, and Ibson, his former teacher. *They all want me dead. Too bad.*

Rainier said while wearing a smile that made Lattimer want to punch him in the face, "That was a nice show. You were a little heavy on the blatant lies and misconception, but it proved effective. Maybe you do have some Remnant in you."

Behind him, he could hear the crier announcing to the crowd the locations of the nearest recruitment offices and when they would open in the morning. Long lines formed where Bellator soldiers had opened their doors to take in any overeager recruits on the spot.

"We need an army. People are flocking to join our ranks. It's a good day." Lattimer acknowledged.

"If only they knew their king was a blood mage that intended to subjugate their minds and turn them into Furies. I think those lines would be a lot shorter." Rose accused him.

"I'm a Malethyan. I'll do what needs to be done and not things twice about it, just like I promised." It came out as a growl, and he continued with conviction. "I have a country to save. I don't care if you care for me or my methods. You will do what I say." He thought of the unbreakable bond he had forged as he stalked past them, heading for his throne room.

"You don't have a choice. Follow me, so that I can decide what you'll do for me next."